LIFE over DEATH

Bruce Aitchison

BRUCE AITCHISON

ISBN 978-1-64299-422-3 (paperback)
ISBN 978-1-64299-424-7 (digital)

Christian Faith Publishing, Inc.
832 Park Avenue
Meadville, PA 16335
www.christianfaithpublishing.com

Although the author researched names and places, all characters appearing in this work are fictitious. Any resemblance to real persons, living or dead, is purely coincidental.

Printed in the United States of America

When one is blessed with longevity, there are those whom are special who will be missed. I would like to pay a special tribute to the following:

James Dye was a lover of westerns who read my first novel, *Last Assignment*, three times. Jim wondered why it wasn't on the NY Time's Best Sellers list. When Jim came down with pancreatic cancer, I gave him a rough draft to proof read of my latest novel, "Life over Death." My hope was to take his mind away from his struggle. Jim became so caught up on the story he scolded me for not giving him all the chapters at once. When Jim finished proof reading, his review was - "I never lost interest from beginning to end." He finished by telling me how the last chapter brought chills up and down his arms! Jim eventually went home to be with the Lord. I wish Jim was still here to see the book he helped edit come into final print!

Bill and Jane Kinnear were my home away from home when I went into the Marine Corp. My parents had moved to Florida after my enlistment and since my high school buddies, since my neighborhood and high school buddies were in my home town, I needed a home away from home. The Kinnear residence was that home. I fondly called Jane, 'Mother Jane.' Bill passed away first and Mother Jane continued to stay in touch via Christmas cards and telephone calls before she went to be reunited with Bill. I still miss them both.

Pastor David Olcott, who promoted my first novel in church, went home to be with the Lord in 2017. My wife Sharon paid a special tribute to him after he made a house visit, commenting, "I've never met a more Godly man!" How true her words were! I actually used his name for the sheriff in *Last Assignment*. I guess one might say his character lives on in the present and into eternity!

As for me, there is one who will never leave or forsake in the present as well as into eternity- Jesus Christ.

CONTENTS

PLATTE RIVER CAMPSITE

C lifford Stokes poured scalding coffee over his tin plate. Watching the last particle of food wash to the ground, he sanitized the job by ladling steaming water over the plate. Unfortunately, his cook was watching. The scowl on Wendell Bartholomew's face indicated a scolding was coming. Cliff knew his cook prized coffee more than food, any waste bringing a lecture. Hoping to head off any reprimand, he handed his plate to the scowling cook with a tactful compliment, "Here, I saved you some time, even cleaned the knife and fork." Cliff added one more diversion, "Wendell, that was some heck of a feed considering how long we've been on the trail. Yes sir, a tasty meal."

His attempt didn't work. Wendell's voice was reflecting exasperation. "You keep wasting coffee for washing utensils, and before this trip's over, I'll be using old coffee grounds."

Eyeing Wendell, Cliff decided on silence. The man's years had caught up with his body. His lean frame had a permanent lean caused by countless hours hovering over cooking fires. Wendell's hair was almost white, and his face covered with a mass of wrinkles. Despite his age, there was nothing old or slow about his brain. What's more, his cook was observant, and despite his propensity to be cranky, he was also quick to compliment. Wendell was a master at using sarcasm. It was his way of making a point, and when he did, it was something needing to be said. Cliff had great respect for the old man's smarts, never hesitating to ask for his advice.

Seeing the wagon master staring in the direction just traveled, Wendell knew what was bothering his boss, saying as much, "I reckon Buchanan's not coming in tonight or he would have been here by now. Who are you going to post?"

Stokes shrugged, not surprised Wendell was reading his mind. "I reckon a combination of youth and experience. I'm thinking of sending young Robinson out on the flats with the river covering his left flank. Sammy will go up on higher ground to the south."

Wendell nodded and asked, "Who's the relief?"

"I figure to use Victor and Taylor, how'd I do?"

Frowning, Wendell checked the sun. "Good picks but you better get started 'cause in a few hours, it'll be dark. Oh, one other thing. You picked two relief men for the outposts, but what about the normal watch?"

"You're right," Cliff conceded. "I'll solve the relief when I get back." Following Wendell's upward stare, Cliff squinted against the diminishing brightness from the cloudless sky. He often thought out loud among those he trusted, a way of letting his inner circle express agreement or disagreement. Wanting more confirmation, he gave his cook more opportunity. "Maybe I should do it the other way around. You know, use Victor and Santana first." He waited for Wendell to have his say. He didn't have to wait but a second.

"Nope, that young Robinson works real good, better you break him in on the first shift. Not much danger on the first shift, unless of course there's a full moon, which there ain't. Besides, the second watch is always the hardest considering how trouble most likely will come just before dawn. Hell, a man's mind has a tendency to wander as the hours drag on, and Victor and Taylor won't be lulled into dozing off before daybreak. Nope, you got it figured out right. Just do it."

Cliff stole a glance at the still hot coffee pot. "Save me some. Be back within the hour."

Wendell leaned over, staring at the still soaked ground where his boss had rinsed off his plate. The cook's response laced with sarcasm, "Coffee, you say, now if that doesn't beat all."

Chuckling, Cliff left his cook bent over staring at the wet earth, his destination a group of men huddled around a fire near the utility wagon, his long strides quickly covering the distance. Standing more than six feet tall, Clifford Stokes had a commanding physical presence. His head was covered with a thick thatch of graying hair—his eyebrows bushy, darker than his hair. He was built stocky, a deep voice matching his stern looks. Nearing the campfire, he could see the men were anticipating his arrival, every set of eyes watching him. Most of the men knew from experience they were about to get an assignment, and they knew why, all except young Mitch Robinson.

Aware his boss was staring his way, Sammy Tillman knew he was about to be chosen, greeting the wagon master, "Where do you want me to post?"

"Lower south slope. Go to the outer edge where those boulders give way to the upper plateau. That should give you some space to maneuver. If you get started now, you should get back in time for one last cup of coffee."

Leaving the comfort of the fire, Sammy grabbed his carbine as he left. Cliff looked at young Robinson. Mitch was always eager to please, a hard worker. Hiring him had been a blessing. The young man had an infectious personality, even better, never complaining; his work always thorough. "Mitch, I've got an assignment for you. Follow me."

Mitch jumped to his feet. His face was square, showing a strong jaw. Thick brown hair covered his head. Robinson's body was blocky with thick wrists connected to muscular forearms. It hadn't taken the wagon boss long to know how to take advantage of the young man's strength along with his positive work attitude. When he first hired him, some of the men mocked the young fellow's exuberance, but that changed when the very same men experienced his willingness to help everyone, including the mockers.

Cliff nodded toward Mitch's carbine. "Bring your rifle." He eyed Victor and Taylor. "You two will be their relief. After these two come back for coffee, follow them when they head out so you'll know where to find them when it's your turn to cover the shift." Turning, he started for the tool wagon, Mitch falling in step behind him. Cliff didn't like to walk and talk. If he had something to say, a stopped man listened better. In his opinion, a busy man should be focused on his chores. The job always seemed to get done faster and a lot more thorough. Talking was a distraction, including during working. Besides, Cliff could always tell by looking into a man's eyes if what he said had gotten through. Socializing was one thing, but giving instructions was another. Idle chatter was acceptable over the evening fire, but concerning work hours, a request should only be spoken once. That was his way and every man knew it, even young Robinson.

Arriving at the tool wagon, Cliff looked at Robinson, gesturing toward the trail just traveled. "In case you hadn't noticed, my scout didn't show up. Unless trouble's afoot, he's always back in time for evening chow. We do have a preplanned understanding. If he's not in before dark, we set out extra outer perimeter guards besides the normal watch, which is going to be your assignment. You are about to have a learning experience along with a dangerous responsibility." Cliff half smiled, adding, "Now, it's possible that Buchanan might still ride in, but we can't wait. And in a few minutes you'll see why." Cliff pointed to a hanging bow saw. "Grab that saw. I'll bring the ax."

Mitch had a hunch they would be collecting firewood, expressing his conclusion, "Looks like I'm going on a wood-gathering detail."

Nodding agreement, Cliff said, "You're right on, but not for your personal warmth. Fact is, I'm hoping you won't have to put a match to the woodpile we're about to build. If you don't have to fire them up, we'll throw the bigger logs in the back of the wagon for tomorrow. I'll explain after we're done."

Watching Mitch work the action of his carbine, ensuring it was loaded, pleased Cliff. The young fellow didn't need to be told everything. Once given instructions, Mitch thought for himself, doing what needed to be done, including taking care of small details relating to any given job. Any boss would be pleased with such a worker. During their many conversations, Mitch was always quoting from the Bible, explaining how God expects a worker to be worth his keep.

What's more, he seemed to have numerous Bible verses memorized for different circumstances. As far as Cliff was concerned, the young fellow had his permission to quote as many verses as he wanted. He had earned that right because of his work attitude. If God existed, young Robinson was a good example of what a god-fearing man should be like. He couldn't help but think; maybe Mitch should become a preacher?

Passing between the wagons, Stokes was aware of the many stares from the folks huddled around their cooking fires, curiosity etched in their faces. Leaving the circled wagons, Cliff stayed close to the river. Several minutes passed before he found what he was looking for. Pointing to a gap between the trees scattered along the river, he gave his instructions. "We're going to pile a bunch of firewood, tepee-style, across that opening. If you get unwanted company, you're going to stick a match to the wood. Once you do, you're going to fall back over to that mound on the other side of those trees. From there you'll fire a warning shot, followed by three more. Even if it's just a lone person, you fire those shots. Anyone sneaking in after dark is trouble. Most likely he's an advance scout for some group up to no good. Now, Mitch, it's going to be pitch-black out there tonight, so you're going to have to use your ears without getting spooked. That's why we're setting up this bonfire. If you need to see who's out there, you'll have an illuminated area."

Mitch had a question. "Suppose the fire won't start?"

"The wood will start, the reason being lots of kindling. The only way the wood won't fire up is if it rains, and judging by today's sky, such a thing isn't going to happen."

Another question prompted Mitch. "I've been wondering why Scott Buchanan hasn't shown up. Maybe we should saddle up and go look for him?"

Appreciating Mitch's attitude, Cliff reasoned, "Nope, be dark soon, not enough time. In case you haven't noticed, the sun's getting low in the sky. I'm sure Buchanan's checking out something. I reckon we'll know by tomorrow morning when he rides in. In the meantime, we take precautions. Until he shows up, we watch out for ourselves."

Mitch frowned, asking, "Suppose he doesn't show up, what then, Mr. Stokes?"

Cliff didn't like to contemplate Mitch's question. He and Scott Buchanan had worked together for a long time, including army service. Over the years, Cliff had come to depend on his scout's skills and instincts. The man was uncanny. Such men were hard to come by. If he ever lost Buchanan, such a loss would be a serious setback for him and the wagon train. Mulling over Mitch's question, he took his time before replying. "We'll give him a fair amount of time before we start looking, which means we'll stay here until late tomorrow morning, be more than soon enough. Right now it's time to get started; we can talk while we work." Cliff laughed at himself, realizing he was contradicting one of his rules, talking while working. Thankfully, there was another saying: rules were meant to be broken. He'd better keep the broken rule to himself.

Gathering an armful of wood, Mitch couldn't stem his curiosity. "How do you search for a man out there? Where do you start?"

Straightening, Cliff explained, "We'll fan out and sweep both sides of the trail, find his horse tracks and follow them. If we don't locate him, we leave him. Besides, Buchanan knows how to handle himself. He not only knows how to follow wagon wheel tracks, as scout he knows our next likely camping location. Trust me, if he's okay, he'll find us."

Mitch changed the subject. "Is it true Indians don't fight after dark?"

The wagon boss rolled his eyes. "Can't prove it by me, especially concerning the Cheyenne and Comanche. Besides, trouble on the trail doesn't always come from Indians."

"I never considered anyone else. You mentioned Cheyenne, what about them?"

Piling more wood over the kindling, Stokes looked at Mitch, remembering the many skirmishes he had with those fierce warriors, vividly recalling fellow comrades falling dead alongside him during the heat of battle. Lost in his own thoughts, he realized Mitch was watching him, still waiting for his answer. Straightening, he gave

Mitch his answer. "The Spanish gave the Cheyenne a name called Komantaa. You know what the name means, young fellow?"

"No sir, can't say that I do."

"That title refers to an enemy who wants to fight all the time and the Cheyenne are good at it. Just ask anyone who served as a horse soldier. Fact is the Cheyenne can flat out fight to the death. You can also lump in the Apache and Comanche, they also fight like hell itself."

For several seconds, Mitch was silent before asking, "You mentioned there were others who could cause trouble. Who are they?"

Cliff spoke reflectively. "If I can remember correctly, when you get near the southern territories, let's start with Mexican bandits, and then there's the Comancheros. You ever hear about the Comancheros, Mitch?"

"Excuse my ignorance Mr. Stokes, but no, I haven't."

"They sell whisky and guns to the Indians while making lots of money. Most have Mexican and Indian blood in them, but not always. Then there are many different Indian tribes like Arapaho, Kiowa, Crow, Sioux, Rees, Arikkaras, Mandans, along with some Pawnees looking for trouble. I almost forgot, the law's always looking for a few fugitives along the trail. How many did I rattle off? Did you keep count?" Not hearing Mitch speak up, he chuckled. "You want more?"

"That's enough," Mitch chuckled back. "All told I think I counted ten."

Cliff liked hearing Mitch laugh, showing he wasn't fearful, complimenting him. "You understand things fast. Someday you'll make a good ramrod, maybe even run your own wagon train. That's of course, if you don't end up becoming a preacher." Stepping back, Cliff eyed the woodpile. "I reckon that's more than enough wood to light up the night. Let's go pick a spot up further ahead for your early warning location." Moving forward, Stokes pointed at a deadfall offering cover and a decent field of view. "That'll work. You'll be sheltered from the breeze coming off the river allowing you to hear. The location is far away from the wood pile allowing time to double back and fire her up. From here, you should be able to detect anyone trying to sneak through. Just to make sure no one slips by you, we're going to spread a bunch of dead sticks out front. Anybody prowling around will step on those sticks. If you hear suspicious noises, you sneak back and light the fire."

Mitch was impressed. "Mr. Stokes, you've thought of everything."

Scattering his last armful of dead sticks and twigs over the bare ground, Cliff straightened. Reaching into his pocket, he pulled out a ball of twine. "Here's another trick. Take this cord and string it to those far bushes, then run it across that opening, next go around that gnarled tree, then back to you. After that's done, you have two choices. One option is to tie the string to your arm in a loose bow. If you feel a tug, you know what to do. Your other choice is to tie the cord to a near branch. If it shakes, you have company. Why two options? If you think you might doze off, better to tie it to your arm. I'm sure you won't doze off because you're conscientious, so a near branch will do. Now, I'm going back to the wagons to check on Sammy. Once you finish stringing the cord, come in and have some coffee. Before I turn in, I'll come out for a visit while walking my late rounds." Handing Mitch the ball of cord, Cliff started to leave, stopping. "Oh, one last thing, when you finish here go over to that knoll and make yourself a comfortable shooting position 'cause you might need it. The reason is you don't want to be close to the fire if there is a prowler, the flames will blind you but not somebody outside the circle of light who's using the cover of darkness. A man sitting near a fire can't see past the blackness, but a man outside the circle of light can see real well. You don't want some sneaking prowler taking advantage from your fire. So you pick a location away from the fire. Here's another tactic, shooting from different spots always puts fear into a prowler. Seeing different muzzle flashes makes them think there's more than one shooter out there." Turning on his heels, he left.

Watching the wagon boss returning, Stephanie Clark sensed something was wrong. Just a short time ago, she had observed a flurry of unusual activity. Based on her observations, it seemed that Mr. Stokes had broken the normal routine while departing the circled wagons with several men. Why had they left the sanctuary of the wagons, and why were they carrying all those tools, including toting rifles, she wondered. Another thing, each group had gone in different directions as if preparing for trouble. Stephanie had another concern. Where was the head scout? In forty-five minutes, it would be dark. The scout was always in camp at least an hour before nightfall. Ever since they had left civilization, she remembered seeing the curly-haired scout arrive just before mealtime to report to the wagon boss. Something wasn't right. Turning, Stephanie voiced her concerns to her father. "Dad, something is wrong."

His mind already preoccupied with worry, Adam Clark's eyes jumped to his daughter, the alarm in Stephanie's voice adding to his concerns. Fearful ever since they had joined the wagon train, Adam's fears were obvious to any bystander. Not known as a man who cursed, he did now, managing to keep it under his breath. Of one thing he was certain: he wouldn't feel at ease until they reached the next town, even better, when they reached their final destination. Above everything that scared him, nothing was more frightening than wild Indians. As they were departing from Fort Kearney, he'd heard the Cheyenne had broken the 1851 treaty. Hearing such frightening news had put the fear of God into him. It was common knowledge that Indians liked white women. Both his wife and daughter were attractive, especially his daughter. Not only was she shapely, it had happened in all the right places. Even if her body hadn't developed in such a way, her face was a magnet. She had full lips accenting her high cheekbones with long auburn-colored hair cascading around her shoulders, complete with almond-colored eyes. Whenever men passed, married or not, they always gave her a second look. For the moment, Adam wasn't concentrating on what Stephanie was saying, his thoughts lingering on the dangers in this heathen land. He wished there was a better way his wife and daughter could join him without crossing this untamed land fraught with danger, but unfortunately for him, he had been unable to come up with another plan. Fretting, he suddenly focused on his daughter, asking her, "What's wrong, Stephanie?"

Leaning forward, her hand on his arm, Stephanie forced her father to concentrate on what she was saying. "Dad, the scout from the wagon train hasn't come in yet. I think something's gone wrong."

"Really," Clark muttered, even greater alarm flooding his thoughts. He glanced at the chuck wagon, not seeing the wagon boss. Unlike previous evenings, he wasn't there. Usually by now, the man was helping the cook prepare the evening meal. Not good, he thought. Trying to suppress the alarm from his voice, he questioned his daughter again, "Are you sure?"

Stephanie pointed toward the far end of the wagons. "The wagon master left the wagons minutes ago with several men carrying rifles." Starting to say more, she stopped. The young man who had departed with the wagon master was walking toward the tool wagon. She watched him disappear behind the wagon. Moments later he emerged, still carrying his rifle, now heading toward the old man holding the coffeepot out. Perhaps she was unduly alarmed, she hoped.

Adam knew there was only one way to settle his nerves, making a decision. "Let's get everything stored away before dark." He looked at his wife Norma, seeing the concern in her face. Masking his own worry, he comforted her. "Don't worry, honey, as soon as we see the wagon boss, Stephanie and I will pay him a visit." Seconds later, both saw the wagon boss at the same time. Adam encouraged his daughter, "Come on, honey, no time like the present. Let's find out if there's a problem. Maybe we'll be pleasantly surprised."

With Sammy following, Cliff headed for the chuck wagon. Out of the corner of his vision, he observed Adam Clark and his pretty daughter approaching, obvious worry etched in the man's face. Why Adam Clark was relocating was beyond his understanding considering the tame life they were leaving behind, especially with two attractive womenfolk, the type who would be more comfortable in eastern surroundings with all the pleasures afforded from city life. Of course, he wasn't complaining, needing customers was his business, including the Clark family. Cliff gestured in the direction of his cook, his voice a command. "Sammy, go get some coffee. I'll be along shortly." Cliff waited for the approaching father and daughter. Compared to the rest of the travelers, Adam Clark's complexion was without color, his face showing no signs of weather related wrinkles. It was evident he made his living far away from the harsh elements caused by out-door life. Adam Clark had told him he was a businessman in the process of moving everything they owned lock, stock, and barrel out west.

Adam's greeting sounded like he looked, indicating serious questions were coming. "Good evening, Mr. Stokes."

Cliff swept his hat off his head, semi-bowing toward the daughter as he spoke, "Evening folks, how may I be of help?"

Clark cast a knowing look at his daughter as he spoke, "My daughter, who is extremely observant, just brought something to my attention. She's wondering where your scout is?"

Impressed, Cliff appraised the young lady, returning his attention back to her father. "She's to be complimented for her keen observations. And the both of you are curious as to why?"

His policy not to dodge questions, much less sugarcoat any-thing, Cliff studied each face as he spoke. "Fact is, I have no idea why my scout's not back yet, but he and I do have an understanding. If, for whatever reason, he stays out, I take extra precautions, including adding to the normal night watch. I'm placing two additional men out on listening posts. It's a precaution we've been doing for years." Seeing the worry remained in Adam's face, Cliff tried to relax the man. It wouldn't be good to have any fears spreading through the travelers. He hitched up his belt as he explained, "Please don't get all worried up, Mr. Clark. What my scout's doing, he's done before. I might add, and on many occasions with my approval."

Adam persisted. "But what does his failure to show up mean? Do you have any idea?"

Sighing, Cliff chose his words carefully, letting a faint smile play across his lips, indicating everything was okay. "Can't tell you what I don't know. Most likely he's uncovered something needing to be checked out. As soon as he figures out what I need to know, he'll report in. Usually by the next morning, which also means I refuse to become worried until noon the following day. Let me repeat myself, we've done this before."

"I see," Adam murmured, still hoping for answers. "Would it be correct to assume that potential danger is lurking out there and your scout has uncovered danger?"

Stokes nodded patiently. "Possibly, but I think I told you in advance of this trip that the land is full of danger. In the worst-case scenario, my scout might be dead. Of course, I doubt it, but I don't exclude any possibility. Now I'm going to repeat myself. We've done this before."

Though he did appreciate the boss man's honesty, Adam Clark wasn't completely satisfied, another question formulating in his mind. What did it mean for them if the scout was dead? Without hesitation, he asked, "If by chance your scout has been killed, how would such a terrible happening affect the wagon train?"

Cliff realized he needed to find the right words to relax the man. He shrugged as if the situation wasn't critical, his voice conversational. "I've got another man who often scouts with Scott Buchanan. I would assign him. I might add, a man who's competent."

Stephanie knew her father wouldn't stop until he was completely satisfied. After all, that was the way he ran his business. Thankfully, the wagon master wasn't being evasive concerning her father's questions, revealing much they hadn't known before. Her father's temporary silence gave her the opportunity to help her dad. She tactfully shifted the emphasis away from the danger to them, instead to the missing scout. Such a change might motivate the wagon boss to reveal even more than he'd already done. She voiced her concerns regarding Scott Buchanan. "Isn't there something you can do now to help your scout? My father and I would like to help in any way we can."

Seeing sincerity in her face, Cliff liked her attitude—her show of concern. Unlike most travelers, she was thinking about the well-being of another. Was her concern genuine, he wondered. He thought so, regardless, she was giving him an opportunity to redirect the emphasis, taking full advantage. "No, and let me tell you why Miss Clark. Buchanan's like a ghost out there. I've often felt he's half Apache and half Cheyenne. The reason I compare him to the Apaches is because he can disappear like they do. As for him being like the Cheyenne, he can fight like them, and I can tell you from my army days, they are fierce fighters. Everything considered, a person might as well mix in some Comanche blood in Scott's veins too. As for any out of control white folks, more than once he's whipped a troublemaker."

"So," Adam interrupted, "he's a violent man?"

"Not really. He doesn't like bullies who take advantage over others. He'd just as soon send them on their way in a like manner they understand."

Adam frowned as he responded, "I see."

Cliff hoped his next statement was the finisher. "I've often contemplated Buchanan would never enjoy life unless he's prowling the land." Laughing suddenly, Stokes hoped his humor would have a relaxing influence. "I reckon a domestic life would be awfully tame for him. Does that answer your question, Miss Clark?"

Smiling back, she nodded.

Adam saw his daughter was done. He knew once this discussion ended, he was going to have to explain their discussion with his wife. Hopefully, he'd be able to extract a more satisfactory conclusion. Persisting, he asked, "Okay, so much for the wagon scout, what about danger to the wagon train?"

Cliff's answer was swift. "I've been taking people west and returning east with folks for a long time. The trail can become treacherous, but my wagon train is safe. As for the Indians, every man working for me is skilled with a gun. I have never left without enough men, which has always helped against being jumped by small groups of Indians. The most vulnerable folks on the trail are single families heading west. You know, Mr. Clark, there is safety in numbers. Fact is, most Indian raids look to jump small isolated groups, which we're not. As for any large Indian war party, usually the army's chasing them."

Clark's fears jumped out. "War party, you say!"

Stokes groaned inwardly, unable to conceal the regret showing in his face over such a tactical blunder, his mind racing to overcome such an inexcusable error. It seemed the more he talked, the more he gave Mr. Clark reasons for concerns. He chose his words carefully. "You know, Mr. Clark, Indians don't like to be killed either. Mostly they hit and run. Their favorite tactic is to ambush some unsuspecting folks and I'm good at avoiding those situations. More than once I've camped out on the trail where I didn't want, thus insuring them scoundrels couldn't use the terrain to their advantage. I might add, that's why my scouts are so important, including staying out until the next day. A good scout knows what's ahead, alongside, as well as what's behind. They are my eyes and ears."

As Cliff talked, Adam recalled how the wagon boss had told him about his military background. Such experience was invaluable, he thought. Remembering their previous conversation gave him a measure of comfort. "I do recall you telling me about your service as an officer in the cavalry. That's very comforting to know, Mr. Stokes."

Finally, Cliff thought he was getting somewhere. "You're right, Mr. Clark. Having army experience is invaluable when dealing with potential problems. My scout, Scott Buchanan, is also an ex-army man, which is why we work so well together. I guess you can say we are in sync."

Stephanie's voice interrupted their two-way conversation. "I'm getting the impression, Mr. Stokes, that you're not overly worried, even about large Indian warrior groups."

"Oh, I'm concerned, all right. My first responsibility is always to you folks and your safety. After the travelers, come, my men. As for myself, I'm always last. Concerning Indians on the prowl, I've always considered the scattered settlers living along the frontier the most threatened. Concerning wagon folks, the greatest danger from Indians usually happens when someone wanders too far from the wagons, especially at dusk. Women are very desirable by those red heathens, children too. Wandering away from safety is a serious no-no. The truth is I'm more concerned with sickness, weather conditions, wagons breaking down, and not having enough food and water. As long as we're near the river, I'm not worried about water, unless of course there's a flash flood. Now, if you'll excuse me, I've got to accomplish a few chores before the night sets in. If you have more questions, I won't be turning in until late. I'm sure you know where to find me." Not waiting for a reply, Cliff tipped his hat, heading for the chuck wagon.

Watching the wagon boss depart, Stephanie spoke to her father. "He seems to have everything under control, doesn't he, Dad?"

Adam smiled, admiring his daughter's keen observations and probing questions. He always considered her his second brain. Despite his worries, he managed to keep his voice light. "Yes, the man's experienced, and you're right, he's very professional. What's more, knowing he has that military background gives me confidence. I guess when we see that scout tomorrow, I'll relax." Adam stole a glance toward his wagon. He could see his wife, Norma, hands on her hips, waiting; her posture indicated she was eager to hear what was said. At least now he had some answers, hoping they were enough. "Let's get back to our wagon so I can try to relax your mother. If I fail, I won't be getting much sleep tonight." Reluctantly, his hand on his daughter's arm, they headed for the flickering fire. Unlike Stephanie, his wife Norma was very much like himself. Both liked everything orderly, including all concerns resolved in preparation for the next day. So far for them, this trip was just the opposite.

TWO SETS OF TRACKS

S cott Buchanan stared at the unshod pony tracks, guessing at least fifteen riders had passed. Dismounting, he settled onto one knee, noting the large granules of sand nestled within the hoof prints. Gently extending a finger, the sand moved at the slightest touch. With a sweep of his palm, he brushed the ground around the tracks, the stiff breeze depositing more coarse sand. Shifting his focus, Scott eyed the dryness around the edges, estimating the horses had passed sometime during the midmorning hours. The question in his mind was what tribe had passed through? Even more worrisome, were they a raiding party intent on plundering and killing? It was not uncommon to encounter roving bands of Indians along the trail at this time of the year, but there was something else bothering him. Earlier this morning, less than a half mile from where he crouched, he had discovered different horse tracks. The tracks were left on the other side of a washed-out gully, but those ponies were wearing horseshoes, indicating white riders. Despite coming near the wagons, the riders chose to remain out of sight. Like the Indian party, they too were flanking the wagon train while remaining hidden. Considering the implications, Buchanan frowned. If they were frontiersmen not looking to cause trouble, why hadn't they ridden over for a friendly visit with the wagon train? Stopping for a visit was a common practice, something to be expected, unless of course, they were up to no good. If that was the case, then not riding over for a friendly visit made sense. There was the possibility they were Mexican bandits. He erased that thought from his thinking. Mostly bandits travel in large groups. Whoever rode those horses were too few in number. Besides, the wagon train wasn't near the southwestern border for such an encounter.

His years of scouting for the wagon train had sharpened Buchanan's instincts. Adding to those instincts was his knowledge of the different tribes, allowing him to think like those he feared and respected. A man had to admire the Indian's ability to live off the land, something he related to as well as being skilled at himself. Buchanan's hand brushed against the butt of his Walker Colt .44. Feeling the gun handle always gave him a measure of comfort, a way to fight back. He studied his surroundings. The land lay flat, patches of trees and bushes scattered in small bunches, the tall prairie grass yellowing from the lack of rain. The soft breeze was strengthening into a steady wind, the grass swaying back and forth. His eyes searched for danger, giving up because of the constant motion.

Buchanan rose out of his grouch, his fingers wrapped around the revolver's grip, his eyes trying to penetrate the tall patches of scrub half hidden by prairie grass. Thanks to the wind, everywhere he looked the grass was in constant motion.

Scott stood a tad short of six feet tall, his body lean and wiry. The hours Buchanan spent in the sun had left his face bronze colored in appearance. More than once he'd been mistaken for an Indian because of his skin color. His constant squinting into the horizon had produced wrinkles pulling at the corners of his eyes. Buchanan's tawny brown hair hung shoulder length, his gray hat pushed down to his ears, the hat bent out of shape. The sweatband showed light and dark stains caused by old and new perspiration. A rust-colored bandana surrounded his neck. Every piece of clothing he wore blended in with the colors of the land, and this was not by accident. In his profession, not being seen out here in the wilds had its advantages. The years on the frontier had taught him seeing someone first was an advantage regardless whether friend or foe. Not forgetting the Indian's ability to suddenly appear, he eyed the direction the horse tracks went before scanning beyond. Long ago he had learned no one could ever be sure when those masters of disappearance might suddenly appear. A mountain man had once warned him how every experience on the frontier is a dangerous lesson about to happen. For Scott Buchanan, such sage advice was something he never forgot.

Buchanan pulled his hat brim lower, shielding his eyes against the sun's glaring rays. He spoke to his dun-colored horse, his voice barely distinguishable over the moan from the wind. "Something's amiss here, old partner, could be dangerous too." He stroked the gelding's neck. Buchanan often spoke to his horse, reasoning things out as he talked. Being alone did that to a man. During those constant one-sided conversations, he had named his horse Buddy. Scott had chosen the young colt because of his color. Like a good camouflage, Buddy's light brown color and dark mane blended into the landscape. Not very pretty, but effective against being spotted by anyone with prying eyes. Buddy was a big horse, standing slightly more than sixteen hands high. Once an aggressive stallion, Scott had been forced to have him gelded. Over the years on the trail, he and Buddy bonded, the gelding knowing what he wanted without guidance, responding to the slightest pressure while being rode. He had often thought how Buddy would have been a great cattle horse. The big gelding could spin on a dime faster than most champion cutting horses. Even better, Buddy had an uncanny ability to sense danger, becoming Scott's other sixth sense.

Reasoning things out, Buchanan's mind returned to the present. It almost seemed like the Indians and mystery riders were following a similar pattern, which triggered the question, were they in cahoots? Reaching up, he grabbed his canteen. A cool drink of water always slowed him down, a habit forcing him to think before reacting on some impulse. Wiping his mouth, Scott hung the canteen back on the saddle horn. For a brief moment, he eyed his rifle. Like his pistol, knowing the Winchester was within easy reach gave him a feeling of security. Scott's hand drifted back to his Walker Colt. Gun in hand, he swung the cylinder open. No empty chambers stared back at him. Rolling it over in his palm, he looked at the revolver fondly. Originally he had been attracted to the gun because of the handle. Knowing the pistol's manufacture, it was easy to see the previous owner had replaced the original walnut with stag-horn boned pistol grips. There was another feature regarding the gun, much more important than the handle. The revolver was perfectly balanced. Wherever he pointed, when he pulled, the trigger was precisely where the bullets hit. Adding to the forty-four's accuracy was the trigger pull. It wasn't touchy, just right. Easing the cylinder closed, Scott dropped the gun back into its holster. Whoever the previous owner was, he must have gotten himself killed. Why else would a man give up such a gun? Of course, there was always the possibility the man had been down on his luck needing some quick cash. Regardless of the man's reasons, if the man still lived, Buchanan was sure the previous owner was skilled with a gun.

Buchanan turned toward Buddy, his hand gripping the pommel. Lifting his foot into the stirrup, he swung up. The gelding turned around, they headed north, his intention to satisfy his curiosity regarding the strangers riding shod horses. Reaching the dry arroyo, Scott allowed Buddy to find his own way down the bank. Crossing, they climbed back up onto the flats. Twenty minutes later, Scott brought Buddy to a halt, studying the mystery riders' horse tracks. Based on what he was seeing, he calculated there were seven riders. For several minutes he considered his options, finally shifting his eyes to the late afternoon sky. There was just enough daylight left to scout out one group, the question being, which one? Hell, he thought, pick the most likely to cause trouble. Just based on the numbers, it figured to be the Indians. If they were a raiding party with bad intentions, he had better find out. Buchanan was fairly sure they didn't have enough hot-blooded young bucks to attack the wagons. Despite not having the numbers, they wouldn't hesitate to grab an unwary woman who wandered too far from the safety of the wagons. At the very least, there were three hours of good daylight remaining before the evening shadows would make tracking difficult. In another two hours, his wagon boss, Clifford Stokes, would be circling his wagons for a night's stay along the south fork of the Platte River. Rubbing his chin, he liked his decision. Hell, he was paid to find out what his boss needed to know. Knowing his ramrod would suspect trouble once he failed to show up gave Scott peace of mind. Years ago, they had reached an understanding. When he stayed out, his boss placed extra men out on listening posts along with the normal watch. Another worry entered his thinking. Was it possible the braves were in some way working with the mysterious riders? With twilight only three hours away, if he got lucky, there might be time to scout out both. Regardless, right now the night sky was just coming out of the moonless stage giving him a tactical advantage. Considering the Indians' uncanny ability to uncover lurking danger, the coming darkness provided him the cover he needed. Of course, there was another option, one he liked, but one he should reject. Tempted, he mulled over reporting in. If he did, the wagons would be alerted and his duty done, not forgetting a hot meal would follow. Even more enticing, instead of him sleeping on hard ground, he would be wrapped in warm bedding for the night. Not a bad option, a very tempting choice. He gave the second option serious consideration. After all, the wagon train would be warned and he wouldn't go hungry. Buchanan sighed, questioning whether a night without food was necessary. Damned if options didn't have a way of making life's decisions more complicated, especially when one choice was more desirable than another. Scott shrugged, conceding how his first responsibility was to inform based on what he knew, not what might happen. He reckoned hot food would have to wait. Besides, the cold night meant the Indians would huddle around their fire for warmth. The reflection from the fire would lead him to their camp. Once he snuck in close, he should uncover what tribe rode the ponies and their intentions. If they were preparing for a night raid, there would still be enough time to sound a warning to the wagon master.

Buchanan turned Buddy with knee pressure. Retracing Buddy's tracks, they crossed the dry wash, finally picking up the Indian tracks. Tactfully following from a distance, he stayed within the lengthening shadows. It was unlikely any braves checking their back trail would discover him as long as he and his horse avoided casting moving shadows, the lay of the land helping as the sun dropped. Occasionally forced away from the shadows, he returned quickly. Once dusk enveloped the land, he would turn Buddy toward higher ground. Up there he could see for miles. It wasn't likely he'd see the raiding party, but one never knew. Patience along with caution went a long way toward rewarding the tracker while avoiding becoming the hunted. Out here on the trail, the constant threat of death was a way of life.

Easing along the base of the steepening slope, Buchanan was pretty positive he knew where the wagons would be camped for the night. If the raiding party was nearby, most likely they'd be somewhere above the bluff overlooking the river. If they weren't, they ceased to be a threat. A nice thought, but his instincts were telling him the savages were hanging around for a reason.

Buchanan's plan was simple enough. He'd circle wide and come in from the south. The greatest danger would be stumbling into their horses. Indians were known to use their horses as watchdogs. If the horses alerted the camp, he would be forced to slip away. If he avoided the horses, he should get close, real close. Another hour passed, the sun inching down, the late setting rays highlighting the tops of the distant hills. The brightness gone from the land, Scott turned Buddy for higher ground. Climbing upward, he swung the gelding west, the plateau waiting. Reaching into his saddlebag as the gelding walked, Buchanan extracted his binoculars. Halting Buddy at the edge of the plateau, he raised the binoculars, scanning for any movement. No moving shapes ghosted across the horizon. In another mile, he would be close to the river and so too would be whoever was following the wagon train. A glance at the sky told him evening was fast approaching. It was time to begin flanking in preparation for his stalk. If his memory wasn't failing him, he recalled large boulders scattered along the bluff. Those monstrous rocks would provide plenty of cover masking his approach. Touching Buddy with his heels, he turned him north, the gelding breaking into a trot, the landscape blending together, the hill flattening out. Except for occasional gusts disturbing the landscape, everything appeared as nature intended.

Seeing Buddy's hide soaked with sweat, Scott reined his horse into a walk allowing for cooling down. No sense in getting Buddy chilled by the night air. Out here, a man had better take care of his horse. If he didn't, he'd regret such a failing. Turning Buddy away from the frontal gusts, they dropped down the southern side of the plateau. Here sheltered from the wind, good grass grew in abundance.

Buchanan slipped from the saddle, tethering the gelding. Reaching into his saddlebags, Scott dragged out a pair of knee-high, mountain-man moccasins. With the coming darkness, the supple leather would muffle in any branches scraping across his ankles, the soft soles allowing him to feel every stick and rock underfoot. Reaching up, he slid the rifle from its scabbard. Out of habit, he worked the lever halfway. Satisfied a bullet nestled in the chamber, he closed the breech. Scrambling up the incline, Buchanan gathered his bearings. If he guessed right, the Indian camp should be located somewhere to the north in the general direction from his right shoulder. The wind becoming sporadic pleased him. Diminishing with each gust, the lessening noise would improve hearing.

Indians on the prowl keep their fires small guarding against being seen from those wishing them harm. Angling deeper into the boulders, Buchanan sniffed for burning wood. Ghosting forward, he cautioned against stumbling into Indian ponies. This was no time to be careless.

The sun was past the hills now, the light fading into gray dusk, the night moving toward becoming pitch-black. Feeling ahead with his left hand, Buchanan brought the Winchester to the front, carefully letting the rifle barrel nestle against his right shoulder. The rifle butt used for balance, he cradled the metal close to guard against the numerous rocks, the night now cloaking everything in darkness. Unable to tell a bush from a boulder, he stopped. His eyes shut, Scott counted to ten. His night vision captured, he eased forward. Ahead a flickering glow penetrated the night. Careful to avoid the boulders, he neared the flickering light. Scott froze, his ears straining, the sound came again. It was made by a horse stomping the ground. Backing up, he flanked around the sound. Sure the wind was in his face, he neared the flickering flames, barely able to see the huddled shapes around the glowing embers.

Too far away to hear, Buchanan dropped close to the earth. Guarding against his face being highlighted by the fire, chin hugging the ground, he inched forward. The talk loud enough to hear, he eased up onto his elbows. The faint light from the coals showed faces without war paint. The language they spoke was Kiowa, their conversation laced with humor, making fun at the expense of one of their own. Occasionally, one of the bucks would give off a soft devilish laugh, mocking whoever was being singled out. Confident they were posing no immediate threat, Buchanan slithered away. Sure he was a safe distance, he jumped to his feet. Threading his way between the mammoth rocks, he cleared the boulders; a sliver of moon gave him a touch of light to follow. Shifting into a cautious lope, he scrambled over the south slope, dropping down. Alarmed, Buddy shied away, Scott's hand clamping over Buddy's muzzle. Sure the big gelding wouldn't blow, he relaxed his grip, his words soothing, "Easy, boy… easy now."

There were times when it was proper for a man to pat himself on the back, this being such a moment. His horse settled, Buchanan spoke to himself, Buddy included, "Hey, I did real well. I was but a stone throw away and they never heard me." Before he got overly confident, he reminded himself Indians have a way of sensing a person's presence, almost as if possessing animal instincts. As far as he was concerned, they could smell out a man like a wolf pack trailing wounded game. One thing Buchanan was sure of, he wasn't about to spend the night near a bunch of Kiowa on the prowl for whatever reason. Nope, he reasoned, it would be smart to clear the area before he got himself discovered.

Since it was better to vamoose anyway, why not check out those mystery riders. Made sense, that's if he didn't get lost with the night being so black and all. Checking the night sky, Buchanan frowned, the sliver of moon slipping behind some fishtailed clouds. No help there. As he had many times, he would have to rely on Buddy's uncanny ability to find his way in the dark. Slipping the rifle back into the scabbard, he coiled Buddy's tether, stuffing the rope. Rising into the saddle, he urged the gelding well below the crest of the hill. Sure they had enough distance against being detected; he let Buddy pick his way up to the top. The sliver of moon reappeared before disappearing, only the brightest stars casting any light.

Swinging east, Scott tapped the gelding with his heels, his horse barely cantering, as if wondering why his master insisted on traveling on such a dark night. The dry arroyo ahead, they crossed over. Sure he was in the vicinity where he'd seen the tracks, Scott hauled back on the reins, Buddy more than glad to halt. Leaning over as close to the ground as possible without dismounting, he stared hard, the lack of light made seeing impossible. Finally he gave up. Straightening in the saddle, he prodded Buddy in the direction of the river. The gurgling sounds from running water would be their guide, not forgetting Buddy's knack for understanding his master's wants. If he found those riders on this pitch-black night, it would be because of his horse. Scott figured as long as the riders were flanking the wagons, they should be upriver, hopefully a campfire providing a final beacon. Unlike Indian fires, as long as wood's plentiful, most settlers crossing the plains tend to make large bonfires. If the riders had a fire going, Scott was sure it would light up the night. Arriving near the riverbank, he turned Buddy upriver.

Scott marveled at the harsh sounds coming from hundreds of chorus frogs, their singing creating a deafening clamor, as if hearing rusty disk blades grinding through rocky soil behind a team of plow horses. Occasionally their mating cries subsided, replaced by shrill chirping from the insect world.

The night darker than ever, Scott remembered his boyhood years, recalling those evening fishing times when he prowled along the eastern ponds and streams listening to spring peepers as the darkness fell, the frogs serenading the night. Funny, he thought, how escaping into nature had allowed him to survive a troublesome home. His dad was a hard worker, a good provider, the problem being alcohol. When his father drank, you didn't want to be around, when he didn't, he was a joy to be around. When dad was under the influence, it was time to slip away, nature his sanctuary, those early and late excursions into the woods preserving his sanity. During those excursions into nature, Buchanan developed a fascination for the outdoors and everything about it. When his mother died, it was no wonder he journeyed west where wildlife teemed.

Attracted to flickering light, Buchanan's musings stopped. Up ahead, flames were pushing back the night, sparks leaping skyward. Where the river curved, the trees bordering the riverbank obscured the fire. Rounding the bend, the flames back in view, he rose in the stirrups, groaning. The fire was on the far side of the river. Whoever those riders were, they had used daylight to find a way across the river. If that doesn't beat all, he thought, especially with the night becoming chilly. One thing for sure, he wasn't about to get wet fording the river, not at this hour. Resting his forearms on Buddy's neck, he gave his frustration some thought. The logical answer was to bed down this side of the river until the morning. After daybreak, he would locate some high ground, use his binoculars, pinpoint their camp, and then cross for a closer look.

Satisfied he had a plan, one that would keep him dry; all that was needed now was a place to sleep. Turned around in the saddle, Buchanan eyed a black mass, darker than other surroundings, guessing the mass a grove of trees. If they were, he would be sheltered from the damp breeze coming across the river. They approached the mass; Scott pleased his guess was correct. Dismounting, he led Buddy around the leeward side. Here, the grove blocked the damp breeze. The temperature felt like it had risen fifteen degrees. Pleased, Scott dropped to one knee, his hand finding bunches of grass. Good, Buddy had his food for the night. The bit removed, he attached a tether to the halter, Buddy left with plenty of rope for grazing. Pulling the saddle, he ducked under the canopy of branches, his feet sinking into a thick carpet of leaves. The saddle placed where he would bed, Scott quickly cleared away any sticks and stones. Untying the bedroll, he smoothed out the ground cloth, the blanket alongside. Folding his jacket into a pillow, he unbuckled his gun belt, placing it within easy reach alongside the saddle horn, his rifle just beyond the pistol. There would be no groping in the dark if his guns were needed. Adjusting his bedding, he sat. Next off came one moccasin, then the other. Carefully he placed them where they'd be covered by the blanket. Stretching out full length, he dragged the blanket over his body. Thanks to the soft cushioning provided by nature, sleep came quickly.

DAYBREAK

Awakened by the sounds from dripping moisture coming off the canopy of leaves, Buchanan pulled the blanket higher. Several minutes passed before he gave in. Searching with his left hand, he found both moccasins, pleased they had remained under the bedding during the night. It was a lousy feeling pulling on stiff leather compliments from the night air. Rolling onto his side, he exposed one moccasin at a time, giving each a violent shake. Satisfied no creature had found a home during the night, he wiggled into the moccasins. Shifting onto his knees he stood, the dripping sounds louder—*plop—plop—splat!* He shivered as the wet chill surrounded him, compliments from the river sending up a ground mist during the night. Shrugging into his sheepskin jacket, he pulled the collar higher, the large collar warding the chill away from the back of his neck. Next on went his hat, providing more comfort. Not wanting to start a fire potentially alerting whoever was on the far side of the river, he stared into the predawn darkness. Tempted to climb back under the bedding, he convinced himself otherwise. Settling into a sitting position, he waited for the light to strengthen, the pleasant thought of coffee invading his thinking. Funny how civilization spoiled a man, he grimaced, even wagon train civilization. His imagination taking hold, he could almost smell percolating coffee along with frying bacon. What the heck, why not throw in his favorite sourdough biscuits for good measure. For the first time, the light was now penetrating the gloom. Seeing his breath hanging suspended before his face lifted his spirits. Once the night let go, he would locate the rider's camp and cross the river for some eavesdropping. One way or the other, before he slipped away, he would have the information his boss needed.

In the distance, a series of sharp yaps from a hunting fox heralded the sly critter's night of hunting coming to an end. Slowly the near objects took shape. Wrapping his hand around his gun belt, Scott rolled to his feet. Buckling on the belt, he hoisted the saddle. Bent over to avoid the low soaking wet branches, he found Buddy with his head down, the gelding's hindquarters facing the river. Objecting to being disturbed, Buddy snorted at his approach. Speaking softly, Scott stroked him before flipping on the horse blanket, followed by the saddle. Tightening the cinch, he worked the bridle-bit into Buddy's mouth. Wrapping the reins around a sapling, he pulled out his binoculars from the saddlebag. The glasses were large, the type used by sea captains. Ducking under the canopy of leaves, he retrieved his rifle. Skirting along the riverbank, he looked for a vantage point, hopefully an elevated location. Just ahead a once tall yellow birch offered potential. The tree was snapped in half from a strong wind. Still hinged to the main trunk, the tree's top half slanted to the ground. Seeing how the connecting hinge was halfway up, if he climbed to where the tree was hinged he had the elevation needed to see across the river. Yep, he decided, the tree would do—brittle branches and all. Laying his rifle on the other side of the trunk, he grasped the stoutest branch, his other hand finding a like cousin. Cautiously climbing one foot at a time, he reached the hinge. Wrapping arms tightly around the trunk, he squirmed around, staring across the slow moving current.

Scott frowned. Where were the riders? No horses, no anything! "What in the hell," Scott grunted aloud enough to be heard. Still searching with his eyes, a dark spot attracted his attention. Adjusting the binoculars, the spot became an ash pile. Studying the ashes, he was unable to detect even the slightest wisp of smoke. Puzzled, he lowered the optics. Something wasn't adding up, especially with the night being as dark as the ace of spades. Hell, hadn't it been too dark to leave before daybreak? So why had they left so early? Was it possible the mystery riders had just left? Maybe, perhaps some sense might yet come from this. One thing was for sure, staying up in this tree wasn't going to give him any answers. Only the spent coals would provide any clues as to when those riders rode out. Cautiously working his way back down, he settled onto the ground. Grabbing his rifle, he scrambled for his horse. Rising into the saddle, Buchanan headed Buddy downstream. Wherever those riders had forded the day before, that's where they would cross. It didn't take him long to find where the riders had entered the water. Here, the river widened, hardly moving. He urged Buddy into the sluggish current. Reaching the far side, they climbed out. Throwing caution to the wind; he booted the gelding into a trot, the campsite just around the bend. Swinging into view, he came out of the saddle on the run, pulling his forty-four. Sliding to a stop, he studied the near surroundings. Satisfied it was safe, he eyed the burnt coffee grounds scattered over the charred wood. Ready to jerk his finger away, he brushed the ashes, the coals barely warm. Strange, he pondered, still puzzled by such an early departure. Since they were flanking the wagons, why hadn't they waited until the wagons moved up the trail? Because of the darkness, none of this was making a lick of horse sense. Shoving his hat back, he contemplated a worrisome possibility. Could it be their intention to hook up with the Kiowa for the purpose of causing trouble? There was only one way to be sure. He would have to ride back to the Indian camp. His hand still holding the six-shooter, he circled the campsite searching for clues. Nothing of importance jumped up at him. Holstering his gun, he grabbed the saddle horn, vaulting aboard his horse. The brisk air made Buddy eager to run and Scott let him run. The big male broke into a spirited gallop. Splashing across the river, they neared the washed out gully. Cautious again, he reined Buddy down to a walk, looking for new tracks mingling with last night's. Seeing none, he urged Buddy up out of the wash, nudging the gelding back into a gallop. As they had the evening before, they would approach the Indian camp from the south. Reaching the grassy hillside, Buchanan wheeled the gelding around. Sliding from the saddle, he wrapped Buddy's reins, jerking out his Winchester.

Moving quickly, Buchanan reached the boulders before hunkering down. Sucking in deep breaths, he reminded himself this was no time to become a rushing fool. Having spent a night of caution, he had no intention of becoming stupid through impatience.

Even smarter, he'd better follow his lifetime habit of making sure there was always a bullet in the rifle's chamber. The first time a man fails to make sure his rifle's locked and loaded is the one time a rifle isn't ready to fire. He'd heard plenty of empty gun stories happening to others, stories with unhappy endings. Careful not to disturb the natural, he eased the breech halfway. Satisfied, he closed it. Moving forward in a crouch, he followed his previous moccasin prints. Nearing where he'd dropped down to crawl, he strained to hear sounds indicating human presence. All he heard were birds singing and a gentle breeze rustling the hillside. Remaining still for several seconds, he eyed the large boulder where he'd first spotted the Kiowa's fire. Keeping the sun at his back assuring a shooting advantage, he eased behind the mammoth rock. Pushing his hat off, he felt it dangle against his shoulder blades. Careful not to clink the barrel against the rock's hard surface, he raised the rifle clear of the boulder. Standing, he eyed the empty campsite. Quickly bridging the distance, Scott touched the ashes from last night. The coals were cold to the touch. Made sense, he concluded, Indians on the prowl weren't slowed down by a need for morning coffee. They travel light, often eating on the run, mostly depending on dried trail food. During his many contacts with different Indian tribes, he'd never seen a fat warrior, overweight squaws, but never young or old bucks.

Settling back onto his haunches, Scott reflected on what the early morning signs indicated. Despite all of his running around, not much, other than both parties having left early. The early departure of the Kiowa didn't puzzle him. Most likely they had a far destination in mind. If that was their intention, a good sign. What kept nagging at him was why those strange riders left so early. Buchanan stood, studying the direction left by the pony tracks. Like the strange riders, they too were traveling in a westerly direction. The only way he'd know if they planned on meeting was to pick up their trail and see if they joined up. Turning, he walked to the edge of the bluff, not surprised at what he saw below. From up here, he could see every circled wagon, smoke rising from the numerous cooking fires. He shifted his eyes to the ground, eyeing the moccasin prints etched along the rim. Obviously, the Kiowa had taken a good look at the folks below. Again, the question turning over in his mind was whether both parties were in cahoots concerning the wagons? Of course, the only way he could be sure was to spend the remainder of the day following pony tracks, which meant his boss would have to take extra precautions without knowing why? What with him being so close, he decided to check in. Since it was his job to scout in advance anyway, he'd find out soon enough if the two groups meet up again. A smile creased his face, his brain focusing on fresh coffee, including morning chow. For the first time in a day and a half, he felt the tenseness leave his muscles. Flirting with danger kept a man on edge. Rifle over his shoulder, he started back for his horse.

Cliff Stokes had been up and about early. It was his habit to check with his watchmen before having that first cup of coffee. He was pleased, the night uneventful. That part was good—now where was his scout? Sipping coffee, he stole a look at Wendell.

Aware of his boss's look, Wendell spoke his mind, "You had better get something to eat besides just drinking coffee. If you don't, you'll be irritable all day long—that's fer sure."

Cliff fought back verbally. "Since you insist, cook up some grub."

Wendell's reply was laced with humor, sarcasm not excluded. "Lord Almighty, can't you smell food? 'Cause it's already cooked. I sure ain't waiting on you hand and foot. It's bad enough I got to cook it, next you'll want me to chew it for you like a cow chews the cud."

Shuffling over to the hanging pot, Cliff grabbed the long handled spoon, generously piling hash on his plate. Tearing a chunk of bread, he stuffed his mouth with hash followed by bread. Cliff waited for Wendell to offer more advice. He didn't have to wait long.

Wendell knew his boss would let him have his say. Besides him, there were two others Cliff paid heed to. One was his foreman, Stuart Whitman, next came the chief scout, Scott Buchanan. But as of right now, the chief scout wasn't here and neither was the foreman. Therefore, it was Wendell's responsibility to get the boss going. Wendell's voice carried a touch of sass, "What are you planning on doing, hanging around until Scott Buchanan shows up—or try to get something accomplished before he does? You know, there are a few things needing fixing while we're waiting."

Cliff didn't mind he was being scolded while being advised at the same time. "Thanks for jogging my mind loose, Mr. Bartholomew." Placing both hands on his hips, Cliff chided back, "Just where would I be without you? No, don't answer that. I haven't all day. As for your suggestion, I suppose a few wagons do need some attention. Since we're way ahead of schedule, we might as well get it done. If Buchanan shows up before long, we can hold off, which is what I expect will happen. If he's not back by noon, I'll take out a search party. Does that meet with your approval… Mr. Wendell Bartholomew?"

Shrugging, Wendell offered another suggestion via a question, "Are you going to inform the folks what's happened?"

Observing the wagons, Cliff saw most of the people were busy around their fires. "I reckon not. Except for the Clark family, nobody knows what's happened. I'll wait until the travelers are finished eating. Once they have all their pots and pans stashed, then I'll say something." A positive thought jumped into his head. Grinning, he voiced it, "Who knows, maybe Buchanan will come riding in for some morning coffee, not to mention wanting a little chow. We've seen that before, haven't we? You know what, chief cook, sometimes the best moves a man makes are the moves he doesn't make. In other words, give time a chance to work."

Wendell conceded, "Yes, sir, Mr. Stokes, many a time I've seen you use them stalling tactics over the years. Yep, you can make a long summer look like it will never get to winter."

Pouring more coffee, Cliff washed down the salty hash, his eyes wandering toward the Clark wagon, pleased they were going about their normal routine while keeping their promise to keep everything quiet. Noticing Wendell laughing, he asked him, "What's so funny?"

"Take a look out onto them flats."

Turning, Cliff did a double-take. A lone rider aboard a dun-colored horse was approaching. A barely visible smile tugged at Cliff's mouth, a sigh of relief escaping him. Hoping he'd kept the sigh silent so his cook hadn't noticed, wisdom seeped from his voice. "Didn't I tell you that patience works?"

"Yep, you did. But I think a better word might be... hoping? Like I've said, if I've seen it once, I've seen it a hundred times. Whenever you're stumped about what to do, you just wait things out as if that was your plan all along. The truth is, you got more luck than a polecat with nine lives!" With a wave of his hand, he dismissed the boss, talking to no one in particular. "This is going to be mighty interesting." Wendell grabbed a cup. Pouring coffee, he was ready to hand it to the chief scout when he climbed off his horse.

Delighted, Stephanie touched her father's arm as the curly-haired scout passed. "Dad, look who's arriving."

Adam's eyes locked onto the scout, relief surging through his body. For the first time since yesterday, he relaxed. "Thank God," he exclaimed, adding, "Stephanie, we have to find out what happened last night."

Studying the lean rider, Stephanie remembered the wagon boss's description of the wagon scout. The boss man said Buchanan acted like he was half Apache and half Cheyenne. She also remembered Stokes saying he doubted the man would be comfortable in a civilized society. For the first time on this trip, she was becoming interested in this Scott Buchanan.

Pulling back on the reins, Buchanan slipped off his horse. Reaching out he took the coffee from Wendell, eyeing with pleasure the hot vapors rising from the cup. He smiled, thinking how coffee needed to be hot to taste right. Protecting his lips, he sipped, confessing, "A man doesn't realize how much a cup of hot coffee is missed until he goes without. Man, this hits the spot, damn near perfect too." He gestured toward the fire. "What's in the pot?"

Not wasting any words, Wendell answered, "Hash. Here, let me dish you up some."

Amused at the preferential treatment his scout was receiving, a smile tugged on Cliff's lips.

Buchanan found himself a comfortable seat; the hash was saltier than normal. There would be no protest. When a man's hungry, it all tastes good.

Stokes dug into his vest pulling out fixings for a smoke. Rolling the paper around the tobacco, he expertly twisted both ends, wetting it with his lips. Striking a match, he watched the burnt sulfur smoke curl upward before lighting his smoke. Refraining from any show of impatience, he watched his scout feed his face. Outwaiting each other was a game both of them played—usually ending up in Cliff's favor. After all, it was Buchanan's responsibility to do the reporting. Cliff chuckled inwardly, knowing he'd never lost, at least not yet, but then, neither had Buchanan. His scout never rushed giving information unless it was an emergency. It was the scout's way of winning. Cliff had learned to wait for his few chosen words. Buchanan took a chunk of bread from Wendell, mopping the remaining hash off his plate. With no more room for food, Buchanan shifted his attention to the smoking cigarette.

Cliff asked, "Want one?"

"It would be a nice way to finish off the meal."

Handing over his smoke, Cliff rolled another.

Enjoying his first puff, Buchanan got started. "I ran into two sets of horse tracks on each side of the wagon trail yesterday, one bunch was Kiowa. They camped last night on the upper plateau overlooking the wagons. They rode out sometime around daybreak. Before they left, they took a good look down here before heading out. I figured a total of fifteen in that bunch. I'm guessing they're a raiding party. Anyway, they rode west. The other set of horse tracks were shoed indicating white riders. I was sure because all the riders were on shoed horses. They crossed the river about a mile below us. Like the Indians, they left during the early morning hours. Never saw them, just the signs they left. What bothered me was how they have been going out of their way to stay out of sight. Seemed strange how they crossed the river without coming over for a visit, made me suspicious. Don't ask me what they're up to 'cause I have no idea. I decided to use the cover of darkness to check out both groups, maybe get a read on their intentions. I managed to get close to the Kiowa. From what I saw and heard, they weren't planning on jumping the wagon train, at least not yet. They're a small bunch, and besides, they're Kiowa, still dangerous, but not Comanche or Cheyenne. It was those riders that really puzzled me. I never got to see them. I was sure I could spy on them in the morning, but they pulled out before first light. I couldn't figure that out either. Hell, it was pitch-black last night, not much better at first light. I did locate their camp during the night. Unfortunately, they crossed the river during daylight hours. There was no way I was going to do a river crossing in the dark and spend a wet night. That's my report and now you know as much as me."

Digesting Buchanan's report, Cliff talked out loud, having a private conversation with himself including anyone within hearing range, "So we got potential trouble hiding from us." Taking another pull on his smoke, he kept his conversation private. "Since we have Kiowa on this side and strange riders on the other side of the river, I'll activate Wes Santana. That way we'll have two scouts working." Stopping, he eyed Buchanan, including him, "Naturally, God forbid, you'll be in charge." Knowing his scout was touchy about repeating himself, he changed the subject. "You get enough sleep?"

"Matter of fact I did." He liked the boss's choice of Wes Santana, agreeing, "Wes is a good choice. He takes instructions well. I'll scout the south side of the trail using Wes across the river to the north. I want to keep a personal eye on those Kiowa. There are more of them and they can be feisty when they have a mind to be. I wouldn't mind putting a scare into them if I get a chance." Holding out his cup to Wendell, he requested, "I could use some more of that mud, Mr. Wendell. You sure do make a decent pot of coffee."

Cliff was done with planning, giving an order. "Scott, when you finish washing your plate, find Wes and send him over here."

Draining his cup, Scott rose, now holding out his plate to Wendell to be washed. "The boss just gave me an order and I need a favor."

Irony reflected in Wendell's voice, "Yeah, but don't keep expecting this kind of service or before you know it you'll be like our wagon boss."

Grinding the cigarette butt into the ground, Scott laughed, departing to find Santana. Passing the third wagon a voice hailed him. "Excuse us, wagon scout, would you give us a minute?"

Stopping, Buchanan eyed the older man with the pretty daughter standing at his side. "Sure, what's on your minds?"

"We know you didn't come in last night. Because of our concerns, we asked your boss why. Of course, Mr. Stokes wasn't sure. He did explain the way both of you like to operate. I guess you could say, we are downright curious as to why you stayed out. My daughter and I are hoping you wouldn't mind telling us."

Not wanting to offend, Buchanan didn't like breaking with his boss's wishes of letting him deal with passengers. "Well, here's the thing, I have to be careful. The reason I need to be careful is because some folks can go into a panic, which means I usually leave the explaining part up to my boss. Fact is he's more diplomatic than I. Besides, he wants it that way."

The girl spoke up, "We do understand. Last night your boss told us everything, and we promised to keep it to ourselves." Smiling, Stephanie added, "We will do the same with you."

Surprised at her boldness, Buchanan looked into her eyes. One of his abilities was judging character. The way she expressed herself and what the boss had already told them, he gave in. "We had some unknown riders on each side of the wagon trail. One bunch was Kiowa, the other bunch I didn't get a look at. I figured the smaller group to be white riders. Both appear to have moved on. I have no idea what the riders intentions are, much less what the Indians are up to. My biggest concern are the Kiowa, as of right now, they're gone. Just to make sure, Mr. Stokes is giving me an extra man for scouting today. My advice is for everyone to stay close to the wagons, especially womenfolk. Indians love to steal women and children. Right now you know all there is to know. Is there anything else before I go?"

Complimentary, Stephanie thanked him. "We appreciate your forthrightness and we thank you for being forthright with us."

"That's my job, you're welcome. But please, any more questions, ask my boss. Like I said, he wants it that way and I do work for him." Tipping his hat, he left. The father and daughter had caught him by surprise, especially the daughter. She was a lot older than he realized, awful pretty too. Trouble was, she talked like an educated woman. As good a looker as she was, that educated part left him out. The best he could do was read and write a few simple words, better than most, but not impressive enough for those with a formal education. Besides, hadn't he always made it a policy to avoid becoming involved with any of the travelers? Wagon folks come and go and he liked his job. Out here on the trail, he was a free spirit. There was another reason to avoid becoming involved. Scouting allowed him to save most of what he earned. For him, not spending money on the trail was a given. After all, the wagon train provided all the necessary food and shelter, not a bad way to live while saving money. Over time he had managed to save up quite a stash. As for socialization, there were times when the wagon boss's foreman broke out his fiddle for a night of dancing, not forgetting there was always the next town. For the present, just getting to the next destination and meeting up with some of the women would take care of his flirtation needs. Nope, he thought, being on the trail took care of everything. If he ever got attracted to some woman, he would have to leave his profession. As of right now, he had no intentions of becoming domesticated, maybe sometime, but not now. There was something else he liked about being a top scout. People depended on him, giving him a feeling of personal satisfaction.

Crossing the grounds between the circled wagons, Buchanan saw Wes Santana watching him. Considering all the men on the wagon train, Wes was the one man he didn't mind scouting with. The man always did what was asked of him. He did it right too. Whenever Wes asked a question, it was well thought out, worth answering. Even better, the man never talked just for the sake of talking. Out here in Indian country, talking was a distraction away from being observant. Even worse, giving away your presence, a potential recipe for disaster! Most times a wagon scout rode alone, always watchful, not missing anything. Because of Buchanan's tutoring, Santana had become skilled at understanding trail signs. There was another personality trait he liked about Santana. Despite Buchanan's insistence on staying alert on the trail, there were times when Santana's humor broke up the seriousness, providing for a little fun. Out here such an attitude often helped break up the monotony when the days became long and boring.

Watching Buchanan approaching, Wes had a hunch this was more than a casual visit. "Morning, Scott, I noticed you stayed out last night. What's out there?"

"Wes, you got lucky. You're getting relieved from doing chores, work chores, the type you hate. To answer your question, right now we're being flanked by mystery riders on one side and a bunch of Kiowa sneaks on this side." Scott grinned. "My boss thinks I need help and instructed me you're the logical choice. He's waiting to see you. I'll wait here while you go see him."

An ear-splitting grin spreading across his face, Wes knew the chief scout understood how he'd rather scout then be stuck doing everyday jobs. "It's about time, be back in a few minutes."

Chuckling, Scott watched Wes angling near the sixth wagon while sneaking a peek at the three women traveling with the single man. More than once Wes Santana had informed him how he wouldn't mind getting hitched to a gal as long as she was a good-looker, and all three women were attractive lookers. Buchanan also remembered Wes complaining about the fellow in the fifth wagon. It seemed the fellow was a real charmer, a magnet attracting all the single ladies, including a few wives. It was easy to see why. The man's confidence stemmed from his good looks and suave manners. His dark beard was well kept, highlighting square features. The man's name was Tyler Harden. Even worse for Santana, the man had the gift of gab. During the night, everyone visited the fifth wagon, including the three good-lookers.

Stokes wasn't surprised how quickly Santana showed up. "Obviously, Scott told you you'll be scouting."

"He did, said to report to you."

"I'm sure he explained the unusual circumstances."

"Mentioned a band of Kiowa and horsemen staying out of sight."

"Good, now you know as much as I do. I'm sure Buchanan will fill you in on what else you need to know while you're scouting. Now, here's what I insist you understand. I expect two reports a day, one around noon and one by sundown. If one of you has to stay out, it'll be Buchanan, not you."

"Yes, sir, you pay me, not him."

"Good, don't forget that."

"I won't. I've got one favor to ask from you."

"Let me guess, you want me to tell Scott what I just told you?"

"Yes, sir, you know how he is."

Cliff glanced at Wendell. "I guess we all do, don't we, Wendell?" Eyebrows arched, Cliff defended himself against what was coming from Wendell, "All right, all right, but maybe that's why he's good at what he does. It comes from proper training, my training!"

A cackle escaped the cook. "Yepper, we sure do." Wendell pointed at Cliff. "And it was you who trained him. I can remember you always telling him to get to the point, and after he did, then you wanted the details. What's that old saying, not far from the tree the leaf falls?"

"So," Wes leaned forward, intent on making sure his request wasn't forgotten. "You are going to tell him?"

"Yes, Mr. Santana," Stokes assured him, "I will tell the chief scout. Now, you go and tell Buchanan I want him back here. After you've given my message, go find my foreman. When you locate Stuart, tell him we move out within the hour. One last thing, I hope you've fed your face by now?"

"Yes sir, finished about a half hour ago."

"Good. I hope you're ready to ride because I want both of you in the saddle and gone before the wagons depart. Is there anything else I need to explain?"

"Nope, I'm on my way."

Every so often, Cliff liked to remind his cook who was the ramrod, his voice giving an order. "Cook, get those pots and pans packed. We can't expect the people to be ready if we're not."

Not protesting, Wendell got started.

Cliff lifted his face upward, the sky his barometer for judging weather. Right now there wasn't a cloud up there, meaning good trail conditions ahead. Satisfied, he shifted his thinking to the day's events. Despite his confidence in his chief scout, seeing him ride in this morning was a relief. He and Buchanan had overcome many dangers together. As for those strange riders and Kiowa, now that he was alerted, there would be no surprises.

NIGHT CAMP

Stephanie was pleased the way Tyler Harden greeted her parents. Escorting each one by the hand, Tyler found a comfortable seat just the right distance from the fire. Seeing Tyler's lavish attention made her parents feel special, Stephanie was more than pleased. Tyler turned to her, a glint of mischief showing in his expression. Gesturing at the opposite side of the fire, he suggested, "I've got a place for you directly across from your parents." Smiling, almost apologetic, he winked, pointing at two overturned barrels. "That's the best I could do… for us! But they are reasonably comfortable." Turning, he introduced his traveling partner. "Folks, this is my good friend, Mr. James Cooper."

James bowed slightly; his voice owned a captivating quality, "Mighty glad to meet you folks." Cooper was a tall man, shaggy hair hanging down to his shoulders. When he looked at a person, his face showed a keen interest, and he was interested. Such a look had a way of making people want to talk with him. His manner of his conversation was to lean forward, his eyes riveted, as if hanging on every spoken word. Once you had Cooper's attention, it didn't waver.

Stephanie was delighted as Tyler sat down beside her, his voice addressing everyone, "Earlier this morning the Meekers favored me with some cornbread, which I was smart enough to wrap properly for tonight. I've just percolated a fresh pot of coffee, and if anyone is tired of coffee, I've also brewed some tea." Smiling, Tyler, like Cooper, leaned forward. "Right now I'm taking orders. All I need to know is who wants what?"

Sitting near Stephanie's parents were the two Lancaster brothers, Bill and Neal. Next to the brothers sat their wives, Susan and Amy. Susan had black hair tied back into a single ponytail, her fingers wrapped around Neal's hand.

Neal had a wiry build, his neck pronounced with a noticeable Adam's apple protruding from his throat. Neal's appearance was like that of a long-necked water bird ready to swallow a fish, he also had the look of a man full of boundless energy. Constantly fidgeting, Neal was all of that.

Bill's wife Amy had long brown hair cascading down to her shoulders. Like Susan, her hand nestled atop her husband's hand. Except for his neck, Bill's build was similar to Neal's. There was something else about both brothers. It was the physical appearance of their hands. Each had slender fingers, fingers so long it seemed as if they should have been musicians, their fingers perfectly suited to be wrapped around some type of string instrument.

Amy was the first to be complimentary, "How nice, tea or coffee with cornbread. I think I would enjoy tea with my bread."

Bill agreed with his wife. "I'll have the same."

Tyler eyed Neal and Susan, asking them, "How about you folks?"

Neal waited for Susan to decide, her response immediate, "Tea would be a welcome change." She smiled at Neal, who like his brother followed his wife's decision. "Tea also works for me."

Now it was the Clark's turn, Adam speaking for both. "It sounds unanimous, tea with cornbread… well almost!" Checking with Stephanie, he encouraged her, "Well, honey?"

Laughing, Stephanie looked at Tyler, her voice breezy. "It seems that you shouldn't have made the coffee."

Grinning, Tyler agreed, "Next time I'll be smarter and take orders ahead of time. At the very least, the aroma of freshly brewed coffee always enhances the ambience of the moment, therefore, not a complete waste."

The use of the word ambiance impressed Stephanie.

Every head nodded in agreement, smiling faces staring back at him.

Leaning forward, Tyler touched Stephanie lightly. "In the back of the wagon is a tray full of cornbread. Would you please get it for me?"

Thrilled by Tyler's touch, Stephanie stood, her destination the rear of the wagon. As she walked, she reflected on Tyler's relaxed way of speaking.

Tyler pointed at a flat board lying across two overturned boxes. "The teapot is next to the cups, sugars in the tin. If everyone will pick up a cup, I'll pour the tea."

Sipping from his cup, Adam couldn't help but notice his daughter was showing serious interest in Tyler Harden. He wasn't sure he liked this slick-talking fellow. It was time to find out about the man, reminding himself to be tactful. He began, "Tell me, Mr. Harden, where is your final destination?"

Tyler's response was right to the point. "California."

"California, you say. Are you after gold?"

Stealing a peek at Stephanie, Tyler winked before answering her father. "Goodness, no, I believe you earn your gold! Fact is I have a job waiting for me when I get there. I'm a writer for a newspaper in San Francisco as well becoming a partner and senior editor. This was my last trip back east while finishing up some loose ends."

Adam liked Harden's answer. His profession explained his exceptional vocabulary. So far so good, he thought. Now it was time to find out about Tyler's personal life. "Tell me about your wife. Is she already settled in California?"

"My wife died two years ago. She was pregnant with a child. I lost both."

Around the fire, there were gasps of sympathy.

Caught by surprise, Adam voiced sincerity, "My condolences."

Stephanie too was moved. "How terrible, is that why you're moving to California?"

"Yes, Stephanie, that is precisely why I'm relocating out west. There were too many memories staying where we once lived."

Susan spoke with sincerity, "Let me add my condolences, Mr. Harden."

For a moment, the only noise came from the crackling sounds of burning wood, Tyler taking advantage, his words conversational, "I appreciate everyone's sympathetic understanding. I guess we all have our reasons for moving west. Once I gained control over my grief, I became excited about my career again. It was then that I decided to go west. I'll be glad when this trip is over. Doing this twice is a bit much. How about the rest of you? What's drawing you folks west?"

Neal was the first to answer. "For us it was a better opportunity. Unlike some of you, this is our first and last trip. What with young'uns and all, not to mention some Indians along the trail, we won't be making any return trips." He looked at his wife. "Will we, Susan?"

Susan's nod was emphatic.

Norma Clark liked this Tyler Harden, her voice indicating respect. "Tell me, Mr. Harden, why did you choose California?"

Tyler reflected for a second before answering her. "I guess the farther away the better. It was either California or Oregon because of my business connections. I have a friend as well as a former newspaper partner who moved out to California. Another associate of mine settled in Oregon. My closest friend, the one in California, gave me the opportunity to buy in." Tyler grinned, adding, "No interview necessary!"

Adam was impressed. The man had connections with important people, even better, a partnership.

Worried about Indians, Amy voiced her concerns, "Am I the only one afraid of the Indians?"

Expressing understanding, Tyler agreed, "No, you're not the only one. You should be concerned since you have children. But here's some good news. I don't know if any of you realize this or not, but you happened to have picked the best wagon master on the trail." Pausing, he eyed the circle of faces. "I trust you folks are aware of such?"

Amy wasn't, shaking her head no.

His face serious, Tyler continued, "I've traveled with Clifford Stokes before and I'm sure everything will be fine."

Bill spoke up. "You say you've traveled with this wagon master before. Exactly why did you choose him?"

Tyler leaned back. "Prior to choosing this wagon train, I did lots of checking around. We newspaper people call that investigative research, and from everything I researched, Clifford Stokes has an outstanding reputation. Yes, he's pricey, but you get what you pay for." Tyler stopped talking, waiting for more questions.

For Bill, it was obvious the man knew more than the rest of them. After all, he had traveled with this wagon train more than once. Curious, he asked Tyler, "Would you say the Indians pose the greatest threat to us, or are there other dangers along the trail?"

"Everything on the trail can be a test for survival. I understand that and so should you. This wagon master makes lots of small trips, but only one major trip every third year. From what I understand, he has a very successful freight business locally. Considering his local success, I inquired why he goes on extended trips. From what I was informed, he has a sense of adventure about him. Apparently, it's his way of overcoming boredom. He likes a challenge going back to his army days. What gave me confidence about him was his army experience. Another thing, he has a great reputation for making schedule. Because of wet springs, Mr. Stokes leaves in late April or early May, his intention to take advantage of drier conditions. Nothing slows travel down more than inclement weather. During early spring, there can be unbelievable thunderstorms hindering river crossings. If the trail gets mired in mud, travel is painfully slow. That's why he refuses to leave earlier. Besides, accidents produce more tragedies than any Indian tribe ever thought of, especially among young children. The worst thing of all is sickness. If cholera rears its ugly head, look out! The truth is the Indians are the least worry along the trail."

Interesting, Bill thought. Yet it was the wild nature of those heathen tribes which fascinated him the most. He persisted in his interest. "The wagon boss seems concerned about the Indians... but you're not?"

"I never worry about something I have no control over. I'm depending on Stokes and his scouts to warn us. I keep my eyes wide open and my gun handy. But I'm not afraid to ask questions, including to the wagon boss." Tyler gave a spontaneous laugh. "After all, I'm a newspaper man. Personally, I think he should have more men patrolling our flanks and maybe I'll make a suggestion when given an opportunity." Swinging his gaze over his captive audience, Tyler settled his eyes on Stephanie, finishing what he had to say. "I have volunteered my services to the wagon boss, and the same goes for the rest of you, so don't hesitate to ask me or my traveling partner."

Impressed with Tyler's concern as well as his exemplary attitude toward everyone, Stephanie admired his intelligence and courage. Thinking about her father, she smiled. Now that he knew Tyler was an educated man, she was sure he would approve.

Norma Clark's worries had jumped when Tyler spoke the word cholera. For a second, the discussion about Indians stopped, allowing her to express her fears. "Tell me, Mr. Harden, is cholera common along the trail?"

Seeing the worry in her face, Tyler shrugged. He tried not to scare her as he explained, "That and others. It's not uncommon to see graves along the trail. There is some good news though. For whatever reason, Stokes's wagon train never seems to experience unusual sickness problems compared to others. Don't ask me why, because I don't know why." Tyler chuckled. "I've just given all of you one of several reasons why I think Mr. Clifford Stokes wagon train is the best."

Norma felt a lot better.

Impressed with Tyler's talented communicating skills giving him such a captive audience, Stephanie marveled how he didn't sugar-coat anything. He just said what was on his mind. What's more, Tyler always finished by saying something positive. For the first time, she thought he should consider running for public office after settling in San Francisco. Stephanie felt a slight rush, intrigued about high society through marriage. Tyler was handsome and successful. She felt glad knowing his eventual destination was the same as hers.

Neal captured everyone's attention. "You said the wagon boss wasn't using enough scouts and you volunteered. What did he say?"

"He thanked me, telling me he would use me if needed." Stealing a glance at Stephanie, he continued, "I've never talked to any of the wagon master's scouts. I did see Stephanie and Mr. Clark speaking to that long-haired scout last night. Did either of you reach any conclusions after your conversation with him?"

Stephanie keyed on her father, waiting for him to answer. Instead, Adam referred to his daughter. "Go ahead, Stephanie."

All eyes on her, for a second Stephanie hesitated, needing to recall their recent conversation. Satisfied with her recall, she explained, "The scout's name is Scott Buchanan. He seems to be a man of few words, preferring any questions to be directed to his boss. He said that's how his boss likes it. Therefore, that's how he wants it." Always respectful, Stephanie shifted the conversation back to her father. "Dad, why don't you tell them how the wagon master described his scout?"

Clearing his throat, Adam rolled his eyes. "Mr. Stokes considers Scott Buchanan half Apache and half Cheyenne. He said he doubted if his scout could ever adjust to civilization."

Amy gasped. "Oh my god, he's half Apache and half Cheyenne!"

Adam laughed, correcting her. "No, he's not an Indian, but like them in ability. Mr. Stokes told us that Buchanan can disappear like an Apache and fight like a Cheyenne. And I've been told Cheyenne are fearless warriors. That's what he meant, not that he has Indian blood in him."

"Oh." Amy felt relief.

"So," Neal added, "this Buchanan is the best."

"According to the wagon boss, he is."

Stephanie's attention was drawn away, focusing on the wagon master and his scout lounging next to the chuck wagon. Both seemed to be listening to the cook bent over the fire. Looking away, she asked Tyler, "How does this trip compare with your last?"

"So far a lot easier, you might say, a walk in the park. What with the weather being so dry we've avoided wet weather problems. Like I said before, heavy rains can really slow down travel. Also, unlike the last time, I'm only bringing a few personal possessions. My partner's taking even less, so our wagon's light. I guess we could have just ridden our horses, but since we are on a wagon train, we did bring a few things to sell. If any of you have wagon problems during the trip and we can be of help, just ask because we do have extra room."

How smart, Stephanie thought. Tyler knew there was something he could sell in California and he was taking advantage. He and his companion were cleverly recouping some of their travel expenses.

Tyler saw Stephanie's look, elaborating, "Besides, you can't get on a wagon train without using a wagon. James and I figured we might as well make some money. Once we get to our destination, we will sell what's in our wagon, including unloading the wagon at fair price. It is our intention to price it to move it."

Neal wished he was as smart, thinking of another possibility. "Couldn't you two have been hired on as workers?"

Tyler gave the question over to his partner. "James, why don't you answer his question?"

Cooper's deep resonant voice was matter-of-fact. "Couldn't do that 'cause Stokes only hires men who will make the return trip. We did broach the subject."

"Makes sense," Bill injected, "considering the man needs help both ways."

Neal's interest with the Indians returned. He directed his question at Tyler. "On your last two trips, you indicated there weren't any problems with Indians?"

Thankful to be back as the center of attention, Tyler recognized Neal's fascination. Indians had a way of doing that. Although his personal experience was limited to his recent journeys, he would share his limited knowledge. Recalling his previous trip, he explained, "We didn't run into any hostiles on my previous journey. The few Indians we met on the trail wanted to trade. Of course, that was when the tribes were at peace. I did overhear a recent Indian treaty had been broken, which means things could change. From what I've been told, the most dangerous tribes are the Sioux, Comanche, Cheyenne, and Pawnee."

Neal bore in, more curious than before, "What about the rumors regarding a broken Indian treaty?"

Tyler shrugged. "You better ask Stokes or his wagon scout."

Silence settled around the fire, the night seeming darker than before, more ominous because of the shared knowledge concerning a broken treaty.

Tyler's eyes locked onto Cooper, summarizing his conclusions. "From what I've heard from others with past trail experience, the biggest disruptions usually come from within a wagon train itself. If you don't have the right mix of people, you can have a lot of dissension turning into hostility. And from what I've heard, this is why Stokes is very careful about whom he takes. Isn't that right, James?"

Cooper agreed, "If the wagon boss doesn't like the mix of potential travelers, he won't go. I'd say to everyone sitting around this fire, you ought to feel good about your character. Otherwise you wouldn't be with this wagon train. In other words, Mr. Stokes would have done some weeding out."

A night owl hooted in the distance, everyone's thoughts returning to the Indian danger.

Seeing their alarm, Tyler's wisdom comforted them. "It's too dark for Indians to be on the prowl, at least that's what I've been told." Looking at Stephanie, he asked, "When you reach San Francisco, what are your plans?"

The conversation shifted away from serious dangers, the night given over to a variety of topics, politics not excluded.

MOVING OUT

U p in the saddle, Buchanan watched Wes Santana mount up. Nodding at Stokes, Buchanan nudged Buddy forward with his heels. Slipping between the first and second wagons, they used the sloping land to shield their departure. Keeping a horse length behind, Wes honored Scott's code of silence. Leveling off where the second incline began, Scott hauled on the reins, breaking the silence. "Here's how I got it figured. We'll stay together till we pass Twin Buttes. As soon as we do, you'll cross the river and pick up those horse tracks made by the mystery riders. If something looks fishy, double back where you crossed and find me. You shouldn't have any trouble since I'll be following unshod horses. Besides, fifteen horses leave lots of tracks. If all goes well, we'll meet around noon where Fish Creek enters into the Platte. I'm planning on waiting for you up on the bluff. Again, you should have no trouble finding me since you'll be following tracks wearing horseshoes, and I'll be trailing fifteen without." Pausing, Buchanan allowed for concerns. "If you have questions, now's the time?"

Wes smiled, eager to ride. "No, I got it."

"Okay then, let's move out."

The only sound for the next half hour was creaking saddle leather. Occasionally one of the horses blew.

Buchanan liked silence. Working alone allowed him to tune into his surroundings. For him, talking disrupted the natural. He was always amazed how the sounds from nature gave warnings to men who understood the ways of wild creatures. When nature became hushed, it was communicating danger, most likely caused by human disturbance. If the creatures were going about their business creating normal sounds, everything was safe.

Dropping two horse lengths back, Wes was amazed at Buchanan's stealth even while astride a moving horse. Hardly ever talking, the man seemed to see everything without looking. If he did concentrate his stare at something, it was expected whoever was following to pay attention to what was being looked at. Apart from that, Wes knew Buchanan would eventually tell him what he needed to know. Of course, whenever that happened one could never be sure. What Wes did know was Buchanan liked him because he didn't ask lots of questions. And since he liked to scout, he was going to make sure he pleased Buchanan. There was something else, the chief scout appreciated humor, and Wes understood the art of teasing. Knowing tactfully when to break up, the seriousness had endeared him to the chief scout.

Wes went on alert as Buchanan swung wide. Dropping below the crest of the plateau, the chief scout stayed within the shadows from the ridge, Wes falling in behind. Several minutes passed before Buchanan angled upward onto a narrow bench easing along the ridge. Ahead the land flattened out, Buchanan hugging the gradual contour of the terrain, his horse disappearing into a grove of cottonwood trees. Entering the grove, Wes pulled up alongside, staring at the boulder formation called Twin Buttes, the overlook highlighted by the two monstrous boulders.

Buchanan kept his voice low. "The Kiowa went past those two boulders. No way of seeing past them rocks until we clear them. Just to make sure, we'll circle around and approach from the south. Once we're close, you cover me. They're sneaky devils, often doubling back. It only takes one mistake out here"—his voice trailing off—"just one."

Wes didn't miss his meaning, matching the sound of Buchanan's trailing off voice, "Yeah, I hear you. A man can't be cautious enough." Knowing silence would have been better, he grimaced, anticipating a scowl with a reprimand, none coming.

Leaving the shadows cast by the trees, Buchanan turned Buddy east, his intention to flank the mammoth boulders with the sun behind him. Nearing the boulders, he eased around in his saddle making a sweeping motion with his arm.

Dragging out his Winchester repeater, Wes swung his horse wide, his attention riveted on Buchanan and what lay ahead. Out of the corners of his eyes, he saw Buchanan pull his weapon. Knowing any moment the scout would rush the boulders, Wes cocked back the rifle's hammer.

A hundred yards from the boulders, Buchanan jabbed his horse with his heels, Buddy flattening out into a hard run. Low in the saddle, Buchanan readied himself for whatever lay in wait. Reaching the two boulders, horse and rider hurtled past, no lurking warriors erupting. Racing from behind the boulders, he wheeled Buddy around, waving for Wes to come on in.

Wes rode up. "You never forgot that spot, have you?"

Buchanan holstered his gun. "Nope, never will. One brush with death was enough!" Turning, he pointed at the river below. "Right before that bend, that's your crossing. I'll keep you covered until you cross. After that, the only way you're going to find me is by tracking me or when we meet at Fish Creek, any questions?"

Wes shook his head no.

"Good, get going, I'll cover you until you reach the far side." Easing out of the saddle, Buchanan pulled his rifle, heading for a large table-rock; the flat surface would be his rifle rest.

Shoving his carbine back in its scabbard, Wes started his horse down the steep slope, horse and rider skidding, dislodged stones tumbling before them. Leveling off, they entered the sluggish water. Halfway across, Wes remembered Buchanan's constant warnings about river crossings, how such spots make for dangerous ambush locations. He lifted his gun, his eyes locking onto the far side. Reaching the riverbank, his horse surged up and out. Relieved, he holstered the long barreled six-shooter. Shifting in his saddle, he raised his hat toward the table-rock, seeing a raised rifle saluting him off.

Buchanan waited until Wes drifted out of sight. Satisfied, he headed for his horse. Slipping his rifle into the scabbard, he mounted. As was his habit, he talked to his horse. "Come on, Buddy. Let's go find us some Kiowa."

Staying away from the well-traveled wagon trail, Scott drifted south. Twenty minutes later, he picked up the Kiowa's tracks, the hoof prints strung out indicating fast travel. Long ago Buchanan had learned that when the Indians weren't disguising their tracks, it was unlikely he'd be detected. Turning Buddy into the tracks, he booted him into a trot, the trail unwinding as far as he could see. His safety depended upon thinking like those he followed. Indians on the move were like hunted wildlife. Whenever possible, they choose wildlife trails hiding their presence while seeking elevation for safety. Like bedded mule deer, hostiles could detect approaching danger from afar. Right now the Kiowa were interested in covering ground. As long as the tracks were spaced out on level terrain, he was the hunter with the advantage. If he became careless, the blame would be on him.

An hour passed, the sun climbing, the tracks still spaced out, maybe more so. The Kiowa were making no effort at concealment. Buchanan's mind drifted, thinking about Wes. Having trained the man, Buchanan was confident in his skills. Although he preferred working alone, scouting with We Santana was the exception. Over time, the man had developed decent instincts. Out here, thinking alike really helped. Once a man knows how a scouting partner thinks, even when not riding together, decision-making was easy.

For the first time, Buchanan realized the Kiowa's tracks had been slowly drifting toward higher elevation. Looking back, Scott scolded himself for not seeing the subtle shift. A favorite Indian tactic was to gradually change direction luring a pursuer into ambush range. His failure detecting the subtle change of direction was a lack of concentration on his part. From now on, he would observe the tracks without riding in them. If he remembered correctly, soon the terrain would give way to numerous brush-choked draws surrounded by numerous stunted groves of trees. Once he saw those trees he would be near Fish Creek. Being on this side of the river gave him a big advantage. Up there, he would see Wes coming along with any-one else, wanted or unwanted. One thing he was sure of, before any-thing, he'd better make sure the Kiowa were gone. Turning Buddy, he stayed true to his caution by avoiding a direct approach. Turning north before swinging back, the gelding high stepped it through a tangle of scrub brush, entering a small clearing surrounded by scrag-gly trees. A quick glance at the sun showed the morning had little time left.

With the sun almost at its peak, Wes was becoming more aggra-vated by the minute. The strange riders were constantly stopping while barely keeping pace with the wagon train. Even from this side of the river, the wagon train's progress was easy enough to follow thanks to the dry land, the arid air sucking up dust clouds revealing the wagons slow progress. If he was going to hook up with Buchanan at noon, a decision was needed mucho pronto. Wes cautioned against becoming hasty, the mystery riders only a hill away. One careless slip caused by impatience would expose him. Considering the slow rate of travel in relationship to time, he remembered Buchanan telling him it was better to make a decision than hesitating. Wes made his decision. He would double back, cross the river, and track Buchanan. Rechecking the sun, he calculated the hour. To make sure, Wes pulled out his timepiece, glad Buchanan wasn't here to see. If Scott saw him looking at his watch, he would be the subject of serious fun at his expense, most likely around the evening campfire. He could almost envision the chief scout explaining a greenhorns need for a mechani-cal contraption despite a clear sky. He stuffed the watch back into his pocket, his destination the river.

Considering he was a half hour from the river, Wes let his mind wander, thinking about the third wagon, the one with the three women, he being partial to the gal with blond hair. The other two were also good lookers, but there was something special about her. He scolded himself to forget those women, at least for now. Not paying attention to one's surroundings could get a man into a heap of trouble out here. If it did happen Scott Buchanan would have another field day with him, that's if he survived such a blunder.

A brown shape slithering through the underbrush caught Wes's attention. The otter, caught far from the river, slipped into a small tributary. For a brief second, the sleek creature's head broke the water's surface before disappearing, a few ripples testifying to its passage.

Stokes was relaxed. He had two scouts on point and good weather. Long ago, he had come to the realization that if a man got all worried up about everything on the trail, then why be wagon boss? His solution was a simple one. Start out each day the same as the last and adjust as the day unfolded. There was another rule he liked to keep. If at all possible, keep things simple while not forgetting to enjoy the unfolding beauty along the trail. Life had a way of passing a man by if one didn't enjoy his surroundings.

Riding alongside Cliff was his foreman, Stuart Whitmore. Not a hint of fat showed on Stuart's body. Of course, not packing excessive weight was normal for those who made a living on the trail. There was something else that always caught people's attention about the foreman. It was his full-length beard. The beard was as black as the ace of spades, completely hiding his mouth. Made a person wonder how Whitmore could get food past all those whiskers? He had another characteristic. His blue eyes constantly twinkled, indicating a hint of mischief mingling within his personality. Cliff often wondered how Stuart would look if he ever shaved off that beard. Probably be tough to recognize him, he reckoned. The man had become second in command because he was a quick thinker. Along with never getting rattled, he possessed another talent. Stuart was gifted musically, capable of producing high-stepping music with a fiddle. Often he had Stuart break out his fiddle for an evening of dancing. Such activity broke up the monotony along the trail. After an evening of sashaying around to the beat of music, the folks' attitudes changed, the long days on the trail not so burdensome despite the miles yet to be traveled.

Cliff glanced over at Stuart amused at what he saw. As usual, Stuart was slumped over in the saddle like a dying man, a normal way of riding for him. Appearances being deceptive, anyone watching Stuart might think he was dozing. The foreman reminded him of a long-haired dog he once owned. The dog would appear to be sleeping until Cliff got up to go out the door. Hearing the opening door, the dog was up like a shot, barging to the front, intent on leading the way. Whenever returning from the outside, the dog did the same, always having to be first. Stokes studied the slouched foreman, chuckling. It seemed as if the man didn't have a care in the world. Shifting his gaze away from Stuart, he looked back at the trailing wagons, his voice breaking the silence. "Stuart, I'm going to swing back and check on everybody. You have the point."

Stuart straightened in the saddle.

Cliff swung the blond-colored mare around, heading for the second wagon. The travelers always appreciated his visits. It was Cliff's personal way of relaxing the folks, also his way of finding out things. Reaching the second wagon in line, he turned the mare, riding up alongside the rig. The driver's name was Harry Phillips, his wife sitting next to him. Cliff smiled at her, doffing his hat as he spoke. "Good morning, Ma'am, Mr. Phillips. I trust the morning's been uneventful other than a relaxing one."

Avoiding the sudden dip ahead, Harry Phillips pulled the reins to the left. Despite the sudden distraction, he answered the wagon boss's salutation with a grin, "Good morning to you, sir. With the weather being so pleasant, I'm sure not complaining. Tell me, wagon master, how far along are we?"

The question was a common one, Cliff not stumped for an answer. "We're almost halfway, way ahead of schedule. As long as the weather holds, we might surprise ourselves." Cliff admired the pleasant smile radiating from Mrs. Phillips. She was a plump woman. Whenever she spoke, her voice was captivating. Even better, her manners had a way of endearing others to her. Yep, Cliff concluded, Harry had done himself well. The man's wife was a nice person to be around. He nodded at Phillips, pleased with the man's response, say-ing as much, "Glad to hear everything's going without a hitch. If you need anything, I'd be glad to accommodate any needs. Just want you to know my scout has uncovered a party of Kiowa and a small bunch of riders flanking the wagons. We have both under surveillance. It appears they've moved on. If you recall, I told you I'd keep everyone informed, which is what I'm doing." Seeing concern jumping into Mrs. Phillip's face, he assured her, "I don't want anyone to worry 'cause they have moved on. So relax, thank the good Lord for decent traveling weather and leave the worrying part to me and my men." Touching his hat brim, adding a broad smile at his departure, he wheeled the mare around, heading for the third wagon.

The rig was being driven by two brothers, Seth and Adam Harris. Stokes guessed both men were about the same age, not more than two years apart. Misfortune through disease had struck both men, causing a loss of their wives and now the brothers were over-coming past grief by heading west to start a new life. Closing in on the wagon, he hailed both men, "Howdy Seth, Adam."

Both brothers sported long brown hair hanging down to their shoulders. Each man appeared physically fit. Seth was always the spokesman for both, this morning no exception. "Good morning to you, Mr. Stokes. So far so good, we have no problems to report. How about you?"

For the most part, it was Cliff's policy to avoid idle conver-sation with travelers, so he came right to the point by doing just that. "Yesterday we picked up a bunch of Kiowa on our southern flank. We also have some unknown riders staying out of sight on the far side of the river. I sent a second scout along with my chief scout this morning. As of right now, both groups have moved on. We should know more by tonight. Seeing as you two aren't intimidated, be much appreciated if both of you would keep your eyes peeled."

Seth and Adam exchanged quick glances. Eager for some dan-gerous excitement, Adam's voice joined the dialog. "Anything special we can do to help? You know, besides keeping our eyes peeled."

"If there is, I'll let you know. Right now having two alert men like you two helps when wagons are strung out along the trail. I'm not expecting trouble, but both of you look able, which means you're an asset to me and the rest of the folks."

Again, Seth was the spokesman. "You just let us know, Mr. Stokes. Whatever you need, we'll be more than glad to help."

Pleased with their response, Cliff leaned toward his left, his weight shift turning the mare, his voice drifting back. "Much obliged for your offer, stay ready."

The next approaching wagon contained a farming family with two teenage sons and a young girl. Always respectful, Cliff liked to greet families formally; such a salutation made it professional. As the wagon rolled up, he noticed a slight limp in the third ox in the traces. Touching his hat brim, he greeted the husband and wife, "Howdy, Mr. and Mrs. Daniel."

Glen Daniel was a rugged man, broad shouldered with a deep Scandinavian accent in his voice. If Cliff was any judge of character, the man was the type who thrived on work. He also suspected Glen, like most men who make a living off the land, loved being independent. Daniel's booming voice was easily overheard over the sounds from the creaking wagon traces. "Howdy to you, Mr. Stokes. If you're hungry, my wife has extra biscuits from da mornings cooking fire. Fresh biscuits always taste better than stale ones." He laughed, his voice gushing out a sincere request. "So you'd be doing us a big favor if you'd take some afore they go stale."

Daniel's wife, Heddy, reached back pulling forth a covered basket. "Please, Mr. Stokes, we have more than enough."

Delighted, Cliff laughed. "Don't mind if I do, much appreciated, thank you."

Heddy's face glowed with happiness. For her, pleasing someone always made her feel special.

Cliff couldn't help but think it was because of families like this why he experienced great pleasure in providing a safe passage. Helping such people gave his occupation special meaning. Looking at their two boys and one daughter reminded Cliff of his responsibility. "I've got a favor to ask of you, Mr. Daniel."

Daniel waited, his face showing curiosity. "You go right ahead and whatever it is, consider it done."

"I want you to make sure you keep the young ones close to the wagons. We're being flanked by a band of Kiowa. I think you know Indians will steal young ones."

Heddy's hands flew to her face.

Daniel's jovial face tightened into concern. He stared intensely, lips compressing, anger etched in his voice. "Kiowa is it!"

Intending to calm, Cliff spoke quickly. "Right now they have moved on. I'll know more by this evening. Regardless, it's always smart while in Indian country to keep children close by. Just so you know, I've sent a second scout out so we're watching them. I will keep you updated after we camp for the night."

It took Daniel a moment before answering, his voice an ominous growl. "Heddy and I will keep the young ones right by our side, that's fer sure! But I'll tell you this, if one of them there heathens gets near our children, by golly he'll be broke in two!"

Having observed the man's strength before, Cliff believed him. Glen's neck muscles swelled out threatening to break his shirt collar even when he was calm. His thick wrists and forearms showed evidence from years of farming work. Cliff had no doubt if the man ever got someone in his iron grip because of anger, he'd break the unfortunate fellow in half. Agreeing with Daniel, Cliff said, "Of that I have no doubt. All the same, keep them close by." Cliff shifted the conversation. "Something else you should know, your third ox in line has a slight limp. You might want to take a look at him."

"That ox has always limped," Daniel responded. "But he can outpull the others fer sure. I wish I had three more with such a hitch in their stride."

"Good, glad to hear it. I'll see you tonight." Wheeling away his horse, Cliff headed for the fifth wagon. Halting the mare, he waited for the wagon to near. He eyed the man holding the reins, guessing his age around forty years. His name was Cornelius O'Keefe. Sitting alongside Cornelius was another man of about the same age. His man name was Wayne Bennett. Both wore their guns like they were comfortable with them. Each had a rifle propped up next to him. Neither had a tendency toward pleasantries, but instead they seemed to enjoy any conversation on the aggressive side. Stokes suspected they had some wildness in them. Aware both were watching him closely, Cliff initiated the talk, "Good morning, sirs, just thought I would update you on the latest developments. Last night we had some Kiowa nearby, along with some strange riders. Looks like they've moved on, but just in case, keep those guns handy."

Bennett's question registered surprise, "Whites and Kiowa together?"

"Sorry I implied them to be together. One group is across the river, the Kiowa, somewhere ahead to the west of us."

Neither seemed alarmed. Instead, like the third wagon, excitement showing in each face, O'Keefe's voice eager as he leaned forward. "Sounds like you need a raiding party to scatter 'em, be glad to join in."

Almost grinning, Cliff expressed appreciation. "Thanks for the offer. You're the second wagon that's volunteered. As of right now, both groups aren't near us, hopefully miles ahead. Should I need help, you will be considered."

Wayne Bennett pushed his hat back, his voice containing the same enthusiasm as his partner's. "You do that wagon master." Pointing, he asked, "You see those rifles propped up next to us?"

"I see them."

"We hit what we aim at, so don't you hesitate."

Cliff touched his hat. Turning the mare, he held his ground waiting for the sixth wagon. As the wagon neared, he thought about Wes Santana's fascination with the three ladies traveling with this lone man. According to Buchanan, Wes had a fixation for the blonde. Said he was constantly turning his head hoping to catch her attention. His problem being he wasn't having any luck. Stokes had to admit, what a combination. One man and three women, and all three gals were attractive. Even more intriguing, one woman was a redhead, the other had auburn hair, the third a blonde. All that was missing was one with black hair. Cliff chuckled. He never had such a bevy of beautiful women being escorted by a single man on his wagon train before. Such a situation made a person wonder. He almost hadn't taken them until he was assured by all three women, including the man, there would be no trouble because of misbehaving. Even more surprising, once they hit the trail, he was surprised how well behaved they were. The man's assurances there would be no misbehaving had held true. The fellow's name was John Sexton, a tall fellow with kind of blank stare when you did hold his attention. Sitting beside Sexton were the three women.

As the wagon neared, Cliff considered being tactful, not wanting to put Sexton into the uncomfortable position of trying to calm his traveling companions for the remainder of the day. What the hay, Cliff mused; escorting such a group of ladies had to mean the man was capable. It was only a matter of time before they heard about the potential problem overhearing conversations. Therefore, it was best it came from him and now as good a time as any. Hopefully, the women wouldn't become too alarmed.

Sexton's voice reached out, his manner reserved as was his habit. "Good morning, wagon master."

"Morning, Mr. Sexton, ladies. I'm keeping my pledge to keep everyone up to date. I don't want you to hear rumors, I'd rather you hear it from me. Last night we picked up a bunch of Kiowa along with some strange riders staying out of sight." Surprised at seeing curiosity instead of alarm, Cliff continued, "This morning the Kiowa have moved out. The strange riders remain on the far side of the river. Right now we don't know why. We aim to know more by tomorrow. For precautionary reasons, I recommend you ladies stay within the safety of the wagons at night."

Sexton responded with a question, "Are the Kiowa a large bunch?"

"According to my scout, they are decent in size, but not enough to jump the wagons. Still, Indians are masters at thievery, not forgetting they do like to keep their tribal numbers up by stealing women and children, so you ladies stay close to the wagons." Cliff rested both palms on the saddle horn in a relaxed way, portraying a lack of concern. "Besides, staying within the safety of the wagons is a smart practice. No sense in stumbling into a rattler requiring emergency first aid. If you feel the need to wander, bring someone capable with a gun. Above all, don't go far."

Indians were one thing, Sexton thought, but unknown riders not visiting was more than unusual. His curiosity aroused, he asked, "Seems kind of strange to me, those riders not riding over for a palaver. Have they always remained on the far side of the river?"

Hesitating, Cliff answered honestly, "Nope. Whoever they are they crossed late yesterday afternoon. My scouts haven't even seen them yet, which is about to change. So far from what we do know, they're riding shod horses so we figure they aren't Indians. As to why they didn't come over for a visit, that's a puzzle. I'm kind of thinking they might be using us as a buffer between the Kiowa. If that's so, they might be our allies. Anyway, they haven't done us any harm. What's more, they have the same rights of travel wherever they want. What I do know is there are more of us than them, including the Kiowa." Cliff smiled, adding, "My scout did inform me there are only seven riders across the river. Early this morning, I sent a scout to keep them under surveillance. Like I said, I'll know more come tonight. Only reason I'm telling you is because I promised everyone there would be no information withheld, so I'm keeping my word and I've doubled the watch while assigning another scout. On top of that it seems the Indians have moved on."

"Are you planning on taking any defensive action?" Sexton inquired.

"And if them Kiowa return, what then?"

"I consider every able-bodied man on this wagon train as part of our defense. As for you ladies, you can load rifles and tend to any wounded. But as of now we are larger, even if both groups hooked up. We should be fine, wouldn't surprise me one bit if the savages are long gone."

Nodding, Sexton shifted his attention to the ladies with his relaxing voice, "Seems like the wagon boss has everything under control, if you ladies got any questions, now's the time to ask, 'cause he knows more than me."

All three women looked at each other, just a minor touch of worry showed in their faces, no questions coming forth. Despite no real outward signs of alarm, it appeared whatever John Sexton decided was fine with them.

Staring into each face, Cliff was surprised there were no questions coming forth, finally breaking the silence, "Well then, since there are no more questions, I'm going to move on and inform the rest of the folks. Like I said, good or bad, I'll keep in touch."

Reining his horse around, Cliff eyed the Clark family. He was looking forward to this visit. The husband and wife were sitting up front in the wagon, their daughter Stephanie riding her horse alongside. He couldn't help but admire the daughter's beauty, her long reddish-brown hair with a touch of gold reflecting in the sunshine. Cliff was impressed how she sat straight in the saddle, always alert, observing everything. What made the Clark family different from most of the other folks was how they were bringing horses, another being towed behind their wagon. Considering Cliff hadn't seen the father ride a horse, he reasoned through logical deduction, it had to be his daughter who insisted on bringing the horses. Swinging his mare close to Stephanie, he leaned far enough past her in the saddle so he could have eye contact while addressing all, "Good morning, Miss Clark, Mr. and Mrs. Clark, it's my intention to thank you folks for the way you handled everything last night. I really appreciated how all of you avoided camp talk about my missing scout. I was gratified how you folks went about your normal routine. Right now I'm informing the rest of the wagons about our situation. I guess you could say, the secret's out. But again, thanks for keeping everything quiet."

"Our pleasure," Adam Clark responded with a smile. "Any new developments we ought to know about?"

"No, sir, I'll know more by tonight."

Adam's response thoughtful, "Well then, we are thankful how you've kept your promise about keeping us informed. You said you would and you have."

Appreciating the compliment, Cliff returned the accolades, "Easy promise to keep when dealing with trustworthy people. Keeping a person's word gives a man a proper reputation, and out here, a good reputation gets around. More important, proper character is earned. Just as you folks did, I aim to keep mine. I'd say you got a right to feel proud for keeping your promise, my compliments to all of you."

Stephanie smiled, enjoying the compliments; her curiosity never stifled as she spoke, "I happened to notice how you sent out two scouts this morning, Mr. Stokes."

"Miss Clark, you do observe everything. Maybe I should hire you as my second wagon scout, especially seeing as how you do what is asked!"

Stephanie's laugh was soft, a touch of dry humor in her voice. "Why do I think that's not likely to happen?"

"I guess you would be right, probably because you're a woman. But if you weren't, I'd sure enough hire you." Cliff glanced toward her father, including him as he teased, "Mr. Clark, if I had a son, I would go out of my way to introduce your daughter to him, yes, I would."

Stephanie pointed ahead, her eyes full of mischief as she questioned him, "Tell me, Mr. Stokes, would you introduce me to Scott Buchanan?"

Eyebrows arched, staring past her, Cliff needed a response, coming up with one. "Normally I would say one of my scouts wouldn't be much of a challenge for you, Miss Clark, but Scott Buchanan might be more than you bargain for."

"I think for a change I would like such a challenge."

Shaking his head, a quizzical smile crossed Cliff's face. "Miss Clark, I've just rethought what I said. I'm thinking I'd better keep him out on the trail."

Stephanie's response was witty. "But Mr. Stokes, don't you see, that's even more of a challenge."

Rocking back, Cliff's explosive laugh had his mare prancing sideways at his sudden shift of weight. "Now hold on, I can't afford to lose him. You can name anyone else, but not him!"

Amused, Stephanie wondered if the wagon boss would repeat this conversation to Scott Buchanan.

Shifting his attention away from the daughter to her father, Cliff felt the way the family conducted themselves deserved special consideration. When his scouts returned with more information tonight, they would be the first to be informed. "Mr. Clark, tonight I'll stop by and update all of you."

Adam took advantage. "We will consider your presence an honor. I'm going to tell Norma to whip up something special for your visit."

Cliff refrained from objecting. After all, he did owe them a special courtesy considering how they'd kept their word. "You just made it impossible for me not to visit everyone, unless of course, there developed an immediate emergency requiring my presence." He looked at Adam's wife. "Mrs. Clark, you can expect me shortly after dark. Can't be there sooner because I've got to make sure every-thing's in order. I'll be looking forward to my visit tonight." Starting the mare around, Cliff added, "And that special treat!"

Checking the sky, Cliff determined it was almost noon. One more wagon visit would be enough before heading back for the point. The truth be known, he was anxious to hear what was happening out there, and Wes Santana should be showing up any time now. Urging the mare forward, he headed for the eighth wagon. The man holding the reins was Tyler Harden. The fellow sitting alongside him went by the name of James Cooper. Cooper was the older of the two. Both were good talkers, but it was Harden who always seemed to be full of ideas how to do things better. He never hesitated to offer advice as if he knew more than a wagon boss with years of experience. Harden's smile was always infectious when he spoke. His spontaneous enthu-siasm had a way of making someone want to confide. His greeting jumped out as Cliff rode up. "Good morning to you, Mr. Stokes. We seem to be making good time. I noticed your scout didn't show up until this morning. Is everything okay?"

Cliff conceded how a man had to admire such a speaking talent. Unlike the smooth-talking Tyler, Cliff rarely said more than needed. Reining in the mare, he acknowledged both men, "Howdy gents, so far so good. And you're right, my scout stayed out last night. He uncovered a party of Kiowa, staying out to check their intentions. He also uncovered some tracks north of us. Those horses were shod, indicating white riders, maybe buffalo hunters. I dispatched two scouts first thing this morning. Right now I'm not expecting any problems, but if trouble develops, I'll bring both of you up to date."

Showing keen interest, Tyler volunteered, "We appreciate you keeping us updated. Please don't hesitate to use us. We're more than able."

"I'll remember your offer, Mr. Harden."

Tyler smiled. "Please call me Tyler, not Mr. Harden… too formal for me. Let me repeat myself, if you need help we'd jump at the opportunity in any way we can."

Grudgingly Cliff admitted a man had to like Tyler's attitude. Yet there was something about the man that bothered him, like maybe he was too good to be true. Regardless, he didn't forget to express appreciation. "Much obliged, I won't forget. Good day gents." Spinning the mare around with knee pressure, she broke into a canter heading for the lead wagon.

Seeing his boss returning, Stuart slipped in a touch of humor. "You able to pacify them folks like a night rider calming down a herd of spooky steers?"

Cliff chuckled, his eyes drifting up the trail as he spoke. "I got mostly good responses from everyone. That Daniels man said that if any of those red heathens got near his young'uns, he'd break 'em in two."

Giving that statement some thought, Stuart nodded in agreement. "I don't doubt he could, I sure wouldn't want to tangle with him. He's got forearms like a young oak. If Daniels ever got his hands on someone, I suspect it would feel like being in a vise, you know, the kind them blacksmiths use. What did those two lone guns have to say?"

"Funny you brought them up. I got mixed feelings about those two. Why did you ask?"

"Why do you think I asked? So tell me, how'd they respond?"

"Like they'd enjoy some danger, is how."

Just what Stuart figured, his voice reflective, "Can't say I'm surprised, what about that Tyler Harden fellow. How'd he answer you?"

Cliff glanced at his foreman. "If you don't mind me inquiring, why are you wondering about him?"

"I got funny feelings concerning him is why."

Cliff admired how he and Stuart thought alike. "Like maybe he's too good to be true."

"Yeah, a nauseating fellow, all full of ideas and advice, and not just once, all the time! Another thing, he's not shy about reminding us about his previous advice, lest we forget."

Cliff grinned. "You think so?"

"I do. Like maybe he'd like to tell us how to manage the wagon train. For whatever its worth, that's my impression. Fact is, the man seems to be just bursting at the seams."

Cliff's grin became a laugh. "I've got to admit, Stuart, you and I think alike. We surely do."

Lifting his hat for a minute, Stuart ran his hand through his hair, speaking matter-of-factly, "Like two peas in a pod, that's us. Say now, I noticed you weren't gone very long. I'm thinking you didn't visit all the wagons cause you got back awfully fast."

"You're right again, I didn't visit everyone."

"Why? I had everything covered up here."

Staring into the distance, Cliff answered his foreman. "That's because, per my instructions, it's time for one of my scouts to check in. I do admit I'm a touch edgy wanting to know what's going on out there."

Stuart lifted his gaze outward at the plains, the sea of grass hardly moving.

Leaving Buddy behind a stand of cottonwoods to protect his rear, Buchanan picked a shaded spot overlooking the Platte. Up here, he could see for miles, a slight breeze washing across his face.

Like a little jewel-like necklace sparkling in the sun, Fish Creek trickled in the direction of the river. Anyone following the river would be exposed long before they reached Buchanan's chosen observation place. Stealing a glance at the sun, he calculated the hour, knowing only too well how things rarely work out according to the clock in this untamed land. He had told Santana he'd wait at Fish Creek and he was waiting. Buchanan stretched out full length, relaxation seeping into his bones, enjoying the view below, the distant river merging with Fish Creek, both appearing like thousands of sparkling diamonds. The sun warming his body, Buchanan's mind lulled into a lazy feeling.

Almost an hour passed when he saw Wes ride into view. For some reason, Wes had crossed further downstream. Shoving his hat back, Buchanan wondered why?

Riding up, Wes slid off his horse, keeping his voice soft, "Where's Buddy?"

Scott gestured over his shoulder. "Buddy's behind the trees."

"Sorry, I'm late, but those riders were awful slow. They stayed abreast of the wagons the whole morning. I had to double back before crossing."

"So they haven't gotten very far. Where are they now?"

"Just the other side of that humped-backed hill we can see from here. From where I was, I could see the dust raised by the wagons and so could they. After I broke away, I found your tracks easy enough to follow. How about them sneaking Kiowa? You catch up to them?"

"Nope, they're still ahead somewhere, which I hope they continue to do. The way I got it figured, I'm going to send you back across the river again. I want you to keep track of them riders. I'll go on in, give my report, then come back out here and follow those heathens' tracks. You okay with that?"

"Sure, you know me, I'm agreeable to anything you say. One thing though, the boss did say if anyone stays out it should be you, just thought I'd mention it."

"I'm sure he did, but the boss means at night. Since those riders are closer to the wagon train than those Kiowa bucks, you ride close on their heels just in case. You bring any trail food with you?"

"Just like you taught me, nothing very tasty, some dried pemmican and leftover sour-dough bread."

"Glad you listened, can't have a fire while following potential trouble. Why don't you go ahead and eat. After you're done, we'll mount up."

Rising, Wes pulled a wrapped bundle from his saddlebag. "You want some?"

"Hell no," Scott grinned. "I'll grab something at the chuck wagon." Seeing Wes's mocking expression, he laughed softy, adding, "Tomorrow it'll be your turn, so toughen up."

Wes's reply was wry, "Yeah, right. With my luck, the old man will probably pull me in tomorrow and you know it."

Waiting for Wes to finish eating, Buchanan kept his eyes searching. Out here, a man could never be sure when trouble erupted, especially coming from some half-naked savages looking for scalps. Of course, there was always the possibility of spotting a buffalo herd. Fresh meat was always appreciated, bringing special recognition to the bringer. Recently he'd noticed more and more buffalo dung along with numerous tracks meandering away from the river's edge heading toward higher ground. Sooner or later, Buchanan expected to see the herd making those tracks. The tricky part was to see the buffalo before they saw you. The only way that would happen is if he becomes lax. If he remained alert, eventually the wagon train would have fresh meat, he being the hero.

Lifting his canteen, Wes took a long pull. Screwing the cap back on, he wiped his mouth. "I'm ready if you are."

Rolling onto his knees, Buchanan stood. "Like I've told you many times, be careful when you cross the river. I'll see you tonight at the wagon train. If trouble develops, report directly to Stokes."

Chasing away an annoying fly with a wild swing of his hat, Cliff watched Stuart tending to the oxen as they drank. Being so close to the river had its advantages. Once they turned inland, the advantage was gone. One by one each animal drank its fill, Stuart finally pulling on the rope, leading the oxen back to the wagon traces. Dismounting, Cliff helped Stuart get them back in line.

Stuart's soft whistle caught Cliff's attention. "Buchanan's on his way in."

Taking a quick peek, Cliff kept working. As his scout rode up, he grunted, "Just in time for lunch. Climb down."

Buchanan congratulated himself. "Didn't you always say timing is everything? Damn good advice too." Easing from the saddle, he ambled toward Wendell.

Stokes turned his attention back to what needed to be finished, leading the mare to the river's edge, patient while she drank her fill. Water dripping from her muzzle, her head up, sure the mare was satisfied; Cliff led her to the work wagon. Wrapping the reins, Cliff eyed his scout, prompting, "Well?"

Casting a glance Stuart's way, Buchanan kept it simple. "Kiowa are traveling in a strung out line moving fast. Right now they're way ahead of us, still going in the same direction as we are." Rubbing the back of his neck, he finished his report. "Wes is keeping tabs on the riders who are staying out of sight across the river."

Considering Scott's report, Cliff's eyes darted across the river, finally asking, "You reckon they're remaining out of sight on purpose?"

"I do."

"What does Wes think?"

"He doesn't like 'em."

"Why?"

"Considering how they haven't rode over for a visit, he reckons them to be unfriendly until they prove otherwise, making him suspicious."

"How far north are they?"

"The distance from us can't be more than a half mile the other side of the river. Wes told me he could follow the wagon's progress by seeing the dust kicked up from the wheels, the riders likewise able to keep track of our wagons."

"He have a chance to sneak in close and take a look at them?"

"I forgot to ask him."

Every once and awhile Cliff liked to chide his scout, this being such a moment. "You didn't ask?"

"Nope, I didn't. I figured if he had he would have said so. Tonight, you can ask him. I guess that's why you're the wagon boss instead of me."

Stokes got in one last lick. "Appears so, 'cause I never assume, you know what they say about people who assume?"

Shrugging, Scott countered with, "I reckon from the same person more than once."

Cliff changed the topic, talking to himself. "Well, we sure don't own the land. I guess they got the right to travel like they want. Let's go eat."

Unable to lip read from such a distance, Stephanie wished she could hear everything the scout and his boss were saying. Looking at her father, who was staring at her, she spoke with a twinkle in her eyes. "It doesn't look like anyone's alarmed over there, so I guess everything's all right. When the boss visits with us tonight, I'm going to find out a lot more than just the tidbits of what they let us in on."

Norma's voice captured their attention. "I think you two had better finish up, because in another thirty minutes, the wagon boss will start the wagons rolling. He's always prompt about not wasting daylight hours."

Passing beans mixed with salt pork to Buchanan, Wendell's voice was caustic. "I was kind of hoping by now you'd have shot us some fresh buffalo meat. If I recall correctly, that's part of your job description. Be nice to have a change of menu once and awhile, don't you think?"

Buchanan kept his expression bland, grunting back, "Can't shoot what I don't see. Trouble is so many wagons pass along this trail, everybody wanting fresh meat. Animals aren't dumb. They go where it's safe." Stopping talking to eat, he avoided complaining about the salty meat. A hungry man should be thankful for a full stomach. Besides, Wes would have gladly changed places with him. An intriguing thought crossed his mind. "Say, Mr. Bartholomew, you have any treats hidden away to finish off tonight's meal?"

Wendell placed his hands on his hips, giving him a mock stare, silence his answer.

Chuckling, Stokes backed his scout's suggestion. "I'm kind of in the mood myself. How about a surprise tonight… would be kind of nice?"

Continuing to glare at Buchanan, Wendell handled his boss differently. "I got some honey I been saving. That's, of course, if we stop early enough for me to mix up a batch of dough so as I can make up something to smear the honey on, but of course, that depends on our chief scout making sure the trail's safe." He looked at his boss, turning his head slightly to hide a wink. "And as of right now, our safety seems questionable."

Drinking water, Buchanan was tactful. "Tell you what I'm going to do, Mr. Bartholomew. I'll ride out making sure everything's safe before heading back early and reporting. That way, I can help you get your baking fire going first thing." He smiled at his boss. "You know, boss, I can almost taste fresh bread smothered with honey."

Stokes agreed with a nod, no words needing to be added. He watched Buchanan head for Buddy, a sudden thought coming to him. He scrambled to his feet, catching up with his scout.

Grabbing Buddy's reins, Buchanan waited to hear what was on his boss's mind.

Easing alongside, Cliff kept his voice low. "How's Wes doing? It has been awhile since he's scouted."

"Good, if I say so myself. I trained him well, used his head today. He usually does, makes me proud."

"Meaning?"

"He adjusted to his circumstances and acted accordingly. A man can't do better than that."

Cliff liked Buchanan's answer. "Well, if something develops before tonight, keep me abreast. If anything unusual is going on out there, I want to know about it. The sooner the better. Otherwise, I'll see both of you before dark."

Nodding, Scott rose into the saddle. Turning Buddy, he nudged the gelding into a trot, his voice strong enough to be heard by all. "Make sure you remind our master chef to make lots of bread 'cause being out on the trail earns a man his privileges."

In the background, Scott heard Wendell's expletive response, a response not fit to be heard, at least not around the womenfolk.

Watching Buchanan ride off, Cliff was glad his scout had prodded Wendell into making sweet treats for tonight. Having dessert out here on the trail usually meant finding a berry patch and loitering, hoping for no unfriendly company, especially a big bruin or sow grizzly. Knowing dessert was coming with the evening chow sure shortened a man's day with anticipation.

LONE HAWK

Trailing behind the rest of the Kiowa raiding party, Lone Hawk sensed he and his fellow braves were being followed. Compared to his adventurous admirers, his instincts were the sharpest. It was often said by his own people that he should have been a Sioux or a Cheyenne. He never shied from a fight, went on every raiding party, and was fearless in battle. Because of his savage nature, the younger braves often turned to him for advice concerning hostilities. There were times he had contempt for his Kiowa brothers. As far as he was concerned their raiding parties turned out to be nothing more than stealing before running away. There was one exception; the exception was Gray Coyote, the elder leading the group. Once known as a fiery warrior, his age had caught up with him. Despite his constant battle with the years, Gray Coyote was respected by his peers as a crafty leader full of wisdom.

Lone Hawk was sinewy, standing slightly less than six feet tall, his catlike eyes missing nothing. The lines in his face pointed downward, a permanent scowl dominating. Although unafraid by his nature, Lone Hawk knew at times it was wise to be cautious. Turning his piebald mustang away from the rest of the group, he headed for the near hill. Reaching the top, Lone Hawk swung his pony around to the far side. Reining the mustang to a halt, he slipped to the ground. Tethering the pony, he loped to the far side. Finding shade, Lone Hawk settled into the knee-high grass. Legs crossed, he became motionless.

Almost an hour passed before Lone Hawk saw the rider. Easing his body full length onto his elbows, he hugged the ground. Squinting, he studied the white-eyes' every movement. From up here he could see the man's head turning, his eyes tracing Lone Hawk's tracks. Impressed with the white-eyes' alertness, his intensity increased. Perhaps, he thought, this was a worthy adversary, a man he could match wits with. For the longest time, the man remained in one spot, his face suddenly looking up where he lay. Quivering like a mountain cougar studying its prey, Lone Hawk's body sunk lower. The paleface showed himself to be patient, staring up at the very place where he hid. The white-eyes had good instincts, he thought. Despite those instincts, the scout showed a fault. He had already lingered too long in one spot. If it was himself who sensed danger, he would have already slipped away. Staying too long in one spot wasn't wise, especially when one suspicious danger was present. A well-placed shot could easily end a life.

Seeing where the single set of horse tracks had left the main bunch, Buchanan halted Buddy. Why had the brave branched off, he wondered. Alert, he guessed the lone Kiowa brave had left the main group to make sure no one followed. The tossed dirt from the horse's hooves were still damp around the edges indicated the tracks were recent, probably within the hour. Glancing uphill, he considered it likely the Indian lurked nearby. If he did, the high ground provided the perfect location to watch one's back trail. Buchanan had no intention of being careless to the advantage of lurking danger. Reining the gelding around, Buchanan retraced Buddy's tracks. Satisfied he was out of rifle range, he swung Buddy off the trail, flanking the hill, a sparse tree line offering cover. Reaching the base of the hill, he eased out from the saddle, pulling his rifle all in one motion.

Not only was the man alert, Lone Hawk thought, but he acted on his instincts by circling away from danger. Revising his thinking, he respected how the paleface had reacted to what his eyes were telling him. In the future, Lone Hawk would not forget how the wagon scout backtracked before flanking his hiding location. Such knowledge might be useful in the days ahead against this potential adversary. He suspected the wagon scout was very much like himself, a man used to living off the land, a hunter who had warrior blood in his veins. For the first time since the raiding party had left their village, he was excited, entertaining the possibility when he and this paleface who rode for the wagons might clash. Such thinking appealed to him, the only question forming in Lone Hawk's mind was, when? Several seconds had passed since the man turned off the trail. Sure the scout was flanking his position, Lone Hawk waited to make sure the paleface didn't reappear. Leaping to his feet, he ran for his horse with long effortless strides. Leaping onto his pony's back, he headed in the very direction where the paleface had stopped to study his tracks. After all, what could be safer than to ride where the scout no longer lingered? As he dropped down the hill, Lone Hawk gave the white-eyes a name. He called him Eyes-That-See.

Buchanan eyed several shallow gullies winding to the top. If he didn't dislodge any stones, he should avoid drawing any attention until he reached the top. Using the rifle butt for balance, he began snaking his way up, grabbing for any available handhold, his mind thinking like that of an adversary. If there was a bushwhacker up there, most likely he was already on the move, perhaps even stalking him as he climbed.

Nearing the crest, Buchanan hunkered down behind a gnarled bush offering partial protection. Intent, he listened, the hillside absent from any sounds from small creatures inhabiting the natural world. Not hearing any chirping from birds made Scott cautious. Didn't nature have a way of sending a silent warning to its own during human intrusion? Maybe it was his sudden arrival; then again, perhaps it was lurking danger which stilled the sounds from nature? Knowing waiting often forces nervous movement, an advantage for the stalker, Buchanan stalled as he plotted. He recalled a grassy overlook near the south end, reckoning if a lurking brave watched from above, the overlook was the perfect hiding spot. If the Indian was there and hadn't shifted his position, once he investigated he'd know.

Crouching, Buchanan skirted the hill's perimeter, hunkering down among low growing shrubs making sure his footing was secure as he peered upward. Pointing the rifle barrel forward, Scott pressed the stock against his hip. His legs under him, with a slight lean forward, he lunged over the crest. Racing forward, he almost overran the Indian's tracks, skidding to a halt. Wheeling around, he scowled at the moccasin prints. One set of tracks was heading toward the edge of the hill, the second set of prints running in the opposite direction. Buchanan followed the running tracks. Nearing where the hill ended, he stared at the fresh pony tracks heading in the opposite direction. Letting his rifle dangle, Buchanan understood what the signs were telling him. It appeared the Kiowa had departed the minute he began his flanking move.

Wanting something distinctive to identify the savage, Buchanan squatted, laying his rifle alongside the pony's tracks. Judging their length, next he examined each hoof print. He found nothing of importance. Unable to find what he wanted from the hoof prints, he studied the brave's stride and the depth of his moccasin prints, both the running and walking. Peering intently, Scott noticed the Indian's left foot turned inwardly more than the other. Pleased at finding a slight difference, he straightened. At least he knew something about the Indian besides his height and weight.

Walking slowly, Buchanan arrived where the pony tracks went over the crest, not surprised at what he saw. The Kiowa had ridden past the very spot he had stopped to look up. Smart, Buchanan thought, smart and cagey. Chasing away the stored up tension, he shook his muscles loose. Some deep inhaling and exhaling finished the job. Tracking impending danger tensed the muscles, leaving a person with the feeling how any moment all hell was about to break loose. Shoving his hat back, using his sleeve he mopped away perspiration trickling down his forehead. One thing he was sure of, he'd been watched and outflanked. Squinting at the skid marks going down the hill, he reckoned the lone brave would now inform the others they were discovered, which meant within the next twenty-four hours would tell him if the Indians were bent on trouble.

Turning away, Scott retraced his path to the gully. Descending to the bottom, his ingrained cautious nature sent a warning. Not seeing danger didn't mean a thing in this deadly game of hide and seek. The lone Indian could have easily circled around and be waiting in ambush. This was no time to stumble into trouble. If the Indian lurked in the near vicinity, most likely he lay in wait where he'd left Buddy. Melting into the shadows cast by the line of trees, Scott drifted south before circling. Sure he'd traveled a safe distance, he located Buddy's tracks away from the main trail. Except for the gelding's lone hoof prints the ground was bare. Confident the savage was gone, he headed for his horse.

Sure no danger lurked, Lone Hawk let his pony run. He had something exciting to tell his brothers, a story to impress. Eager to catch up and share his latest adventure, he threw caution to the wind. By midafternoon, he caught up with his Kiowa brothers. As he rode up, Lone Hawk saw each brave eagerly observing his approach. Riding to the front with a flourish, he wheeled his mustang around.

One by one the braves semicircled Lone Hawk, the older man speaking, "What excites Lone Hawk? What danger have you uncovered?"

The younger braves laughed, knowing Lone Hawk loved adventure—dangerous adventure.

Enjoying the attention, Lone Hawk took his time, his attention focusing on the weather-beaten face of the leader leading the group. Gray Coyote had a warrior past, a skilled tactician admired by many chiefs from different tribes, one who was even respected by his past enemies. Finally Lone Hawk answered the old warrior, "A scout from the wagon train has been following us."

Considering the implications, Gray Coyote asked, "How far back is this wagon scout?"

Lone Hawk spoke respectfully, "One drop of the sun, Gray Coyote."

Having mastered the art of being a good listener, Gray Coyote digested even the smallest detail as he listened. He studied Hawk's bronze-colored face along with its perpetual scowl, already anticipating Hawk's intentions. He chose his words deliberately, "This wagon scout, is he always staying back one drop of the sun or sneaking closer?"

Shrugging, Lone Hawk answered him, "For now he stays back one drop of the sun."

"Good, he is but one man. Even better, no threat because of the way he follows us. Go, and if he spends the night among the wagon campfires, he is no cause for alarm. It will be good if we know such things. You will be our eyes and ears."

Gray Coyote's wisdom pleased Lone Hawk. The wily leader understood how Lone Hawk liked to hone his fighting skills alone. He knew every man on this raiding party, as well as how to take advantage of each brave's strength, while at the same time never forgetting each man's weakness.

Gray Coyote dismissed him with a wave of his hand. "We will see you after the sun goes down."

Lone Hawk started his horse back down the trail, nodding at each brave as he passed. When he returned after dark they would be eager to listen, excited to hear what he had to say. Pleased, his mind shifted, planning ahead. This time the wagon scout would not know of his presence. Unlike the last encounter, there would be no tracks to see. He would hide his signs by riding into the tracks left by others. Knowing the land was Lone Hawk's great advantage. Excited, he prodded the piebald mustang with his heels, thinking it was not by accident that the name Lone Hawk had been given to him by his peers. Besides, didn't a hawk look down from above and see its prey before swooping down for the kill. Yes, this time he would toy with this man who scouted for the wagon train. A sudden idea crossed Hawk's mind, a more dangerous game to play. Why not leave just enough signs of his presence so that the paleface would understand he lives because Lone Hawk allows him to have life? The idea intrigued him, a strong possibility. Liking such a challenge, Lone Hawk became more excited by the minute. He would think about this tactic some more.

For the rest of the day, Buchanan constantly checked for any unshod pony tracks branching off the main trail. Several hours had passed since he'd uncovered the lone Kiowa's maneuver. Scott was sure that any changing pattern from the Kiowa raiding party wouldn't come until the following day. As the afternoon slipped away, Scott saw no signs of pony tracks leaving the main group. Stealing a glance skyward, he judged the hour by the sun's location. In another hour, the evening shadows would start stretching across the land. Remembering Wendell's promised treat for tonight, for a moment his mind wandered, almost tasting the fresh bread smothered with honey. He scolded himself to remember his soldiering days, how ambushes often occurred when returning behind friendly lines. Getting waylaid by an enemy army during war was one thing, at least the sound of gunshots going off provided some warning, but Indians kill silently. Calvary soldiers called it "whispering death." This was no time to become careless. He decided to make one more check on his back trail before heading in.

More and more Lone Hawk was excited as the afternoon wore on. He had chosen his hiding places well, watching the wagon scout pass close enough to kill with the bow, the man unaware of his lurking presence. Delighted with his stealth, almost cocky, he considered himself more than a match for this paleface. It was he, Lone Hawk, who now scouted from behind, always maintaining the advantage. Despite his success, Lone Hawk always looped wide insuring none of his tracks would be discovered. Knowing the terrain as well as he did, each time his chosen location had been the right one. Since the wagon scout was constantly looking for tracks branching off from the main trail, the scout was totally unaware of Lone Hawk's presence. Keeping the paleface in sight before slipping ahead was the answer. Like the mountain cougar stalking his prey, every time Lone Hawk stalked ahead his potential victim remained in sight. Once he picked his chosen spot along the trail, he made sure he was close enough to spring into action should he want. The trick in gaining closeness to any rider was to find a blind spot where the trail curved. A rider always looked ahead in anticipation of what might come into view around the next bend, any ambusher hiding just before the trail straightened was overlooked as the road opened for distant viewing. Lone Hawk was pleased with his stealth and cunning. Like counting coup, there were times when he could have rushed forward touching the scout. An exciting thought entered his thinking. It would be a great victory for his reputation if he hung this scout's scalp from his lodge pole. Eyeing the descending sun, Lone Hawk knew before long shadows would cover the land. Soon the white-eyes would turn back for the safety of the wagon train. He must not forget Gray Coyote's request to inform him if the scout returned to the wagons for the night. He urged his mustang upward where he could spy from above.

Buchanan let his horse work his way along the jumble of loose rocks strewn along the base of the hillside. Turning Buddy, they climbed. Once above the trees, the land stretched out allowing a man to see for miles. Gently pulling back on Buddy's reins, the gelding stopped. Using his binoculars, Buchanan swung the optics in a slow arch, sudden movement catching his attention. Adjusting the focus, he watched three mule deer ambling out from behind a tree-covered arroyo. Content, the deer grazed out onto the grassy slope. Hell, he thought, if the deer weren't nervous, it was doubtful danger lurked nearby. Turning, he scanned the horizon, noting the sun's position. Starting to swing his head away, he froze. The sun was rapidly descending casting lengthening shadows revealing something looking like human footprints. Wondering if his eyes were playing tricks on him, Buchanan brought the binoculars up. Focusing on a far patch of bare windswept ground, he grunted, "Damn, they do appear human!" Urging Buddy in the direction of the knoll, he stared down at the fresh moccasin prints. A sudden breeze rustling the grass sounded like a hissing arrow. Cringing, Buchanan rolled out of the saddle, his gun appearing in his hand. Crouched like a coiled rattle-snake, his eyes darted everywhere, no attack coming. Ready to shoot, he straightened slowly. Again, the slight breeze rustled the grass. Remaining alert, his finger still planted against the trigger, he moved forward. Grim, Scott eyed each moccasin print, noting the left foot had a slight inward turn to it. Settling onto one knee, he spread his palm, touching the crushed grass where the Kiowa had laid. The blades of grass were still warm, warmer than the surrounding grasses.

Buchanan felt a prickly feeling going up the nape of his neck. Only minutes ago, the same Kiowa brave who had outflanked him earlier, just moments ago, the same brave had slipped away. And like before, there were two sets of tracks. One set of prints coming, one going.

Frowning, Buchanan followed the moccasin prints, halting where the horse had waited for his master. Not only had he been stalked, even more alarming, the Kiowa had been within killing range. The significance of what had happened caused his jaws to clench tight. The first time he had been watched, this time stalked. Had this lone buck wanted, he could have easily stuck an arrow through his shoulder blades. The color draining from Buchanan's face, a slow foreboding captured his mind. During his army years he'd seen many an arrow slice into someone's chest, the results always fatal. His expression tightened as the full realization sank in. The Indian had been toying with him. Edgy, he turned back for his horse. The gelding's head was up. Standing placidly, his horse watched his approach. If the Kiowa had maneuvered around, which seemed to be his habit, Buddy would have warned him. Holstering his gun, he rose into the saddle, his destination the trail below.

It was time to rendezvous with the wagon train. Leaning backward as Buddy worked his way downhill, Buchanan tried relaxing. It didn't work, his mind mulling over the danger from this lone warrior. Not only had the Indian played cat and mouse with him, it had been no contest.

Surprised he had been discovered for a second time, Lone Hawk watched from a distance. Once again, Eyes-That-See had uncovered his presence. Now that the wagon scout was aware he had been stalked, how would the paleface react? Watching the scout drop out of sight, Lone Hawk removed his hand from the mustang's muzzle. Concern entered his thinking, a scowl knitted across his brow. Just as quickly his expression immediately replaced because of his warrior mentality, his face intense. A hot fire grew within him. It would have been very disappointing if his adversary wasn't a capable foe. Besides, hadn't he considered leaving signs showing the white-eyes lived because Lone Hawk allowed it! His warrior mindset fueled, he waited until he was sure the paleface was gone before mounting his mustang. It was time to join up with his brothers and report to Gray Coyote. He had much to tell, but before revealing his story, he would satisfy his hunger while keeping the young braves waiting. Eating before talking assured him a captive audience, the young bucks always eager to listen to his adventures. One day in the not too distant future, age would catch up with Gray Coyote. When this happened, Lone Hawk would become their leader.

Lone Hawk's mind returned to the wagon scout, the intensity stirring up again. Despite his caution, the paleface had discovered his presence. Mulling this over, he came up with a positive. Had this not happened, his story would have lacked greater danger to himself. Because of this, he had a more important story to share. Once Gray Coyote and the others listened, not only would he have a captive audience, they would understand why he must kill such a worthy adversary. Killing another with a strong spirit was the way a warrior strengthened one's own spirit. This could only happen if a foe was a capable warrior. If he successfully killed this wagon scout, his reputation would spread among the different tribes. Once the tribes heard of his exploit, they would tell others. As the story was spoken, his legend would grow. Only a dangerous foe could make such a legend possible. Even more exciting, riding into danger showed he was a brave warrior fit to lead others. Thinking such thoughts erased Lone Hawk's concerns regarding the Eyes-That-See discovering his presence.

Nearing where the wagon train would circle up for the night, Buchanan couldn't shake his jumpy feelings. Constantly glancing back, all he saw was lengthening shadows. To satisfy his jitters, he decided it would be smart to do one more check. Riding between two merging slopes, he turned Buddy, the gelding working his way up a narrow draw staying hidden from view. Topping the draw, Scott reined Buddy to a halt. From here he could see afar.

Up here the land serene, almost void of life, the sun barely brushing the hilltops, the land below pretty enough that he almost forgot why he'd rode to the top. Content to be still and enjoy the serenity, he forced his eyes to search for danger. Buddy, sensing his master's more relaxed mood, his tail barely twitching, muzzled his own chest, horse and rider succumbing to the tranquility. A sudden jerk from Buddy caused by a blood-sucking mosquito brought both back to the present. The darkening dusk was sending up swarms of mosquitoes from the river below. Except for the whining insect hovering near Scott's ear, the land lay quiet. Once the cool of the night prevailed, those annoying pests would cease their aggravating assault. Right now moving would help. Starting Buddy back down, Buchanan's thoughts shifted away from himself to Wes Santana, anxious to hear Wes's report. Reaching the bottom, only twenty minutes of gray light remained, the hills hardly contrasting against the blackening sky.

Approaching the wagon trail, Scott turned Buddy onto the road, the numerous horse and oxen droppings still fresh. Just ahead he heard men's voices along with the tantalizing odor of cooking food. As much as he liked being out in this untamed land, returning each night gave him a special feeling of appreciation for the shelter afforded within the wagons, not forgetting the company of people along with a warm bed. Such things didn't cost money, but they sure were precious. Being out in the elements all day made a man appreciate the basic comforts the civilized world took for granted. Scott's eyes searched out the chuck wagon, seeing Wes standing beside Cliff, the foreman next to Wendell, all three watching his arrival. Riding up, he kicked his right foot out of the stirrup. Lifting his leg up and over, he landed feet first.

Wendell already held out a cup of steaming hot tea, Scott reaching out with both hands, the radiating heat from the cup warming. Aware all eyes were on him, he thanked Wendell, "As usual, much obliged, Wendell." Locking his stare onto Wes, he asked, "What happened after I left?"

Wes shrugged. "Not much to tell. Shortly after we split up, they moved out. They pretty much kept pace with the wagons. It almost seemed to me like they was using the wagon train as a buffer against the Indians. Hell, they could have easily distanced themselves since they aren't encumbered by wagons. Speaking of Indians, how about you?"

Taking his time, Scott figured a reaction was coming, one he didn't want. "Things were a little different this time. One of those Kiowa was shadowing me and got real close more than once."

Cliff didn't miss the implications. Curious, he probed, "If I heard correct, you were outmaneuvered by an Indian."

Shrugging, Buchanan sipped some tea before responding. Hoping his answer sounded matter-of-fact, he was careful to keep any concerns out of his voice. "I got to admit the brave's good at it. Fact is, I didn't catch on until late."

Wes was also taken back, a slight alarm in his voice. "I'll be damned! What do you think he was up to?"

"Hard to say, I reckon I'll know better by tomorrow."

"So," Cliff interrupted, "by tomorrow you mean?"

"I figure by now the brave has warned the others, which means they'll either place more daylight between us, or stay about the same. If they stay about the same, I'd consider them potential trouble."

Wendell had heard enough. Keeping his thoughts to himself, he drifted away but stayed within hearing range for more tidbits of information. He would have his say later.

Casting a glance at Wendell's leaving, Cliff asked his scout, "You said you didn't catch on until later, how come?"

Having ridden the trail with Cliff long enough Scott knew his boss was already anticipating what action might be necessary. Locking his focus on his boss, he answered him, "I uncovered his tracks when he broke away from the main bunch. He picked a perfect location overlooking their back trail. No doubt he was making sure they weren't being followed. Of course, I wasn't sure he was up there but I had my suspicions. So I circled around, climbed the hill, and Walla… my instincts were right on! After he knew I was onto him, he slipped away. I might add, nervy enough to ride past the very spot where I looked up the hill when I became suspicious. I figured he would report to the rest of his raiding party. Instead, he fooled me. Later in the day, thanks to my cautious ways, including some luck, I uncovered how he hid his tracks while keeping a close watch on me."

Wes didn't like what he was hearing, especially considering he was out there scouting himself. "You said more than once, how do you know the Indian wasn't a different one?"

"I rode up on high ground just before dark to check things out before heading in. The sun's rays were casting shadows, elongated shadows. That's when I noticed his moccasin prints. I rode over to make sure my eyes weren't playing tricks on me. It was then I realized how I'd been stalked. As for him being a different Kiowa, his left foot leaves a different print from his right. His tracks were the same ones I saw in the morning. He's the same Kiowa all right!"

Mulling over what they'd just heard, for several minutes no one talked, each man keeping his thoughts to himself. A nighthawk called in the distance, everyone thinking Indian, all heads jerking toward the sound.

Stokes broke up the mood. "Was he near enough to stick an arrow into you?"

Buchanan rolled his eyes before answering. "He was when I found them prints in the dirt."

Alarmed, Wes thought, no one was better than Scott Buchanan at prowling around, and if he could be outflanked by a lone Kiowa, what did that mean for the rest of them? Wasn't Scott like an an Indian himself, a real good reason for more than just casual concern? Another thought invaded his thinking. What did this dangerous development mean concerning their upcoming plans for the morning? He had better find out and now. Trying to hide any outward signs of being afraid, Wes asked the wagon boss, "What about tomorrow, this change anything?"

Fair question, Cliff thought, unsure himself. "Why don't you ask the chief scout?"

Buchanan's response was quick. "Hell if I know, I haven't had much time to think about tomorrow. The good news is that he didn't stick an arrow into me, for which I'm forever grateful. Besides, I always think better after I eliminate the hungries. After I do, then I'll think about tomorrow."

"Hungries, where'd you come up with that word?" Cliff chided.

Grinning, Scott made a point. "When I'm famished, it's called the hungries!" He stole a glance in the direction of Wendell, the cook bent over the fire. "The first thing I'm going to do is settle my horse for the night. Once that's done, I'm heading for that cooking fire to feed my face. If any of you have suggestions, I've got a good set of ears." Grabbing Buddy's reins, his voice drifted back, "See yo'all at the fire." Glancing at the nearest wagon, he noticed the pretty daughter who had asked him all those questions was looking at him. He liked her show of interest, surprised at himself.

Stephanie wished she could overhear the conversation between the two scouts and their boss. If someone wanted to know what was going on, listening to their exchange would provide some valuable answers. She was sure whatever the wagon boss decided, his decisions depended on the information he received from his scouts. There was something else motivating her. She was becoming intrigued with the Scott Buchanan, recalling how the wagon boss had told her he was untamable. She wondered if that was true. Stephanie sighed, thinking how there were now two men on this wagon train attracting her interest. Tyler Harden was one, and now there was the wagon scout. One who was very sophisticated, the other more comfortable among the savages. As she watched Buchanan leading his horse away, their eyes met. He stared at her for a moment before looking away. Well, she smiled, that was progress. A thought crept into her mind. Tonight, when Mr. Stokes visited their campfire, she was going to pry out more information about Scott Buchanan. Chuckling, knowing how her father constantly told her how persuasive she was, tonight she would give it her best effort.

The sky rapidly darkening; everywhere one looked folks were hovering over low-burning fires. Wendell smiled, watching Stokes and Buchanan devouring the fresh bread smothered with honey. Sitting cross-legged, Scott nodded at Wendell, his voice gushing out, "Whew, I was thinking about this all day."

Not about to bask in the compliment, Wendell came back with, "If I recall, you was going to come in early and help me with the fire for some baking."

"That was my intentions, but I'm sure you understand, I had to deal with a distraction."

Wendell knew this was his opportunity to have his say regarding the Kiowa brave. He slipped his dig in. "Maybe that's why that Kiowa made a fool out of you? Instead of paying attention to business at hand, you were thinking about dessert pleasures."

Knowing the cook wasn't given much too casual conversation, Scott knew Wendell was prying, wanting more than what was told. There was no doubt Wendell was going to keep asking until he dragged out the information wanted. Might as well give it to him, Scott decided, admitting his concerns, "I was careful, Mr. Bartholomew. Despite my caution the buck got the best of me despite my awareness he was lurking about. My gut's telling me this Kiowa is trouble—serious trouble. But come dawn, it's a new day. In the morning, I'll allow for a change in tactics. However, right now I'm not letting that stop me from enjoying the moment regarding your baking talents." Shifting his gaze at the rear of the chuck wagon, he could see more tins, his voice almost pleading, "Say now, Wendell, you wouldn't have more bread and honey stashed away in them tins, would you?"

Casting a chastising look, Wendell scolded him. "My God, we still got a long trail ahead of us. You already done ate half a loaf yourself."

Cliff Stokes chuckled, breaking up the two-way conversation. "Listen here chief scout, if there's any more left I got rank here, not you."

Laughing, Buchanan rocked back, conceding, "Well now, you can't blame a man for trying." Rising, he swept his plate clean. "Wendell, if you'd keep that teapot hot I'll be back later for another cup. I've got to mosey over to compare notes with Wes." Not waiting for a reply, he left. Walking slowly, his mind pondered about those strange riders. He had better have all his ducks in a row before approaching his boss about tomorrow's plans. Cliff always wanted to know his scout's intentions in advance. Once he talked to Wes, he would be ready for the boss man.

Santana watched Scott approaching, gesturing for him to sit.

Choosing the three-legged stool next to the fire, Scott balanced himself.

Wes pointed toward the teapot. "Want some?"

"Sure, why not. After we discuss our plans, I can tell the boss our strategy for tomorrow. You know how Cliff is, he does have the final say."

Wes nodded, pouring tea as he spoke. "He surely does. I must admit, I'm a little unnerved about that Kiowa ghost. He has got me to worrying considering how close he got to you, especially with your instincts. He did it several times without you knowing which is troublesome to me." Fixing his stare on Buchanan, he waited for an explanation.

"The only thing I can tell you is what I uncovered and what my instincts say. I had the feeling he was testing me, wanting to see how I reacted." Relaxed, Buchanan took a sip of tea before continuing. "Here's what I do know. Based on the depth of his tracks along with the length of his stride, including the matted grass where he lay watching me, I got him pegged at about five feet, eleven inches tall, probably weighs about one hundred and fifty, maybe add another ten pounds. Last but not least, he's stealthy, making him dangerous. I'd say he's wiry like a coiled rattlesnake and can run all day." Serious, Scott finished with, "That's what I calculate, and what I suspect."

Wes always marveled how Scott could read signs better than anyone he'd ever known. A man had to admire such a gift. Being able to judge the size of a man without seeing him by reading ground signs was something he hadn't mastered yet, maybe he never would.

For a moment quiet settled over the fire, each man lost in his own thoughts. Breaking away from the hypnotic influence from the flickering flames, Buchanan studied his scouting partner's face, figuring it was time to find out what Wes thought, so he asked him, "How about those mystery riders? You come to any conclusions why they're staying out of sight?"

Wes liked his questions, allowing him a chance to express his opinions. Whenever the wagon scout asked for a person's opinion, that showed he respected you. Another thing, Buchanan was a good listener. Clearing his throat, Wes answered the scout's questions. "I think they're trouble, that's what I think! Just a hunch I got. Here's the thing, if they were friendly, they should have rode over for some conversation by now. A friendly visit would be normal—to be expected! Since they haven't come over for a visit, I got them pegged as sneaks." Wes stared into the night, agreeing with himself some more, "I don't like sneaks. Such activity makes a man suspicious. I guess that pretty well sums up my conclusions about them."

Lots of horse sense there, Buchanan thought, agreeing, "I'd say you're right on, couldn't have said it better myself."

Wes was pleased, flattered. He had kept his conclusions brief and to the point. Unable to shake the potential danger from the Kiowa from his mind, he returned to what bothered him. "What about that Kiowa sneak who's been dogging you? What are you going to do about him?"

"I don't know. Whatever I decide, I'll need the boss's permission. For all we know he could be long gone. Here's the thing, Wes, those strange riders have gotten hold of my curiosity. We need to get a good look at them. After we do, it might get real personal between me and that Kiowa, that's if he's still around… a big if? Regardless of whatever we decide, I still have to go and consult with the boss man. Like I said, he's in charge, not us." Holding his cup out, he watched Wes give him a refill while giving him a chance to respond.

Still unable to shake his concerns, Wes stayed on his primary concern with a suggestion. "I been thinking we should gang up on that sneaking Kiowa. Two against one is a big advantage, don't you think?"

Although Scott trusted his instincts more than his partners, it wasn't smart to reject another man's concerns. It was obvious Wes was more worried about the Kiowa brave than those mystery riders. If Wes had his way, they would take action against the savage. Taking a sip, Scott pondered a course of action for the morning. Despite his curiosity about those strange riders, Wes's suggestion had merit. Finally he reached a conclusion, making it known, "You're right on all counts. Trouble is I can't shake my curiosity about those strange riders. We need to get a line on them and pronto. Of course, like I say, the boss will have to approve. The way I'm thinking is once we scout them out and tell Cliff what he needs to know and then we can gang up on the savage. There is the possibility he's long gone, which is all the more reason to check on those mystery riders. They won't up and disappear like the savage. Still, considering how you might be right, I'm going to tell Cliff what's bothering you and let him make the final call, if that's okay with you?"

"Hell, whatever you say is okay with me."

Rising, Buchanan stared over at the third wagon, noticing the pretty daughter and father talking with his boss. He rubbed his chin, thinking how Stokes wasn't much for socializing, which meant he should be leaving soon. Scott figured he wouldn't have to wait long. Turning his attention back to Wes, he noticed him staring at the sixth wagon, the wagon with the three attractive women and lone escort. He decided to have some fun. "If I have my way, we'll be leaving just before first light. Getting an early start means turning in early, so you better forget about them three ladies you keep gawking at."

Wes stretched out his hands, palms open, a grin plastered across his face. "I got to admit, just like out on the trail, you don't miss much, always good at reading a man's mind. There is one thing I'm not liking though, hoping you have some savvy advice. Have you noticed the suave fellow in the fifth wagon? It seems like he's impressed them ladies so much that they fall all over themselves trying to catch his attention. He's a real charmer, that's for sure."

"Yeah, I've noticed him. And you're right, he's got a way about him. The man's name is Tyler Harden. He's got the gift of gab, never at a loss for words with the womenfolk, does pretty good around the men too."

Wes didn't try to hide the jealousy in his voice. "It's frustrating watching all them women flock around him."

"Well," Scott chuckled, "maybe he'll stumble and not look so dashing before this trip ends. Besides, any woman falling for him might not be the type of gal you'd want to settle down with anyway. You know, a man needs to be careful about whom he gets serious with. Kind of like when the horse you're riding steps into a gopher hole and takes you down. The way I figure it, if a woman constantly pops up in a man's mind, it's time to ride for the hills."

Not buying his reasoning, Wes challenged him. "You saying you ain't ever planning on getting hitched?"

"I didn't say that. But I'm not very comfortable around them real pretty ones, the types who draw men like a magnet picks up nails. Besides, never-ending competition can become troublesome. Then there's my lifestyle. I reckon I'd have to give up prowling the land. Once you give up being free, life's never the same. I guess what I'm saying is this, I'm not ready to be domesticated yet."

"How about physical needs? A man has got to take care of that, don't he?"

Frowning, Buchanan considered this conversation was getting overly complicated; the tables were being turned on him. He answered as best he could. "A man doesn't have to be married to solve that."

"Is that so? Why don't you go tell that opinion to the young man studying to be a preacher?"

"I'm not talking to a preacher. This here conversation is between us two, nobody else."

Wes laughed, retorting, "Would you be interested in courting some gal that slept around?"

"No, I don't consider I would."

"So, you'd make her unfit for another man just to satisfy yourself?"

"Supposing she's already of that type, nothing I've done to corrupt her."

"But would you marry her?"

"Can't say I know." Buchanan decided it was time to change the topic. "I'm going to mosey over and catch up with the boss. As soon as I find out what he decides, based on a more intelligent conversation, I'll be back."

As he took the cup from Buchanan, Wes whispered, "Coward."

Chuckling, Buchanan wondered why his boss was still chatting with the Clarks. Mostly his boss did brief visits before moving on. Lingering longer than usual, it appeared the wagon boss wasn't in any rush. With a change of plans in mind, if he and his partner were going to get an early start on the trail come the morning, he couldn't wait any longer to talk things over. Hopefully, when Cliff saw him sauntering over he would depart from his socializing. Didn't the boss always stress there was a time for business and a time for leisure? Right now was time for him and the boss to talk business and forget socializing chit-chat. Besides, he was in no mood to get in a conversation with the pretty daughter. She had a way of asking too many questions. If he could avoid her, he would. Reluctantly Scott started walking slow, still hoping when the boss saw him coming he would move away.

Stokes had intended a brief visit, but he never had a chance. Norma Clark was the reason. Even before he knew what that something special was, the tantalizing odor permeating the campsite had its effect. Whatever she had prepared, gave him his excuse to linger. Besides, it would have been rude for Cliff to refuse after his earlier promise.

Adam winked at his wife. "Norma, where are those special treats you baked for Mr. Stokes?"

Curious with anticipation, Cliff spoke without sounding convincing, "I've already eaten, so don't feel obligated."

"Mr. Stokes," Norma scolded, "I've prepared my mother's favorite brown-bread recipe. I might add, a handed down recipe from the old country from generation to generation. I can't wait to see your face after you've tried it."

"Well then," Cliff grinned, "I reckon I will."

"That's not all," Adam gushed. "We've just opened a fresh jar of strawberry preserves. What's more, I've smelled the brown-bread all evening. Norma made it special—and not for me. Here, let me pass you a cup of tea or coffee, whatever's your preference, while my daughter passes the goodies."

Cliff didn't have to pretend he was whipped. "Strawberry preserves and brown-bread, my goodness, I guess I do have more room."

Adam waited for the wagon boss to finish his portion before starting his small talk with more meaningful intentions to follow. "Please don't be shy, help yourself to more, because if you don't, I will and I've already been scolded twice."

Rolling his eyes, Stokes managed to speak between bites, confessing, "Mrs. Clark, if I informed my men how delicious this bread is, my cook would be getting all sorts of requests. What with Wendell being so prideful and all, I'm thinking we wouldn't want a contest happening, especially one he'd lose."

Watching the wagon boss enjoy the brown-bread, Norma's eyes sparkled with pleasure.

Adam kept his tone conversational. "Tell me, Mr. Stokes, what have your scouts uncovered lately, anything new, perhaps exciting?"

Attentive, Stephanie suppressed a smile, knowing the game was on. Her father's opening question was just a starter. It was just a matter of time before her father prepped the wagon master with more serious questions.

Purposely taking another bite, Cliff stalled. He wasn't a wagon boss strictly because of his savvy along the trail with all of its potential problems. Long ago he'd learned the art of people motives. One thing he was sure, Adam Clark wasn't interested in excitement, if anything, just the opposite. It was only a matter of time before what was really on his mind made its way into the conversation. Gaining time, he apologized. "Sorry, I can't seem to stop myself. This brownbread just might be the best I've ever eaten." Bowing toward Norma Clark, a twinkle in his eyes, he included the topping. "Not forgetting the strawberry preserves." Finishing with a sigh, he answered Adam Clark's question, "As for excitement, right now the Kiowa are at least a day's ride ahead of us. By this time tomorrow, I expect they will be even further away. We'll know more by late tomorrow. As for those mystery riders, I'm going to send my scouts to have a look-see in the morning. At the very least, I want to know what they look like. Let me add this, you can tell a lot about people by how they look." Seeing curiosity in Clark's face, Cliff cocked his left eyebrow as he explained, "Folks up to no good have a look about them. Of course, we don't own the trail, which means whoever they are they can travel wherever they want and how they want." Seeing Buchanan approaching, he ceased talking.

Stephanie was excited. She was about to hear the scout and his boss speak to each other, the man described by his boss as half Apache and half Comanche.

Doffing his hat with a flare, Buchanan semi-bowed toward the ladies as he spoke, "Evening ladies, please excuse me for my barging in."

Adam couldn't have wished for a better development, acknowledging the wagon scout with enthusiasm, "Glad you stopped for a visit. We were just discussing yourself and the other scout."

"You mean, Wes Santana?"

"If that's his name?" Adam questioned.

Extending the platter containing the bread and preserves, Stephanie insisted Buchanan join them. "Please, I'm sure Mr. Stokes will attest to how delicious the bread and strawberry preserves are."

Glancing at his boss, Scott chose a slice covered with jam. Nodding at Stephanie, he thanked her. "What a treat, thank you, ma'am."

Well, Stephanie thought, the scout spoke with some social graces.

Adam cleared his throat, directing his curiosity to the scout. "Tell us, Mr. Buchanan, what did you uncover out there today?"

Looking up from the morsel in his hand, Scott shot a look at Cliff, surprised at seeing his boss's head going up and down giving him the go-ahead. Measuring his words he kept his eyes on his boss as he spoke. "Thanks to fair weather the trail's good, we're making good time mileage wise. As for the Indians, they're farther away than yesterday. Even better, no accidents and all the wagon folks are healthy."

Such a generic response wasn't acceptable for Stephanie. "What about those riders on the other side of the trail, Mr. Buchanan?"

Scott didn't have to answer. Cliff answered for him, "I told them you're going to ride over and check them out in the morning. I explained once you scout them out, we'll have an idea as to their intentions. Just getting a good look at the cut of folks often says a lot about them, kind of like reading trail signs, which you're very good at."

Stephanie turned her attention back to Buchanan.

Keying in on what Cliff said, Scott agreed, "Mr. Stokes is right. Seeing how people look often reveals character… good or bad."

Stephanie didn't miss a beat. "Sounds kind of discriminatory to me. You know, judgmental. Why wouldn't you just ride over for a visit?"

Seeing as how he was now on his own, very aware how Stephanie Clark seemed kind of touchy about judging people, probably because of her eastern education, Buchanan gave her his reasons. "Out here things aren't so black and white. It's better to keep the odds in your favor. Not scouting in advance can get a man killed. As for appearances, it's not whether they look Mexican or half breed, but little things like how they wear their guns, do they keep looking over their back trail, how they talk, which I aim to hear without them knowing I'm near. Things like that.

Supporting his scout, Cliff interrupted, "Especially since it is common for most riders traveling along the trail to drop in for a visit."

"So," Stephanie suggested, "they may be up to no good?"

Not answering, Cliff and Buchanan eyed each other.

"I'm surprised," Stephanie pressed on, "that the Indians aren't aware you're following them. After all, they are Indians."

She was a smart one all right, Buchanan thought. No quit in her. He saw a slight smirk around Cliff's mouth. At this point, the boss was letting him come up with answers on his own. He responded truthfully. "If they stay around long enough… they find a person out."

Tossing her auburn hair, Stephanie persisted, "What then, Mr. Buchanan?"

For sure she was herding him into a box canyon with no way out. If he was going to get rid of her noose, he had better make his move now. He got right to the point, speaking matter-of-factly, "The boss and I have plenty of experience from our army days. We have more than enough knowledge about Indian ways and their intentions. So we keep an eye on them, stay alert, and make sure they're not up to mischief. If they are, we scatter them."

Well, Stephanie congratulated herself. She certainly had him talking—even better, he was giving up information. Hoping for more, she asked him, "Suppose they get reinforcements?"

Buchanan's answer jumped out. "Let's not suppose something unless it happens. No sense in causing worry unless there's a reason for it. Besides, if they do, I'll know."

"And how will you know?"

Fighting off exasperation at her persistence, Scott realized she was using one question to lead to another. Hiding a frown, he wondered about her motives. Was the motive to get him to talk, maybe relieving family concerns? Perhaps something about him interested her. Whatever her motives, it was time to throw her off track. He chose his words deliberately, making sure to keep the subject focused on the Indians and not on himself. "White or Indian, nobody walks around out here without leaving signs of their passage. Indians ride horses, and horses leave tracks. Tracks give out lots of information to those who can read trail signs, which I'm good at that. As for the different tribes, Kiowa are fighters, but not as fierce compared to Comanche or Cheyenne. Mostly they like to trade, but not always."

Using what he said against him, Stephanie pressed on. "By saying not always, what you really mean is they are dangerous." She smiled, waiting.

"They can be. Other than that, Kiowa raiding parties pick their fights. This group doesn't have enough numbers to threaten us."

With his scout engaged and holding his own, Cliff saw his chance, excusing himself politely, "Mr. and Mrs. Clark, Miss Stephanie, thanks so much for the refreshments. It's time for me to make the rounds. Unfortunately, I only visited with half the folks yesterday. So tonight I'm going to catch up with the rest of the people." He glanced at Scott, giving him his out. "I'll see you in about a half hour." Wheeling on his heels, he left.

Stephanie knew this was the moment. If ever she was going to find out about this man the boss called half Apache and half Cheyenne, there wouldn't be a better opportunity than right now. Obviously, the best tactic was to keep him talking without appearing too pushy. She backed off tactfully, thanking him, "My father and I are feeling a lot better now, thanks to you."

Watching his boss walk away, Scott answered her, "Glad I helped." He shifted his eyes to his hand holding the bread covered with jam, realizing he had yet to take a bite. "Miss Clark, I've been holding this treat in my hand for some time now. If you give me a second, I'm going to enjoy my treat. After I do, I will then answer any more questions you have." He threw in a dig. "Or any more you might come up with."

Smiling, she feigned disappointment. "How rude of me, please excuse me."

Finished, Buchanan addressed Mrs. Clark, "Ma'am, that was something special."

Norma's expression beamed back at him. "Please help yourself, there's more."

"Thanks but, no, thanks. Truth is, I can't talk with food in my mouth, and after I finish answering Miss Stephanie's questions, I have to get going. My boss did say we are to meet in a half hour." He studied Stephanie's face, gearing up for what was yet to come. His expression told her to go ahead and ask.

"Tell me, Mr. Buchanan, about the other tribes and how you would deal with them compared to the Kiowa?"

Taking his hat off, he twirled it slowly, attempting to remain casual. It was then that he made a mistake. "There are exceptions. Fact is I had a Kiowa brave stalking me today." He grimaced at his blunder. Too much talking had a way of causing a man to reveal more than one intended. The effect was immediate.

Father and daughter stared at each other, Stephanie's voice serious. "Stalking you!"

Damn his mouth, Scott thought, the girls got me blabbing my fool head off.

Adam Clark's response was quicker than the fangs from a sidewinder rattler striking at his prey. "Was he trying to kill you, Mr. Buchanan?"

"No sir, he wasn't. He got close, close enough to try, but he didn't. I figured he was checking to see if they were being followed, that's all." It was time to change the direction the conversation was heading. "We should be near a frontier town in a few days. By then I'm sure those Kiowa will be gone. Like I mentioned before, mostly Kiowa are traders. I wouldn't be surprised if we didn't see the same bunch in the next town looking to barter." He smiled, hoping to excuse himself. "Now, I've got to go and huddle up with my other scout before meeting with the boss man." He smiled, not forgetting to repeat his compliment to Mrs. Clark. "Ma'am, much obliged for the dessert." Starting to walk away he was aware the Clark daughter was following him, her voice turning him around.

"Tell me, Mr. Buchanan, how did you know he wasn't intending you harm?"

Thanks to his big mouth he needed to explain. "I found out by accident at the end of the day while riding up to some high ground to check my back trail. If he intended me harm, he had his chances, which he didn't take. It won't happen again."

"And how do you know it won't happen again?"

Not wanting to be rude, Buchanan assured her, "Now that I know what he's up too, I won't be making the same mistakes. Miss Clark, I really do have to get going. Good day to you." Turning, he walked without stopping. This time there would be no ongoing conversation.

Frustrated but amused at his polite rudeness, she watched him leave. Stephanie crossed her arms, thinking a better word for his departure was—fleeing. As he walked away, she couldn't help but notice the way he moved. His movements were lithe, like he seemed to be floating over the ground. As she watched, Stephanie concluded the way he walked probably had something to do with his profession requiring stealth. As for his personality, perhaps it was his occupation which developed such an attitude. It would be interesting to see when they reached civilization if he became a different man. She liked such a thought.

Making the Rounds

Passing numerous campfires, Cliff acknowledged every invitation with a wave of his hand without stopping. Reaching the ninth wagon, he halted, his voice bridging the distance, surprising the busy wife and husband. "Evening folks, mind if I interrupt for a moment?"

The man hovering over the fire straightened. Lean and wiry, his body showed no indication of overindulgence concerning food or drink. His hair was kept, his mustache neatly groomed. Seeing the wagon boss, the man's face lit up with pleasure. Seeing such a man of importance, enthusiasm reflected in his hello, "Mighty pleased to have company, come and sit awhile."

One thing Cliff admired when he met a man was his appearance. You can tell a lot about a man by how he kept himself. Although not money folks, both he and his wife were always dressed clean, making every effort to stay well groomed during this dusty journey. Most men on the trail for extended periods let their hair and beards grow long, almost disheveled, but not Warren Jamison. His wife, Bernice, a slender woman, seemed to have a new dress for every other day. From what Cliff knew, she was barren. Despite their possessions being few, both were very attentive to each other's needs, a very admirable trait Cliff respected.

Responding, Cliff refused the invitation, "I can't stay very long. I'm trying to catch up with my promise to keep everyone informed."

Always polite, Warren nodded. "My wife and I appreciate you keeping your word. We surely do." Turning, he spoke to his wife. "Bernice, would you bring the coffeepot over."

Holding up his hand, Cliff refused politely, "If that's for me, thanks but, no, thanks. I've already had my fill. Anymore and I'll be up all night. I'm here to update you on the latest goings on. Two days ago my scout uncovered some unknown riders flanking both sides of the trail. One group is a small party of Kiowa, another bunch riding shoed horses. Right now we haven't seen who's riding the horses wearing horseshoes, much less why they haven't ridden over for a visit. We aim to find out tomorrow. If they appear to be a problem, you'll be informed."

Face tightening, Warren's voice was deliberate. "If you need help, you can count on me for some straight shooting. I've been hunting and trapping for most of my years, what's more, it's a rare thing for me to miss with a rifle." Eyes squinting, he added, "Even if my target's on the move, distance never been a hindrance to me, and that's a fact."

Knowing the man as he did, Cliff knew he wasn't bragging. Men who live off the land are self-sufficient, shooting no exception. Not doubting him, Cliff said so, "If I ever need someone who's a sharp shooter, it'll be you. Another thing, you're one of the few travelers qualified to scout for me in an emergency. I won't forget that either. Right now the Kiowa have drifted away. Hopefully they'll keep on distancing themselves from us. As for those other riders, like I said, we're placing them under surveillance in the morning. When I know more, you and your wife will know more. In the meantime, make sure you keep Mrs. Jamison close by."

Gesturing toward the coffeepot as if the wagon boss might change his mind, Warren poured another cup for himself. "Freshly brewed, sure I can't pour you a cup?"

Shaking his head no, Cliff excused himself, "Perhaps another time. As usual I'm running late. One of these evenings I'm going to surprise you." Touching his brim, he departed for the tenth wagon.

The two men in the tenth wagon were transporting furniture to San Francisco; their special cargo was round oak tables complete with claw feet. Such tables were highly prized in west coast cities. They owned two Conestoga wagons, both wagons were packed tight. If ever there were two men with opposite personalities, it was these two. Often they openly stated how their differences were their number one assets. Leonard Henderson was the bookkeeper, a man blessed with the ability to calculate figures. His partner was Frank Carlson. Unlike Leonard, he needed to push himself away from the food table, his round frame carrying way too much weight. Frank's gift was his persuasive tongue as a salesman. Both men had two things in common, making money and being unskilled with guns.

Nearing the wagons, Cliff dodged numerous oxen droppings before singing out, "Evening, gents, thought I'd drop by and update you on what's going on."

Carlson, the salesman with the gifted tongue, was the first to acknowledge the wagon boss. "Good evening to you, Wagon Master." Coughing momentarily, he added, "Considering the dust we're kicking up, I'd say we're making exceptional time."

Cliff confirmed Carlson's observation. "Better than expected for this time of the year. What with the weather holding and all, we should continue to roll up more miles than normal. I'm here with the intention of informing you regarding a recent development."

"You mean about the Indians?"

Cliff's surprise showed. "You know?"

"Yes, we know. We also heard something about strange riders." Carlson smiled, explaining, "Overheard some campfire talk. Not purposely eavesdropping, you understand, but certain folks spoke across their campfires on the loud side."

"My apology you didn't hear it from me first."

Including a shoulder shrug, Carlson waved his hand as if it didn't matter. "A man can't be everywhere at once. We figured if it was serious enough you would have informed everyone at the same time. The only concern Leonard and I have is one thing."

"Go ahead, what is it?"

"Would those heathens burn a man's wagons?"

Almost laughing, Cliff refrained. Knowing the value packed into the two wagons, laughing wouldn't be wise. For most folks, any Indian presence meant a serious threat to life and not possessions. But to Frank and Leonard, there was a fortune to be lost if fire destroyed their cargo. Still, it didn't hurt to warn them about a worst-case scenario. Besides, prevention made sense. If something did happen, they would be forewarned. Cliff kept his response simple. "If they got serious and attacked, I'd expect some wagons might be set on fire. Of course, I'm not expecting such a happening. It is possible, remote, but a possibility. You might want to fetch a few buckets of water from the river just in case."

Both faces tightened, each squinting at each other.

Hoping to relax them despite what he'd said, Cliff added, "Don't go getting overly alarmed. As of right now they've moved ahead of us. Another thing, we've got them under surveillance. What with the river being so near, having some extra water on hand makes sense no matter what."

Frank and Leonard nodded in unison, the possibility of all their investment going up in smoke was a horrifying thought. Folks in San Francisco paid dearly for eastern furniture, and round oak tables brought premium prices.

Cliff offered another assurance. "I'm telling you because anything's possible, though highly unlikely since Kiowa don't go picking fights with groups larger than themselves. Indians aren't foolhardy to attack unless they have the numbers."

Despite Cliff's calm demeanor, it was obvious the thought of a potential fire wasn't very calming to both men and it showed.

Trying a more relaxing approach, Cliff encouraged, "If I was you, I'd be more concerned about keeping your cooking fire under control than about those Kiowa firing up your wagons. Anyway, I've got to finish making the rounds. If anything changes, I'll let you know."

Watching the wagon-ramrod depart, Leonard was the first to speak. "Where did we pack those extra pails?"

"The only place we had empty space, in back of the second wagon." Both started for the wagon containing the pails.

Cliff had a special fondness for the next two men he was approaching. Within their wagon were two tents, digging tools, along with several large pans. Extra clothes with blankets and lots of dried food filled out their inventory. Both men were prospectors heading west to find gold. Tied to the back of their wagon were two mules. Cliff enjoyed Jack Yates and Bill Cody because of their fun attitudes. Both were always full of the devil. If ever there were two men who knew how to have fun and relax, it was the two miners. When a man started up a conversation with either one, he'd better be alert because of what was coming. Long ago they had mastered the art of turning around a man's words faster than a ricocheting bullet. As he neared, Cliff decided to become vulnerable. Not that he had much choice anyway. He was sure they were about to have fun at his expense. Even from this distance, he could see them planning mischief. "Evening, gents, an old Irish friend often greeted me with, 'How are you making it?'" Knowing he was about to get corrected, not sure how, but sure it was going to happen, he held his breath.

Cody's head swiveled around at Yates, his partner following suit. As if something was amiss, both showed an exaggerated frown. Bill kicked off his humorous response with, "We ain't making anything, least not that I know. Jack, didn't Mr. Stokes say making?" Both men laughed at the partner's cleverness.

Not disappointed, Cliff chuckled, considering giving both another opportunity. "All right, all right, just forget that I asked. You two have anything you might need some help with?"

Wide eyed, it was Jack's turn, the same mischief in his voice. "And what do you have in mind, wagon boss?"

"I was thinking about going over a map with you. You know, help you get started in the right direction where all that gold's buried."

Both questioned each other in perfect unison, "A map, what happened to our map?" Bill's hands flew to both sides of his face. Looking skyward, he rolled his eyes as he rubbed his forehead, his voice perplexed as he peered at the wagon boss. "Come to think of it, we were so worried about someone stealing our map, I went and hid it. Just hours ago I told Jack, I can't remember where I stashed it."

Playing along, Cliff raised his voice a notch. "I'd say that's a serious problem, be only glad to begin the search. Where do you suggest we start?"

Astonishment filling his expression, Bill looked at his partner in desperation, urgency in his voice. "I'll be darned, Jack, I just remembered where I stashed it! It's under the train trestle back in St. Louis!"

Fully enjoying himself, Jack added, "I guess we need to ask the wagon master to hold up the wagons for a few days until you return with the map."

Bill asked, "Well, Mr. Wagon Boss?"

"Of course, how long before you get back?"

"Considering going and returning, it shouldn't take Bill more than two to three weeks if he rides one of those mules." Gesturing toward the mules, both miners roared with laughter.

Just looking at the two, their hair disheveled from rubbing their heads, Cliff joined in.

Hearing the spontaneous laughter, the nearest wagon folks stopped doing chores, curiosity in their stares.

Raising his hand, Cliff became serious. "We have a party of Kiowa on our southern flank, also some strange riders tagging alongside on the far side of the river."

The humor gone from his voice, Bill's response was fast. "How near are them Injuns?"

"Farther away than yesterday, maybe a half day's ride."

"How many?"

"My scout figures fifteen."

"But moving away?"

"Seem to be."

Digging into his pocket, Jack pulled out fixings for a smoke, asking the wagon boss, "Want me to roll one for you?"

"I appreciate the offer, too hot, besides, my mouth's dried out. Find me a cigar for tonight around the evening fire and I'll thank you."

Bill shrugged. "Don't have any cigars, cost too much. Well, considering them Injuns, we both shoot straight with a fair amount of accuracy. We've both had a few scrapes with different breeds, and so far our luck has stayed with us. Be glad to share such luck if you need us. All you got to do is give us a yell." Casting a quizzical eye at the wagon boss, he asked him, "What about them strange riders?"

"I'm sending out two scouts in the morning. When they come back, I'll get the information to you."

Jack liked the way the boss man kept them abreast. The man said he would and he did. A man couldn't ask for more than that. He looked at his partner, offering, "We're available, including standing night guard."

Shocked at such an offer for night watch, Cliff almost stammered. "Talk about volunteering, much obliged!" Such an offer confirmed what Cliff knew about these two. Few men were willing to stand guard during the night; the hours seem to drag on forever while the world slept. And if that wasn't boring enough, come daylight, the remainder of the day left a man exhausted. Yes, sir, Cliff thought, Yates and Cody were fit to ride the trail with.

Lifting his hat, Cliff ran his fingers through his hair, conveying how much he appreciated such an offer. "Not many men would volunteer such service, which means your character has lots of sand in it. If I need a helping hand, I won't forget your offer, but it won't be for night guard. You've earned better because you two have thoroughbred blood in your pedigree."

Jack and Bill shrugged in appreciation.

"Tell you what," Cliff continued, "when we reach the next settlement, I'm going to purchase a box of cigars for you two. That way when I need one, I'll know where to go."

Yates and Cody chuckled in unison. "We ain't overly proud to refuse such a gift."

"Your volunteering earned such an offer. Right now I'm going to mosey over and talk with the folks behind you and then catch up with my scouts." Departing, he said, "We should know more tomorrow, I'll keep you posted. Like I said, I'll know more after tomorrow."

Walking away, he reflected on the two miners, recalling his father's advice years ago. More than once his old man explained how the people business can harden a person's attitude toward some, making a person not want to help those deserving it. If a man developed a hardened attitude, there would be missed opportunities to assist someone deserving, reminding Cliff of his father's words. His old man was right; the just made offer by Yates and Cody confirmed his father's wisdom.

The glowing light reflecting from the campfire showed numerous faces, oriental faces. They spoke a language Cliff didn't understand. They were Chinese folks, bound for San Francisco to reunite with relatives. Whenever he stopped for a visit, the men and women were always courteous, treating him almost as if he were royalty. Fortunately for him, a few spoke broken English allowing for communication. Cliff felt a tremendous respect for their manners. Another thing, whenever he was in their presence they never spoke in their native tongue, such a habit showing courtesy, more than that, a show of class. Cliff always considered foreigners speaking another language around someone who didn't understand a sign of rudeness, but not these people. The man leading the group went by the name of Geming.

As Cliff entered the circle of light, all talking ceased, the elder rising with a bow, his voice reflecting genuine pleasure, "Please, Mr. Stokes, sit among us." Pushing a stool he'd been sitting on forward, he said, "You honor us with your presence. We have made fresh tea if that is your wish."

Spreading his legs, Cliff settled on the stool, a small dainty cup placed in his hand. He studied the cup's golden scroll inscribed on the translucent china. Sipping, Cliff had to admit oriental people know how to brew tea better than anyone, including the British. Made sense, it was part of their culture. This group had three wagons. A father and mother accompanied each wagon, including children and grandparents. The number of children born to the parents varied. All the children were well behaved, only speaking when spoken to. Smiling, Cliff broke the temporary silence. "The tea tastes special, much obliged."

"Tell us, Mr. Stokes, how else may we show our appreciation?"

Every face smiled back, acknowledging the older man as their spokesman. Geming gestured toward the pots. "We have much food."

The aromatic smell of rice and vegetables hung in the air, not Cliff's favorite food compared to steak and potatoes, but then again, without such food scurvy can become a haunting problem for travelers. There was something else to be considered attesting to their health, never recalling overweight Orientals. What's more, whenever he visited they made it difficult for him to refuse their humble hospitality. It was very important he didn't offend them.

Tactfully, Cliff declined; making sure his voice expressed humble regret. "The next time I visit I'll be sure to arrive with an empty stomach. Unfortunately, I'm plum full from overeating, perhaps in the near future." Finishing the tea, both hands gently wrapped around the cup lest he break it, he found a safe place for it on the ground. What he said next shifted their attention away from hospitality to serious concerns. "I'm here to warn you to keep your women and children within sight at all times. We have a band of Indians nearby, not to mention some strange riders within several miles of us. I'm not expecting trouble, but Indians do steal women and children. You need to stay alert."

Most of the folks didn't understand English, Geming translating. When he finished, all eyes turned back to Cliff, their leader asking, "Tell me, Mr. Stokes, why do Indians steal another man's property?"

Cliff found it strange how Geming referenced children as property. It had to be their culture, he reckoned. Careful to avoid a cultural argument, he chose his words carefully. "It's because of constantly suffering population losses caused by sickness and from warring tribes. By acquiring another man's women and children, they keep their tribal numbers up. Of course, stealing another tribe's women and children causes ongoing raids."

"Ah-so, I understand. Thank you for giving me better understanding." Turning, Geming repeated what he was told. Some of the faces showed curiosity, many alarmed, a few showing casual concern.

Cliff waited until Geming turned back to him. "Just so you understand I'm not expecting trouble from them. I'm sure you know a few Chinese proverbs regarding caution. We also have some sayings; one of them being an ounce of prevention is worth a pound of cure." Cliff grinned, waiting for the host to translate.

Geming was brief, his group smiling as he finished.

Bending over, Cliff gently picked up the porcelain cup as he stood. "I wish I could linger and enjoy your hospitality but I must counsel with my scouts in preparation for tomorrow. I will let you know if any changes occur. Please remain alert. Thank you for the tea."

Taking the cup, Geming bowed as he spoke. "As you suggest, we will follow your instructions remaining alert. You have spoken wisely."

Excusing himself, Cliff suggested, "When I visit again, you must share your ancient wisdom with me."

Smiling, Geming returned the compliment. "That will please me. In such a way we will learn from each other."

Seeing Buchanan heading for the chuck wagon, Cliff quickened his strides. Joining up, they strolled toward the campfire. Cliff kept his voice hushed. "Have you thought about tomorrow?"

"I have."

"And?"

"I've got mixed feelings."

"Meaning?"

"Meaning those strange riders need to be scouted out. Despite what I'm planning for tomorrow, I've got a bad feeling in my bones about that Kiowa sneak."

Cliff pondered his scout's concerns. Despite Buchanan's worry, he needed to know about the strangers staying on the far side of the river. He made his decision. "The way I see it, we can't wait any longer. I need to know about them riders before they become a problem. Since Wes knows where they're camped, he'll ride with you. Once you have a good look, you can report back. As for the Kiowa sneak, he's only one, which drops him into second on the priority list."

Buchanan remained quiet.

Eyeing his scout, Cliff said, "Not knowing what those riders are up to can make for a dangerous situation. We may not be horse soldiers, but right now our needs aren't different. Whoever they are, they need to be scouted out by someone with experience, meaning you. Hell, one of your primary functions was reconnaissance when you scouted for the army. The same is true now."

Hearing his boss's concerns, Scott felt a little better. It was the wagon master's final decision, not his. He wondered who Cliff would choose as his other scout, asking him, "Who are you going to use to keep a watch on this side of the river?"

"Pat Morgan."

Nodding, Scott approved. "Good choice."

"I thought you'd approve."

"What are you going to tell him?"

"Same thing you'll tell him. Be cautious and swing wide when he rides out. Since you're going to instruct him first, I'll confirm your instructions. You have a better approach?"

Relating to his boss's old officer rank, Buchanan grunted, "Sounds to me like you're quoting from our old manual on scouting tactics."

"As good a source as any, like I said, you can refine any instructions you want. I suggest you tell him to wait until the wagon train starts moving up the trail. That should create enough of a diversion should any savage, or savages, be lurking nearby. Whatever you say, I'll repeat. Since I want you and Wes to leave before sunup, I'll double remind Pat before he heads out."

Sighing, Scott wasn't going to argue, "Seems like you got everything figured out. If all goes well, I'll be back by noon to relieve Pat."

The scout's worry was rubbing off on Cliff. Mulling over what was bothering his scout, he gave Scott's concerns more thought. The Kiowa outfoxing Buchanan was making his scout jumpy. If Scott had a better plan, now was time to hear it. Swinging around, he stepped in front of Buchanan. "I'm sensing you have a premonition. If you have a better plan, I'm all ears."

Buchanan stared into his boss's face. "I wish I did. I haven't thought that far in advance. I just don't like the notion of Pat dealing with such a skilled prowler."

"Anything else?"

"Yes. Be nice if Pat had more Indian experience, is all."

"You told me he makes good decisions."

"I know I have. What's more, he likes to scout."

"There you have it. We're not asking him to do something he doesn't want to do."

"True. It's just that my instinct is telling me this Kiowa is someone who likes to kill. I got a bad feeling in my bones. I think this sneaking savage has a warrior mentality. Those types believe they can acquire another warrior's spirit by killing another warrior. Indians bent on killing think in such a way."

Cliff stroked his day old-whiskers, wondering how he could protect Pat while finding out what he needed to know regarding the mystery riders. Nobody was better than Buchanan about deciphering potential danger. Wes was decent, but not Scott Buchanan. The man's instincts were uncanny. He had the ability to see what others missed. Nope, Buchanan needed to go with Wes. Besides, this wasn't the first time they had used Pat Morgan for scouting. What's more, the man did a decent job. Yes, Scott's concerns bothered him, but so did those strange riders. It was time to reconnoiter them, the sooner the better.

Staring out into the sea of grass, Cliff expressed his decision. "Right now that Kiowa is only one brave, probably long gone while catching up with the rest of his Indian scoundrels. For all we know, we'll never see him again. Right now I need to know why those strange riders are staying out of sight while keeping pace with us. I'm not going to wait any longer without knowing something. But I hear you. Tell you what I'm going to do. I'll keep Pat Morgan close to the wagons while he's out on point. I won't let him roam overly far with the added precaution of having him check in at regular intervals. When you return, you can relieve him. That should keep him safe from danger. Besides, he's a grown man, can't keep treating him like he needs to be watched over like a puppy dog."

Feeling a tad better, Scott agreed. "You have a point there. I reckon Pat has more than just a smattering of experience. It should be enough."

Hoping to nail down any further concerns, Cliff shifted all responsibility to himself. "I don't like placing a man in harms way either, but that's why I'm the boss. When I was an officer during the war, I never liked telling my men to charge into enemy lines. Notice I said, my men. But someone had to give that order. Since it was my responsibility, I gave the order. Same is true here, end of discussion. You go tell Morgan he's in our scouting plans. After you do, then escort him to me for more of the same. Before you and Wes ride out in the morning, we'll both repeat our instructions. Now, get going."

Stephanie watched Tyler Harden approaching. She was pleased and it showed.

Harden had rehearsed what he was going to say, his voice flirtatious, "I've noticed something about you, Stephanie. Something I see all the time."

Anticipating a compliment she feigned surprise. "Really, and what is that, Tyler?"

"I keep noticing how at the end of the day you look the same as when you started out in the morning. Kind of like a pretty sunrise followed by a pretty sunset. You know, something a man finds himself attracted to before he starts out, then again at the end of the day."

A crimson blush spreading slightly, Stephanie accepted his compliment graciously, "Why thank you, Tyler Harden."

Overhearing their conversation, a pleased Adam Clark emerged from behind the wagon. It was increasingly obvious the man was showing keen interest in his daughter. Now that he knew about the man, Adam wasn't worried about his intentions. Just the same, it was his responsibility to make sure any suitor conducted himself in a proper manner. After all, he and his wife hadn't raised Stephanie without concerns for her future. Although he now approved of Tyler, proper protocol would be followed. He had to admit, he liked knowing Harden was successful, the type who could take care of his daughter very comfortably. Even so, Stephanie's beauty had attracted other suitors before. There was one youthful exception, the rest all successful men. Knowing his daughter would never be without suitors, there was no need to be in a rush. Despite his intended guidance, her age gave her the right to make her own decisions, something she was very competent at doing for herself. At least for now the man had impeccable qualifications. He greeted Tyler enthusiastically, "Good evening, Mr. Harden. Please visit with us for a while."

Tyler flashed his smile. "Thank you. I have to admit I was hoping for such an invitation. I accept."

Looking for support, Adam eyed his daughter as he spoke. "What can we offer, Mr. Harden?"

Before Stephanie could answer, Tyler interrupted with a chuckle, "How about information? Tell me, has Stephanie noticed anything unusual lately? She seems to have developed the uncanny ability to notice everything regarding life on the trail."

Unable to contain himself, Adam's laughter was spontaneous, prompting his daughter, "What about it, Stephanie? Have you detected anything out of the ordinary within the last twenty-four hours?"

Enjoying the attention, Stephanie studied Tyler's expression as she talked. "There is something new."

Keenly interested, Tyler asked her, "And what is that something new?"

"There's an Indian stalking the wagon scout."

Tyler's expression jumped, his voice gushing out, "Really!"

Adam confirmed his daughter's statement. "He did say so, didn't he, Stephanie?"

Shifting his eyes away from the glow cast by the fire into the night's surroundings, Tyler mused, "I wonder what that means? I guess it could mean several possibilities. One of them having the element of danger since it appears Kiowa is lingering for a dubious reason."

Not liking what Tyler said, Adam's fears returned. "Which would indicate what?"

Shifting his gaze back toward the wagons, Tyler wasn't sure. "It's plausible the Kiowa are scouting out the wagons for thievery, the other question is, are they in cahoots with those strange riders?" He looked at Stephanie. "What else did Buchanan have to say?"

"The information he gave kind of slipped out. He's very guarded about what he says."

Tyler didn't doubt that. "That sounds like him, all right. He wants Stokes to do all the communicating." His hand rubbing his chin, Tyler followed up with, "Since he's so closed mouthed, how did you get him to reveal about the stalking Indian?"

Casting a glance toward the camp wagon, Stephanie recalled her sudden interest in Buchanan, remembering her intentions to get the scout to talk about himself. She would keep her personal interest private. "I decided to ask questions on top of questions." Laughing, she added, "And it worked, at least temporarily. Once you get a person to talk, you can use what they say to ask more questions. After our talk, he just about fled."

Intrigued, Tyler asked her, "It seems like you rattled him pretty good. If you don't mind me asking, I'm curious about your reasons?"

Was Tyler a little bit jealous? Stephanie wondered. Cautiously omitting the personal interest part, she said, "It seems whenever the wagon boss makes a decision, he depends on the information he receives from his chief scout, and Scott Buchanan is the chief scout."

What she said made sense, Tyler thought, shifting his thoughts away from the wagon scout. Since he was an opportunist, now was the perfect time to endear the family to him while gaining Stephanie's favor. He was quite sure her father lacked protective skills. It was time to take advantage of the current circumstances. He turned his attention toward Stephanie's father, questioning him, "How are your skills with a gun?"

"I only know what they look like," Adam admitted. "I guess I do know where the trigger is."

Tyler had the answer he'd hoped for. "If you wouldn't mind, I think from now on you would be wise to keep your wagon in line right behind ours. If any trouble develops, I and my partner are proficient with guns, if that's okay with you?"

Stephanie felt her emotions stirring. Not only was Tyler charming and handsome, also unafraid, a man who cared about others.

Adam accepted the offer without hesitation. "We accept. I'll have to ask the wagon boss if he minds us moving our wagon's position in the line with yours."

Tyler waved his hand. "Don't, I'll talk with him."

"Thank you."

Searching with his eyes, Buchanan approached the huddled workers, quickly locating Pat Morgan. He wiggled his finger for him to come.

Standing, Morgan joined him. "What's up?"

"Tomorrow morning you're becoming a wagon scout at least for a day." Knowing he liked to scout, deciding to have fun, Scott teased an eager Pat Morgan, "Are you up for it?"

"Are you kidding? I can't wait."

Holding on to his arm, Scott steered him toward the chuck wagon. "Let's stroll over and join the boss and Santana. While we're walking, I'm going to give you some important instructions, so listen carefully. Yesterday I played cat and mouse with a Kiowa brave. The worst part was he could have bushwhacked me more than once."

Startled, Pat pulled up. "You say an Indian got the best of you!"

"He did, but it won't happen again. At first I didn't know he was stalking me. I kind of found out by accident. As of right now, Stokes wants me and Santana to scout out those strange riders on the far side of the river. He intends to have you ride the point. You will be covering the area where that sneak was. Pat, you have to be careful. We think he's gone, but you need to be watchful. Am I understood?"

"Yea, I hear you. Stop worrying."

"I will stop worrying if you do what you're told. All we're asking is for you to make sure no one has slipped back looking to cause trouble. Cliff's going to instruct you to stay close to the wagons while you ride the point. When I return, I'll catch up with you, hopefully by noon. You understand how it goes out there. Things rarely work out time wise, especially when avoiding detection. Not being seen requires caution by not rushing, so no telling when I get back. As for that Kiowa sneak, you know how it is with Indians. Just when a man thinks they're not around, look out! Now, Pat, you have to promise me you'll be cautious, no daydreaming! These are the same instructions you're going to hear from the boss, so pay attention because there's a reason why we've already talked it over. All you have to do is follow our instructions. If you do what you're told, no Indian will get the jump on you."

Pat interrupted, "If I didn't feel able, I wouldn't go."

"Good, you just made me feel better. Here are more instructions. In the morning, you're going to wait until all the wagons are moving up the trail. Why, because it's a diversion tactic? Once you ride out, you backtrack down the trail before swinging wide for higher ground. You'll be looking for horse tracks, especially a single set of horse prints." Buchanan leaned forward, his eyes boring into Pat's face. "Especially unshod horse tracks. By circling you should detect any prowler. Like I've already said, as soon as I get back I'll catch up with you. I know I'm repeating myself, just the same, some things are worth repeating."

"What you said is easy enough to remember. You have my promise."

"Good, and Pat, don't be overconfident out there. If you see anything, anything at all, hurry back to the wagons and warn Cliff. That way you'll be safe and so too will be the rest of the wagon folks. Which I might add, is your primary purpose out there."

Pat nodded.

"Let me repeat myself. The most important tactical part is to swing wide when you head out. After you've backtracked far enough, you ride up to the high ground. Once up there, you stay as high as possible. I think you know why, don't you?"

"Yeah, I know why."

"Why?"

"Because Indians spy from the high ground. What's more, the best ambushes come from above."

Pleased with Pat's response, Scott relaxed slightly, encouraging the new scout, "It's pretty tough for savages to get the jump on someone when you know in advance they're in the vicinity, especially when you have the terrain advantage."

Staying silent, Pat nodded.

Stokes could see Scott and Pat were having a serious discussion. Even better, Pat was concentrating on what was being said.

Scott stopped talking as they neared.

His eyes on Pat, Cliff questioned his scout, "You finished briefing him?"

"I have."

"Pat, you have any questions?"

"None I can think of."

"Good. Here's the thing, Wes and Buchanan will slip out just before dawn. You won't leave until the first wagon rolls onto the trail. Better yet, wait until all the wagons are headed up the trail. If anyone's spying, they'll be distracted by all the wagon movement. I want you to ride back down the trail for a good half mile before swinging wide. Don't go straight out. After you've circled, you head uphill, coming back in from the south. If anyone snuck in during the night, you'll see their tracks. By making a wide swing, you'll be flanking any potential bushwhacker, something Indians are good at. Take your time. Once you take over the point I want you in constant communication with me. When Scott returns, he'll ride out and get you. Pat, if you have any questions, now's the time to ask."

"Just one."

"What is it?"

"I was kind of hoping you'd need me for more than a day."

"Do this right and you might get your wish." Looking at his chief scout, Cliff asked him, "Have I overlooked anything, something you said I missed? I'm sure you warned him good and proper about the Kiowa sneak."

"I did."

"You explained why we want him to circle wide?"

"Like you just said, word for word."

Cliff shifted his attention back to Pat. "Tell me Pat, when you ride out what's the first thing you're supposed to do? Or should I say, you're going to do."

"Backtrack before circling for the high ground."

"What are you looking for?"

"Unshod horse tracks."

"How about any kind of horse tracks?"

"Any kind of horse tracks, then."

"Why?"

Thinking seriously, Pat took a second before coming up with a reason. "Indians steal horses, and a stolen horse could be wearing horseshoes."

Satisfied, Cliff instructed, "After you assume the point, you're to stay in regular contact. I'll go over everything again in the morning. As for now, let's everybody get a good night's sleep. Scott, I'm sure you'll be up before first light. I'll see you and Wes first thing in the morning. If either of you think of anything we haven't discussed, I'll pass it on to Pat. As for you, Pat, you'll be rousted early. I suggest you hit the sack as soon as possible."

For a moment all talking ceased, the only sounds coming from the crackling fire. The night was pitch-black, a solitary coyote's howl breaking the silence, followed by another.

Hypnotized by the fire, Cliff yawned, content in knowing both he and Buchanan had gone over the same instructions. In the morning, they would repeat those same instructions, making sure Pat fully understood every precaution down to the smallest detail.

Matching his boss's yawn, Buchanan stretched. The boss's suggestion of hitting the sack sounded like good advice. Tomorrow promised to be an interesting day. Excusing himself, he nodded to everyone, "I'll see you all in the morning. Pat, get a good night's sleep 'cause somebody's going to be shaking your bedding before you know it. Since you've joined the scouting fraternity, you'll be eating with the boss man before heading out. I always figure a brain works better after being refreshed during a good night's sleep, not forgetting a proper feeding. Like the boss said, you'll be instructed again."

Grinning, Pat defended himself. "Just make sure I've had my second cup of coffee. That's if you want a fresh brain."

"When I roust you, I'll stick a cup in your hand. You can get the second cup from Wendell."

The popping sounds from the fire captured the night as they turned in, only Cliff remained to mull things over.

AMBUSH

Noting the spring in Pat Morgan's steps, Cliff Stokes took another sip from his coffee cup before greeting him. "Howdy Pat, have your coffee yet?"

"Yep, one cup, compliments of Buchanan."

"I'm sure you remembered you're having morning chow with us."

"I did."

Lifting the coffee pot, Cliff poured Pat a cupful. "Last night I told Wendell to cook up some extra chow. Now let's see if he listened to me."

Taking the cup, Pat grinned. "Much obliged. A morning without coffee means a man is off to a bad start."

Cliff gave a curt nod of agreement. "I'll be right back," finding Wendell rummaging through the rear of the tool wagon. "Wendell, we have enough chow to include Pat?"

Stepping back from his searching, Wendell toned down the sarcasm in his voice, "Well now, are you accusing me of becoming senile? Even if you forgot to ask, knowing you helps me anticipate everything you want... or might want." Walking his boss back to the fire, he chided him, "I not only have enough chow, the foods already cooked. How about you, Mr. Boss Man, you eat yet?"

"I'll eat with Pat."

Watching Wendell pile on the food, Cliff grasped both plates, approaching Pat. "It seems my cook has a memory. Claims he can anticipate what I want regardless if I ask. You ever notice how he's a master of shifting all compliments in his direction? Considering such, I have to admit such anticipation by him has happened more than once. Anyway, food's hot, maybe not tasty, but hot." Grimacing at his careless mouth, Cliff glanced sheepishly back at Wendell, breathing a sigh of relief. His cook was back behind the work wagon rummaging for whatever he hadn't found before. Cliff smiled inwardly, thinking how he'd dodged a bullet. It didn't pay to be critical of Wendell's talent. He had a way of making you pay for any criticism no matter whether warranted or not. If Wendell became irked, he would get even through his cooking.

Finishing off his plate, Cliff started in on Pat. "I have some early chores to do, so here are your instructions for the day. When you head out, I want you to scout the south side of the trail, not forgetting the first thing you do is make sure you backtrack down the trail. Once you've traveled a safe distance, you climb higher than normal before you circle around. If you cut no horse tracks, then and only then, are you to assume the point. Every so often make it a habit to circle ahead looking for strange tracks. If you find any, make sure you use the same tactics before checking them out. If everything appears okay, go back to the point. If you get suspicious for any reason, double back here and report to me. You got that?"

Pat downed his coffee, thinking how his boss worried too much. He waved his free hand as he spoke, "I can't think of any, you and the chief scout have repeated yourselves pretty good."

"I hope so. Did Buchanan tell you what you need to know about that Kiowa stalker?"

"He did."

"Pat, be careful. If that Indian buck got close to Buchanan, he can do the same with you."

"You know, Mr. Stokes, I'm not exactly a stranger out there. By the way, where's Buchanan and Santana?"

"They rode out after Buchanan rousted you from the sack."

"Oh."

Cliff wondered if he was forgetting anything critical. He thought of caution. "I don't want you to be in a rush out there. I'm dead serious when I say the slower the better. The only way you can give yourself a margin of safety against a potential ambush is to inconvenience yourself by not being impatient. Taking your time forces folks up to no good becoming the impatient ones. When that happens, the advantage swings toward the one who's not in a rush. As for any savage on the prowl, right now he's nothing more than a sneak, which means we don't want him to become a successful bush-whacker. Am I getting through to you?"

Pat spoke his favorite saying for emphasis, "Most certainly."

"I hope so. The reason we want you to swing wide when you ride out is to make sure no one snuck in close during the night, especially that Kiowa sneak. Again, if you cut any tracks, get back here pronto. Only when you're sure there's no one prowling around are you to take over the point. Like I said yesterday, I expect you to check in on a regular basis, every three hours seems about right." Cliff shook his finger in Pat's face. "If you don't report like I want, I'll send someone out to relieve you... and that's a promise."

Pat liked scouting. It was a choice job, one that got him away from boring work. He had better avoid sounding overly cocky. Hoping to relax the wagon boss, he dragged out his words. "You know, Mr. Stokes, I've done this before. There isn't any lone Kiowa going to get the best of me. Maybe if you had said Comanche or Cheyenne, maybe even Apache, then I might worry. Besides, you and Buchanan bent my ears pretty good last night. Like you just mentioned, he told me the same things you're saying. You can be sure I will take precautions—so stop worrying."

Frowning, Cliff corrected him. "Don't think for one moment Kiowa can't fight like Comanche or Cheyenne."

"Ain't no Injun crazier than a Comanche, but I hear you. I'll do like you say and that's a promise."

Cliff appreciated Pat's confidence, but not his attitude. Careful to avoid shaking the man's confidence, he added, "I know you have experience or else we wouldn't be sending you out there. But remember, it just takes one mistake through carelessness. If my chief scout was concerned about the Kiowa, so should you. We've both told you what you need to do. Let's go over this one last time, you answering me. How are you planning to ride out?"

Pat was ready, saying, "Backtrack before circling up to higher ground."

"Correct. The moving wagons will act as a distraction. As soon as we're strung out, that's your cue to ride. Head back about a quarter mile before circling. I can't stress that enough. Once you're on the point, what are you supposed to do?"

"Once and awhile circle ahead."

Pleased, Cliff asked, "How often are you to check with me?"

"Every three hours."

"I'll be timing you," Cliff warned. "When Buchanan returns, I'll send him out to see how you're doing. If you're doing what you've been told, we just might leave you out there. That's all I got to say 'cept we fed you, got some wake-up coffee in you, and now all you have to do is get your horse ready. Oh, one other thing. Make sure you have bullets in every chamber. Pat, do this right and we'll be motivated to use you more often than not."

Walking away, full of confidence, Pat's voice drifted back. "Stop worrying, Mr. Stokes, I'll be careful and check in, just like you want."

Shrugging, Cliff glanced over at Wendell.

Wendell could see his boss was on edge, couldn't say he blamed him either. If the Indian had out-maneuvered Scott Buchanan, there was plenty of reason for him to worry regarding Pat. Wendell attempted to settle his boss. "You know, Pat ain't half bad at scouting. If you didn't send Santana out with Scott, Pat would be your other scout, isn't that right?"

A valid point, Cliff conceded. "You're right, Wendell. What's more, he's a grown man who has experience and has been taught and told right. Like I often say, you can only puppy-train a dog for so long, same with a man. Let's get packed up so we can move out."

Finishing the cleanup, they hooked up the oxen, the middle ox giving some difficulty. That was strange, Cliff thought. By nature, the third bull was a very placid animal who never gave them trouble before. Was that an omen of something bad about to happen, he worried. His concerns returning, lips compressed, he eyed the rest of the wagons, pleased to see everyone was looking at the lead wagon. Cliff chased any bad thoughts from his mind. Rising into his saddle, he nodded at his foreman. "Move them out, Stuart."

His hand raised high; Stuart dropped it as his horse started up the trail. Behind came the shouts from human voices, oxen surging into motion, followed by sounds from straining leather and grunting animals leaning into their traces. Cliff always enjoyed trail sounds indicating progress. For a brief second, he looked back, eyeballing a lone figure astride his mount. He gave a curt nod to Pat Morgan.

Seeing the wagon boss's nod, Pat touched his hat brim. The slight breeze freshened. Thanks to the cool morning air, feeling frisky Pat's bay blew loudly from his nostrils.

The sun touching the hilltops was a pretty sight, the distant slopes as clear as a bell. Pat thankful he had an interesting day ahead of him. He hoped Buchanan didn't get back too early, the later the better.

Finally the last wagon entered the trail, rocking briefly as its wheels adjusted to the ruts. Pat tempered his eagerness, waiting before starting his horse across the flats, the land gradually gaining in elevation. As the last wagon rounded the far bend in the trail, Pat urged his horse up the gentle incline, the bay climbing easily. One thing he didn't need to be told was to seek high ground. Having served in the army, Pat understood terrain strategy. If a man occupied the high ground, danger would only come from below. Nearing the crest of the first hill, glancing back, Pat suddenly realized he hadn't followed instructions. Caught up with the beauty of the morning he'd forgotten to backtrack before making his swing. Scowling, he considered turning back. Looking downhill, he hesitated. Shifting in his saddle, he studied the upper hillside. Just before him was an easy way up, it was too tempting. As soon as they topped the hill, he'd backtrack. He urged the bay up the incline, the hilltop looming ahead. His horse dropped into a slight hollow before surging upward. Leaning forward, Pat straightened in the saddle as they leveled off. He blinked; something was coming at him in a blur.

The arrow punched into Pat's chest, his face contorting into surprise, blood spraying across the horse's withers. His body rocked back, the arrow tip stabbing into the horse's spine, the bay bolting. Falling backward, Pat slammed against the ground, his breath knocked out of his lungs. He managed to raise his head, disbelief taking hold. Pat focused on the feathered shaft protruding from his chest. Bright crimson blood was spreading through his shirt. Wrapping his fingers around the arrow shaft, he tugged, feeling a rush of warm blood soaking his chest. Alarmed, he stopped, a strange sensation coming over him. He felt no pain, just a numbness producing a weakening grip, a foreign ringing filling his ears, the bright sunlight fading. "Damn it to hell," Pat groaned. "Why oh why didn't I listen!"

Lone Hawk approached, surprised, then angry. This scout was not Eyes-That-See. He was not the one who would give him bragging rights, the warrior he wanted to kill. He stole a glance in the direction of the departed wagons. Good, he reasoned, they had no idea what had happened. He returned his gaze to the lifeless body. Despite Lone Hawk's disappointment, his ambush had been brilliant, his shot true. Pulling his knife he quickly lifted the man's scalp. The bloody scalp hanging in his hand, he eyed the man's horse. The animal stood almost sixteen hands high. Such a strong horse was a great prize to show his Kiowa brothers, so too were the man's guns. First, he must capture the horse. Lone Hawk laid the scalp on the ground. Approaching the horse slowly, the bay lifted his head, nostrils flared, nervously prancing backward. The smell of bear grease smeared over Lone Hawk's body scared the horse. He stopped, waiting for the horse to settle down. Making sure his hand was held low, a raised hand a sign of aggression, he crooned soothingly. Taking one step at a time, he made sure to keep his hand well below the stallion's muzzle. Avoiding quick movements, he gradually gained the bay's confidence. Stroking the calmed horse, Lone Hawk pulled the rifle. Grasping the bridle firmly with his free hand, he loosened the cinch, dumping the saddle to the ground.

Sneering, Lone Hawk stared at the saddle with disdain. Such a cumbersome weight always allowed an Indian warrior to outrun the palefaces invading their land. Didn't a lighter horse run faster for a greater distance? Only the white-eyes needed such a cumbersome burden. With one lithe movement, he lifted the saddle, slinging it into the tall grass below. Tying a rope to the bridle, Lone Hawk secured the other end to his mustang. Unbuckling the man's holster from the lifeless body, he draped the gun belt over his shoulder. Attaching a leather sling to the man's rifle, he slung it over his back. Satisfied, he leaped onto his horse, urging the mustang into a trot, the bay following.

Lone Hawk wondered if Eyes-That-See had altered his routine because he sensed danger. Another thought nagged at him. Was it possible the wagon scout's spirit was stronger than his? When he had left the raiding party, he was confident the man he hunted would fall to his arrow. It had been his intention to show Gray Coyote that no white man was a match for Lone Hawk's prowess. Instead, his bragging rights were muted. What would he say now? If he did not tell the truth, Gray Coyote would know. The old leader was uncanny, always able to separate truth from deception. Besides, if he spoke with a forked tongue, he would be like those double-talking people overrunning the land. They promised one thing while doing another. No, he would not be like them.

Several miles passed as Lone Hawk contemplated the coming meeting with the Cheyenne. Even more exciting, they were being led by the legendary war chief, Two Moons. He snarled outwardly, angry about his missed opportunity. It had been his plan to show his warrior mettle before such a great leader. Now he was denied such an opportunity, yet there was still hope. Hopefully, the Cheyenne were still several days away. He was sure the Great Spirit would allow him to kill the man he wanted, and after he did, he would tell of the dangers he'd encountered. Another pleasing possibility interrupted his thinking, a very encouraging thought. Perhaps this temporary failure meant he was destined to have an even greater story to share. Instead of one death to brag about, there would be two. Yes, such a happening would be an even greater opportunity adding to his legend as a warrior. Lone Hawk's scowl departed, replaced with composure. Despite Eyes-That-See's good fortune, hadn't he killed an enemy invading their land, wasn't success against any foe always a great achievement? Yes, he had earned the right to brag about the scalp he was bringing back to the raiding party. As the afternoon wore on the shadows lengthened, the tracks from the Indian mustangs stretching out before Lone Hawk. He was sure his Indian brothers would soon head for higher ground. Several minutes later, he congratulated his anticipation. The pony tracks had turned, swinging toward a cluster of stunted tree-lined draws. Sure that Gray Coyote's band lurked in one of those draws, he would know which one when he saw where the tracks passed the farthest from, the wily old leader making sure the tracks they left passed their hiding location allowing for ample warning. Whoever followed the raiding party would be looking ahead, leaving Gray Coyote's men time to escape, or attack without warning. Guards would be posted overlooking their trail until dark. Once the night claimed the land, the lookouts would come in and gather around the fire. Lone Hawk could hardly wait until the right moment to give his account of his success. Already his chest swelled out anticipating becoming the center of attention. Besides, what story did the others have to tell? Only he, Lone Hawk, had a captivating adventure to share. He imagined the gasps coming from the circled braves as he told them how the unsuspecting paleface rode into the path of his arrow.

The tracks Lone Hawk followed veered sharply, bypassing a series of draws, continuing west. He pulled on the reins, no longer following the pony tracks. Instead, he rode directly for the first draw. Riding past several boulders, Lone Hawk expected to be challenged at any moment. Dropping into the draw, two dark forms rose, the nearest speaking, "Lone Hawk, you have killed the scout who has Eyes-That-See!"

Holding up his bow, Lone Hawk acknowledged them with a warrior's salute. Continuing on, he reached the camp. Slipping from his horse, he watched the men gather around the dead man's horse. Standing with his arms crossed, he waited for the questions to begin as several of the younger braves pointed to the scalp.

It was Gray Coyote who spoke first. "You have scalped success-fully. You are a great warrior. I see you have returned with the dead scout's most valuable possessions."

No reply came from Lone Hawk, just a nod.

Gray Coyote was surprised, by now Lone Hawk should be gushing with enthusiasm. Why was he not bragging? Gray Coyote decided to find out. "This is not like you, why is your tongue quiet? Isn't this the one you hunted?"

Aggravated inwardly, Lone Hawk geared himself for what was coming. The leader always seemed to know what had gone wrong without being there. Always eager to hear what Lone Hawk had to say, the braves closed in as Lone Hawk explained, "My ambush was good, my aim true, but the scalp is not the one I wanted."

A soft gasp escaped the group, one of the young bucks questioning him, "You did not make sure the one you shot was the one you wanted?"

His eyes defiant, Lone Hawk's retort was sharp. "There was no time because of my hiding spot. As soon as the scout came into view, I was at full draw, the arrow gone. My trap was set in such a way."

A sinewy brave named Spotted Pony spoke what was on his mind. "So you are not yet finished."

Lone Hawk liked what the brave said, repeating it, "I am not yet finished."

A puzzled look in his face, one of the younger braves asked, "But why?"

Gray Coyote answered for Lone Hawk. "Because Lone Hawk's victim did not possess what he craves. He wanted to kill the one who has a warrior spirit. But that is not all. The man he hunted will now stalk him. Isn't this so, Lone Hawk?"

Crossing his arms, Lone Hawk considered Gray Coyote's con-clusions. He hadn't thought of being hunted by the wagon scout. Not wanting the others to see how much smarter Gray Coyote was, he kept his face expressionless. Pretending to have considered such a possibility, he replied, "If the white-eyes fails to come after me, I will be disappointed. But no matter, Spotted Pony is right, I am not yet finished."

Gray Coyote had another suspicion, revealing it, "I think there is another reason."

A young brave next to Spotted Pony asked, "What reason?"

Lone Hawk's brow tightened. What was Gray Coyote about to say? He was sure he was about to be chastised, waiting for it to happen.

Gray Coyote ended the suspense. "He cannot yet brag to our Cheyenne brothers, this is why!"

All faces swung toward Lone Hawk.

Lone Hawk didn't like it when Gray Coyote exposed his inner thinking. What he said was true. How he responded needed to impress the listeners. Deliberately taking his time, Lone Hawk stared into each brave's face, his gaze returning to Gray Coyote. "I do not disagree with what you say. I must kill the wagon scout so that I may share my success with our red brothers, the Cheyenne."

Despite admiring Lone Hawk's manipulation of his words, Gray Coyote determined Lone Hawk's attitude was not good. He was a fierce warrior on a pride path, a very dangerous trail to travel. Instead of Lone Hawk helping them, he was feeding on his own ego. As much as Lone Hawk frustrated him, they still needed his warrior influence. The younger braves admired his fearless courage, volunteering to come on these raiding parties hoping to see Lone Hawk's reputation in action. Rarely were they disappointed. Gray Coyote knew at times like this there could be no reasoning with Lone Hawk. At least, not until his now damaged ego was satisfied. Lone Hawk lived for his reputation. This was how the man was. If you rode with him, it took much wisdom to harness his lack of fear for the good of the raiding party. So be it, Gray Coyote decided, it was his turn to be tactful. "Come, let us go eat. You must tell us how you sprung your trap so well. After we have satisfied our hunger, we will discuss your plans for tomorrow."

For the moment, Lone Hawk's ego was placated. As he fell into step alongside the old man, Gray Coyote had more to say. "Since the white-eyes now is aware you hunted him, he will be ready to fight. You no longer have the element of surprise. I'm curious about your plans?"

Keeping step with the wizened old warrior, Lone Hawk's aggravation surfaced again. He had not thought that far ahead. Normally his face expressed bold confidence without doubt, but not now. He quickly changed his expression, hoping none of the others had seen his momentary frustration.

Gray Coyote hadn't missed the look. Keeping his voice low, he said, "You had not thought of this, have you?"

Aggravated for a moment, Lone Hawk glared at Gray Coyote. Aware the leader wasn't purposely embarrassing him by keeping his voice to a whisper, Lone Hawk gained control over his anger. Biting his lip, he confessed, "You are right, the next time I must set my trap differently."

"A wise decision," Gray Coyote agreed.

Lone Hawk had to admit the old man thought of everything, leaving no stones unturned. It was not by accident that year after year Gray Coyote was chosen to lead on these forays. He was like the old mountain lion prowling the land using his cunning and stealth while avoiding other hunters as he secured his prey. Despite Lone Hawk's jealousy regarding Gray Coyote, it was obvious the wily old leader was not yet ready to crawl into his Hogan and die. Until he did, his years of wisdom would be sought by others. As much as the eager young bucks admired Lone Hawk's fierce fighting ability, they were equally spellbound by the old man's knowledge and decisions. If in the future Lone Hawk was to lead these raiding parties, he would have to wait for the passing of such a respected leader.

It was not often one heard Lone Hawk confess, a slight smile teased at Gray Coyote's lips. Conquering it quickly, he maintained a face without expression. If Lone Hawk thought for one second he was being mocked, his fiery anger would become impossible to control, a serious threat to himself and the rest of the raiding party. A warrior had to go into battle using cunning. It was Gray Coyote's intention to impart such thinking to Lone Hawk. Studying Lone Hawk's face, he kept his voice to a whisper, "Have you studied this wagon scout, Lone Hawk?"

"I have."

Nodding, Gray Coyote asked, "What did you see?"

"There was one thing I noticed. When the scout senses danger he lingers too long in one spot."

"Ah, you saw your advantage. As we eat you may remember seeing other habits preparing you for victory. But first we must listen how you chose your ambush location so well."

Lone Hawk's face glowed with anticipation.

DEATH IN THE SKY

Darkness clinging to the land, Buchanan and Santana slipped between the lead wagons. Heading north, they traveled in silence, a faint light gaining a toe-hold over the gloom. Reaching the river, they crossed. Exiting, both horses dripping wet, Buchanan reined in Buddy. Shifting in his saddle, he eyed Santana, keeping his voice hushed. "Seeing as how you know where the riders are camped, lead out."

The light now bright enough to reveal horse and rider movement, Wes moved past Scott. Sure of his bearings, he skirted the numerous arroyos, purposely avoiding the skyline.

Impressed with Wes's savvy, Scott appreciated the way his partner used the terrain to hide their movement. A mile passed before Wes pulled up, his gaze fixed on a distant outcropping. Turning, he waited for Scott to ride alongside. Leaning over, Wes kept his voice to a whisper. "Those riders are camped just south of that outcropping."

Buchanan squinted at the rocks, his voice hushed. "What's it like on the far side?"

"The land kind of drops away into a large trough surrounded by rocks and grass, springs seep through the grass making the hillside spongy. Dig a hole and you can get all the water you want. The low ground keeps the riders out of the wind; the rocky slope gives them high ground to post a lookout."

Impressed, Buchanan complemented Santana, "Nice job, real thorough. Even better, the approach you used kept us out of sight. I couldn't have done better myself. If I were a betting man, I'm sure someone is posted in those rocks. Here's my plan. Right now they have the terrain advantage, which means we need another location so we can sneak in close. If I recall the lay of the land from my previous trips, I've got a hunch where they'll stop. But first I need to know how fast they're moving. Once we know their speed of travel, I can calculate a likely location for their noon stopover. If we do this right, I should be able to get us close enough for a good look as well as hear their talk." Shifting in the saddle, he eyed his partner. "If you have a better plan, I'm listening."

Beaming at the compliment, Wes gave himself a pat on the back. "That's exactly what I'm thinking, seems like you and I think alike."

Half smiling, Buchanan teased, "Considering how we both think alike, you have any specific location in mind where they'll rein in?"

Knowing Scott was having fun at his expense, Wes countered, "We'll scout ahead and find a place with lots of shade and water."

"Not bad, describes lots of locations around here. How about being more accurate?"

Grinning, Santana suggested, "If it was me, I'd stay near the river."

"I have to admit you think fast, used logic too. Right now I'm going to further your scouting skills by giving you an education how to use time as an advantage. Once we know how fast they're traveling, I can judge where to look for that shady spot along the river you mentioned."

Biting his lip, Wes kept his tongue quiet.

Nudging Buddy around, Buchanan stayed below the skyline. In another ten minutes, they would be hidden by a series of rolling hills. Once behind the hills, they would ride hard. All he needed was to find an elevated location to gauge the speed the strange riders pushed their horses. If those riders were keeping pace with the wagons, Buchanan already had an educated hunch they'd halt for their noon lunch. Seconds later, the hills obscured their movement. Buchanan leaned forward, lightly slapping Buddy's shoulder; breaking into a trot, Wes keeping a horse length behind.

The sun breaking over the horizon, fingers of sunlight etched across the grassland. Despite the cold air, heat vapors rose off the horses' hides. The terrain melted away, the sun reaching the eight o'clock position, Scott turning Buddy toward a domelike hill, the slope gradual. Reaching the top, he reined Buddy in behind an erosion-caused drop-off. Dismounting, he pulled his binoculars out. Below the river curved west. Waiting for Wes to come out of the saddle, he marveled at the view. Up here, surrounded by rim-rock, the land gradually fell away into a shallow basin stretching to the river's edge.

Wes gasped at the view.

Knowing elevation allowed human voices to travel for miles; Buchanan kept his voice well below the sounds from the stirring breeze. "We got the sun shining right at us, meaning our faces are lit up like oil lamps. We might as well be saying, look at us, here we are. Be a good idea if you pulled your hat down."

Grunting, Wes complied.

Satisfied, Buchanan headed for a clump of sparse bushes bent over from the constant wind.

Using the stunted bushes to hide their silhouettes, he dropped down to one knee. Brushing the ground free from stones, he settled into a sitting position. Crossing his legs, elbows tucked against both knees, he brought the binoculars up. Barely visible smoke shimmered from the distant outcropping, finally dissipating in a southerly direction. Bringing the lenses down, Scott told Wes what he saw. "Looks like they got themselves a hot cooking fire going, we have lots of time, might as well stretch out and get comfortable."

Wes picked his spot, mindful to speak low. "When do you think they'll ride out?"

"Most likely they'll wait until the wagons head up the trail. Of course, it's possible they could move later considering horses travel faster than wagons. No matter what they do, we'll stay with our game plan. Movement always gives away someone, so we'll let those mystery riders do the moving. Besides, if your observations about them keeping pace with the wagons are correct, I doubt they'll be in a rush. If they stay with their pattern, we'll loop ahead. Should they ride off in a northern direction, most likely they're not much to worry about. If they do, we let them go. If they cross the river, we follow."

Comfortable, Wes pulled a pouch from his breast pocket, asking, "Okay if I roll a smoke?"

"As long as you don't care about your sense of smell, neither do I."

Sprinkling the shredded tobacco into the curled paper, Wes deftly rolled the ends together. Dragging his thumbnail across a match-head, the flame brought the cigarette to life. Taking a deep drag, Wes rolled his eyes in pleasure, making a statement of correction. "I've seen you smoke before."

"I don't deny it."

"So?"

A sudden apprehension flooded Buchanan's mind, his body tensing, a hiss of breath expelling loudly.

Wes saw and heard. "What spooked you, you see something?"

"Not a thing, but something just went wrong somewhere. Don't ask me what or why, 'cause I don't know."

"You think something went bad back at the wagon train?"

Scowling, Scott grunted, "I'm not sure, wish I knew."

The feeling stayed, taking a deep breath didn't help. Scott's mind jumped to Pat. Squeezing his hands, trying to settle down, he stared in the direction of the distant river. Right now there was a job at hand and he needed to think clearly about what they were doing. He tried to shake the premonition. Whatever bothered him wasn't going away. His years on the trail had sharpened his instincts, those instincts so often an advanced warning. Such a sixth sense often steered him clear of trouble. More often than not, his premonitions turned out to be justified.

Dear God, he thought, don't let it be Pat! If it was him, it would be tough to forgive himself. Sure something bad had happened, the question was what? Aware Wes was still staring at him, he shifted his gaze in the direction of the far outcropping of rocks hiding the strange riders. Pushing against the premonition, he tried to distract his mind away from what bothered him. "It shouldn't be long before the wagons start out."

Wes wasn't over that look, persisting, "I've seen you have that look before, kind of uncanny. You have any idea what spooked you?"

"Can't be sure, it doesn't pay to speculate. Better we stay focused on what we're doing."

Taking another puff, Wes dropped the subject. If Buchanan didn't want to talk about it, neither would he.

The sun was higher now, the stretched-out shadows gone. Concentrating on the business at hand, Buchanan brought the binoculars up. Smoke no longer curled upward. Cocking his head towards Wes, Buchanan kept his voice low. "No more smoke. It appears either their fire has gone out, or it has been reduced to hot cooking coals. Best we keep a sharp eye out just in case. Be kind of stupid if we let them catch us napping."

Both saw the distant riders at the same time.

Buchanan frowned. Eight black shapes disappeared before reappearing. Again they dropped from sight.

Seeing Buchanan's frown, Wes snuffed the cigarette into the dirt, a questioning look in his expression.

Seeing the look, Buchanan asked, "How many you count?"

"I counted eight."

"Yeah, me too, when I first cut their tracks two days ago, I figured seven. I must be slipping. Unless they picked up another rider along the way, and if they did, things might get dicier than we figured. Maybe my premonition was caused by this eighth rider, I hope so."

Wes said what was on his mind. "Your premonition was about Pat, wasn't it?"

Buchanan admitted as much, "He did cross my mind."

Wishing he hadn't asked, Wes changed the subject. "Maybe there were always eight riders."

"Possibly, but I don't think so."

Peering at Buchanan, Wes decided to have a little fun. Hopefully, a little humor would offer some relief from the scout's worry. What the heck, one of the reasons Buchanan liked his company was because of his dry humor. Cocking an eyebrow, he let the humor fly. "First that Indian scout up and outflanked you, and now you're not sure you can count horse tracks correctly. Maybe it's time for you to consider becoming domesticated. You know, find a nice woman, settle down, and raise a family."

Keeping his eyes glued on the distant riders, Scott countered, "Like one of those three fillies you keep gawking at."

Congratulating his instincts, Wes kept the distraction going. "Yeah, nothing wrong with that group. Just so you know… I got dibs on the blonde."

"Does she get to choose or have you already made up her mind for her?"

Wes smiled. "Once she gets to know me, the fellow won't have a chance."

"You seem to be doing an awful lot of worrying about that other fellow," Scott chided. "You better hope that Harden goes and makes a fool of himself, otherwise after this wagon train reaches its destination she may be riding off into the sunset, and it won't be with you."

Wes gathered his thoughts. Needing a response, he quickly came up with one. "I ain't worried about him. It seems like he has taken a fancy to the Clark daughter. Even better, she's taken a fancy to him."

Not sure he liked what Wes said, Scott couldn't help but concede to his point. Gradually the riders were nearing. He nodded at Wes. "Time to ride."

Dropping onto the valley floor, Buchanan grimaced. Not a breath of air stirred down here.

Both men felt the soaring humidity, indicating a heat-stifling day on the way. With the early morning coolness gone, Buchanan followed the shady side of any trees. Finally they started up. The higher they climbed, the more the breeze stirred. Not much relief, but a lot better than being down on the valley floor. Cresting the hill, Scott dropped out of the saddle. "We'll sit tight here and time them when they appear. I hate to tell you this, but I don't think we'll need your location 'cause I already figured out a likely spot." Winking, he pulled out his pocket watch.

Wes eyed Buchanan's watch, a touch of getting even in his voice, "I thought you was a look-at-the-sun man to judge time."

"That's so, but I don't need to know what time it is, I just need to know how fast they're traveling. Let me know when they reach the flats, also, the minute they leave the flats."

Not giving up, Wes couldn't let this opportunity pass. "If I recall, you also mentioned how you could determine the hour by the length cast by the shadows."

"That's a fact, but right now we're going to be very precise. So keep your eyes peeled, be thankful you're about to learn something."

For the next few minutes the only sounds heard came from the ticking secondhand sweeping across the watch's face.

Wes finally broke the silence. "They just hit the flats."

"Let me know when they leave."

Several minutes ticked by before Wes grunted, "They're off."

Staring at the timepiece for a second, Buchanan shoved the timepiece into his pocket. Surging to his feet, he grinned at Wes. "I think I got them pegged. Come on, partner, time to show you that shady spot you thought about without knowing where."

If Buchanan's memory hadn't forsaken him and his addition was accurate, he recalled where three ridges merged near a bend in the river. Even better, a long sandbar extended out into the water right where the bend forces the spring currents to surge against the far side, a perfect location for a noon meal. It was there they would wait for those strange riders. Rising into the saddle, they dropped back down to the valley floor. Turning with the sun at their backs, Buchanan and Santana stayed within the shade whenever possible. Right now Buchanan was sure the riders had no reason to cross the Platte. If they did, he and Wes would be stuck until they found a different crossing.

The sun was almost past midmorning, the valley floor without a breath of air. Untying the bandanna from around his neck, Buchanan wiped away the sweat trickling off his brow. Nearing the first ridge, Buchanan steered Buddy through a narrow gap where two game trails merged, a lot cooler here thanks to the light breeze funneling between the ridges. Ahead, a small glade opened up offering more shade. Dismounting, reins in hand, he led Buddy into the clearing. Here the grass was lush, compliments of the water seeping off the ridges. Satisfied, Buchanan broke the silence. "Lots of lush graze here along with shade for our horses." Tethering Buddy, he eyed the top of the north ridge. "When you get your horse secured, we're climbing yonder ridge."

Doing what he was told, Wes didn't talk. Quickly falling in behind Buchanan, they started up. Reaching the top, soaked from perspiration, Buchanan broke into a mile-eating stride, the ridge opening onto a windswept overlook. Below, the river sparkled like jewels in the sunlight.

Gasping at the beauty, Wes gushed, "Lord Almighty, it sure enough is pretty down there."

"Sure is, we can see for miles too. This is where we wait. What's more, from here we can move in any direction. Find yourself a spot and get comfortable."

"Ride and sit, ride and sit, is this how it works?"

"Keeps a man from becoming saddle sore, nice scenery too."

Wes settled under a tree, marveling at a red-tailed hawk spiraling on the air currents below. Captivated by the bird of prey, his mind drifted, forgetting why they were here.

Buchanan too watched the hawk, his brain recalling his earlier premonition. Needing something positive, he came up with one. Didn't boss Stokes say that if a man worried about everything along the trail, such thinking would shorten a person's life sooner than necessary, such stressful thinking being the culprit? The wagon master often liked to emphasize percentages regarding worry. The boss was of the opinion that only eight percent of all worries required fixing. One thing Scott was sure of, there wasn't a thing he could do until he checked back with the wagons. Until he did, it was time to concentrate on the business at hand.

The sun slowly reached its zenith, the day sultry, Scott and Wes saved because of the steady thermals rising from the river. Far below, two long-legged cranes waded across the shallows at the outer tip of the sandbar. Suddenly both birds were airborne, their long wings beating slowly as they followed the curve of the river. Alert, Buchanan squinted upriver against the glare bouncing off the water. Just as he anticipated, the mystery riders rode into view. The lead rider dismounted, the others following him out onto the sandbar.

Buchanan winked at his scouting companion, bragging, "Ain't I the genius, just like I figured. Let's work our way down and have us a look-see. One thing though, we have to be careful against kicking any stones loose sending a warning. Stay directly behind me while I remove any loose rocks."

Down onto his hands and knees, Scott started down, occasionally removing a rock. Sure it would stay, he moved methodically down. Finally the slope leveled off. Just ahead voices were heard; ahead a clump of prickly bushes offered concealment. Guarding against the nasty thorns, Scott slithered through, easing his way to the outer edge. Waiting until Wes wiggled alongside, he rose onto his elbows, eyeing a burly fellow sporting long mutton-chop sideburns. The way the man was commanding everyone's attention, he appeared to be the leader.

Another man attracted Buchanan's attention, the fellow leaner than the others. He wore his gun holster in a cross-draw way, the gun butt protruding out from his left hip. If ever a man had the look of a gunfighter, the lean hombre did, his steely look gave him the appearance like a coiled rattlesnake.

Scott shifted his observation to a fellow sporting a handlebar mustache. The burly man's deep voice made hearing easy as he listened and observed the man.

"Russ, I'm in the mood for some tea, get some driftwood and start up a fire. That damn wagon train is traveling slower than some trail cook pouring black-strap molasses on a cold winter morning."

The mustached fellow agreed, "Makes a man wonder if a team of oxen can run a'tall. I swear they're going slower than yesterday. I'd love to inquire why?"

Muttonchops grunted back, "Other than asking, which I'm not about to do, I haven't the slightest idea." He shifted his look toward the lean one with the cross-draw holster, speaking to him, "Maybe

they dispatched someone over this side of the river for scouting pur-
poses. Hell, it's possible the wagon boss doesn't like us being here.
Could be it's time for us to pay them a visit."

He got no response.

The man named Russ asked, "You think they uncovered our
tracks?"

"I learned long ago, anything's possible."

As if not interested in the talk, the lean one turned away. Moving
over to a flat rock offering shade, he made himself comfortable.

Buchanan observed each man, how they wore their guns, manner of dress, how they were shaved, hat condition, including their
alertness. He checked their horses, studying the gear lashed behind
the saddles.

A heavyset man pulled his six-gun, spinning the cylinder. The
man's voice had kind of a whine to it, louder than necessary. "How
we doing with supplies, boss?"

"Damned if I know. Ask Mel."

Buchanan eyed the man called Mel.

Mel had a pock-marked face, his black hair long and stringy.
Something about the man suggested a person had better be careful
how you spoke to him.

The heavyset man looked at Mel, asking, "Well?"

Mel kept it simple. "We're okay," offering no further explanation.

The heavyset fellow had a protruding gut. Not liking Mel's
answer, the man suggested, "I'd sure like to get something fresh to
chew on, like newly baked bread. More often than not I can smell
fresh baking drifting across the river. Like the boss said, maybe it's
time to check out that wagon train."

It was obvious the man liked his food, Buchanan thought.

The lean one stared at the man with a mocking look. Reaching
into his vest, he pulled out fixings for a smoke. Rolling the brown
paper around the tobacco, he licked the paper, twisting both ends
closed. Satisfied, he placed the one end in his mouth. Lighting a
match, he brought the flame up, smoke curling from the glowing tip.
Taking a drag, he made it a point to focus on the man's protruding
gut.

Buchanan suppressed a chuckle.

The man saw the look, defending himself, "Yeah, I know Raymond, you never eat."

Raymond took his time answering, his voice soft but piercing, "Here's the thing, Josh, I only eat when I'm hungry."

Soft laughter spread outward from the circle of men.

Josh wished he was as fast with the gun as the lefty. If he was, he would shoot the man right where he sat. Be a real thrill to blow the gunslinger's brains all over the flat rock he was perched on. Trouble was, if he tried, he'd be the dead one.

Obviously done with any more conversation, the left-handed gunman took another pull on his smoke. Head back, he blew a circle of smoke out, his expression deadpanned.

The men ceased talking, watching the man called Russ returning with driftwood.

Buchanan pulled his eyes away from the men, focusing his attention on the horses' saddlebags. There was something about those saddlebags that was odd. Man alive, he thought, they were stuffed so full, seemed like they were threatening to split apart. Scott stole a glance upward, noting the sun's position, the time to be around one o'clock. Right now the riders were only killing time. Unable to erase his worries about Pat, he nudged Wes. "Follow me." Clearing the bush, he swung around. Crawling for another hundred yards before stopping, he waited for Wes to come alongside. "I have to return and relieve my worry about Pat. Besides, I saw enough, plus you're still here, meaning you're going to sneak back down there and listen. Once they ride out, you pull back and follow from a distance like you been doing. Tonight, you can bring me up to date. You okay with what I said?"

"Not a problem. Based on what we saw, what do you think?"

"They're a tough-looking bunch. Did you happen to notice how their saddlebags were bulging?"

Surprised, Wes stammered, "Can't say that I did. Probably food, don't you think?"

"A possibility, but I don't think so. The fellow with the gut seems to have concerns for decent chow. Whatever's in those bags, they're stuffed pretty full."

Frustrated with himself, Wes groaned inwardly. Buchanan noticed everything, why didn't he? Wondering why Buchanan didn't think it was food, he asked him, "How can you be sure it isn't food in those saddlebags?"

"Usually trail food's a lot more bulky."

"Oh."

"Besides, if they were carrying bulky food provisions, they'd have a pack horse."

"I hadn't thought of such."

"I'm thinking they're carrying something besides food in those saddlebags. Anyway, you sneak back down there and do some more eavesdropping. I'll see you tonight."

Watching Buchanan's stealthy departure, Wes scolded himself for not being more observant. A proper scout would notice everything, not just the obvious. This time when he snuck back he would study even the smallest detail, maybe even surprise Buchanan when they met tonight. He liked that possibility. Turning, Wes retraced his path down the hill.

Safely distancing himself, Buchanan shifted into a loping run. As he ran, he worried about the sudden appearance of the eighth man. Had he miscounted? Was it possible there were more men joining those riders? The sudden appearance of the eighth man puzzled him. Regardless, he had to consider the possibility there were more riders lurking in the area with ulterior motives? Once he reached his horse, he'd be smart if he crossed further downstream before doubling back. Concerning Pat, despite his worry, at least now he was taking action against something bothering him. If his premonition had nothing to do with Pat, then he could relax. Slipping and sliding down the ridge, Buchanan trotted into the glade. Loosening Buddy's reins, he vaulted up, urging Buddy into a gallop. Retracing their previous path, they broke out into the open. Turning Buddy away from the river, he let him run until they were way past the original crossing before splashing across the river. Nowhere did he see any tracks indicating more riders on the prowl. Entering the wagon trail, he slowed Buddy to a trot as the wagons came into view. His timing was perfect. The wagons were stopped for the noon break. He could see Cliff along with Stuart observing his approach.

Buchanan wheeled Buddy behind the chuck wagon, coming out of the saddle lickety-split. Hurrying toward them, he dusted off his pants. Near enough, he straightened, giving his report, "We got close, close enough to hear along with having a good look. They're a tough-looking bunch. One of those fellows looks married to his gun. I figure him to be the most dangerous."

Watching the dust still settling off Buchanan's britches, Cliff wondered why Wes wasn't with him. "Where is Wes?"

"Wes is still keeping them under surveillance. I couldn't get Pat out of my mind."

"How much did you hear?"

"Enough."

"Go on, I'm listening."

"Heard some grumbling about wanting fresh food, one of the complainers mentioned how smelling our cooking fires makes him hungry. He thought they should pay us a visit, and not a cordial visit."

"In other words, not by invitation."

"More like, help themselves. I'd say they bear watching. From what we overheard, there's nothing to hang a hat on as to why they're out there. I'm hoping Wes will have more info by tonight. Another thing, they picked up another rider."

Surprised, Cliff asked, "Where did he come from?"

"Your guess is as good as mine."

Stokes drained his coffee cup. "Want some?"

"No, thanks, I want to sleep tonight. How about Pat, he still out on the point?"

Stokes's face tightened, concern etched in his eyes, followed by a hint of anger. "I don't know where Pat is. I told him to stay in touch every three hours, but he hasn't checked in, not once. I might add, before he left, I went over our instructions again, leaving nothing to chance. I also told him to take his time and not be in a rush out there.

I was just about to send out someone to check on him. Glad you're back, bring him in for not following orders."

Buchanan frowned, considering how it wasn't like Pat not to follow orders. He felt his earlier eerie premonition returning. Shrugging it off, he lifted himself into the saddle. "Shouldn't take me long. Don't wait for us 'cause I know where you're going." Giving Buddy a tap with his heels, Scott turned the gelding's head in the direction of the southern flank. Clear of the camp, he booted the gelding. Sensing his master's urgency, Buddy bolted, the gradual terrain rising fast. Hoofs pounding, they thundered to the top where Scott could see for miles. No dark shapes appeared in the distance. Slowing the big male down to a trot, they covered another mile, finding nothing. Swinging wider, Scott didn't find a single horse track, not even wildlife tracks, much less hoof prints. Strange he worried, by now he should have cut Pat's trail. Swinging Buddy around, his body became rigid. High in the distance buzzards were wheeling in lazy circles in a cloudless sky. A hard pit developed in his gut. Staring at the circling scavengers, he tried subduing his worry.

Buchanan's mind exercise didn't work. For sure, something had died back there. He started Buddy in the direction of the distant birds. Staying in the open to avoid any lurking danger, he used the terrain to mask his approach. Constantly checking on the wheeling birds until they were no longer just specks in the sky, he reined Buddy to a halt. Shifting around in his saddle, he realized he wasn't far from last night's camp, more alarm flooding into his brain. Starting Buddy forward, he searched for horse tracks, finding a single set of hoof prints. If this was Pat's trail, it appeared he hadn't followed orders. From where he sat in the saddle, it appeared the horse tracks came straight up the hill without circling like he was told. From here the land kind of funneled, providing a natural way up. Shifting in his saddle to stare at the vultures, he pulled his six-gun. The pistol grip firm in his hand, he rested his thumb on the gun's hammer as Buddy started up.

Close now, Buchanan grimaced at the god-awful noise from squawking vultures. Pointing the gun barrel toward the noise, he urged Buddy over the rise, the grotesque scavengers launching themselves skyward. Pat Morgan's body lay stretched on his back, his eyes pecked out from the vultures, blood soaking the ground in two places. Eyeing Pat's missing scalp, Buchanan went numb, shock flooding his brain, his body sagging. Several seconds passed before his brain accepted what he saw. Sure the ambush was meant for him, his words came out with a hiss. "Damn you sneaking heathen!" Groaning inwardly, his anguish replaced by anger, now it was personal, more personal than ever. Slipping to the ground, his thumb still rigid on the gun's hammer, he wanted to scream at the ghostlike Indian who had killed Pat. It took several minutes for his rage to ebb, replaced by a sick feeling saturating the pit of his stomach. Pat was too young to die; somehow his death had to be avenged.

Pulling his eyes away from Pat's mutilated body, Scott studied the ground, staring at the left moccasin track with its turned-in impression. He returned his look at Pat's body. At least death had come quickly, the arrow shaft still imbedded in Pat's heart. Judging by the way Pat lay and the angle of the shaft, the arrow flight appeared to have come from a nearby knoll. Following the moccasin prints, Scott approached the knoll. Feeling the breeze blowing at his back told him the ambusher had made sure the wind wouldn't give away his scent. The Indian had chosen well. The only thing that could have saved Pat's life was if he'd circled wide and uncovered danger signs like he was warned. Frustrated, Scott returned to Pat's body. Seeing the blood still oozing from the missing scalp was hard to take, his fury boiling over again. Scott fought it off, such extreme anger kept a man from thinking straight. Right now it was important to remain clearheaded. Several circling shadows passed overhead reminding him he had to get Pat's body away from those nasty scavengers. After that was done, he could think about avenging Pat's death. One thing was sure, that hot-blooded Kiowa buck wasn't going to escape from what he'd done. Bending over, he gently pushed Pat's eyelids over the empty sockets.

Straightening up, for the first time Buchanan saw the saddle strewn in the tall grass below. He had completely forgotten about Pat's guns and horse. If nothing else, when he located Pat's horse and hardware, he will have found his killer. For now the saddle would stay where it lay. If the wagon boss wanted, he could send some riders back for it. After he delivered Pat's body, he was going hunting, Indian hunting. He and the Kiowa killer had an appointment with death. Bending over, knees flexed, oblivious to all the blood, he dragged Pat over to Buddy. Keeping his back as straight as possible, he lifted the limp form, draping Pat's body as far forward as possible. Struggling into the saddle, Scott let Buddy work his way toward the flats below.

A PROPER READING

Only three hours of decent light remained when Buchanan spied the dust kicked up from the wagons. His face covered with prairie dust from alternately riding and walking, he relieved Buddy of his weight; quite sure Buddy appreciated the weight loss. Rubbing Buddy's neck and shoulders, reins in hand, he angled to intersect the wagons.

Stuart saw Buchanan first, signaling the lead wagon to pull up, the long line of wagons slowing to a halt. Cliff sat stiff in the saddle, not liking what he was seeing—sure he was about to see Pat Morgan's dead body. His face stoic, he tried to prepare himself. Such moments like this reminded him of his war years when viewing fallen soldiers. His face taunt, he and Stuart started their horses forward. Nearing Buchanan, both dismounted, waiting to hear what they didn't want to hear.

Wondering why the wagons had stopped, Stephanie swung her horse away from the wagons. Up ahead, she saw a body draped over a horse, a lone man leading the horse. She recognized the horse's color; it was the wagon scout's gelding. Stephanie tore her eyes away, yelling at her father, "Dad, something terrible has happened!"

"What is it, honey?"

"Someone is dead. I'm going to ride up and see who. I'll be right back." Not waiting for her father's reply, she started toward the gathering group, several riders galloping past her. As her horse trotted forward, Tyler joined her.

Cliff remained tight-lipped. He was sure Buchanan wouldn't waste time, not this time. He wasn't wrong, Stuart standing shoulder to shoulder with his boss, both mouths compressed, their eyes steely.

Buchanan's voice bridged the distance as he neared the wagons. "Kiowa bushwhacked Pat at point-blank range, stuck an arrow in his heart. Pat never had a chance."

Stuart couldn't stop the profanity flowing from his mouth. "Damn that Indian!" Staring at Pat Morgan's lifeless body, he swore some more, "Damn him to hell, and then some!"

Seeing Buchanan was alive, Stephanie felt relief, followed by sadness. What she heard next startled her.

Buchanan kept his eyes focused on the lifeless body draped over his horse, declaring his intentions, "I'm leaving tonight. Won't be back until I kill Pat's ambusher."

Aware a gathering crowd was surrounding them, Cliff didn't argue. It wouldn't do any good anyway. The shock of seeing Pat didn't immobilize his thinking, he barked out orders. "You men give Stuart a hand with Pat's body. We're going to give him a proper burial along with a scriptural reading. We might as well do it now. Hell, this is as good a place as any."

Sammy Tillman stepped forward, addressing Buchanan. "Scott, you can count on me if you need help hunting down that heathen."

Buchanan thanked him. "Much obliged, Sammy, but I think you're going to be needed here."

Tyler Harden leaned over from his saddle, stealing a glance at Stephanie before he spoke, his voice capturing everyone's attention. "Mr. Stokes, I'm here to volunteer. Whatever you need, just ask. If you need another point man, I can handle such an assignment."

Wondering if Harden was putting on a show for Stephanie, Buchanan couldn't help but notice how Harden always seemed to look at her whenever he spoke. Mr. Bravado, he thought. His dislike for Tyler grew.

Stokes held up both hands, asserting command. "Let's everyone settle down and not let our emotions overrun us. First, we're going to give Pat a proper burial. After we do, I'll give out assignments to my men—not travelers." Cliff eyed Harden, suggesting, "If you want to help and since you're still sitting on a horse, I'd be obliged if you'd go fetch Mitch Robinson."

Wheeling his horse, Harden stole another glance at Stephanie as he rode away.

Not knowing how, Stephanie wanted to help in some way. Perhaps the wagon boss knew a way, asking him, "Mr. Stokes, I'm so sorry. Is there anything I can do?"

Cliff knew sincerity when he heard it. Watching Mitch approach, he thanked her, "Can't think of anything, but thanks anyway."

Seeing Pat's body stretched out, Mitch masked his frustration.

Cliff was glad he was organizing things, being busy helped a burdened mind. "Mitch, I'd like you to say last rites over Pat."

Staring at the lifeless body, Mitch recalled their last conversation; glad it was fun talk, answering his boss. "My privilege, I'll go get my Bible."

Forming a circle, the wagon folks watched the men dig, their shovels grating through the soil, followed by thumbing sounds from tossed dirt hitting the ground. An occasional murmur broke the solemn quiet. Using a hammer, Stuart fashioned a crude cross. The hole finished, the wooden cross was tapped into place. With sweating faces, the men lowered Pat Morgan gently, his hat covering his face. Cliff nodded at Mitch.

Stepping forward, Mitch's right hand held the Scripture pages open. In no rush, he scanned everyone, his way of gaining everyone's attention.

With all heads turning his way, Mitch began, his voice solemn, "If everyone will form a circle around the grave, we'll commence." Waiting until the circle was complete, Mitch instructed, "After I give last rites, all those who want to honor and are physically able, you can form two lines and place a shovel full of soil over Pat's final resting place. If at that time you have a eulogy to share, please do." Mitch paused to see if there were any questions. None coming, Mitch's voice became reverent, "It is time to bow our heads and honor Pat Morgan's passing. Heavenly Father, we are surely grieved over the loss of this hard working man. His enthusiasm affected us all. Truth is he's going to be missed. We trust some good will come out from this. As your word declares, we brought nothing into this world and we can take nothing but our souls. We now commend Pat's body to you, dust to dust, ashes to ashes, for out of the fertile ground we came and back to the dust of the earth we shall return. Amen."

Slowly dirt filled the grave, a few having something to share, finally the grave mounded at the top. People began drifting away, only Stephanie lingered. Reaching out, she touched Buchanan's arm, her voice throaty. "I hope you're not blaming yourself."

His eyes still looking at the grave, Scott answered her, "Kind of, I figured that Kiowa was after me."

Stephanie didn't like his answer. "I heard you say you intend to stay out there until you shoot the one who killed Pat. Why, because of vengeance?"

Looking for a clue to help him answer her, Buchanan studied her eyes, seeing only concern. "That alone is a good enough reason. I'm sure he killed Pat by mistake. I was his bragging rights, not Pat. You need to understand about warrior types. Failure isn't acceptable. It leaves them with no story to tell."

"You really believe that?"

"Miss Clark, if there is one thing I do know is how an Indian thinks. Their ways are unlike ours."

"But you can't be sure, can you?"

"I'm sure. Here's another thing, when Indians aren't up to mischief, they disappear. This Kiowa buck hung around for a reason. Braves like him have a killer mentality, and warriors gain strength by killing other warriors. They believe if a warrior kills a man who has a strong spirit, the dead man's spirit strengthens their own spirit."

"And you have a strong spirit."

"He thinks so."

"Wouldn't he be satisfied with Pat Morgan's spirit?"

"Normally, I would say yes, but he was playing cat and mouse with me, not Pat."

"Why is that so important? Explain."

"I'll try." Maybe if he explained this proper she would understand. "He was testing me by leaving enough signs to see if I was a worthy adversary. Once I discovered him, he considered me to be a worthy warrior for his bragging rights. It is a great feat to kill such a foe. I'm sure he's already bragged to his peers about his intentions. Now do you understand?"

Crossing her arms, Stephanie wasn't ready to concede. "And if he has left the area, then you're wrong."

Buchanan gestured with a roll of his eyes. "Your reasoning really doesn't matter, Pat's death needs closure."

"But you will admit you're wrong?"

"I won't have to. I wish I was wrong, but he's still out there waiting for me."

"You're sure?"

"I'm positive."

Seeing he wasn't about to budge, Stephanie sighed, giving up. "You're a brave man, Scott Buchanan."

"Depends on your definition of brave. Do you know what it means to be a brave man, Miss Clark?"

"Tell me."

"A brave man is a fearful man."

Puzzled, Stephanie questioned him, "How can a brave man be a fearful man?"

For the first time, Buchanan smiled. "No fear, no bravery. When someone's afraid, it takes courage to fight. Fear is a healthy thing as long as it doesn't bind a person up. It forces a man to keep his wits about him."

Stephanie hadn't thought in such a way. Admiring his reasoning, she dropped the subject. "When will you depart? I recall you saying tonight."

"Yes, tonight."

"Why tonight? Why not wait until the morning when you're rested?"

"Because the Kiowa killed Pat first thing in the morning. He used the cover of darkness to position himself near the wagons. I'm not going to give him the same chance. If he repeats the same ambush tactic again, his raiding days are over."

"And if he's gone, will you return to the wagons?"

For the first time, Buchanan sensed Stephanie's interest more than a casual concern. He felt his emotions stirring.

"Well?" she asked.

"Just because he's not there in the morning doesn't mean he's rode off. He might try another way, maybe farther up the trail. By me staying out he can never be sure where I am. Regardless, I aim to see he pays for Pat's death."

Stephanie's eyes locked into his. "I'll be glad when you come back. Is there anything I can do, anything at all?"

Surprised, he took a minute to think. "There is something you can do. That's if you're up to it."

"Tell me."

"Keep a watch fire burning for me."

"What is a watch fire?"

"A watch fire burns all night providing a lighted path to follow. Just seeing it in the distance strengthens a man's inner spirit."

Stephanie tossed her head slightly, her hair bouncing. "If that will help, I'll do it."

Buchanan took off his hat. Running his fingers through his hair, he reckoned it was only fair to explain the difficulty to keep such a fire going, especially to a woman not versed in frontier ways. There was something else; a watch fire was an indication of interest. He kept that thought to himself as he responded, "Keeping such a fire going isn't easy. You're going to have to get up during the middle of the night to keep the flames alive, and if it's windy, maybe more than once."

Stephanie understood the implications, "Anything else?"

"Are you sure you want to do this?"

"Yes."

This Stephanie Clark was quite a gal. Not many women would be willing to become sleep deprived. Admiring her grit, Scott showed his appreciation promising, "While I'm out there, I'll be keeping an cyc out for that fire."

Stephanie's eyes didn't blink.

Reaching out, he touched her arm, surprised at his boldness, wondering if he wasn't becoming enamored with her beauty and heart attitude. Smiling, he finished by saying, "If you keep it going, my spirit will be strengthened. Now, if I'm going to get an early start tonight, I've got to get ready since I'll need some provisions. Good night to you, Miss Clark, and thank you." Giving her arm another slight squeeze, he headed for the chuck wagon. Aware Cliff was waiting he crossed the distance keeping his voice low. "She asked me about every question under the sun. I have to admit, I kind of liked it. Fact is… she's more than fit to ride the trail with."

Damned if Buchanan didn't mean it, Cliff believed, a smile tugging at the corner of his mouth. Careful to avoid Stephanie Clark seeing his expression, he matched his scout's hushed tone, making sure what was said remained private. "Can't say I blame you, she's awfully pretty too." Becoming more serious, he moved closer. "So what is your plan?"

"First of all, just because I'm on a mission doesn't mean I won't be out there scouting. I understand my obligations, an obligation I aim to keep. As for the Indian, the way I got it figured, he wanted me, which means he'll be back. I've got to make sure he doesn't get the jump on me like he did Pat. After I eat, when the campfires die down, I'll sneak out. The moon's been growing bigger lately allowing me enough light to find a location for a fight. Once I'm satisfied, I'll hunker down for the night. Come daybreak, if the ambusher is out there, he's got a surprise coming. Regardless if he's gone, I'm planning on finding him. While getting rid of that killer, if I see something you need to know, you can be sure I'll get word to you."

Seeing how Scott had thought of everything, including any objections he might have, Cliff didn't argue. When Scott Buchanan made up his mind, no one could stop him anyway. The only thing to do now was ask him what he needed. Cliff did just that. "What do you need?"

"Trail food."

"See Wendell for your food. What else?"

"Nothing else, most likely I won't be far from the wagons considering the Kiowa expects me to be still scouting. Like I said, even though I'm out there on a manhunt, I can still warn you should I see trouble on the horizon. Tell me, who are you going to use for taking my place?"

Cliff didn't hesitate. "Sammy Tillman."

Nodding, Buchanan agreed, "Good choice."

"I thought you'd approve."

"How long ago did you plan on using him?"

"Knowing you, the minute I saw you riding in with Pat's body."

Not surprised, Scott asked, "If possible, can we eat early? That way I can slip out before the moon starts climbing. If the Kiowa happens to be near, he won't see me leaving."

"I'll tell Wendell, speaking about the man, look who's heading our way."

Both watched the cook's gangly approach.

Cliff greeted his cook. "We're starting the cooking fire early so our chief scout will have a good meal before slipping out for some night stalking. You have any special vittles you can whip up before he heads out?"

Figuring a little humorous sarcasm was in order to relieve tensions, Wendell dug his spurs in a touch. "Special vittles, you say. If I recall, part of our scout's job description is shooting fresh meat whenever possible? I'd call them special vittles. Can't remember throwing any fresh steaks in the pan for some time, but of course, there's a few hours of daylight left. I'm thinking it's not too late for our chief scout to use his hunting skills. I understand there's wildlife roaming out there—probably over the next hill? Most likely if our scout left now he could return with some fresh buffalo or antelope steaks before dark. If he was to do that, then I could really whip up something special." Besides his propensity to use sarcasm, Wendell's fun nature often did help to relieve stress. With that intention in mind, he directed more sarcasm at Scott's expense to his boss. "You go ahead and get that fire going early, and as soon as it's fit for cooking, I'll come up with something despite our scout's diminishing skills."

Scott laughed. "If you point me in the right direction, I'll start hunting, but just in case you send me in the wrong direction, I'm trusting you have something special stashed in those tins. The ones you guard with your life."

Looking up at the sky, Wendell held his hands high, pleading to the man above. "Lord, I reckon I'd better come up with something because it doesn't sound like we're going to get any fresh meat today, tomorrow, or anytime in the future."

Unable to contain himself, laughter bellowed out from the wagon boss. Yes, sir, Wendell was in rare form today.

His hands coming down, Wendell suggested, "How's sourdough biscuits sound?"

Scott grinned, "Better than me going on a wild goose chase."

"Yeah, not that you were going to anyway!"

Enjoying Wendell's shenanigans, Scott forgot the impending mission for a moment. Knowing the cook knew how much he loved sourdough biscuits, he thanked him, "Thanks, Wendell, they are my favorite."

Scott's gaze settled on the distant hills. For a moment, he hoped the stalker was gone, but only for a moment. Pat's death had to be avenged. He was sure the Kiowa buck was a bad one, bent on satisfying his savage nature, especially since he had killed the wrong man. No, the savage wouldn't abandon stalking him, of that he was sure. What puzzled him was why the savage hadn't stuck him with an arrow when he had the chance? Why did he wait to kill until the following morning? Perhaps when he met this adversary, he'd learn why.

WHY DEATH

Saddened from the burial ceremony, Mitch Robinson neared the utility wagon hearing his name called. Looking in the direction of the voice, he observed Stephanie Clark hustling toward him, almost skipping as she walked. Removing his hat, he swung facing her.

Stephanie smiled, her words encouraging, "Mitch, I wanted to tell you how thoughtful your prayers were during the burial ceremony."

"Thank you, Miss Clark, it was a sad moment."

"Yes, it was. I wonder if you would join my folks, I'd like to ask you a few questions?"

"Sure, I'll be glad to. First I'm going to secure my Bible and then I'm at your disposal." Placing the Bible at the top of his bedding, he turned, falling in step beside her. "Exactly what is on your mind?"

An even better idea excited her, deciding to extend a dinner invitation. "If you will join us for the evening meal, then I can ask you more questions… a lot more questions."

Mitch hesitated. Being an unexpected guest was rude.

Sensing the reason for his not accepting, Stephanie persisted, "We have more than enough food, and since my parents love unexpected company, please say yes?"

"Only if you're sure I'm not inconveniencing your folks."

What a considerate young man Stephanie admired, almost scolding him, "Mitch, I wouldn't have asked if my mom and dad weren't excited about you joining us." Seeing her mother and father watching, she called out, "Mom, he said yes, we have company for supper."

Despite not knowing in advance, Norma was delighted, her voice reflecting enthusiasm. "What an honor, Mr. Robinson. We do so enjoy company."

For Norma, unexpected guests meant potential for a fresh conversation breaking up the monotony along this tedious journey. Norma was sure the young man's presence offered a distraction away from her husband's constant fearful concerns around the evening fire. More often than she liked to admit, the potential dangers on this trip dominated the conversations. Another topic often discussed was the constant discomforts from such a dusty and bumpy journey. Knowing Stephanie, for a brief second, she wondered if her daughter had an ulterior reason for inviting him, but only for a moment.

"Thank you, ma'am," Mitch responded.

Adam Clark pointed to a small wooden chair. "Please be seated, young man." Aware Mitch was aspiring to become a preacher, Adam used the proper vernacular. "Your visit is a blessing. Since we were just about to enjoy some tea, may I pour you a cup?"

Nodding enthusiastically, Mitch took the cup. He couldn't help but notice Stephanie's eager expression. Apparently she wanted to get started so he accommodated her. "You mentioned you have some questions, Miss Clark. What sort of questions?"

Stephanie decided to be tactful. "First we want to know about you, and after, I would like to discuss God. I hope I'm not putting you on the spot. From what we know about you, a godly vocation is in your future. If I'm making you uncomfortable, tell me and I'll stop."

Not expecting godly questions, Mitch was surprised. "I hope I can satisfy your interests." Pausing, he sipped the tea while allowing for a silent prayer for the Lord's guidance. It wouldn't be good if she stumped him. Eyebrows raised, his eyes locked intently onto her face, his expression encouraging her to begin.

Adam interrupted, warning Mitch, "I hope you're ready because my daughter is a teacher with a fancy vocabulary who likes to ask lots of questions, followed by more questions."

Mitch laughed, appreciating her father's humorous warning. Once they were done with whatever questions needed answering, he had something to share with her regarding teaching. Information he was sure would both surprise and please her.

Intentionally, Stephanie shifted her emphasis focusing on Mitch's personal life. By relaxing him, she was sure he'd open up, allowing for a more serious conversation to follow. Stephanie was confident her teaching training and motivational skills would overcome any reluctance on his part. In a casual way, she asked him, "Mitch, do you have a girlfriend, someone you're courting?"

Surprised, Mitch's face radiated enthusiasm. "Yes, as a matter of fact, I have her picture." Digging into his breast pocket, he extracted a brown leather case.

Eureka, Stephanie glowed, knowing she'd hit pay dirt. Getting him to confide about his personal life without being overly prying was working.

Parting the folded leather, Mitch passed over the picture.

Taking the picture, Stephanie's eyes widened seeing the girl's beauty. She had dimpled cheeks along with elegant features highlighted by gorgeous red hair cascading over her shoulders. Gasping, she passed the picture to her mother, exclaiming, "Mom, isn't she gorgeous? Mitch, what's her name?"

"Shannon O'Leary."

Stephanie rocked back, delighted, teasing him, "Why am I not surprised at her name?"

Pleased with her spontaneous reaction, enjoying the moment, Mitch smiled from ear to ear.

"Tell us, Mitch, where is Shannon living?"

"Right now she's living with her mother and father while finishing school. After she graduates, we're going to get married."

For the life of him, Adam couldn't help but wonder why Mitch was working on a wagon train while being separated from such a beautiful girl. Perplexed, he asked him, "You're not going to continue traveling around with the wagon train as an evangelist after you get married, are you?"

"No, sir. I'm planning on the return trip so we have enough money. Then we'll settle down and tie the knot."

"I'm curious, why a wagon train in the first place?"

Mitch liked the question, one he would have asked a stranger himself. "For one thing, all room and board is provided. For another, being out on the trail keeps a man from spending what he earns. Last but not least, I've always had the urge to see the country before I settle down. Hopefully, before I return, I'll find a town needing a preacher."

"But aren't you scared out here in this savage land?"

"No, sir, God will provide."

"I see. You mentioned you haven't finished your schooling yet?"

"That's correct. I'll be going back to school."

Impressed by the way Mitch spoke, Stephanie summarized he already had sufficient education, probing, "Mitch, you're well spoken. How much more education do you need?"

"I only need one year to finish up my apprenticeship requirements to be ordained. My fiancé only needs one more year in school to become a teacher. I guess you could say our timing is perfect. We are very excited."

Stephanie's eyes opened wide at the use of the word *teacher*.

Norma, who was listening intently, broke up the talk. "Food is ready. Please fill your plates before it gets cold."

Gathering around the wagon, Mitch was astonished at such variety. The smell of grits and potatoes mixed with ground pork was tantalizing. He complimented Mrs. Clark. "Ma'am, this is a real surprise so far from civilization."

Norma beamed. "Thank you, Mr. Robinson. We would be pleased if you would say grace."

"I'll be glad to, let's bow our heads and acknowledge the Almighty." All heads bowed, hands clasped, he continued, "Dear Father God, we are forever thankful as you meet our needs. It is our desire to be mindful of such a blessing. We so appreciate the food before us and the hands that prepared such a bountiful selection. I thank the Clark family for their hospitality. We pray for your protection as we journey toward our final destinations. Also, we dare not forget praying for our wagon scout, Scott Buchanan, who now faces the threat of death as he protects us. Let your ever-present spirit harness our fears while our prayers bear fruit through your presence. In the precious blood of our Lord and Savior, Jesus Christ… Amen."

Mitch's prayer reminded Stephanie of the serious questions she intended to ask him. "Tell me, Mitch, how do you reconcile two men trying to kill each other with God?"

Alarm flooding Norma's face, her eyes flashed a warning at her daughter.

Seeing her mother's concern, Stephanie explained, "Mom, I lured Mitch here by telling him I had some serious questions regarding God. He agreed."

"Oh," Norma responded, casting a nervous glance at her husband.

Adam smiled, curious himself.

Glad he wasn't stumped, Mitch's answer was spontaneous. "I personally don't approve men killing men because the scriptures say to repay evil with good, but the Bible does say that any man who plans to take another man's life shall pay with his own life. Since it was the Kiowa who lay in wait to kill, he brings the curse of death upon himself."

"So," Stephanie persisted, "that justifies killing?"

"No, but then the Indian wasn't trying to kill me. The Bible does condemn murder. Laying in ambush to kill is premeditated planning to commit murder. Such a crime means the killer is promoting death upon himself, not God."

Digesting his answer, she pressed on. "But suppose it's the Kiowa who kills Buchanan and not the other way around? How would that square with God and be right?"

Mitch gave a generic answer. "According to the Bible, God's final judgment in the last days will resolve all questions regarding death. Besides, since man brought death upon himself and since it is man who murders man, people shouldn't blame God."

Adam interrupted Mitch, "How about the whites driving the Indians off the land causing them to fight for their freedom? Who is at fault there?"

Guarding against the talk becoming strained, Mitch enjoyed a sip of tea before answering. "God is no respecter of persons, which is why we're to treat others as we want to be treated. In other words, two wrongs don't make a right. Blessings and curses are self-inflicted, meaning good or bad is the final consequence. One of the reasons the scriptures are so profound and prophetic is because they answer all those tough questions from God's viewpoint. In the very beginning, God gave man blessings with responsibility, and if a man rejects those blessings, then it is the man who brings a self-inflicted curse on himself. If all humanity applied God's virtues toward others, we would all live in harmony. Something I try to apply to myself."

"Interesting, but doesn't the land belong to the Indians?"

Mitch pursed his lips, saying, "No, sir, not really."

Intrigued, Stephanie took her father's side. "Why doesn't it belong to them, Mitch?"

"Since God's the creator, all the land belongs to God, not man."

Arguing logically, Adam challenged Mitch. "But wait a minute, weren't the Indians here first?"

"Yes, sir, I guess they were. But the reason they came to this land goes all the way back to Babylon during ancient times."

Wanting clarification, Stephanie's voice was curious. "Babylon, I've often heard Babylon mentioned. Where exactly is Babylon?"

Her father answered her. "Babylon was an ancient city in the Middle East where the people built a tower toward the heavens called the Tower of Babel."

Mitch nodded, adding, "Yes, and God scattered the people because of rebellion against Him. They used that tower to worship the stars and the sun god, so God confused their languages, causing the people to become nomadic. But no matter where they traveled, all the earth is still God's. Since it is, God can give the land to any people he wants. I might add, for His divine purpose."

Stephanie had been sure Mitch would be stumped trying to explain such questions. Impressed, she asked him, "And you believe that's why people settled in different lands?"

Nodding in confirmation, Mitch was glad her father knew ancient history. "Yes, as I said earlier, the Bible does give answers for everything." Intending to keep the atmosphere compatible, he added with a smile, "I must confess, knowing how the scriptures answer all those difficult questions assures me the writings are divine. I like that."

Fascinated with the young man's answers, Norma Clark complimented Mitch. "You are very mature at such a young age."

Mitch appreciated the compliment. "Thank you, ma'am, but I still have a lot to learn."

A lone wolf's howl distracted their conversation. All heads turned, staring out into the night. Despite the blackness, a faint glow was penetrating the sky announcing the moon's arrival.

Adam restarted the conversation. "Did divinity school teach you how to answer such questions?"

"Not at first, our teachers always quoted scriptures, but mostly they focus on the formal part of education."

"Why is that Mitch?"

"If a man's going to be a pastor, he has to know how to manage a church. Once he's mastered management, he focuses on advanced studies covering spiritual knowledge as well as theology."

Stephanie was fascinated. "Tell us more."

"Divinity school teaches like any school. We have debates followed by writing a thesis relating to those debates. Next we do oral presentations, and in between, we have written tests."

"Tell me," Adam asked, "why does a preacher man need such formal education? I didn't think they needed it since they're called by God."

"True, a formal education is not God's requirement. A man can become an evangelist simply through a calling inspired by God's Holy

Word. However, since I'm marrying a teacher, my fiancé impressed upon me the advantage of a formal education."

Adam liked his response, murmuring, "Good advice."

Suddenly distracted, Stephanie's body tensed, catching a glimpse of a lone rider and his horse slipping into the night.

Everyone saw her reaction, Adam Clark the first to react. "What is it, Stephanie?"

Stephanie sighed, concern etched in her voice. "I just saw Scott Buchanan riding out."

Mitch couldn't help but think how life was riding out seeking death, a very unsettling thought.

Purposely wanting Buddy's tracks to mingle with the day's horse and oxen tracks, Buchanan backtracked down the trail. Thanks to the moon's glowing influence the road was easy to follow. Soon the flickering campfire shadows no longer interfered with the soft glow from the rising moon. Sure he had backtracked far enough, he urged Buddy along the shadowy side between both hills. They climbed steadily, his destination the second hill behind the first. By staying low before starting up, they avoided casting moving shadows, a dangerous giveaway. Halfway between both hills, he turned Buddy upward. The land brightened as they neared the top. Turning Buddy just below the crest, the gelding's surefootedness took them to the far side. Dismounting, Scott lifted his gun. Tugging on the reins, he started for the crest. If they stumbled into the savage, the advantage in this deadly game belonged to the Indian. If not, he would find a likely location placing him within easy rifle range covering the first hill. If the Kiowa intended to lay his trap as he had previously, it made sense the murderous stalker would choose the first hill. If the savage did, the ambusher would become the ambushed.

ON FOOT

The long night finally ended, the dawn saturated with a raw dampness. Buchanan stared up at the gray overcast, wishing the threat of rain would go away. Slowly the gray clouds dissipated, the sky brightening. With the clearing sky came a strengthening breeze developing into a blustery wind. Scott groaned, glad for the clearing atmosphere, but frustrated because of the moaning wind. The unsettled landscape made detecting movement all but impossible. Every stalk of grass bounced back and forth, the trees and bushes shaking violently. The front brim of his hat flattened from the force of the gusts, Buchanan tightened the hat string by sliding up the bead under his chin.

What a morning to be on the lookout for a ghost, Buchanan grimaced. Trying to think of something positive, however weak, he came up with one. Despite the conditions, if the Kiowa was about, it was him, not the Indian, who held the terrain advantage giving him the edge in these god-awful conditions. Needing another positive, considering the morning weather, it was unlikely the Kiowa would suspect he was lying in wait. A third advantage to be considered was how the night had been calm before daybreak. If the savage traveled during the night, most likely he lurked nearby. Made logical sense, Scott thought, at least if the savage planned on using the same ambush tactics as before. Had the weather been as violent during the night as the early morning, it was doubtful the Kiowa would have ventured out. Such a consideration helped keep him alert.

Frustrated by the constant movement, Scott cautioned himself against becoming overly distracted by the heaving landscape. If he allowed himself to be distracted because of the lousy conditions, his ambush advantage would be wasted. He'd better keep those eyes going. Another concern jumped into his mind. It was doubtful the scalping Indian would appear until the wagons were on the move, which meant he had time. Despite having time, Scott reminded himself such thinking wasn't a good excuse to relax. Even if the Kiowa had already had selected his ambush site, because of the terrain and weather conditions, it was possible the savage would expose himself by shifting to a better location. The thought inspired him to keep his eyes going. There was another consideration, maybe Stephanie was right, the Indian might be long gone. Nor was it unreasonable for the savage to wait out the windy conditions hoping for more favorable weather. Regardless of all the possibilities, Scott reminded himself to remain alert, here he was and here he'd stay, at least until the wagons were gone.

Shifting to relieve his cramped muscles, Scott focused on the hill overlooking the circled wagons. Except for the shifting landscape, he saw no signs of human movement. From where he was hunkered down, his chosen location was well within rifle range. Finally a positive consideration seeped into Scott's mind. With the wind in his face, should the Kiowa ride his way, calculating rifle windage left or right was eliminated.

The minutes ticked by, the gusts further apart now, the front passing. Aware of the diminishing wind, Scott tried thinking like his adversary. Dealing with Indians had taught him to anticipate the unexpected. An annoying thought returned replacing the positive. The savage might wait farther along the trail, if he did, the advantage shifted to the Indian. On the other hand, the savage's ambush had been successful, so why change. The next few minutes were going to answer those questions. If the savage didn't change his tactics, all hell was about to break loose.

Slowly the sun's warming rays touched Buchanan's back. Placing his palms against the damp ground, Scott eased around checking the sun's position. Good, he thought, by now the cooking fires from the wagon folks should be getting doused with water. Once the fires went out, Cliff and Stuart would be getting ready for the wagons to start up the trail. Shifting back around, his hands fondly closed around the Winchester. Scott knew his first chance would be his best one. Confident he'd picked the right spot, his mind went over every possibility again. Was it possible the savage might stalked him from behind? Knowing Buddy was hidden at his rear, he dismissed any danger coming from behind. Despite knowing how things can go sour fast out here in the wilds, it was time to shrug off all negative worries. He was in good rifle range allowing for shifting if the situation called for scrambling into a better shooting position. If he had to move, the terrain over to his left offered decent concealment. Not so to his right side, but it was doubtful the savage lurked there. If the Indian came from his right, the savage would be nakedly exposed, an easy target. Nope, danger wouldn't come from over there. Even if the savage came from that direction, once the wagons started up the trail the Kiowa would be lured his way. Confident he'd considered all the negatives, Scott ceased thinking about what might go wrong. Recalling last night, for a brief moment, he almost wished the Kiowa was gone, the feeling brief. The savage had killed a person who was fun to be around. Pat's carefree ways needed to be avenged. Even if the brave wasn't bent on returning, he would be hunted down.

Faint voices reached Buchanan's ears. Straining to hear over the blustery wind, as if a few inches would help, he leaned forward. Briefly the gusts abated, shrill voices reaching him. The sounds were children shouts, full of energy, excited as the wagons started up the trail. Scott's anticipation heightened. A subtle sound off to his left shoulder caused his head to whip around. He stared into the eyes of a gray-feathered bird. Alarmed, the bird darted back into the underbrush, its clucking sounds fading.

His heart thumping, Buchanan breathed again. If he didn't get a handle on his breathing, his long-range rifle advantage wouldn't help. A steady eye along with breath control was critical for rifle shooting. Regaining his composure, he worked on his breathing. Now was the time to think like a hunter and not be distracted about what might go wrong. Hunting a man from ambush was like hunting from a deer stand requiring patience. The timetable was up to the hunted, not the hunter. Believing one had chosen the right spot was critical for success. The unsuspecting quarry coming to the hunter made for the perfect opportunity.

The rising sun's height reduced the elongated shadows from the land. The gusts ebbing, fading voices indicated the last wagon in line was on the trail. A flicker of movement caught his attention, Scott's body stiffening in anticipation. A different type of shadow ghosted across the hill. Jerking impulsively, he snatched up his binoculars, scolding himself for his impulsive reaction. Fortunately for him, the shifting landscape disguised his sudden reaction. Restraining his arms to move in slow motion, he focused on the moving figure. Two feathers adorned the back of the Kiowa's head, the feathers canting sideways in the stiff breeze. The Indian's lower body covered with buckskin leggings, a reed vest covering his torso, his face smeared with black and vermillion paint. Coming his way, the savage and his horse dropped from sight below the crest of the first hill.

Head held high, ready to drop his cheek on the rifle stock the minute he saw his target, Buchanan slipped his hand directly under the rifle's forearm. If the prowler topped the hill directly in front of him, his stalking days were about to end. For a second, there was a glimpse of movement. Steadying the rifle, he breathed deeply, letting half out. Seconds passed with no target appearing. Something wasn't right. Half raising, Scott swore. The brave was moving away following the curve of the gully.

Coiling into a crouched position, Buchanan waited. The minute the Kiowa's head dropped from sight where the gorge steepened he would scramble into position for a long-range shot. Seconds later, the Indian's head and shoulders disappeared. Lunging up, Scott raced toward the edge of the drop-off. Ahead a toppled tree offered a place to steady his rifle. Reaching the tree, he dropped into shooting position. Steadied by the stout tree trunk, Scott sucked air back into his lungs. Taking one last deep breath, he let half out. Eyes steely, a desire to kill surged through him. Here on the leeward side of the hill, the wind ebbed, no longer a factor.

Minutes later, feathers bobbed into view, followed by the brave's head, finally his torso, then his horse. Buchanan's rifle came up smoothly, his mouth curling into a snarl. He thanked the savage for being out of the wind, the brave's tactic about to cost him his life. Barely keeping the front blade ahead of the Kiowa's bobbing chest, his trigger finger began tightening ever so slowly. A gust of wind buffeted him. Red dust swirled in his eyes, the front blade wavering off target. Blowing the dust out of his mouth, he blinked furiously, realigning the front and rear sights. Finding the Kiowa's chest, the front blade now steady, Scott's finger tightened, the rifle's recoil slamming against his shoulder.

Lone Hawk's horse stumbled, the hidden gopher hole breaking the mustang's stride, the sharp crack from a rifle shot washed over him, a lead messenger hissing past Lone Hawk's torso, a white puff whining off the nearest boulder. Rock fragments stinging his face and arms, the savage instinctively dropping alongside the far side of his mustang. Lone Hawk's face and body shielded, the mustang exploded into a flat run.

Lurching to his feet, Buchanan tried to find the Kiowa in his sights, the Indian hidden behind his pony. Only an arm and leg showed. In another fifty yards, the mustang and Indian would be gone. Face tightening into a grim look of determination; Scott shifted his sights onto the pony's back. If his shot creased the animal's spine, the mustang would crash to the ground. His other choice was to kill the savage's mount. Soft hearted despite the dangerous moment, Scott chose the first. Trying not to rush, making sure of the sight alignment, he squeezed the trigger. The pony squealed, flopping over, dust flying. For a moment, the Kiowa was pinned. Suddenly out from under, the savage darted between two boulders. Hurrying now, Scott rushed his shot, rock fragments flying off the boulder to the right of the darting Indian. Seconds later, the Indian was gone.

Throwing caution to the wind, Buchanan ran. His right foot landing on a loose stone, his legs shot out from under him. Managing to land on his butt, slipping and sliding, he hit the gully floor.

Seeing Buchanan's arrival in a cloud of dust and rolling stones, the alarmed mustang's hooves clattered across the rock strewn ground, his destination the next territory.

Taking a deep breath, Scott eyed the broken bow wedged between two rocks. The last thing he remembered seeing was the savage's empty hands. Without weapons other than a knife, it was time to press his advantage. If the savage was armed at all, it would be with a belt weapon, maybe a tomahawk? Nearing the two boulders, he reminded himself a cornered brave with a knife was the equivalent of a puma with razor-sharp claws ripping and tearing. Pulling up, he hesitated. If the Indian lingered, another step would expose him. Eyeing a large boulder five feet distant offering cover, Scott tucked the Winchester against his body. Dropping to one knee, he rolled over twice, reaching the monstrous rock. Easing his head around to see, the Indian was nowhere in sight. Sure the savage was on the run, Scott stumbled up, searching for signs telling him the direction the savage fled. He didn't have to search far. Thrown pebbles and scuff marks indicated the Kiowa had headed toward a line of scraggly trees bordering the rim. Cursing, Scott started up. Whatever had caused the Indian's horse to stumble had saved the Kiowa from his bullet.

Running hard, Lone Hawk gained distance along with time between himself and the white-eyes. Reaching the top, he avoided the sun's rays by staying within the shadows cast by the trees. Racing along the gully, Lone Hawk sought hard ground to hide his passage. Having escaped death, the savage was encouraged by his escape. The white-eye's ambush had failed—Lone Hawk's warrior spirit was still strong, more powerful than that of the wagon scout. Despite losing his bow, including his mustang, Lone Hawk began plotting a fight to the death with this invader who brought unwanted palefaces to their land. For now his weapons would be his skill and cunning. Since his youngest days, Lone Hawk had the heart of a warrior because he was without fear of men. Nor did he linger in one spot as were the paleface habits. The next battleground would be different, one of Lone Hawk's own choosing. Once he made good his escape, his adversary wouldn't be safe even if the scout slept in his own bedding surrounded by the security afforded by the wagon people. Anticipating such a remarkable deed, Lone Hawk's snarl turned into a sneer of distain. He would kill the scout where he slept. The white-eyes wouldn't experience his presence until he drove his knife deep into his heart within the sanctuary of the paleface's own camp. There was one thing he must get back; he needed to find his mustang. If he failed to recover his pony, Lone Hawk would steal one from the slow moving wagon train. Once aboard his pony, his escape assured, then the white-eyes would die.

Half turned in his saddle, Stuart was about to offer a suggestion to the boss, his voice cut short by a distant crack from a rifle shot. Muffled by a sudden gust of air, a second shot followed, then a third. Grimacing at the sound of the third shot, he pulled back on the reins, staring at Stokes, a question in his expression?

Stokes leaned forward with each bark from the rifle, less confident with each ominous discharge. Hearing horses, Stokes turned, observing approaching men. He spoke to Stuart in a matter-of-fact way, "Too much shooting. I don't like it. If it's Buchanan, he doesn't miss."

Not liking the number of shots either, Stuart nodded in agreement. His boss was right. The scout was a deadly shooter, rarely needing more than one shot. Deciding to keep those thoughts to himself, Stuart suggested, "You want me to circle up the wagons till we find out who's doing all that shooting?"

"Nope, we'll stop when it's time for lunch and not before. Keep them moving forward, Mr. Stuart."

Up and down the wagon train all heads turned toward the distant hills, everyone thinking like thoughts. Stephanie feared the worst. Mitch did his thing, murmuring a soft prayer. Tyler Harden separated from his wagon, riding toward the Clark family.

Out on the point, Sammy Tillman swung his horse around, facing in the direction of the gunfire. Hoping to see something, he saw nothing. From where he was, Sammy judged the shots came from the general vicinity where the two distant hills merged. He wondered if he should leave the point and check things out. Sammy rejected the idea. Mr. Stokes had been emphatic about him staying out on point. Besides, the wagon boss had other men he could spare. He looked back at the wagons. They were moving again. Reluctantly he turned his horse, occasionally glancing back.

Huffing and puffing, Buchanan reached the top. Dropping to one knee in case the savage had doubled back, he waited, no threat coming. It was time to get up and move. With the savage on the run, it was important to push him. If the Kiowa escaped, the crafty killer would return to kill again. Right now the savage was hurt, had lost his bow along with his horse, and was fleeing on foot. Despite the Kiowa being weaponless, he was still dangerous. Pursuing without caution wasn't good, but right now caution wasn't to Scott's advantage. If he didn't hurry, the Indian would find his pony first. There wasn't much choice. If the red devil found his mustang while his pursuer was still on the ground and far from his own horse, the savage would be in control. If that happened, the danger was immense. Scott had to find the horse before the Kiowa did. He was certain of one thing, if he found the mustang before the savage, both would meet. Perhaps not grabbing the brave's pony right away may have been a stroke of good fortune, the fleeing animal a magnet leading him to the murderous bushwhacker. Unless of course, he ended up on the ground while the Kiowa rode.

Rifle over his shoulder, Buchanan broke into a loose-jointed trot. Skirting the gully, he scanned both sides for the Indian's pony. The only signs were the savage's scuff marks following the rim. Drifting away from the rim, the land opened allowing him to quicken his pace. He was sure once the mustang settled down he'd meander out into the prairie seeking to graze. The only question was which side? Salty perspiration trickling down Scott's forehead, he brushed aside the sweat, doubt invading his mind for a second. Maybe the Indian's head start had already allowed him to find the mustang. Scott pushed aside the thought. He was sure the crushing weight of the pony had taken its toll. If that didn't give Scott the edge in a footrace, so be it. Again second guessing himself, he wondered if he had lost his advantage by not going back for his horse. To hell with that, it would have taken too long. If he didn't come upon the savage's mustang soon, he would go back and get Buddy. Rounding where the ridge tapered toward the flats, Scott saw the dark form of a mustang moving out into the tall grass, the pony's head down as it grazed out on the prairie.

Relieved the brave's mustang was on this side of the gully, Buchanan plunged into the knee-high grass, the long grass stems grabbing at him. A line of trees attracted his attention, a lone figure emerging running with a limp. The Indian too had spotted his pony. Despite the running savage being closer to the grazing animal, his pronounced limp slowed his ability to cover ground with ease. Scott was thankful the savage was hurt. It was tough to beat an Indian in a footrace. Unburdened by weight was the brave's only advantage in this race to the death.

Adjusting arm and rifle into a pendulum-like motion so not to impede his running, Scott leaned forward slightly. Lengthening his strides, he gained speed despite the added weight from the cumbersome rifle. Angling to close the distance, he was thankful the wind was pushing from behind.

Lone Hawk ran well despite the limp, his biggest problem the pain stabbing at his ribs. Earlier the numbness had helped, but not anymore. Each breath caused a sharp pain. Slowing to a trot helped. For the first time, he looked over his shoulder, grateful at seeing no sign of pursuit. He had been wise by hiding his tracks on the rocky ground. Swinging his focus back to the feeding mustang, he tried running without drawing deep breaths which helped reduce the pain. Stretching out his strides also helped, the less bounce, the less discomfort. His pace slowing, he ignored the throbbing pain. Ahead his grazing mustang loomed larger.

Guarding against becoming overanxious, Buchanan began planning how this would end. So far, the warrior had yet to see him. If Buchanan started sprinting, when the time came for shooting, his breathing would become ragged affecting his shooting. His eyes shifted to the Indian pony, thankful the mustang was feeding away from him, his head still buried in the tall grass. If the pony continued in the same direction, it was unlikely he'd become alarmed in time to warn his master of his presence.

Not seeing the gopher hole, Buchanan pitched forward, the ground dropping away. Skidding onto his elbows, he surged up, checking the rifle's muzzle. The barrel was free from dirt. Forgetting his bruised elbows, he ran. Ahead, a mound of grass rose higher than the surroundings. Calculating distance, Buchanan decided it was time to swing his rifle into action. Once atop the mound, he could shoot over the grass, his main worry his labored breathing. If he didn't control his breathing, no telling where the bullets would fly. If the mound allowed, he would drop into sitting position using his knees to lock his elbows to steady the rifle.

Lone Hawk concentrated where each running step landed. If he fell, the pain would be fierce. For a second he glanced back, wondering where was the white-eyes? He decided he must have gone back for his horse. Confident he would catch the mustang before his pursuer showed up, he slowed. Awed with his survival ability, Lone Hawk again congratulated himself. He had gotten away by not lingering as was the white-eye's habit. Hadn't the mustang's stumble saved him, revealing the Great Spirit was still with him? Once Lone Hawk mounted his pony, he vowed to take the wagon scout's scalp before sunup. Hopefully, by then, his Cheyenne brothers would arrive to hear of his feat.

Hearing running footsteps, the mustang jerked his head up. Seeing his master and another man, nostrils flared, he threatened to bolt.

Sucking in gulps of air, his chest heaving, Buchanan settled into a sitting position, dropping his elbows against his knees.

Lone Hawk saw his horse staring in another direction. Whipping his face around, he saw the white-eyes dropping into shooting position, his long gun coming up. Lone Hawk forgot the pain, bolting for his horse. A booming sound washed over him, his right leg caving out from under. Pitching forward, he felt a warm sticky feeling oozing down his leg. Staggering up, half turned, another force slammed him backward, a second booming sound enveloping him. Lone Hawk's chest went numb, his breathing ragged, a whistling sound escaping his chest. Flopping to the ground, he tried without success to sit. His strength fading, he coiled into a fetal position, the sunlight turning to twilight, then into night, a final gurgling sound escaping his mouth.

Ready to shoot again, chest heaving, Buchanan rose. Barely able to see the stretched-out body lying in the tall grass, he jacked another cartridge into the chamber. Knowing how Indians were masters at playing possum, he cautioned himself to stay where he was. Once he walked off the mound, he'd lose sight of the prone brave. Almost a minute ticked by, the obscured form not moving. He started off the mound. Approaching the motionless body, he saw a face with a lifeless stare. Studying the man he'd killed, Scott took a deep breath. The Kiowa's facial features had a fierce look, like one who relished killing, one who was unafraid. And yet as Buchanan's intensity ebbed, adrenalin no longer fueling his anger, he felt a moment of remorse at the savage's death. He always admired the Indian ways of thinking, the way they spoke, so in tune with nature and yet unafraid to die. To him, they were like a kindred spirit. Well, almost. They were on the savage side. Forget the kindred spirit stuff, he scolded himself. Hadn't this brave killed someone who had done him no harm, a good man? The savage deserved death. Scott felt better thanks to his reasoning. He shook his shoulders loose, chasing away the tension. Glad this duel to the death was over; he eyed the pillow-like clouds scooting across the blue sky, wondering about the finality of death. Was death the final end, as he believed, or did warriors depart to live among their ancestors as they believed? Was there a happy hunting ground? As for Scott, he reckoned such beliefs to be wishful thinking. One thing he was sure of, it was better he lived than his stalker.

A snort pulled Buchanan's eyes away from the dead Kiowa. He eyed the watchful mustang. The pony was alert, ready to flee. Half turning away, Buchanan dropped his head in a nonthreatening way, keeping his body posture relaxed. Animals that are hunted sense danger through intensity. Both ears up, the horse watched him. Scott circled slowly, speaking softly, almost crooning. As if he had all day, Scott avoided any sudden movements. Nearing the mustang, he turned away in a nonthreatening position, the animal nervous but not fleeing. For the first time a plan began formulating in his mind. Bending over, Scott grasped the dangling rope. Continuing to talk soothingly every step of the way, he gently led the mustang over to its fallen master. Stopping next to the dead body, he rubbed the mustang's shoulder. Confident he'd gained the horse's acceptance, he dropped onto one knee. Withdrawing the Kiowa's sheath containing his knife, he stuffed it behind his own. Bent at the knees, he lifted the limp brave up, wrestling him over the mustang. Coaxing the skittish pony into remaining still, he passed the rope under the pony's belly, quickly lashing the dead brave's hands together, followed by both feet. Smelling blood, the mustang backed away, ready to buck. Scott spoke soothingly, reassuring the nervous pony, "Whoa boy… easy now." Again rubbing the mustang's shoulder to quiet him, the pony settled down. Drawing the rope tight, Scott was sure the body was secure. Retrieving his rifle, he led the pony in the direction of the distant gully.

Tillman stared in the direction he heard the shots coming from. This time the sounds of gunfire were closer—a lot closer. Squeezing both hands around the saddle-horn, he stood up in the stirrups. The only thing he saw was empty grass. Despite his boss's strict instructions against leaving the point to investigate, he considered disobeying. Knowing Mr. Stokes's temper, he decided against going. Not obeying meant a demotion, and he much preferred riding the point. It would be smart for him to do what he was told. Settling back into the saddle, he had an idea. There was more than one way to skin a cat. He would ride up to higher ground. By doing that he was still on point. His last instructions were to report anything out of the ordinary. If he saw something to report from up there, it was okay to leave the point. Pleased with the genius of his thinking, Tillman urged his horse into a gallop toward higher ground.

Cliff sat still in the saddle, Stuart doing the same, both horses fidgeting. Cliff had a hunch his scout was in a fight, maybe needing help? This was the second time gunshots had erupted, this time the shooting coming from farther west. He needed to find out what was going on.

Seeing the wagon boss's mind was preoccupied, Stuart interrupted Cliff's thinking. "Those shots weren't very far from where we heard gunfire earlier. A little more to the south. Want me to ride over and check things out?"

Cliff rubbed his chin, his response quick. "Nope, your job is wagon foreman. I'm giving that job to Victor." Turning his mare around, Cliff ordered, "You stay right where you're at. I'll have Victor hook up with Sammy, which is why he's riding the point. Between the two of them we should be able to find out who's causing such a ruckus." Trotting the mare past the line of wagons, he spotted Victor, wheeling his horse abreast of the utility wagon. "Vic, ride out and locate Sammy Tillman at the point. When you do, I want the both of you to find out who's doing all that shooting. As soon as you know what in the hell's going on, report back to me. Notice I said… you! If it's something real dangerous, both skedaddle back. If not, tell Tillman to ride back at the point."

Victor was pleased. The shooting had made him curious, and now he could do something satisfying his curiosity. "Sure thing, boss, be back as soon as possible."

Watching Victor gallop away, Cliff started back to the lead wagon, aware every face was watching him. Tonight he would have some explaining to do with no way out because of his policy of keeping everyone updated. Hopefully, it would be good news. Nearing the lead wagon, he observed Tyler Harden and Stephanie Clark heading his way. Sure Tyler would be the first to speak, Cliff kept the mare at a slow walk. He wasn't wrong, Harden's statement bordering on the obvious.

Tyler sounded excited, "We figured that shooting has something to do with Buchanan."

No surprise there, Cliff thought, the man always impressing anyone within hearing. Avoiding being sarcastic, Cliff kept his response brief. "Your guess is as good as mine. We'll know more shortly, if not, by nightfall." His answer met silence, the only sound coming from a horse's snort.

Stephanie broke the silence. "We noticed you sent a rider out. Not wanting to sound foolish, I'm thinking he's investigating who's doing all the shooting."

Somehow, unlike Harden, Cliff didn't mind answering her, his voice modulating slightly, "Yes Ma'am, that's my intention. But there is a lot of ground to cover out there. Regardless whether the news is good or bad, I intend to keep moving. As soon as I have information, I share it. Like I said, by nightfall everyone will know as much as I do."

Stephanie couldn't help herself, a touch of emotion seeping into her voice. "You do think that shootings involving Buchanan, don't you?"

Tyler Harden wasn't sure he liked Stephanie's subtle show of emotion.

Shrugging, Cliff answered her. "He is out there and we know why, don't we? Anyway, until we find out more, it is my intention to keep us on schedule regardless of who's doing all that shooting. Hopefully, my scout will be showing up shortly. If he does, I'll let him do the explaining. If not, like I said, as soon as I know more, so will everyone else." Prodding his horse, he rode away.

Wendell greeted Cliff with a statement. "My rifle is locked and loaded."

Despite his concerns, a grin split Cliff's face. "I notice. You know, Wendell, most folks would be standing around wondering what in the hell's going on, but not you. No, sir, my cook knows what to do. He grabs a rifle and gets ready for trouble." Leaning forward, Cliff rested his arms on the mare's neck. Confiding in his cook, the humor was gone from his voice, he complained, "We both know Buchanan doesn't miss when he shoots. If it's him in a fight, I sure wish I was in on it."

Wendell kept his tone positive. "Sending Victor out was smart, you done right. Now we just got to wait and see."

It didn't take Victor long to find Tillman. Riding up, he hailed him. "Sammy, did you hear where those shots came from?"

Sammy pointed. "Over that way. Is the boss allowing me to go look?"

Victor stared where Sammy pointed. "You have his permission. I'll follow you."

Excited, Sammy grunted, "It's about time, come on." Swinging abreast, both rode through the belly-high grass, their eyes scanning for signs of a fight. Not seeing anything, Sammy made a suggestion. "Let's fan out a little, we'll cover more ground that way." Keying off Sammy, Victor eased away, his eyes searching. A half hour passed when he saw Sammy gesturing. Riding over, Victor saw what his partner saw. A single set of unhurried horse tracks angled west, the tall grass pushed over. Moving their mounts on each side of the tracks, they followed at a slow walk, the trail easy to follow, the meandering tracks indicating a feeding animal. Another hundred yards passed when Victor hauled back on the reins. Breaking the silence, he pointed at human tracks merging with the hoof prints. "White or Indian, whoever he is, he's running." Half rising in the saddle, he checked in the direction the lone man came from, seeing what looked like more disturbed grass slightly to the north. Settling back in his saddle, his voice stopped Sammy. "Hold up here, I see something needing looking at by that humped-back mound over there. Give me a minute." Nearing where the ground rose, Victor squinted at the grass flattened into an oval impression. Something was shining between the blades of grass. Riding closer, he eased out of the saddle, picking up the brass casing. Sniffing the freshly spent powder, he rolled over the empty cartridge checking the caliber. Stuffing it into his pocket, he climbed back into the saddle. Riding back, he told Sammy what he'd seen. "Somebody sat down on that mound over there and did some shooting." Extending the spent cartridge, he asked, "You think this is a load Buchanan shoots?"

Sammy studied the empty cartridge. "All I know is that he shoots a Winchester, besides this caliber is common enough." Lifting his stare toward the distant mound, he understood the advantage the shooter used. "Whoever he was, he picked a good place to shoot from. Let's follow them horse tracks and see if the shooter hit something."

They didn't have to ride far, both horses snorting at the smell of death, the grass wet with blood. Easing from the saddle, Sammy skirted around the blood. Finishing a wide circle, he came to a halt.

Here, human footprints and horse tracks mingled at the bloody scene. Eyeing the direction the tracks went, he looked up at his partner. "If I'm reading the signs correct, somebody died here. From this point on, we have a man on foot leading a horse."

"So," Victor mumbled, "whoever got shot must be draped over the horse."

Sammy agreed, "That's what I'm thinking." Reaching up, he wrapped his hand around the saddle horn, pulling himself back into the saddle. "Whoever he is, the trail's heading to the top of yonder hill. Maybe we'll get lucky and catch up. If not, maybe uncover some clues up there. Let's ride."

Stopping at the ravine, both realized the sunbaked ground obscured any tracks, Sammy grumbling, "Tough to follow tracks here, ground's hard and rocky. No telling where they went."

Victor agreed with a nod. Moving his horse up the edge of the steep sides, he offered a suggestion. "Why don't we ride along the edge in opposite directions? If I find anything, I'll give a sharp whistle. You do the same."

"Sounds like a plan. Let's do it."

Sammy hadn't traveled more than two hundred yards when he heard a sharp whistle. Turning, he rode back. "You found something?"

"I did. Hoof skid marks went down here. From up here I can see lots of dislodged stones piled up at the bottom."

Frustrated, Sammy sighed, "We could be trailing for hours. Even worse, never catch up. I'm thinking we should call it quits. Besides, if it was Buchanan doing all that shooting, by now he may have returned to the wagons."

"Suppose he's not?"

"If he's not, we'll let the wagon boss decide."

Victor pushed his hat back, staring across the gully at the far side. "You got anything special in your thoughts concerning what you want me to say when I get back? Hell, you know how the boss wants nothing but details. Be smart if we're both on the same page. I'm sure he'll cross examine you by asking the same questions tonight."

"Heck, we both saw the same thing—somebody killed somebody. Like I said, by the time you get back, Buchanan will be there.

If he's not, don't forget to show Mr. Stokes that shell casing. I reckon he'll know if it belongs to Buchanan or not."

"Yeah, shows we done a good scouting job. If Buchanan's back, I'll ride out and give you the good news. I reckon you'll be going nuts wanting to know."

"I sure will."

"If he's not, I'll see you tonight."

Spinning his horse around, Victor booted him into a gallop.

Taking one last look across the ravine, Sammy headed back to the point.

NOON CONFERENCE

F or the longest time, Cliff studied the sluggish current, the water clearer than normal for this time of the year compliments from a dry spring and early summer. Watching his mare drink, his eyes became hypnotized by the river eddies, each with its own swirling pattern, each producing a different sound. Tearing his eyes away from the gurgling water, he pulled on the mare's reins, leading her up to the rope line next to Stuart's horse. Mulling over the day's events, he wrapped the reins. Aware he was being observed, Cliff removed any show of concern from his face.

Wendell didn't miss Cliff's sudden change of expression. Despite feeling the same, he wasn't about to give in to such thinking, at least not yet. He studied Cliff's face, admiring his boss's ability to hide worry. Except for the wagon boss's inner circle, for the most part the ramrod kept his thoughts private. Knowing this, Wendell had mastered artful ways of engaging the boss in conversation with the intent of getting him to loosen up, perhaps even reveal his inner concerns. Sometimes such an approach worked, usually not. Wendell had a hunch this time his efforts would be fruitless. Still, it helped to talk things out. He caught his boss's attention with a positive statement. "The worst thing to deal with is waiting, especially if one's anxious.

The way I got it figured, when Morgan gets back we'll know something. Until then, we should keep our worry under wraps." Wendell's expression quizzical, he cocked his head, driving home his point. "Don't you think?"

Glancing toward the distant hills, Cliff rubbed his chin before answering, "Can't argue with such reasoning. I have to admit, not knowing what went on out there makes a person jumpy. Truth is, I'm feeling kind of edgy myself, like anxious. If it was Buchanan, by now he should be here."

"Maybe so, but until we know more, nothing's happened tragic to our scout. Besides, I recall you telling me Buchanan isn't an ordinary scout, best we all remember that."

"I do recall saying such." Wendell was throwing his advice back at him. Cliff thanking him, "You're right, thanks for reminding me what I should remember." A touch of humor entered his voice. "You have any more sage advice?"

"May I quote another one of your famous sayings?"

"Might as well, you're going to get it out anyway."

"Let time work things out."

Cliff couldn't hold back his boisterous laugh. A man had to appreciate how Wendell was a master of recall, and now the cook was applying reverse psychology on the originator. What goes around comes around, Cliff conceded. It sure didn't make sense to argue against his own logic. As usual, his cook had found a way to relax him. Uncapping his canteen, he took a long drink.

The muffled sounds from a walking horse turned everyone's attention. Seeing Morgan arrive, Cliff steadied himself, his worries returning.

Dismounting, Victor got out what he knew. "There was a fight out there for sure, the truth is Sammy and I don't know who was involved, much less who fought. We were hoping when I got back to camp our chief scout would be present, but I'm not seeing him."

Not what Cliff had hoped to hear, he asked Victor, "What did you see out there?"

Taking the water Wendell handed him, Victor spoke deliberately lest he forget anything. "We found two sets of tracks along with lots of blood. There was a single set of human footprints leading a horse away from the scene." Pausing for emphasis, he added, "Weren't anybody in sight."

Cliff and Wendell looked at each other, Cliff glad the news wasn't worse. Hopeful, he asked for some details. "Were those human footprints wearing boots?"

Victor didn't lack for an answer. "The grass was too thick to see tracks, the ground too hard from lack of rain. Wish I could tell you more, but I can't. At first we figured, all that shooting was from Buchanan. But then we recalled how that Kiowa got hold of Pat's guns, so who knows. For all I know, it could have been a shootout between both—or maybe somebody else."

Digesting the information, or lack of information, Cliff grilled Victor, "You think to follow those tracks further?"

"We did."

"And?"

"At first we hoped the horse and rider were headed back this way, but no such luck. Those horse tracks led us away from where the fight took place, eventually to a steep gully."

"And you couldn't tell the difference between boots or moccasins on the ground, or whether the horse was shoed or not?"

"Nope, couldn't be sure, especially knowing Buchanan often wears moccasins himself. Besides, that scalping savage got Pat's horse, so whether the horse is shoed or not wouldn't confirm anything."

Victor was right, Cliff conceded. Because of his Indian-like ability, only Buchanan could decipher such signs. Unfortunately, Buchanan wasn't here. "Anything else catch your attention, maybe something positive?"

"We found this." Reaching into his pocket, he handed Stokes the empty cartridge. "We weren't sure if Buchanan shoots such a caliber. We thought you might know."

Cliff rolled the shiny case over. "He does shoot this caliber, but so do a lot of others, including most of us."

"Yeah, we was afraid of that. As I was riding in, I gave some thought as to what we didn't see."

Cliff cocked his head. "Go on."

"There should have been two horses, instead there was only one. Which means whoever survived the shootout had to go get his horse before coming here. If it was Buchanan's horse, we figured he should be back here by now. I promised Sammy that if he was, I'd ride back out and give him the good news. From what I'm seeing, I don't have any good news to tell."

Pondering the implications, Cliff shifted his attention to Stuart, then back to Wendell, exasperation in his voice, "More waiting for us." Refocusing on Victor, he asked, "Did Sammy come to the same conclusions as you?"

"Pretty much, we both concluded that somebody got killed. Blood was everywhere. Nobody could lose that much blood and live. As for them two empty bullet cartridges, they don't mean much 'cause the Kiowa did get hold of Pat's guns when he ambushed him."

"Did you think to pick up that other shell casing?"

"I gave it a brief thought, but there was only one shooter, so it didn't seem to matter."

At a loss for more questions, Cliff checked with Stuart. "I miss anything?"

Stuart thought for a moment before replying. "Indians don't use saddles, too much weight. I'm wondering, is it possible to ride bareback with another body with all that blood and without a saddle? That might explain why the fellow who led the horse didn't ride. All that blood would make it difficult for two people. If that's the reason, it might mean a dead Indian."

Encouraged, Cliff frowned. "You're thinking because there was no saddle it was an Indian pony. Here's another consideration, one I like. If it was the Indian, he'd use the horse to drag the body."

"Correct."

Stuart followed with, "Savages mostly leave a scalped body to rot in the sun."

"I like that thought, and you didn't see any sign of a body being dragged."

Victor interrupted. "One thing we both noticed, at first there was blood dripping from both sides of the horse. Three hundred feet farther, the bleeding stopped. Whoever the survivor was he still could have climbed aboard and rode double if he wanted."

Stuart didn't think so, saying as much, "When the Kiowa shot Pat, the only things he took was his horse, guns, and scalp. The way I see it, we have until nightfall before we start worrying ourselves over what happened out there. And that goes for everyone, not just me. In the meantime, wagon boss, what are you going to tell the folks?"

Cliff looked over at Wendell. "My cook tells me I'm a master at stalling, accuses me of letting time save me from decision making. There is some truth to his astute observation. Considering such, maybe my scout will show by then so I won't have to come up with anything. In the meantime, wagon foreman, go tell the folks that I want at least one person from every wagon in attendance right after dark."

"Suppose Scott shows up by then?" Stuart suggested.

"Then he can give the report."

"Good answer," Stuart chuckled. Wheeling around, he departed as instructed.

Cliff heard his stomach growl, glad for such a positive sound. Losing one's appetite wasn't good, meaning worry was in control, not the man. "Wendell," he barked, "I need some food before we move out. What's on the menu?"

"Just hardtack and tea."

Cliff made a face. "Pass the hardtack."

"How about the tea?"

"Whatever."

Wendell had heard enough, departing for the rear of the wagon to pass out the hardtack.

Caught up in their own thoughts, the men chewed on the hardtack, washing down the meager meal with a bitter tasting tea. Finishing, they made themselves ready to mount up. Cliff tossed the cup's bitter contents to the ground, growling, "Stuart, whenever you're ready."

Happy to be on the move, the sounds from creaking harnesses pleased Cliff. At least they were making good time. Each mile covered brought them closer to their final destination. Hoping to see a lone rider, Cliff found himself constantly searching the horizon. Despite his concerns, the unfolding trail helped alleviate what bothered him. In another hour, the sun would near the western hilltops. Just ahead and not far from the river a grove of trees offered shelter from the wind. He nodded at Stuart. "Turn them by those trees. We won't find a better place to spend the night."

Slowly the wagons wheeled into a loose circle, livestock unharnessed and fed, wood gathered, fires springing to life. Despite Cliff's frustration, the fires were a cheery sight. Assigning the night guard, he occasionally snuck a peak down the trail. The evening meal finished, he helped Stuart and Wendell with the cleanup. Finally the chores over, Cliff hung up the drying towel. He fixed his eyes on Stuart. "Go pass the word."

People began trickling in, everyone quietly forming into a loose circle. Aware there were a lot more than just one person representing each wagon, Cliff waited until there were no more stragglers. He stepped forward, his voice capturing everyone's attention. "I thought I'd update you folks and when I'm done, you will know as much as me." He paused, making a point. "Please don't ask me to tell you what I just told you. It's not my intention to be picky. I just don't like repeating myself being how it's a waste of time." Letting silence magnify his reasoning, he studied the circle of faces as he cleared his throat. "As most of you know, we lost one scout to a sneaky savage. My chief scout went after that murdering heathen. I don't think I have to tell you he's not back yet. Truth is, because of his intentions he's not overdue, but as of this minute, I don't know whether he's dead or alive."

A nervous man began coughing.

Cliff waited for the man's hacking to subside. "Earlier this morning we heard some shooting. I'm sure most of you folks did also. I sent a couple of my men to check things out. They found some blood, some tracks, two empty shell casings, but no dead bodies. We had hoped Buchanan would show up after the shooting, but he hasn't, which brings us up to the present. Buchanan told me he'd stay out until he kills the bushwhacker who murdered Pat." Again, he paused, hoping everything he explained was sinking in. "What's more, he plans on tracking the savage even if it requires him leaving the area. In other words, it could be some time before he returns. If Scott's not back in a week or more, I'm planning on him not returning. I've got to plan it that way so we keep heading toward our final destination. Here's what I want you to hang your hat on. Whether Buchanan's dead or alive, I'm not stopping this wagon train for anything, including personal tragedies. The only reason I ever stop is to fix a broken wagon and even then not for long. Why, because it's bad luck. We have a destination to reach and we're going to reach it regardless how many obstacles hinder us, including personal tragedies. As you've seen, I'm not heartless. We'll take time to grieve, bury the dead with reverence, and then move on. Here's some cheery news. We have been covering some serious miles thanks to cooperative weather. We have to continue to take advantage of dry conditions. As for our chief scout, I wish I could tell you more but I can't. If you folks got questions this is the time, 'cause that sums up what I have to say."

A voice at the far end of the circle called out, "Doesn't your scout being on a personal manhunt jeopardize the wagon train?"

"That's a fair question. My scout's sure that heathen sneak is nearby. What's more, he's usually right. With that being the case, he's still scouting for the wagons while hunting down the killer. Told me if he sees danger, he'll get word to me."

Another hand went up at the opposite end of the group.

"What's on your mind, Bill?"

"You said we were making good time. How soon before we reach the nearest settlement?"

"The way we're covering ground, about a week and a half. At the most, not more than two weeks."

A murmur of excitement swept through the group.

Another hand rose.

Cliff eyed Cornelius O'Keefe. "What's on your mind, Connie?"

"Any more signs of more sneaky Kiowa besides the lone bushwhacker?"

"Here's a word of caution. I doubt that lone Kiowa would hang around unless the rest of that bunch isn't very far away. On the other hand, if he's gone so are the rest. Regardless, everyone stay alert. Anyone with women and children, keep them close by."

Cornelius wasn't done. "How about them strange riders?"

Cliff had to admit the man was asking intelligent questions. "Here's my thinking regarding those strangers. They have the same travel rights to the trail as we do. As long as they don't cause us any trouble, I have no problem with them. Just so you folks know: we're not taking them for granted."

A man in the center asked, "You have any idea why they haven't rode over for a visit?"

"None whatsoever, as long as they keep their distance, that's fine with me. Like I said, we are keeping them under surveillance."

Tyler Harden spoke up. "Please don't forget to ask if there's anything the rest of us can do, we're more than willing to help."

Cliff eyed Harden, thinking the newspaper man ought to be called, Mr. Volunteer. The man wasn't about to let go of drawing attention to himself. If he had a middle name, "Look-At-Me" would fit nicely. Cliff fought against expressing his opinion. "I won't forget, Mr. Harden. Anyone else have more questions?"

Silence ensued.

"Well then, that's it, thanks for coming."

Cliff watched everyone moving away, everyone except Stephanie Clark. He wasn't surprised. "What is it, Miss Clark?"

She stared at the ground before lifting her gaze. "I asked your wagon scout what I could do to help. He suggested I keep a watch fire going for him. I agreed. Tell me, Mr. Stokes, will keeping a fire going really help?"

Surprised at Buchanan's request, Cliff's face showed it. Smiling, he encouraged her, "If he told you a watch fire was important to him, you can rest assured he meant it. As for whether it will help, a good scout always checks from higher elevations. You can be sure if Buchanan's around he'll see the fire from afar. But I must warn you, getting up during the night to keep a fire alive isn't easy. If you can endure some sleepless nights, go for it."

Smiling, Stephanie was encouraged. "I'll manage." Turning, she walked away.

Watching her depart, Cliff didn't doubt she would keep her commitment. Getting up in the wee hours of the night had a way of dragging a person into a condition of fatigue. The Clark girl had some grit in her. An alarming thought crossed his mind. Was Scott Buchanan testing her, seeing if she was really interested in him? Apparently his scout and Stephanie were having some serious conversations. A growing concern entered his thinking. Cliff wasn't sure he liked any romantic inclinations being entertained by his chief scout. It was tough finding experienced scouts that weren't fiddle-footed, especially one as good as Buchanan. Cliff selfishly needed him for a few more years.

Seeing Wendell beckon, Cliff headed for the cook. As he walked, he gave more thought to what he'd learned. Knowing Scott Buchanan like he did, if the man had serious intentions regarding Stephanie, when the time came, nothing would stop him short of death. Therefore, there was no sense in worrying about something he couldn't prevent. If Buchanan wanted to settle down, that Stephanie gal was as fine a mare as a man could throw a lariat over. A grin split his face. She just might be more than Buchanan's wild nature bargained for. Besides, she had more than one man trying to corral her during this journey. Tyler Harden was the other stallion showing his pedigree.

LIFE OVER DEATH

Letting Buddy find his way up and out of the gully, for the first time in hours Buchanan felt spent. Skirting the ridge they turned west, a long rope attached to the dead Indian's horse. Scott had a plan requiring the element of surprise. Knowing Indian ways fueled his planning. He would use the dead warrior's body for negotiating. Right now there was no time for returning to the wagons. If he didn't find the Kiowa within the next twenty-four hours, he'd be dealing with a rotting corpse caused by rising temperatures. Not knowing how far away the raiding party had traveled required him to cover distance at a rapid pace. Hopefully, the raiding party would be found just southwest of the river somewhere along the foothills. If Scott moved quickly, he should find the raiding party before dark. If successful, Scott still needed the element of surprise for his plan to work. Once the Kiowa were located, he'd negotiate depending on being positioned before first light while surprising them with an unexpected morning powwow. Once again, the dark of night would be his ally.

As much as Scott wanted, informing the wagon train would have to wait. At best his plan was a calculated gamble, but then so too was life out here in the wilds. Buchanan's instincts had served him well. He wasn't about to change now. After all, part of his job as scout was to insure safety for the wagon train.

Gray Coyote rose before anyone else. Each year he ate less, slept less, his body aching more. Despite his body protesting, he refused to concede to age, especially before others from his tribe. If he gave in to what bored him, life would cease to excite him. Despite his advancing years, he was still known as a man who prowled the land with cunning. Gray Coyote appreciated what life's experiences had taught him. Often sought out for his wisdom, counseling others gave him a feeling of importance besides surviving old age. Many tribal visitors had informed him how his name was often mentioned respectfully around different council fires, even more satisfying, among the different warrior tribes.

The still quiet morning allowed him to reminisce back to his younger days, those years when he was given the name, Gray Coyote. A man earned his title by being given a name by those he rode with. Once a man was named, he had his reputation.

Slipping quietly among the sleeping men, Gray Coyote selected the one fire still showing faint signs of life. Spreading dry buffalo chips, blowing hard, he coaxed the coals back to life. He settled cross-legged before the fire, facing east. He always appreciated seeing the first signs of dawn, glad the others still slept allowing him time to meditate. Just the other day, they had uncovered fresh buffalo signs. Bringing fresh meat back to the camp was far better than raiding some village along the trail. This morning, Gray Coyote would instruct his braves to locate the herd. As for him, he would let the eager ones find the herd while he trailed from behind. In this way, their back trail would be guarded.

The sky brightening, the men rose. Joining Gray Coyote, each brave muttered a soft greeting. As was his habit, he acknowledged each by their earned names. Sticks holding impaled rabbit caught by snares hovered over the fire, the smell pleasant. Finishing, they tossed the burnt sticks into the fire, watching the flames hungrily attack the charred wood. All talking ceased, each brave focused on Gray Coyote. It was time for their leader to speak.

His head bobbing in agreement with what he had to say, Gray Coyote measured his words. "Before the sun went down yesterday, we came upon fresh buffalo tracks. This is a good sign. Before the night returns, we will have fresh meat for our lodges."

Tall Oak spoke, "What about Lone Hawk?"

"He will find us as he always does. Besides, he knows where our village is."

Red Fox agreed. "You have spoken wisely. It has been a long time since the Great Spirit has shown us fresh tracks leading to buffalo."

Gray Coyote nodded. "Yes, while the Great Spirit is leading we must not wait. The sooner we cover the one fire still burning, the sooner we find the herd. Once this is done, we can go back to our lodges." He began tossing dirt onto the sputtering flames. The fire smothered, the braves gathered their horses, waiting.

Leaping onto the back of his horse, careful to disguise his inner pain, Gray Coyote groaned inwardly. Such a discomfort was more bothersome during the first hours of daylight. Once the day warmed, his bones left him alone.

The young bucks watched him, awed with such agility despite his age.

He liked that. Starting his horse forward, Gray Coyote headed him up the side of the coulee, the braves falling into a spaced-out line behind him.

Seeing the white-eyes, Gray Coyote reined in his horse. His eyes shifted to the second horse, the horse carrying Lone Hawk's body. A low hissing sound came from behind him, the braves forming a semi-circle alongside their leader. Observing how the white-eyes sat atop his horse, he waited until everyone was in place, starting his horse toward the white-eyes. Slowly approaching, Gray Coyote halted. The paleface sat tall, unafraid. Gray Coyote broke the ominous silence. "Speak, for I am the leader of these warriors."

Making sure he showed no sign of nervousness, Buchanan eyed each brave separately before answering. "I am returning one of your own."

"Why?"

"You have your ways of taking care of the dead. We have our ways."

"This is so. Is that all you have to say?"

"No, I have other reasons."

"Tell us, for you are one among us. We can easily slay you."

"What you say is true. As for myself, I have no desire to kill. More deaths will solve nothing. If I must, I will. But before I die, I will take you and one of your younger men. This I must do. In that way, the younger brave will not see a full life… as your fallen warrior did to one of our younger men. But first, I will kill you to avenge myself."

Gray Coyote saw the man's hand fingers around his gun, his strong words showing he was unafraid. Gray Coyote too was without fear. He questioned the white-eyes. "I have lived long, why should I fear death?"

Buchanan maintained his calm stare. "I can see you have lived long. Since it will be you who decides for death over life, a man of many warrior years should get what he wants. I know warrior ways. I also know you would not be leading these men if you had not been chosen because of your past. There is one other thing for you to consider. I intend to kill more than two before I die."

Gray Coyote was impressed. Certainly, the white-eyes had warrior blood in his veins otherwise he would not be sitting astride his horse in such a way. "Tell me, what else do you wish, for then I can decide?"

"I want life over death. It is not my wish for death, not now, not before. But I did not make that choice, so I fought that I may have life. He had his chance, I had my chance. That I lived was fair for he was the one who stalked first, not I."

The old leader nodded. "It is as you say. I know this because Lone Hawk told me so. He also told us you have a warrior spirit. He wanted your spirit for a greater spiritual strength for himself. He respected you. That is why he named you Eyes-That-See."

Buchanan took advantage of what he was hearing. "So this means that I have acquired Lone Hawk's warrior spirit. I think I would like to keep the name he gave me. Tell me, what is your name?"

"My name is Gray Coyote."

"Ah, because your name has meaning, you are as I thought. You are a cunning leader who knows how to skirt danger while being a successful warrior." Turning, he pointed at the dead body. "He fought well, but at times, life is meant for the thinker over the one who is bold. Lone Hawk's strength became his weakness. Weakness can become strength as long as fear doesn't become the master. I suspect you know that, and that is why you still sit astride your pony while he no longer rides."

Gray Coyote knew he was hearing wisdom, agreeing, "You speak well. You understand the ways of my people."

Buchanan found common ground as he spoke, "If my ancestors weren't from a distant land, I would be like you, living off the land. Living off the land makes one part of the land. There is no better way of life."

Gray Coyote liked this warrior man. Making his decision, he gave a sharp nod with his head. "You shall live. You are unafraid and will have the name you earned in battle, the name Lone Hawk gave you. Your name is Eyes-That-See, a blood brother to the Kiowa." Gray Coyote drew his knife, drawing the sharp blade across his palm, extending his hand.

Buchanan pulled out his knife, drawing blood from his own hand. Moving forward, he grasped Gray Coyote's hand palm to palm. "I am pleased to be a brother of the Kiowa. Take Lone Hawk's body. Take his horse, his weapons, including his broken bow. Give him a proper burial."

With a positive shake of his head, Gray Coyote said, "This will be done." Turning, he spoke to a tall warrior. "Tall Oak, go and fetch the horse taken from the white-eyes killed by Lone Hawk. Bring his short and long guns. Eyes-That-See has returned our slain brother to us with his possessions, we will do the same." Turning back, Gray Coyote pointed south. "We have found fresh buffalo sign. You are welcome to hunt with us if you wish."

Thoughtful, Buchanan searched for an answer showing respect, artfully dodging, "My chief waits for me so I must return. The people who travel with us are bound for a distant land."

A touch of bitterness crept into Gray Coyote's words. "These people keep coming, when will they stop?"

"This I do not know. But these are a soft people not fit for the land. They will not stay near your fires. That is good for you and your tribe. When I return, I will seek you out. We will spend time together, but for now I must return."

Gray Coyote gave the peace sign. "So be it. We will see you when you return. Soon I and my men will meet up with our Cheyenne brothers. I will tell these warriors you are leading strange people to a distant place. You and your wagon train will have safe passage, this I can promise you. Since you are now one of us, go travel with the Great Spirit as we do. When you return, we will smoke the pipe."

WATCH FIRE

His red-brothers watching his departure, Buchanan felt exhilaration, the trailing rope pulling at Pat's horse. A mile passed. For the first time, he felt a need for solitude, a place to unwind. The question was, where? His palm smarting from the blood-brother ritual, he recalled a distant stream with its banks covered with reddish clay, a type of clay full of healing properties. Yes, he would use such a spot for his quiet place. Once he reached the stream, he would find some herbs to mix with the clay. After the clay was prepared he would cover the wound, a wet bandana around his hand preventing the clay from hardening allowing for his cut to heal. After he attended to his hand and settled the horses, then he could unwind. As for the wagon train and his boss, they would have to wait. He knew Stokes would be anxious, but for now he needed solitude, a time to recover from dealing with death. His memory where the stream was located not failing him; Scott arrived at the exact location.

Sparkling in the sun, the stream meandered through the meadow, disappearing into a grove of cottonwood trees. Dismounting, Buchanan enjoyed the sounds coming from the gurgling brook. The stream's surface, warmed by the sun's rays, triggered a feeding frenzy as brook trout feasted on the numerous mayflies rising from the clear water. A swirl on the surface was followed by a flash of silver as an emerging mayfly was sucked under the surface. Buchanan smiled. Tonight he would dine on trout. Reaching into his saddlebag, he pulled out a beat-up tin cup. Moving away from the pool, he stooped low, gouging the clay lining the stream's bank. The cup full, he stood. Now all that was needed was a few herbs, the type found in pockets of sunlight. It didn't take him long. Crushing the herbs into the clay, he returned to the brook, gently washing the cut. Untying his bandana, he soaked it under the water. Wringing it gently, his eyes settled on a near log not yet covered by moss. The dry log would provide him a comfortable place to lean against while dressing his wound. Settling against the trunk, he let the air dry his hand, gently working the clay over the cut. The cooling effect gave immediate relief. Wrapping the wet bandana around the clay, he used his teeth and free hand to secure the knot. Already the wound felt as if it was healing. Satisfied, he relaxed, fascinated with the swarms of mayflies completing their mating ritual. Hundreds of the light-colored mayflies fluttered over the water, their whitish color contrasting against the green background cast from the cottonwoods. There were surface swirls everywhere, at times the hungry trout leaping out of the water.

As Buchanan watched the feeding trout, he recalled an elderly Ojibwa who had taught him the art of observation. The old man had instructed him to watch the way the flies flew as they mated. He then asked him to explain what his eyes saw. At first not seeing anything significant, Scott had done as he was instructed. Sure there was an important lesson to be learned, he kept watching. Finally he saw what he thought he was supposed to see, noticing the mayflies always flew upstream. When Buchanan explained what he had seen to the sage Ojibwa man, he was told this was why the mayflies never wash away into the great bodies of water. The elderly Indian explained; if the mayflies constantly flew with the current as they mated, so too would all their eggs wash downstream. If this pattern continued, there would be no mayflies inhabiting the upper reaches of the small brooks and streams. But because they flew upstream, there would always be mayfly nymphs providing food for the trout.

The Ojibwa concluded this was how the Great Spirit blessed all living things, allowing not only for survival, but also food needed for the living. What the old Indian said made sense. As Scott's eyes followed the frenzied mating, he remembered his conversation with the old Ojibwa man. Most of all, he never forgot the greater lesson, the art of observation.

Relaxed, Buchanan became hypnotized by his surroundings. Briefly forgetting the last few days, he became content to watch the mayflies and the trout. As their activity ebbed, his mind returned to what bothered him. He understood the need to hunt for food. The mayflies were food for the fish, which was understandable. But one man killing another man for greatness was another matter. As a hunter, he'd developed admiration for his quarry. Often he'd experienced regret after a successful hunt. Despite such regret there was never a guilty feeling. Even if a bad buckaroo deserved death, taking human life wasn't right. Considering how individuals bring death upon themselves, what a complicated world, he grimaced. Predatory animals kill to survive, which means they're excusable. Men who justify killing others as an honorable way of life is wanton killing. Taking Lone Hawk's life was unavoidable because Scott had been the hunted one, so he had killed to stay alive. Vengeance too had merit. Pat's killer had to be brought to justice. Out here on the frontier there were no courts, no juries, not forgetting having to deal with the Indian norms of justice. Such justice as they practiced often was very torturous. There was another strange phenomena regarding killing, one he'd experienced. It could become very exhilarating, almost intoxicating. To kill a worthy adversary fueled the warrior mentality. A man had to guard against such feelings, if he didn't, all restraint could be lost provoking murderous intentions. When he had studied the fallen Kiowa's face, he saw features indicating cruelty, someone who loved to kill, further justifying the Kiowa's death. Buchanan wasn't burdened by his conscience. The Indian had gotten what he deserved. And yet, didn't the Kiowa warrior have a family with wives and children? Didn't the brave have a mother who loved her son? Certainly, she would grieve his demise?

Unable to settle what bothered him, he considered his love for hunting. Killing was part of hunting. Then why did he love hunting? He reckoned as a hunter he was part of nature, not just some alien observer who didn't belong. Because wildlife avoided him, his skill needed to be greater. Because of his instinctive animal-like ability, he was integrated into nature, making him part of the land he loved.

Scott's thoughts drifted onto the young worker who was always talking about God's love. One of these days, he was going to have a serious conversation with Mitch Robinson. He was going to ask the young fellow some difficult questions, and when he did, he was going to challenge the young believer to explain about God and killing. Such a conversation should bring about a stimulating disagreement. It would be quite interesting to see how the young preacher answered such questions. After all, if God was a God of love, why did he allow for murderous happenings? Buchanan was sure Mitch wouldn't be able to answer the impossible. The way he saw it, nature was the survival of the fittest, and that was where humanity fit in.

Buchanan's mind switched away from death, his thoughts focusing on the different types of people traveling with the wagons. His thoughts drifted to Stephanie Clark, causing him to frown. Such a woman made a man think about settling down, a very scary thought. Life on the trail allowed him to do his own thing. Constantly being on the move in this wild land was exciting, a special occupation, something few people were skilled at. Out in the wilds, he was respected highly for his frontier skills. Another thing, Buchanan constantly met new people, folks who valued such skills, their respect leaving him with a feeling of importance. For a second, he almost laughed. If a person traveling with the wagon train was ornery, it was the wagon boss who had to deal with such a problem maker. Even better, if Buchanan didn't like one of the travelers, at the end of the trail they departed never to be bothersome again, at least not to him. As for the good folks, if they liked you, often an invitation was extended to visit. In other words, he had a nice option to see someone again if he liked them. Now, if a man settled down and had a troublesome neighbor, he couldn't ride away from such a nuisance.

Buchanan's mind refocused on Stephanie Clark. Was his golden rule in danger, he wondered. It had always been his intention to get past a certain age before thinking seriously about a woman, any woman, and once a man settled down all that would change. There was something special about Miss Clark. More and more she was in his thoughts. Not good, he concluded. What about that Harden fellow? Stephanie seemed to like the handsome, slick-talking professional, who was obviously courting her while using his educated vocabulary. For a moment, he felt a twinge of jealousy. Even worse, it wasn't going away, indicating his free lifestyle might be in jeopardy. Of course, there was the possibility Stephanie was more attracted to Harden instead of a rough and tumble wagon scout. For a second, Buchanan felt a measure of relief. Then there was always the possibility she wasn't interested in either of them. He chuckled to himself, thinking if that was the case, both were eliminated, temptation through jealousy no longer a concern.

The day slipping by, Buchanan lifted his gaze toward the sky, captivated by the large fluffy white clouds, some higher than others. Each seemed to be ghosting along in different directions, in between were patches of blue, the higher clouds moving faster than the clouds below. Hypnotized by the three dimensional movement, he forgot time. His mind drifted along with the clouds, Buchanan content to let the day slide by until disturbed from a growling stomach. Giving consideration to hunger, if he was going to cook some trout before dark, he'd better start a fire before fishing.

Hauling himself into a standing position, Buchanan removed the bandana, laying it over a small branch. It didn't take long before returning with an armful of dead wood. The fire ignited quickly. Avoiding casting his shadow along the brook, Buchanan treaded softly, seeking a place where the stream banks were shade covered. Just ahead the brook sharply turned, no longer bathed in sunlight. Sure the far bank would be undercut because of the current swirling at the bend before the stream straightened, if ever there was ideal shelter for wary trout, it would be there. Dropping onto one knee, he stretched out full length. Propped up on his elbows, he crawled to the edge. Rolling up his sleeves, Scott slipped both arms into the water. Slowly his hands rose and fell with the current. Waiting until his hands adjusted to the cold, he let them sink deeper, the current pushing them under the overhanging bank. Moving them a few inches at a time, he felt a trout. The fish drifted away. Keeping his hands limp as if they were nothing more than part of the pulsating current, the trout stopped moving away from the fingers subtle touches. Accepting the gentle caress, the fish relaxed. Ever so slowly Scott's fingers located the head and tail. Quickly closing his hands, he flipped the trout onto the bank. Moving further downstream, he repeated his success. Soon four brook trout flopped in the grass. Smiling at such skill, he acknowledged how the clay had more than one purpose besides healing. The trout would be packed in clay, and when the fire was reduced to hot coals, he would push the trout deep within the red-hot coals. Once the clay hardened from the heat, the skin would peel off with the clay, the fish moist and cooked to perfection. Retrieving his tin cup, Scott returned to the stream, gouging out more clay, wrapping each fish. Satisfied the fire was ready; he pushed each fish under the hot coals. Retrieving the tin cup, he returned to the stream for more healing clay. Back at the log, Buchanan worked the clay around the cut. Satisfied, the wet bandana was wrapped around the already half-healed wound.

Finished eating, his stomach full, Buchanan fluffed his jacket into a pillow. Leaning back, totally relaxed, Buchanan was pleased for the first time in days he felt free from tension. Closing his eyes, sleep claimed him.

The moon rose flooding the darkness with a soft light. His horse snickered, nudging the master's prone body. Buchanan's eyes opened, staring at the surroundings bathed in moonlight. Surprised at himself for falling into a deep sleep, feeling chilled, he rubbed Buddy's muzzle. Reaching for the bedroll, Scott changed his mind. With the night so illuminated, it would be smart to take advantage of what the Indians call: the Stalking Moon. Slipping into his jacket, hands on the pommel, he rose into the saddle. Gently nudging Buddy with his heels, he turned the gelding in the direction of the wagon trail. Entering the road, thanks to the luminous light, travel was easy.

Higher and higher the moon climbed, finally hovering overhead. He and Buddy made good time. As the hours passed, the descending moon was in his face. Unlike the sun's rays which blinded, the light cast by the moon provided a softly lit pathway easy to follow. The moon now descending toward the western horizon, shadows appeared like fingers stretching towards him. Enjoying the surreal ride, Buchanan's body adjusted to the steady rocking motion from Buddy. As the moon dropped, as if seeking to touch, the shadows stretched out closer and closer. Had there been a breeze, he was sure the ride would be eerie, perhaps unsettling. As the moon slipped lower, the contrasting tree trunks merged obscuring the pockets of moonlight. Knowing every one of Stokes's favorite camping places along the trail, Buchanan turned Buddy for higher ground. If the wagons were camped where he suspected, he saw no sense in alarming the lookouts. Disturbing the sentries in the wee hours of the morning would cause too much of a commotion. Besides, once he showed up there would be lots of explaining to do. Nope, he concluded, it would be smart to ride in when everyone was up and about. Shifting in his saddle, he observed a slight touch of light in the eastern horizon. Dawn wasn't very far away, the wait manageable. Reaching the top, he reined Buddy around, staring downhill.

A lone fire cast its flickering flames on the third wagon behind the cook wagon nestled within the circled wagons. The watch fire stirred his emotions. Stephanie Clark had kept her promise.

BACK IN CAMP

Awakened by her promise, Stephanie's eyes opened. Exhausted, she peeked out at the night. Judging by the moon, she guessed the time to be around three in the morning. She had made a promise to Scott Buchanan and so far she was keeping it. Not wanting to leave the warmth of the blankets, she stared at the hardly alive watch fire. Pushing aside the covers, her stumbling steps brought her over to what was left of a shrinking woodpile. She dragged a gnarled chunk of wood to the fire. Hovering over the dying fire, the smoldering flames barely illuminating their wagon, she arranged sticks over the flickering coals, followed by larger branches. The fire sputtered to life, the flames ate hungrily at the new fuel. Kneeling, she rolled the chunk of wood into place. Satisfied, she watched the flames grow, the black of night receding. Sure the fire will not go out; Stephanie shuffled back to the wagon, leaping into her bedding. Dragging the blankets over her head, she snuggled, thankful for the warmth. Unable to fall back to sleep right away, her mind wandered. She hoped the scout's superstitions were real. Unless Buchanan returned, keeping the fire going was an exercise in futility. It will be a sad moment if he failed to return. But for now, she was determined to keep the watch fire alive, at least until the wagons reach the next settlement. If he was not back by then, she will have to concede something terrible happened. Sleep finally relieves her from thinking.

Voices awakened Stephanie, the morning coming too soon. Throwing the blankets back, she can see her mother busy over the fire, her father gesturing for her to stay in bed, his voice admonishing, "Honey, you look exhausted. I'll wake you when everything's ready."

Yawning, Stephanie rejects his advice, wrapping one blanket around herself; she struggled out from the wagon, her destination the wagon tongue. Sitting, she stared blankly, still not quite awake, a vacant look in her eyes. Facing east, the sun's rising rays are blinding. Briefly her mother's shadow blocks the sun, a steaming cup of coffee placed in her hand. Thankful, Stephanie's voice whispered, "If this doesn't wake me, nothing will."

Seeing the fatigue lines in her daughter's face, Norma expressed concern, encouraging, "You should listen to your father and go back to sleep. We can manage. I think keeping the watch fire going is wearing you out."

Guarding against burning her lips, Stephanie wraps both hands around the cup, her voice barely distinguishable. "Too late now, I'm awake."

Hearing louder than normal voices coming from the lead wagon, shifting around, Stephanie raised her hand to ward off the sun's blinding rays, a horseman towing a rider-less horse approaching the wagon boss, the rider's horse a light colored dun.

His coffee cup falling from his hand, Cliff almost catches the cup before it bounces off the ground. Relief flooding his brain, he picked up the unbroken cup. Straightening, he sees Wendell with a smile plastered across his face. Regaining his casual demeanor, he makes a face at Wendell, ordering him, "Here, pour me another cup."

Wendell retorted with a snicker, "I only got enough for one more cup, Buchanan's cup."

"It figures," Cliff retorted. Considering what he's seeing, Cliff's sure the trailing horse belongs to the deceased Pat Morgan. This is going to be one hell of a story, he reckoned.

Slipping from the saddle, Buchanan accepts the hot coffee from Wendell, his face radiating pleasure, words gushing out, "Damn, Wendell, it's been over three days since I've had me some coffee. I'm going to enjoy this brew." Holding up his free hand, he looks at his boss, pleading for a second, "Just one sip." Finishing with a sigh, Buchanan doesn't push his boss's patience. "Sorry it took me so long. Dealing with death has a way of changing schedules. I would have come back right away, but my brain came up with a way of using that Kiowa's dead body for the good of all of us." Pausing, he sneaks in another sip before continuing, "My instincts were in charge, not me. That and how hot weather can start a dead body to stinking."

Aware people were crowding around, a few folks muttering hellos, Buchanan acknowledging each hello, keenly watching Stephanie's arrival for a moment before speaking loud enough for everyone to hear. "The killing savage is dead. You probably heard the shooting. The reason I didn't come right back here was because I used his dead body for negotiating. What with the rising temperatures and all, things could have gotten pretty smelly. I caught up with the dead Kiowa's raiding party after dark. I needed the element of surprise, so I waited until the morning. I figured if I caught them before they had their wits in gear, it would allow me a chance to talk before things turned ugly. It worked, too. I positioned myself so when they moved out at first light I was smack-dab in their path. They recovered pretty quick, surrounding me, but I got them to listen. I told their leader that if they chose to fight, before they killed me, he and a younger brave would die along with some others. I explained I really desired life, not death. But if they wanted death, everything will be even. I would kill one old and one young. Two for two, maybe more. So I gave their leader a choice. He could see my hand on my gun knowing I meant what I said."

Fascinated, Stokes asked, "What made you think of using the dead body?"

"I needed an edge. I figured them seeing a dead body of one of their fiercest warriors would give me time to negotiate. I told the leader they had their ways to honor their dead and we have our ways. I was honoring them by returning one of their own."

"What was their leader's name?"

"Gray Coyote."

Stokes nodded. "Apparently he respected your reasoning."

"As you can see, he gave me back Pat's guns and his horse. Something else happened. Because I honored their ways and was a man of courage without fear, we made a blood covenant. I have a new name, a Kiowa name. My name is… Eyes-That-See."

A murmur swept the listeners.

Stokes pointed at Buchanan's hand. "Is that why your bandana's wrapped around your hand?"

"It is. We each drew blood, palm to palm."

"How's it healing?"

"Good. It's really time to take the dressing off. Gray Coyote told me I was given that name by the brave who hunted me. I asked him if I could keep it."

"Smart thinking."

"Knowing he understood I was honoring their ways, I thought so. Before I left, Gray Coyote said they were meeting up with some Cheyenne warriors. Since I was now a blood-brother to the Kiowa, he would speak for us."

Wendell's enthusiastic voice broke up the two-way conversation. "If that don't beat all," he cackled, "yes, sir, this is a story to tell kinfolk."

Pushing his hat back, Stokes rolled his eyes, agreeing, "Maybe legendary. You look like you rode all night."

"Pretty much, I didn't want to disturb the folks until the morning."

"I'm thinking you must be hungry."

"I could use some chow."

"Tie your horse to the back of my wagon. After you chow down, climb in and get some sleep. I've been looking for an excuse to have a party. You just gave me a reason. What's more, I know just the right place to stop for a night of two-step dancing. Yes, sir, we got ourselves an excuse for a celebration. Stuart, tonight you're going to break out your fiddle." Stokes laughed, pointing his finger at Buchanan. "Now you go get some food and sleep, that's an order."

Turning, he addressed the on-lookers, "The rest of you folks finish eating and get your wagons ready to move out, 'cause we're stopping early for a good old fashioned—hoedown!"

A soft cheer went up. Eager anticipation in their faces, everyone hustled for their wagons. As the folks left, many cast a second look at Buchanan, several touching their hat brims, a few smiling.

Smiling back, Buchanan saw Stephanie leaving, his voice reaching out, "Hold on, Miss Clark." He closed the distance. "I want to thank you."

Thinking she knew why but not sure, Stephanie waited.

"When I saw the watch fire, I felt special."

Eyebrows arched, Stephanie repeated his observation. "You saw it?"

"I sure did. You kept your promise. Not only are you downright pretty, more important, you're special. I'm glad I've gotten to know you."

Moved, a touch of emotion flooded her face. "When did you see it?"

"About an hour before dawn, what with the moon being so bright, I traveled during the night. When I saw the fire, I knew it was you. Do you know what that watch fire told me about you?"

"What did the fire tell you about me?"

"The watch fire showed your spirit is a pathway of light showing what's within you."

Touched, she remembered the wagon boss telling her how he considered Buchanan to be half Apache and half Cheyenne. Yes, Stephanie thought, what Mr. Stokes said was probably true, but she was seeing something else about this frontiersman. The man showed sensitivity and was appreciative. She replied softly, "Thank you, Scott Buchanan."

"No, Stephanie, thank you. Now, I have a request."

Wondering what it was, she studied his face.

"When Stuart strikes up that fiddle tonight, I'd be honored if you would grant me the first dance."

Delighted, Stephanie laughed. "I'd like that, make sure you come over and ask before someone else insists."

"I'll do that. Right now I'm going to go eat, grab some shuteye, and get ready for tonight." Bowing, he turned, his destination the chuck wagon.

Watching Buchanan go, Stephanie experienced elation and exhaustion at the same time. She was glad she had tended the watch fire, pleased the scout was alive, and now, like him, she was going to take her mother and father's advice and catch up on some sleep. Even better, there would be no tending the watch fire anymore. Turning, she half skipped, laughing softly, anticipating the first dance and more.

Wendell watched Buchanan approach, handing him a plate piled high with hash. "Well, young fellow, all of us were pretty worried. How about some details how you killed that Kiowa sneak?"

Seeing the wagon boss heading their way, Buchanan stalled, "Wendell, how about giving me a chance to digest a little food before the boss arrives. Once I gain control over my growling stomach, I'll give both of you the lowdown." Shoving some meat and potatoes into his mouth, he chewed, the hash tasting special. Bringing the coffee cup up, he decided against it. He had better drink some water instead; otherwise sleep might not come easy. Swallowing his last mouthful of hash, he took a swig from his canteen. With Cliff in hearing range, Buchanan updated both. "Wendell asked for some details concerning the Kiowa ambusher."

Leaning against the wagon, Cliff gave Buchanan his attention.

"The morning broke windy, tough to see anything. The Kiowa didn't pull out from his hiding spot until the wagons started up the trail. I had to run into position to get a clear shot at him. I would have shot him dead, but just as I squeezed the trigger, his mustang stumbled. When my shot missed, his pony was off and running. I got lucky. My shot clipped his mustang across the spine, knocking him and mount to the ground. The savage wiggled out from under, darting behind some boulders. I had a brief second shot, but missed. I caught up with him when he tried to get his mustang back. We had us a running foot race, my edge being my rifle. After I plugged him, it was then that I came up with the idea of catching up with his raiding party. I have to say it worked out better than I expected."

"You don't usually miss. How about the last two shots we heard? All told I counted five."

"You counted right. I was breathing hard, not very steady. My first bullet took his legs out from under him, my second shot finished him."

Looking over at Wendell, Cliff rubbed his chin, asking, "You've accounted for two days. What about the third?"

Staring back with a slight smile, Scott answered his boss. "I needed some time alone to unwind. I knew you'd be anxious, but I needed some tranquility."

"It help?"

"Yes, I dozed off waking up to a full moon, so I started to ride. I pretty much knew where I'd find you."

"You see Miss Clark's watch fire?"

"As a matter of fact, I just thanked her. Even better, I have the first dance tonight. And now, I'm going to take your advice. You know, enjoy a good sleep. If I don't grab some shuteye, come tonight I'll be stepping on someone's toes."

Stokes laughed, pleased with his decision for a hoedown.

Wendell took Scott's cup and plate, watching him head for the back of the utility wagon, whispering to his boss, "He sure enough thinks like them Injun heathens, don't he?"

Whispering back, Cliff agreed. "Yeah, but that's because he admires them and their ways. Because he does, he speaks their thoughts to them. If Buchanan ever settles down, I'm going to miss him, can't find many scouts with such skills."

Wendell jumped all over Stokes's words. "If he does, it just might be because of that gal Stephanie. He's taken a fancy to her."

"Yeah, I've noticed as much. Maybe we should root for that slick-talking charmer, Tyler Harden."

Wendell gave a violent shake with his head. "Speak for yourself, I sure won't."

Cliff had to admit, he and his cook agreed on most things.

HOEDOWN

Stephanie couldn't help but admire how handsome Tyler Harden looked. He was attired in finely striped black pants showing off a white ruffled shirt. His black boots shined in the subdued light. The man's hair was swept back highlighting his square features. Several women stared coyly as he passed, hoping he would look their way. Having become quite smitten by Tyler's constant showering of attention toward her, her pulse quickened at his arrival.

Trying not to stare, Harden failed. Stephanie looked absolutely beautiful in her flowery skirt accented with a white blouse, the blouse fashioned out of intricate lace. Her hair cascaded down, shoulder length, several ribbons highlighting her auburn hair, the curled ribbons matching the color of her skirt. Tyler's voice gushed out, complimenting her, "Stephanie, you most certainly do take a man's breath away." He smiled, confessing, "I wasn't going to say so but I couldn't help myself. You do have a way of drawing a man out despite himself." He laughed, giving another confession. "We men folk don't like to give the impression we're overly eager... even if we are."

Almost blushing, she thanked him. "Why thank you, Tyler. As you can see, I'm dressed for a night of dancing."

Tyler's response was quick, "With that in mind, it would be my pleasure if you'd grant me permission to escort you, even better, a great honor to have the first dance."

Smiling, Stephanie responded tactfully, "I'd be delighted with your escort—as for the first dance, I've already been asked. You shall surely have the second dance."

Surprised, Tyler recovered gallantly. "Knowing your beauty, I should have asked sooner." Semi-bowing at the waist, he expressed more chivalry. "Though I'm disappointed, being your escort allows me certain privileges, of which I will take every advantage. And one of those privileges will be the second dance. May I also add, perhaps more than just the second dance?" With a pained look in his expression, he followed up with, "Since I'm somewhat of a competitor by nature, may I ask who was smarter than I to have already requested the first go-around?"

Stephanie's eyes twinkled, her voice coy, "The man whose return we're celebrating, Scott Buchanan."

"Ah, the man who is half Apache and half Cheyenne. I guess that's only right since he's our excuse for a good time. Were you surprised when he asked you?"

Surprised by Tyler's use of the word *excuse*, Stephanie hesitated before answering. She wasn't sure she liked the inference. Discarding her momentary concern, she answered truthfully, "Yes, I was surprised. Quite honestly, I really didn't think he was the dancing type."

A thoughtful expression on his face, Tyler reflected, "From what I've heard, it's quite common for mountain men to dance around like wild Indians while attending a trapping rendezvous. Usually they're pretty liquored up. I guess dancing isn't an isolated activity for just the educated. Since he's a man of the wilderness, we shouldn't be surprised, should we?"

Stephanie defended Buchanan indirectly by questioning Tyler. "You don't think Stuart's going to play mountain-man music, do you?"

"No, I wouldn't think so."

"Neither do I," Stephanie smiled. "Therefore, I expect Buchanan knows a step or two."

Tyler's perception told him to drop the subject. He did.

Both heard the sounds from the fiddler warming up his instrument. Folks were drifting past, gaiety in the air.

Not forgetting etiquette, Tyler remembered Stephanie's parents. "Shouldn't we wait for your mother and father?"

Silently scolding herself for forgetting her parents, Stephanie replied, "How thoughtful of you, I'll ask."

Admiring the back of Stephanie's figure as she departed, Tyler's eyes shifted to the passing crowd. Some were dressed to the hilt in their finest. Others wore the same clothes they traveled in. Hearing Stephanie return, he swung around.

"Mom and Dad thanked you, said they'll catch up." Stephanie's face radiated excitement as she hooked her arm through Tyler's. Approaching the gathering couples, her eyes searched the crowd. Not seeing Buchanan, she wondered where he was.

Ribbons were hung from a sagging rope, the rope stretched into a large circle. Unlit oil lamps hung between the ribbons waiting for the night.

Oh my goodness, Stephanie admired, everything looked so festive. Apparently, Mr. Stokes knew how to throw a shindig out here in the wilds. Her gaze went everywhere seeing Stuart Whitmore standing on a small wooden platform adjusting the strings on his fiddle. He was dressed in a black suit complete with tails. Seeing the second-in-command dressed for such an occasion, Stephanie was impressed. To the right of the platform was the refreshment stand. Behind the stand sat Wendell Bartholomew, he too formally dressed in black. A large crystal bowl was on the table, a pink-colored liquid filled the bowl, complete with a long-handled ladle. Stephanie shifted her attention to the arriving people, including the three women from the fifth wagon who were escorted by the man chosen as their guardian. The women were dressed in pretty dancing outfits.

The sky darkening, the lamps were lit. A slight breeze brushed the dangling ribbons, their movement reflecting in the flickering light creating an atmosphere for celebration. Cliff Stokes stepped forward. The crowd hushed, waiting for his announcement.

For the first time, Stephanie saw Scott Buchanan just beyond the wagon boss. He wore light-colored jeans, his blue denim shirt partly covered by a dark vest. A long black bandana matched the color of the vest. His boots, chestnut colored, matched his belt, the boots shining from a recent buffing. Scott's bent hat was gone, and like Tyler, his hair combed straight back. Unable to hide her surprise, she admired how different the scout looked.

Cliff's voice captured everyone's attention. "We're using Scott Buchanan's return for a reason to celebrate, but we shouldn't be forgetting the man we were forced to leave behind. Pat Morgan was as good a man as I've ever known. His unfortunate passing is a real tragedy." Stokes paused, his words deliberate for emphasis. "The men and I are going to miss Pat Morgan." Quiet for a moment, he continued on. "To honor his passing, I'm going to ask for a moment of silence, perhaps a quiet prayer if you're of mind. We'll start now." Removing his hat, Cliff bowed his head, quiet descending over the crowd, the only sounds coming from a slight breeze rustling the ribbons.

Satisfied, Cliff raised his head, breaking the silence, "The trail's been long and dusty, it's time to break up the monotony and have a little fun. Besides, Pat would want that." Cliff turned, eyeing his fiddler, he asked him, "You about ready, Stuart?"

Stuart grinned, answering back, "Whenever you stop talking, I'll strike up the music."

Everyone laughed, someone in the background shouting, "Let's do it!"

Holding up both hands, Cliff had more announcements. "I have two more things needing saying. "We got some punch mixed up special at the refreshment table to cool you folks down from all the dancing, courtesy of Wendell. Even better, no charge for the beverage, it's on the house. One more thing—we don't like whisky showing up. Alcohol has a way of creating trouble. If any of you have some libation, save it for when you reach your final destination. That's all I have to say. Stuart, you go right ahead and strike up the music."

Ready for the music to begin, people began drifting into the circle.

Seeing how Tyler had escorted Stephanie, Buchanan began second-guessing himself. Had he made a mistake with his big mouth by asking her for the first dance? No matter, he decided. Since he had asked, he'd better make good his request. Crossing the hard-packed earth, Buchanan smiled at Stephanie, giving Tyler a nod of recognition. He was relieved seeing Stephanie's face light up with her infectious smile. He wondered how Tyler would respond, especially since he was her escort. Scott's instincts told him Stephanie would settle things. He was right, her response perfect.

Smiling demurely, Stephanie said, "I told Tyler I was being rewarded the first dance with you for keeping my watch fire promise." Continuing to smile, she held out her hand. "I hope that wasn't your only reason for asking me to dance?"

Tyler masked his surge of jealousy. As if not bothered, he smiled broadly.

Scott couldn't help himself, his head rocking back, he laughed Looking at her escort, he bowed slightly, expressing civility toward his competition. "If I were a betting man, I'm sure someone has already made sure they have the second dance." His hand enveloping hers, he was unable to stop himself, mischief coming out of his voice. "I hope the first dance is slow, that way we can get to know each other better."

Again, Tyler hid his frustration.

Subtle humor still in Scott's thoughts, he rested his hand on the small of Stephanie's back, deftly guiding her into the center of the waiting circle.

Intrigued by the way the scout was moving her toward the middle of the waiting couples; Stephanie sensed Scott Buchanan may very well be an accomplished dancer. She spoke her mind. "I have a feeling you're not uncomfortable on the dance floor."

A twinkle in his eyes, Scott smiled.

Poised with his fiddle, Stuart's eyes didn't miss who was escorting Miss Clark out among the waiting couples. Knowing the scout had been promised the first dance with her; Stuart reckoned it was time to have a little fun by playing cupid. Brushing the strings on his fiddle with a soft sweeping motion, his loud declaration gained everyones' attention. "Before I strike up the music, I have an announcement, so everyone listen close. I'm going to start with a high stepping tune titled 'Turkey in the Straw,' followed by 'My Old Kentucky Home.' Consider them one song, and all you folks who have the second dance… you'll just have to wait!"

Stokes laughed softly. Stuart didn't miss much. He was making sure Buchanan had the edge over Tyler. Yep, he congratulated himself; his selected crew was top draw—the best.

The fiddle came to life.

Leading her perfectly, quickstepping to the beat of the music, Scott seemed to float over packed dirt.

Intent on where he was leading her, Stephanie stayed in step, whirling bodies everywhere. Finally the music slowed, the fiddle's melodious sounds changing over to 'My Old Kentucky Home.' Brought together, Scott kept his conversation light. "I'm betting you didn't think I could dance, did you?"

Stephanie answered honestly. "I must confess, not at first. You were almost right about something, but not quite right."

"And what is that something?"

"You said after we had a slow dance we'd get to know each other better, but I learned a lot more from the first dance."

Admiring her wit, Buchanan smiled as he came back with, "Miss Clark, you do indeed have a quick mind." Turning Stephanie in a slow circle, he leaned her backward slightly, his mouth near her ear. "But I'm about to learn more about you during our slow dance."

What an intriguing response, Stephanie pondered as he brought her up. This man called by his boss as half Apache and half Cheyenne was not at a loss for words. It appeared the wagon scout had more polish than she expected. Staring into his eyes, she asked him, "And do you like what you're learning?"

"Yes, and no."

Surprised, she inquired, "Meaning?"

Buchanan decided it was time to up the stakes, something he hadn't planned on. Hopefully, he wasn't about to make a fool of himself. He tried to be tactful, hoping for the right results without appearing vulnerable. Winking at her, he kept his voice light.

"Maybe I'm getting a little jealous over the competition, you know, the one who was supposed to have the second dance."

Enjoying his teasing, Stephanie was disappointed the music was ending.

Buchanan turned, escorting her toward Tyler. As they weaved their way, she squeezed his hand, encouraging him, "Don't forget about me for the rest of the evening... I like a little competitive jealousy through dancing."

Tyler was complimentary at their approach. "You surprised me, Buchanan. You are an accomplished dancer."

Scott bowed slightly, his voice chivalrous, "Thank you, now we're even."

Eyebrows arched, Tyler wondered why. His voice matched Buchanan's chivalry. "Please, explain to me the part about us being even?"

"I'll be glad to. You've had the pleasure of escorting Stephanie, and now one dance which counts for two. Since I had the first two dances... now we're even."

"Ah, interesting arithmetic. I never thought of counting in such a way. Thank you for making me aware. Since you have, I had better guard against equality."

Stuart's fiddle captured the night with another slow song, Tyler sweeping Stephanie toward the pulsating crowd.

Scott drifted toward the refreshment table. As was Wendell's habit, extending a cup of punch to Buchanan. Showing his thanks, Scott nodded.

Standing slightly to the left of the refreshment table, Stokes commented, "You surprised her, didn't you?"

Shrugging, Scott acknowledged as much. "If you mean by my dancing ability, yes. As for our conversation, she can tease with the best." He glanced at his boss. "I will admit she did show some interest."

"What type of interest?"

"I guess a good word would be *flirtatious*."

"Do you think she was serious?"

"I'm not sure how serious, but serious enough to be encouraging. Her attitude kind of caught me by surprise."

"Here is the bigger question: did you like it?"

Taking a drink, Scott made a face as he answered. "More than I should have, especially considering I'm violating my golden rule."

Stokes kept a straight face, understanding all too well, teasing his scout, "Yeah, and if I remember correctly, you once said if a man gets interested in a woman, he ought to keep riding. Another thing I recall you saying was if a man gets to the ripe age of thirty, he might be able to go all the way. Tell me, you have a change of heart?"

Buchanan laughed. "I guess I meant it when I said it."

Cackling, Wendell joined in on the fun. "Hey, mister wagon scout, Miss Clark just looked over this-a-way. Why don't you give her a big wink? I think she'd like that."

Refusing the advice, Scott passed back his cup for more punch. Keeping a straight face, he countered, "Is that so and now you're playing Cupid. Here's some advice for you, just pour me a little more punch and leave the playing Cupid up to the funny guy with the bow and arrow."

Head rocking back, Cliff roared with laughter.

Not about to stop having fun at Buchanan's expense, Wendell pressed on. "You know, sooner or later, a man's got to settle down, and that gal ain't half bad. She might even teach you some etiquette. Fact is, what with Tyler Harden being so attracted and all; I'd surely like to see you upset his applecart."

Scott eyed his boss. "You see any apple carts around here? I don't."

Cliff was enjoying the banter, deciding to be tactful for his own interests. "Nope, can't say I have. Now Wendell, don't you go encouraging losing a good scout because of some filly heading for civilized society."

Wendell fought back. "Yeah, but we both was married and he's entitled to his turn, don't you think?"

Cliff had to admit, Wendell had scored a valid point. It would be better he shut up letting silence be his best response. Besides,

Wendell had a knack for getting the last word in, rarely leaving little room for argument.

Folks were starting to arrive for refreshments.

Buchanan eased away, having promised to relieve the guards for some dancing. It was time to honor his promise. Later he would return to take advantage of Stephanie's suggestion of not to forget her. Out of the circle of light, he saw Wes talking with the blonde gal from the fifth wagon. It would be interesting to see what might develop between those two during the night of dancing. The music started again, bodies whirling, laughter dominating as he slipped into the night.

The music coming to an end, breaking away from the dance floor, Tyler kept his arm around Stephanie. Nearing the refreshment table, Tyler saluted the wagon boss, his voice complementary, "Your timing for breaking up the routine for a little gaiety is perfect."

Not speaking, Cliff smiled.

The music starting again, Stephanie caught Cliff by surprise. "Mr. Stokes, if I'm not being too forward, perhaps I might have the pleasure of the next dance with you?"

Cliff responded graciously. "You're a very thoughtful woman, Miss Clark, I might add, for more reasons than one. I would be delighted to have the next dance." As Cliff escorted her toward the moving dancers, he considered how she was including everyone. A person had to appreciate such an attitude in a young lady. Obviously, her parents hadn't spoiled her.

Stuart, always watchful, knew how to mix up songs strategically. Seeing his boss walking out onto the dance area with the Clark daughter, he slowed the music allowing for small talk.

Stephanie wasn't surprised how smoothly the wagon boss led her to the beat of the music, commenting, "You and your scout are very accomplished dancers, Mr. Stokes."

"Thank you, Miss Clark. You seem to have mastered the art yourself."

She laughed. "Did you teach Scott Buchanan?"

"My first wife Teresa taught him. I guess you could say we kind of adopted him after he was discharged from the army."

"Now I'm beginning to connect you two. Apparently, both of you served together in the army." Not waiting for his reply, she followed up with, "And how long have both of you been running a wagon train?"

"Yes to your first statement, as for the second question—ten years. After my wife died, it was a way to stay busy and see the country while earning a living. Mostly, I do short trips. About every three years, I do a cross-country trip like this. After this trip, I may retire. I'm getting a little tired of all the adventure and I do have a prosperous freight business."

"Did you remarry?"

"Yes."

Separating slightly, Stephanie slyly asked, "Was Scott ever married?"

Cliff's face lit up in mock gesture. "Him, no way, he doesn't have to. Buchanan shows up every Sunday and enjoys my wife's cooking."

"So your new wife also adopted him."

Cliff rolled his eyes as he spoke. "Despite his wild ways, he does have the knack of endearing himself to others. He can be very charming, that's of course, if he wants."

Interesting, Stephanie wondering where was the wagon scout. "Tell me, Mr. Stokes, where is your illustrious scout? He appears to be among the missing."

Impressed with Stephanie's keen observation despite all the dancing distractions, Cliff complimented her, "As is your constant habit of being observant, if I remember correctly, he said he was going to relieve the two night guards so they can come in and have some fun. He always comes back before Stuart takes his second break."

"You're sure?"

"I'm sure. You know, Miss Clark, we've been doing this a long time. He will show up. As you mentioned, he is an accomplished dancer. I'll tell you a secret. My scout likes the dance floor. When he appears, please corral him into another dance. We'd consider such a happening would be pleasing to us."

"Exactly who represents… us?"

"My fiddler Stuart, then Wendell, followed by yours truly."

Interesting, Stephanie thought. Despite the wagon boss's description of Scott's supposedly wild nature, it appeared Buchanan had a threesome encouraging his socialization. She wondered why. Without pursuing why, she asked, "Speaking about dancing, do you think Wendell would like to dance?"

Cliff couldn't help but conclude Stephanie was a woman who was more than just brought up right; she was a gal who cared about people. "Thanks for your thoughtfulness, Miss Clark. My answer to your question is yes. Wendell's surprisingly agile and loves to dance. What's more, I'm going to relieve him at the refreshment table for that go-around on the dance floor. You know, Miss Clark, Wendell has a devilish sense of humor and enjoys a good time. When he wants, he can be the life of the party. Fact is, he's going to be tickled pink. One thing I need to inform you, you'd better hang on because he can two-step with the best of them."

The music ending, Tyler's gallantry greeted them, "I would feel remiss if I didn't compliment the both of you for your dancing skills. I must admit, the more I watch, the more I realize how all the hired men on this wagon train are exceptional dancers. Tell me, Mr. Stokes, is dancing a prerequisite for being employed by you?"

"Most assuredly." Cliff laughed.

Tyler shifted his attention to Stephanie. "You are the belle-of-the-ball. I'm hoping the next dance is mine?"

A twinkle jumped into Cliff's eyes. "Miss Clark just informed me the next dance is reserved for Wendell." He smiled at Tyler. "As you said earlier, patience is a virtue, and when someone escorts the belle-of-the-ball to a hoedown, even escorts are often forced to wait. Regarding a prerequisite, I'm sure you understand why I can't allow my men to go stale."

Recovering quickly, Tyler agreed, "Of course." Smiling at Stephanie, he said, "How thoughtful of you, Stephanie. And you're right, Mr. Stokes, patience does reward those who are willing to wait—as frustrating as it might be."

Honoring Tyler with a curtsy, Stephanie's words soothed his disappointment. "When the music stops, the next dance will be ours."

Guiding Stephanie around the long line to the side of the refreshment table, Cliff elbowed Wendell aside, giving an order. "Wendell, you're being relieved for the moment. Miss Clark has requested the next dance with you despite my protests."

Wendell's face lit up. Handing Cliff the ladle, he grinned like an old tomcat that had just fought off a younger suitor. With a spring in his step, he dragged her toward the moving bodies.

Seeing who was entering the dance circle, Stuart immediately began playing Wendell's favorite up tempo two-step music.

Stealing a glance at the crowded dance floor, Cliff enjoyed the scene. The dancers were now forming a circle around Stephanie and Wendell, clapping as they watched the couple promenading in an ever widening circle.

Cliff was pleased how everyone was having a fun time. Most of the folks standing in line for refreshments joined in with the clapping. The song went on for some time. It was obvious Stuart was making sure Wendell got his money's worth. Finally the music ended, Stuart announcing it was break time. Cliff fought against laughing out loud. It appeared Tyler would have to demonstrate greater patience by waiting until the music started again. He checked his watch, surprised to see the big hand settling on the ten o'clock number. The night was slipping away. Yes, sir, there would be no early start on the trail tomorrow morning. It was time to unwind, a time for some fun. Observing the look on Wendell's face as he escorted Stephanie back to the table, gave Cliff a special feeling of satisfaction.

Stephanie's voice gushed with enthusiasm, "Mr. Stokes, Tyler is right. Everyone working on this wagon train is an accomplished dancer!"

All laughed as they watched Scott Buchanan arrive.

Stephanie kept up the gaiety. "Scott, I've just received some dancing lessons from Mr. Bartholomew."

Buchanan liked what she said, indicating she hadn't been swept off her feet by Harden. His smile lit up the night as he responded. "I've seen Wendell do that before. And after he does, I want to go back to being a wallflower."

Though frustrated, Tyler grinned, adding to the banter, "I can understand after watching Wendell. Just so no one forgets I've reserved the next trip to the dance floor with Stephanie."

"Ah"—Scott chuckled—"you're learning about life out here on the trail." He shifted his look to Stephanie. "Perhaps I might be rewarded with a dance after Mr. Harden?" Out of the corners of his eyes, Scott saw Tyler's face tighten ever so slightly. Tempted, he refrained from expressing what he saw. There was no sense in rubbing salt into a wound. After all, the man had done him no ill will.

For the first time, Tyler wondered if there was a conspiracy.

Stuart arrived, receiving applause for his musical talent.

Stephanie's eyes widened as her mother and father approached. "My goodness," she exclaimed, "I haven't enjoyed myself this much in such a long time."

Adam added to his daughter's enthusiasm, "Your mother and I have observed your different dancing partners. We are wondering who's wearing you out the most. Is it Mr. Harden, Mr. Stokes, Mr. Buchanan, or could it be Mr. Bartholomew? Your mother and I have come to the same conclusion: it is none other than Mr. Bartholomew."

Wendell beamed from behind the table.

Stokes's laughter was contagious, everyone joining in.

Finishing his punch, Stuart mingled with the crowd. A half hour passed before Stuart began playing again. Reaching out, Tyler took Stephanie's hand, leading her away into the swaying circle of light, whispering into her ear, "Finally."

Giggling, she snuggled into him.

Stokes and Buchanan heard the sudden commotion at the same time, their eyes meeting. Voices, loud voices, were coming from the far end of the wagon train. Both moved quickly, Scott skirting around behind the gathering crowd, his boss moving directly toward the disturbance.

John Sexton stood between three women, his glare fixed on Wayne Bennett.

Wayne's voice slightly slurred, he complained, "Get out of the way, Sexton. You can't hog all the women on this wagon train."

Sexton held his ground, retorting, "You have no rights to some-one who's not interested in your advances."

Shouldering between several bystanders, Buchanan saw the bulge under Bennett's vest. Shifting over further, he made out the handle from a six-gun protruding from his belt beneath the vest, Bennett's hand creeping toward the bulge. Scott checked his boss's eyes. When it was time to make his presence known, his sudden move would be triggered by his boss's signal.

Cliff stepped forward from the crowd, his voice drawing Bennett's attention. "What seems to be the problem here?"

Angry, Bennett growled back, "Man's trying to stop a fellow from having a good time, is all."

Cliff could smell the whisky. "Wayne, you been drinking?"

"Maybe, but I can handle it. You and Sexton step aside, 'cause I'm going to have me a dance with one of them pretty fillies the man's been hogging for himself."

Cliff took a half-step forward.

Bennett stiffened, his hand brushing aside his jacket, his fingers wrapping around the gun handle.

The half-step his signal, Buchanan launched himself, chopping viciously onto Bennett's gun hand, his right shoulder driving into the small of Bennett's back, his forward momentum slamming both to the ground.

Bennett's gun spun loose, Cliff sweeping the six-shooter away with his foot, his weight pinning Bennett's chest. He eyed Scott. "You ready?"

"Ready!"

Stokes heaved upward, his strength unbelievable, Buchanan keeping Bennett's arms pinned behind him. All three standing, Cliff's voice lashed out, "You got two choices, Wayne. We can hogtie you for the night and find that whisky you been drinking, or you can cooperate now and show me where you got it stashed. That way you'll get it back when you reach your final destination. Either way you're going to cooperate. I suggest you choose the second, but one thing's for sure, you ain't going to ruin tonight's fun. Now which is it?"

Buchanan could feel Bennett's muscles going limp; the realization of his situation was setting in, Bennett's voice reflecting his mistake. "I reckon I just made a fool of myself, didn't I?"

Liking what the man said, Cliff encouraged him, "Yeah, I reckon you did, which is why I have a rule against alcohol. It can make a man downright foolish. Why don't you go ahead and apologize to the women folk and Mr. Sexton. That way we can forget this happened, how about it?"

Bennett nodded, looking at Sexton, then at the three women, his voice contrite, "I'm sure enough sorry. I wish I'd listened to the wagon boss the first time."

Sexton nodded, accepting the apology, "That's good enough for me. As far as I'm concerned, this never happened."

Pleased, Cliff offered a solution. "I'll tell you what Wayne, just to make sure we'll keep your gun and give it back to you in the morning. Now, if you'll show me where that whisky is, I'll store it into safekeeping until tomorrow." Shifting his stare, he saw Santana watching him. "Wes, go ask our cook to brew up a pot of black coffee fit for roof tar. We're going to sober Wayne up so he can enjoy the rest of the party. As for the rest of you folks, we got a couple of hours of high stepping music left, and if my ears aren't deceiving me, I hear the music starting up again. Let's everyone get back to some dancing."

As Bennett started to turn away, one of the redheaded gals with Sexton stepped forward. Touching his arm, she said, "Once you finish with the wagon boss and have some coffee, if you escort me over to the dancers, we'll have that dance you want."

Bennett's face beamed, his night no longer a disaster.

Watching the crowd break up, Stephanie waited for Buchanan, stepping in front of him. "Scott Buchanan, it's your turn."

Grabbing Stephanie's hand, Scott led her toward the center of the moving dancers.

Resting her head on Scott's shoulder, her mouth near his ear, she congratulated him. "You're a brave man, Scott Buchanan."

Aware Tyler Harden was staring at them, Scott turned her toward the far side of the dance floor. Considering her statement, he suggested, "Brave or foolish, I'm not sure which. Besides, it's part of my job."

"Do you like that part of the job?"

Scott laughed. "If it turns out okay."

"You seem to be good at it."

"You don't always get the cards you want. At times, the people business can be tough."

"So then you act on instinct."

"Yes and no."

"That's a little confusing?"

"Let me explain it this way… the wagon boss and I use body language."

Studying his face, Stephanie probed, "So you knew when to act?"

"This time I did."

Suddenly Stephanie felt like finding out more. "Tell me, Scott, do you consider yourself a good judge of human character?"

"Somewhat."

"You're a tough man to get a straight answer from. I'm thinking if you were educated you'd make a good lawyer. But since you did say somewhat, I'm curious about someone. What do you think about Tyler Harden's character?"

What a loaded question, Scott thought. He gave careful consideration to his response. Why was she asking him about Tyler? For him, such a question had red flags flying all over the ridge top. It would seem Stephanie's question had ulterior motives. Was she playing a game with him, trying to see how he responded by showing his serious side, maybe his jealous side? Right now he needed a diplomatic answer. Another thing, it wasn't good to speak badly about someone. Saying something negative regarding someone always made the person who said it look bad. He had better turn this conversation around and fast. It would be better to let Stephanie reveal her own thoughts about the man. Satisfied with his thinking, Buchanan responded with a suggestion. "He seems interested in you."

"That's not what I asked you."

Continuing to dodge, he asked her, "Do you like him?"

Not wanting to give in so easily, Stephanie kept her voice light, "You first."

"Why are you asking me?"

"Because of so much danger out here, you seem to be an excellent judge of character. So out here in the wilderness, I'm curious. What do you think about him?"

Conceding to her persistence, Buchanan remained tactful. "It's tough to tell. From what I know about the man, he's successful, quite polished, not forgetting he's very smart. I reckon in high society, Tyler will do quite well. I think a better way to judge someone is in their proper element. Most women would want a man where they intend to settle down. Tell me, don't you?"

Studying Scott's expression, Stephanie realized he was an artist at not being pinned down. Yet, he had answered her and now it was only fair to answer him. "Yes, I like him."

Scott nodded. "You know, Stephanie, certain things are only revealed over periods of time. The same is true about a person's character. We get impatient. It's better to go slow when judging others. More than once, I started out not liking someone but ended up in a strong friendship. So I avoid quick judgments. Over the years, I've seen how time can reveal more than first impressions ever will. Making snap judgments can be embarrassing and I don't like being embarrassed. I'd much rather say good things about a person. If they deserve a bad reputation, let them do it in front of others, that way they've earned their reputation." He paused, intent on wrapping up this give-and-take conversation. "I think it is better that way. Keeps someone from becoming a gossip."

Stephanie knew Buchanan had again skillfully maneuvered around her questions. To his credit, what he said was profound. Good for him, she thought, her words complimentary, "I like the way you reason, Scott Buchanan. You are a man of character."

"So," Scott chided, "even a wild man can have character."

Stephanie smiled, teasing back, "Only time will tell."

Both laughed as the music ended, Scott escorting Stephanie toward the refreshment table, she kept her hand in his.

A sudden question invaded Stephanie's curiosity about the wagon scout, she asked, "Please don't misunderstand what I'm about to ask you. I'm really not prying into your personal life. I am curious relating to your occupation. Have you ever seriously thought about getting married?"

Buchanan's eyebrows knit together in surprise. "Of course I've considered it."

"And?"

Almost ready to flirt, he didn't. The look in her face told him she was serious. He reckoned he'd better answer her the way he was asked. "The truth is, Stephanie, I don't know."

Keeping her eyes on him, Stephanie hoped for a further explanation.

Seeing she expected more, Scott accommodated her. "You know, Stephanie, out here I'm in my own element. Now in high society, that Harden fellow would be quite the man." Mischief suddenly slipped into his voice. "Here's another thing you probably already know. You'd be a temptation to any man... anywhere... anytime."

"But," she teased back, "not to you?"

"I think I just said... any man! But I'm also a realist. You're heading to the west coast to settle in a cultivated way of life. I wouldn't be much good among those types of folks."

"If you don't mind me asking, why not?"

"Because I've spent some time among such folks. Don't misunderstand me, they're not bad people, but what they talk about and the things they get caught up in... I just wouldn't fit in. Like I said, out here I'm in my element."

Needing a response, Stephanie couldn't think of one.

Buchanan rescued her. "If I thought for one minute I could get your father and mother all riled up without causing any of them a heart attack, I surely would."

Intrigued, not sure what he meant, she asked him, "And just what do you mean, Scott Buchanan?"

Pushing her toward the waiting group, devilishness showing in his eyes, he whispered in her ear, "Because I'd propose to you right now. Can you imagine the shock to your parents if you said yes?"

Delighted, Stephanie enjoyed the playful exchange. "Can you imagine the shock to you if I said yes?"

Rolling his eyes, a laugh was Scott's response.

Stephanie kept the teasing going, "Was that an almost... proposal?"

"I think I'm in deep water."

"Right now you're treading water," Stephanie laughed. "As for Tyler, I do like him a lot, but I alsos appreciate your advice about time. Thank you for such wisdom."

Recovered, Scott found himself enjoying the banter. "Here's the real question, where do you want to live? I already know, but do you?"

Not answering, Stephanie squeezed his hand. She was sure her squeeze would convey affection as they worked their way back to the refreshment table. She noticed her parents standing next to Tyler Harden. More and more her parents seemed to enjoy Tyler's company. It seemed he had gained her parents' approval as a potential suitor. One thing she was sure of, Scott Buchanan would never be their choice.

LEFT-HANDED GUN

T he landscape dripping wet from a heavy ground fog, Cliff stared at the sputtering fire. Hunching over, cheeks puffed out, he blew the smoldering coals into life, the damp twigs and broken branches hissing, the flames finally gaining advantage thanks to the newly added dry kindling. Satisfied, he stood. Except for Stuart and Wendell, along with his two scouts preparing to ride out, the camp had yet to come to life. Most of the folks were still sleeping soundly from the evening of dancing. Cliff spoke softly, not wanting to disturb the quiet. "Scott, I'm shifting you across the river so we can keep an eye on them strange cowboys, or whatever they are. Wes, you're going to scout this side of the river. I want you to report back to the wagon train sometime between two and three in the afternoon. If you're wondering why, it's because we got a few wagons needing attention, and since the good Lord blessed you with skillful hands, I'm going to use your wagon repairing talents. Right now the weather's holding, but yesterday I noticed dark storm clouds to the north. Saw some in the western sky as well. Noticed a shift in the breeze too, so whatever's in those clouds is heading our way. I figure to head for higher ground and get some repair work done. The upper plateau has some rocky ground, and since I don't like working in mud, we're heading for hard surface. If it rains, we'll be high and dry. Even better, no chance of getting bogged down. We got about a week before we hit a small settlement. Once there, we'll pick us up a few needed supplies. In the meantime, I aim for us to avoid getting our wagons stuck in mud. Scott, before you two split up, make sure you point out the upper plateau to Wes. I want him to know where to meet the wagons. That sums up what I have planned. If you two have anything to add, I'm all ears."

Buchanan answered, agreeing, "Nope, nothing complicated about what you said. As soon as Wendell feeds our faces, we'll ride out." Turning, he suggested, "Wes, since it will be a couple of minutes before the chow is cooked, why don't you get your gear and horse ready."

With a nod of his head, Wes departed.

Wendell placed the iron brackets on both sides of the fire, hanging a large pot over the now hot coals. Satisfied, he found a spot for the coffeepot.

Studying his cook, Cliff was careful to avoid conversation. Wendell never spoke until food was ready, unless of course he became aggravated. If he was to speak at all, Wendell struck up a private conversation with himself, often mumbling something needed doing, at best brief and to the point. God forbid a man tried to use Wendell's mumbling as a reason to talk. Another thing about Wendell, it was sacrilegious to talk while eating. Since he was the last to eat, it didn't pay to engage him in conversation. Besides, Wendell wouldn't talk anyway.

Finished eating, Wes broke the silence, "One of the benefits of scouting is not doing chores before eating Wendell's food in the morning."

"In other words," Buchanan contributed, "you're spoiled."

"Something along those lines."

The rest of the camp stirring to life, Cliff eyed his scouts. Now that their hunger was satisfied, he wondered if anything new had popped into their brains. "You two think of anything I should know before you ride out?"

Buchanan shook his head no, heading for his horse. Grabbing the pommel, he hesitated, grunting at his partner, "Come on, Wes, it's time to earn your breakfast, no freeloading here." Rising into the saddle, he waited until Wes was aboard his horse. Pat's death still fresh in his mind, he turned Buddy in the direction the wagons had already traveled before swinging wide, still paralleling the trail. Recalling ambush attacks from his old army days, such memories had a way of making a man pay attention to self-preservation. Hell, he thought, life is full of problems, not excluding danger. After all, solving problems was part of life. A man won't have things going his way all the time without the bad happening on occasion. Having some luck also helped.

It was time to instruct Wes. Reining Buddy to a standstill, Scott waited until Wes came alongside. "When we reach where I'll cross over, I'm going to show you from a distance where the boss plans on stopping. After I do, you keep riding until you arrive. If you take your time, it should take most of the morning, and I want you to make sure it takes you all morning. Out here being in a hurry isn't healthy, matter of fact, downright dangerous. A man just doesn't see what he should when he's hurrying. Wes, do you understand what I'm saying?"

"Loud and clear, chief scout."

"Good." For a moment, Buchanan stopped being serious. "Since you know where you're going, you shouldn't need to keep peeking at that pocket watch you can't get along without. In other words, you'll arrive on time by relying on your frontiersman skills. A man feels a lot better out here using his sixth sense, not forgetting you should learn how to use the sun's position to tell you what your rate of travel is." Laughing at his cleverness, Scott congratulated himself by adding, "I've taken all the worry out of your decision making, can't make it much easier for you."

Respectful, Wes changed the subject, "If trouble happens, our signal the same?"

"Yep, no reason to change it, two shots, three seconds, two shots, three seconds, and two more shots. You remember why our signal is different?"

"So we know it's not coming from some stranger using the standard signal, three shots, three times, with two pauses in between."

"You got it, time's wasting, follow me."

Hearing the bird's singing heralding the morning always quickened Buchanan's spirit. More and more the land was appearing withered from lack of rain. Pockets of brown Cow Vetch gave off rattling sounds, the dry stems banging against the brittle stalks caused by the steady breeze. The once green grass was now yellowing in color, waving stiffly back and forth, pushed by a breeze growing stronger by the hour. The smell of rain was in the air. Climbing higher, the two rode through a series of rolling slopes, Scott reining in his horse. Half turned in the saddle, he pointed as he spoke, "See that yonder gap between them identical hills?"

Wanting to make sure he was seeing the same, Wes made sure, asking, "You mean the two hills covered by a bluish haze near the top?"

"Yep, the base of those hills is your final destination."

"I was wondering," Wes asked, "what's so different up there to make Mr. Stokes want to take the wagons so far out of the way? Isn't there hard ground closer?"

"Lots of hard ground up there, is why. Another thing, after the wagons needing fixing are finished, the wagon train can move down the far side while cutting off a few miles."

Squinting at the far hills, Wes pursued, "How far away are those hills?"

"I really don't know. If you push hard, you'll get there when the sun is a little after eleven o'clock in the sky, which I don't want you to do. In other words, if you arrive before noon you traveled too fast. Hell, Cliff won't arrive with the wagons till later. Regardless, make sure you approach from the right and slightly above the gap between them hills."

"You're saying the hill over to the right at the north end?"

"Exactly, Wes, don't ride directly into the gap. It's an ideal location for someone lying in wait." Shaking his finger at Wes, Scott voiced a stern warning, "You do like I'm telling you 'cause we don't want any more tragedies on this trip."

Wes gave him the thumbs up, assuring him, "I ain't planning on adorning anyone's lodge pole, much less having some bandits tearing through my saddlebags. Of that you can rest assured."

"Good answer."

"Any water up there?"

"There are springs at the top producing seepage working down the slopes on the far side. It is not unusual for some Indian hunting party to be camped there, which is why I want you to come in from above at the north end. If by chance you see some horse tracks, you can investigate from on high. Wes, if you become suspicious ride back and warn Cliff. If not, pick a vantage point, relax, and wait for the wagons to show up."

"Any best way my horse can climb reaching the upper gap?"

"Not really, same rolling terrain we just rode through. If I recall, there should be some game paths to follow 'cause there's proper bedding locations up there. Game animals leave trails leading toward water, but so do hunters, the type you want to avoid. When you get fairly close, like I said, swing wide and take your time. If you jump any deer, most likely ain't no humans present. Now, Wes, I've got to get going. If you have no more questions, I'll see you back at the wagon train."

"Asked all I could think of."

Turning Buddy, Buchanan headed for the river.

An hour later, close enough to hear human talk, the left-handed gunman and his companion watched the wagons departing off the main trail, winding their way for higher ground. Raymond Floyd wondered why he didn't see the wagon scouts. He looked at the man sitting on his horse next to him, expressing his concern, "I'm not seeing them wagon scouts."

As if he calculated every word's meaning like he didn't hear, Floyd's dark bearded companion had a habit of never rushing to speak. When he did speak, Floyd appreciated whatever he had to say was worth hearing. Of all the men he rode with, other than the ramrod himself, he respected the dark-bearded man the most. The man was unafraid with a cold way about him. A man had to respect such a person.

Finally the dark-bearded one spoke. "We've seen all we need to know, seems like they're planning on heading for them faraway hills with some work to do. Even better, they're stopping early." Grinning, he said, "Busy people don't pay much attention, easy to get the jump on. We better get back to camp and inform Burke. It's his call. As for those scouts, once the wagons stop them scouts should report back early. If they do, they'll be just as surprised as the rest of them travelers. Let's go."

Raymond nodded in agreement. "He ain't boss for nothing, sure knows how to connive better than any man I ever met. Still, I'd like to know where those scouts are. Hell, Burke will ask us, he wants to know everything. Be a good idea to have some answers ready."

The bearded man thought a minute before rejecting his partner's worry. "Get over it. Some things are impossible to know. We can tell the boss and let him decide."

The left-handed gun dropped his concerns. Wheeling their horses around, they headed back for the river, splashing across.

Studying the tracks left by the strange riders, Buchanan frowned at what he saw. Why were there only six horses? What had happened to the other two? Alert, he turned Buddy north, backtracking. Once he discovered their night camp, he might uncover some clues as to what happened to the missing riders. A half hour later, he found where they'd spent the night, the horse tracks telling him what he needed to know. Two riders had separated from the group riding in the direction of the river. If he were a betting man, he suspicioned they were spying on the wagon train.

Buddy's ears perked, his body becoming taunt. Alerted, Buchanan strained to hear, at first detecting nothing. Seconds later, he heard the faints sounds from horses coming his way. Easing Buddy around, they melted into a grove of cottonwoods. Leaning over, he clamped his hand over the gelding's muzzle.

Seconds later, two riders appeared. Not speaking, they passed within a horse length distance from the cottonwoods. Both riders never looked left or right, disappearing from sight.

Buchanan remembered the left-handed gun. The other fellow had a look about him—a mean look. Both horses were dripping wet from crossing the river. The more important question was—why? What other reason but to check on the wagons, he guessed. Sure the riders were gone, he removed his hand from Buddy's muzzle, rubbing his horse's neck in appreciation for the early warning. Except with the morning being so still and thanks to Buddy's ears, they would have ridden right up on him. Leaving the shelter of the trees, a question nagged at him. Why had they changed their pattern? He wondered if last night's music attracted their curiosity. A more troubling thought crossed his mind. Were they about to make a move against the wagons? He gave his premonition serious consideration as he turned Buddy into the horse tracks left by the riders. The only way to know was to stay close in case they were up to no good. With a fresh set of tracks to follow, trailing would be easy.

Deciding they could use some fresh provisions, Burke tossed the reused bitter coffee grinds to the ground with disgust. Drinking coffee made from old grounds left a bad taste in one's mouth. Considering last night's music coming from the wagon train, until they reached a settlement, the only place he could think of fresh anything was from the wagon train. Last night's music sounds indicated the wagons weren't lacking. Hell, he thought, it was tough throwing a shindig without plenty of provisions. His mood foul, he watched the bearded one and the gunslinger riding in. Setting down on a rock, he waited for them to dismount.

Eyeing Burke, the bearded one spoke first, "Seems like their wagons need some repairing so their ramrod is moving them to higher ground."

"Why higher ground?" Burke growled. "Why not work on them where they are?"

"Their ramrod thinks bad weather's coming. I guess it's better up there."

His left arm draped over his left leg, right hand on his hip, Burke digested the information while meditating out loud, "Which means they will be preoccupied." He looked at both men, his mind already planning ahead. "I think their ramrod's right, the wind's picking up with lots of dampness in it. How about you, Raymond, you have anything to add?"

"Just this, their wagon scouts must have ridden out at first light because we never saw them. We haven't the slightest idea where they are."

Mulling over the lefty's concern, Burke rubbed his two-day old whiskers while considering the information. Eyeing the lefty, whose instincts he respected, Burke conceded their absence might be a problem, saying as much, "Not knowing where they are could cause us some trouble."

Raymond responded, "Zack doesn't think so."

Burke focused on Raymond's partner, asking, "Why so, Zack?"

"I'm figuring they'll check in early. Most likely they'll have scouted out what they need to know. Besides, their boss told his foreman he needs one of those scouts repairing skills, which means at the most, only one will stay out. Since they're stopping so early, I'm betting both will check in early."

Nodding thoughtfully, Burke took his hat off, spinning it around before placing it back on his head. He looked up at both, asking, "How many able-bodied men do we have to deal with?"

Zack didn't hesitate. "At the most, I figured a dozen."

"How about you, Raymond, you agree?"

"Considering how the rest have women and children, Zack makes sense."

Digesting the information, Burke reflected, "We could sure use some fresh provisions and with everyone busy working on wagons, I can't think of a better time to sneak up on them." Knowing greed appealed to his men, he included stealing as a motivator. "After we ransack them for coffee and food, no telling how many valuables we'll find. Folks relocating to a new life bring lots of jewelry and whatever money they own with them. Besides, with all that promenading last night, most likely they'll be half numb. Let's gather everyone around for a mutual agreement decision. Zack, go round the men up."

Watching the approaching wagons, Wes marveled at Buchanan's calculations. The man was uncanny. Who knows, maybe someday he'd be as good.

Seeing Wes waiting, Cliff complimented him, "Wes, you did good, real good."

Wes grinned, wanting to take all the credit, his honesty keeping him from doing it. "Yeah, but I have to admit, Scott told me how to time you, not to mention where you'd be."

"This means you followed instructions. Out here on the trail, doing what a man is supposed to do means you can turn your back and know it's covered. You're to be commended. As soon as I get the wagons circled up, I'll lay out your work responsibilities. For starters, I want you to block up the rear of the chuck wagon and look over that left rear axle. While you're at it, inspect the wheel rim. Something's causing that wheel a slight wobble. Not bad yet, but slightly more pronounced every day."

Despite the compliments from his boss, Wes scolded himself for not noticing the wobble.

Keeping the wagons in repair was part of his job assignment. Just like Buchanan, the wagon boss noticed everything, no details escaping his keen eyesight. Shaking his head in frustration for not seeing what they did, he rationalized, coming up with a convenient excuse. Hadn't he been distracted by his latest scouting assignment? Despite the answer being yes, wanting another excuse, he came up with one. He blamed the blond gal in the fifth wagon. What the heck, he reasoned. Didn't women have a way of distracting a man? He came up with a third excuse. He wasn't the wagon boss, just a worker following orders. Realizing he was pushing the envelope by coming up with one lame excuse after another, he stopped. The truth was he should have seen that wheel's wobble before anyone. It should have been him informing the boss, not the other way around. Being on top of things brought respect. Unfortunately, it was the boss who noticed the problem. What was done was done. The next time he'd do better. In the meantime, it was time to go to work.

Looking for potential problems, Cliff made the rounds, over-seeing inspections on every wagon. Except for the chuck wagon, all needed repairs were minor. Knowing which wagon parts take a pounding on the trail helped avoid more serious delays. Conestoga wagons were built tough, rarely breaking down. Another advantage was how most of the men folk were handy, the worksite now filled with the sounds from busy workers.

Inspecting the last wagon, Cliff was bent over when he felt the barrel from a six-shooter jammed into his back, the voice behind the gun deadly. "Go for your gun and you're a dead man."

Cliff felt his gun being lifted; his arms pulled back, his wrists lashed tightly behind him. Allowed to turn, he grimaced. All work had stopped, guns pointing at everyone. The mystery riders had quietly slipped in getting the jump on everyone, lashing each man to his own wagon. He counted seven men, two of them herding the womenfolk to the center of the circled wagons. Disturbed for being so preoccupied without paying attention to his surroundings, Cliff boiled with angry frustration.

The man with the mutton-chopped sideburns spoke, his booming voice menacing, "You folks cooperate, no one gets hurt. You try something stupid. We'll take us as many women as we have men. In other words, no man will be without. Since we're going to take all the supplies we need anyway, if you care about your women, you'll do what you're told."

One of the men eyed Stephanie. "Say, boss, how about one exception for the trail?"

Keeping herself from cringing, Stephanie stared back defiantly. If she could get her hands on a gun, she would shoot him dead.

The mutton-chopped man with sideburns growled at the speaker, "That's up to them, 'cause they sure enough got a passel of pretty gals. Fact is, better than most wagon trains." Grinning, he purposely eyed the three gals huddled together with different colored hair, seeing concern on the faces of the captured men as he eyed their women. "Remember what I said, you folks don't cause trouble and your womenfolk are safe. In other words, it's up to you." He pointed his finger at two of his nearest men, giving orders, "You two check yonder chuck wagon and get what's needed. After you do, go through every wagon. Raymond, you stay here and keep watch with me. Sal, you and Carlos cut out some extra horses. We're going to need them."

Stephanie eyed her father's fearful expression. Where was Scott Buchanan? Had these outlaws also gotten the jump on him?

Stokes eyed his cook, their eyes meeting, their thoughts the same. Both Wendell and Stuart knew he had assigned Buchanan to watch these strange riders. If they hadn't captured him, he had no doubt his chief scout was nearby. Anticipating he was, the question was, what could he do to help?

Testing the rope, Stokes grimaced. He was tied tight, real tight. If he couldn't loosen the rope soon, his hands would be numb, leaving him only the use of his brain. The brutal answer to his question about helping was obvious, he couldn't physically. Not prone to give up, he tried to think of something. Maybe when the time was right he could create a diversion with his mouth. He had better not be obvious, if he was, it would only alert these thugs.

Nestled against a scrubby bush on higher ground, Buchanan peered down, surprised how the riders had so easily gotten the jump on everyone. At first critical, he changed his thinking. After all, the Indian scare no longer being a primary concern, Cliff hadn't needed guards. With every man being busy and no guards out, their leader had picked the perfect time. Obviously, the leader was cunning and dangerous, not someone to underestimate. Here, slightly above and well hidden in the weeds, Buchanan's mind raced, needing a plan. He squinted at the sky, contemplating what to do. Based on the sun's position, he reckoned at least five hours of good daylight remained before the sun nudged below the horizon.

Buchanan calculated possible advantages regarding the present. One reason to act now was preoccupation. Two of the men were busy going through the strung out wagons, another two cutting out horses. A third man was among the missing, probably guarding the outlaw's horses. Scott gave more thought to the missing man. Right now the man not being present reduced the odds in a gunfight. If he waited too long, the man would probably show up. Since the missing fellow was probably assigned to watch the horses, most likely he was not as dangerous as the remaining thugs. He could be dealt with later. That left four on the lookout for trouble. Scott had no illusions. The remaining four were no doubt the most dangerous. Right now the left-handed gun stood beside their leader. If Scott shot from here and took out the lefty, then the boss, the rest would run for it. At least he hoped so. Of course, if they remained, there was a possible hostage situation.

A tall fellow walked in the direction of Stephanie. Stopping, he eyed her with lust in his eyes.

Squinting, Scott studied the man who had ridden past him with the gunfighter, changing his mind. The man looked like he relished a shootout, meanness written all over his face. Such a ruthless character wouldn't hesitate to inflict harm on the wagon folks. Scott's gaze settled on the bearded one. If he had to shoot three men, the bearded fellow was next. Sure he had chosen the right targets; all he needed now was a plan. There was one other option. He could wait until dark. If he waited, he could slip in under the cover of darkness. Scott rejected waiting. In another hour, the rest of the scoundrels would no longer be busy. His best opportunity for surprise was to take advantage while so many were preoccupied.

Another worry crossed Scott's mind as he watched the tall one leering at Stephanie. If he waited too long, despite what the ringleader said, the women might get molested. If that happened, the odds would become more complicated, a lot more complicated. From up here, the ringleader and the gunfighter were within easy rifle range, but again, a potential hostage situation.

The tall fellow turned, walking away.

Relieved, Scott's mind considered another idea. He needed an edge besides himself. Eyeing each wagon, he considered possible help. If successfully sneaking under one of those wagons from whomever he chose, Scott reckoned he could free up some help, the only question remaining, which men? He needed at least two skilled shooters who were brave and proficient in a gunfight. He ruled out his boss and the foreman, they were too close to the ringleader. Checking the wagons, Scott focused on the two men tied to the sixth wagon. Adam and Seth Harris claimed to be handy with a gun, both having volunteered against the Kiowa threat. As long as the thieves were busy, freeing Seth and Adam would cut the odds in half. Even better, he wouldn't be the lone target. Hell, there were only eight thieves, one not present. Using the element of surprise along with additional help, Scott's odds improved dramatically. Getting close wasn't going to be easy, but doable. If Scott was discovered before freeing anyone, his life would be cut short. Not an encouraging thought, he grimaced.

The lefty gunfighter was now talking with the tall fellow before returning to the boss man.

Buchanan didn't doubt the lefty gunslinger would enjoy pumping some lead into him. His decision left him with one last problem. What was the best way to slip down and arm his help? He'd have to use his rifle while giving both men his six-shooters. Fortunately, Scott had an extra pistol stored in his saddlebag. Satisfied with his decision, he paused, wondering if there was something he hadn't given proper consideration? With no other possibilities coming to mind, if he was going to take advantage while the scoundrels were busy, now was the time. Once the men ceased rummaging through the sixth wagon and left, he needed to be close enough to initiate his plan.

Slithering around, Buchanan headed back for his horse. Pulling the extra revolver from the saddlebag, he loaded the cylinder. Finished, Scott shoved the gun barrel under the back of his belt. Pulling out his rifle, he cautioned himself against making noise as he eased open the action. Satisfied, he rechecked his own pistol, holstering his gun. Leaving Buddy, he neared the scrubby bush stretching out full length. Hat off, he raised himself one click at a time, eyeballing the lefty shooter and his boss. Both men were exactly where they were before, chatting away as they watched the two men cutting out horses. Pleased their attention was drawn in the opposite direction, Scott shifted his eyes, pleased at what he saw.

The two men who had been rummaging through the wagons were now heading toward the sixth wagon, the one where his chosen help was.

Casting one last look at ringleader and gunslinger, both still facing away, Scott started down. Cradling the rifle in the crook of his right arm against scrapping against stones, he pushed through the brittle grass, noisier than normal thanks to the dry conditions. He cringed how much noise he was making. Nearing the wagon, he hugged the ground. Listening intently, he detected murmuring voices fading away. His greatest danger now was avoiding detection caused by sudden movement. Ever so slowly, lifting his head high enough to see, Scott froze. One of the men assigned to search the wagons was behind the seventh wagon watching his rummaging companion. No doubt he was making sure he wasn't going to miss getting his share of any loot being pocketed.

Buchanan stole one last look in the direction of the boss man and along with the gunman, stiffening. Both were now looking Scott's way. If they started toward him, there was no choice but to come up shooting. It seemed like forever before they looked away, his breath expelling with a hiss, Scott's hand moving away from the rifle trigger. Riveting his attention over at the seventh wagon, he watched the one man climb out, both hands empty, the two departing for the next wagon. It was time to attract help without being seen. Fingers digging in the soil, Scott snaked his way forward, positioning where he'd be seen by his chosen helpers.

For a split second, recognition flooded Seth and Adam, quickly disappearing. Outwardly calm, they kept their body language relaxed, their expressions passive.

Encouraged by their composure, Buchanan raised a finger to his lips. Working backward, he rolled under the wagon, crawling over to the men's legs. Scott matched the sound of his voice with the breeze stirring the canvas, his voice barely a hiss. "Don't look down, just listen. I'm going to cut you two loose. When I do, let me know which hand you want a gun in by wiggling your gun hand. As soon as I know, I'll stick a loaded gun in it. Just so you know, both guns are loaded for business. Before I do, I need to know one thing. Are you two up to this? Clench both fists if you are."

Both clenched their fists.

"Good. Don't go doing anything rash until I take action. I'm going to come up shooting so we need to be on the same page. Once I come out from under this wagon, I'm taking aim on that left-handed gun and his boss man, one of you shoot the black-bearded tough leaning against the wagon wheel. He's a bad one, hangs out with the lefty. The fellow with the pockmarked face by the outer edge has to be taken out. Adam, you're to the right, you gun-down the bearded fellow. Seth, you shoot the one by the outer edge. After you shoot your men, both of you help me with my targets. Also, make sure you shoot whoever I miss. If you don't, we'll all be dead. What's more, don't stop shooting until no one's left standing. These are bad hombres with no conscience, so don't go soft 'cause we're only going to have one chance. Remember, shoot to kill until they're all down, no exceptions. I'm not interested in capturing anyone, just freeing our people while staying alive. You two understand what I've said?"

Two thumbs went up.

"Good. Now spread your wrists as much as possible so I can free your hands without cutting any flesh. Once you're free, let me know when you have feeling by wiggling your gun hand."

Opening his palm wide, Adam wiggled his gun hand first. Handle up, Scott slipped the six-shooter into the hand. Waiting for Seth, he cast an eye at the gunfighter, then his boss, no longer standing side by side. Not good, he groaned under his breath. Better for them to be together, made for easier shooting. Scott shifted his stare to the dark-bearded fellow leaning against the wheel. He was staring at the women with lust in his eyes. Good, Scott thought, keep looking 'cause it's going to get you into a heap of deadly trouble.

Sudden motion caught Scott's attention, Seth now wiggling his left hand, opening his fingers wide. He eased the pistol into Seth's hand, whispering to both, "Locked and loaded—get ready. Like I said, as soon as I stand I'll be blazing away, you do the same. And remember, don't let up. I want one more thumbs up so I know when you're ready."

Again, both thumbs went up.

Easing his rifle into the crook of his arm, Buchanan eased over to the edge of the wagon, stealing a glance at his targets. All three were distracted in different directions. Hesitating for a second, he located the man with the pock-marked face. Marking the gunman's position to memory, he stole a last look at his help. Both men had their fingers wrapped around the pistol grips, their thumbs on the hammers. Seth's hand was gripping too tightly, his knuckles showing white, not relaxed as he ought to be. Too late now, Scott thought, telling himself to forget the white knuckles. It was time to focus on his first target, the one most likely to put a bullet into him—the lefty fellow.

His heart pounding, Buchanan locked his stare onto the gunslinger. Shaking the tenseness out of his muscles, he wanted his body to come up smooth and deliberate, his survival depending on fluid accuracy along with surprise. Knowing all hell was about to break loose, he eased closer to the wagon's edge. Dragging in one last deep breath, Scott let half out, his fingertip touching the trigger, his thumb ready to cock the rifle's hammer.

Scott stole one last peek, satisfied; he rolled out into the bright sunlight, surging up.

The ominous double-click coming from a cocked hammer being armed, all heads swung toward Buchanan.

Startled, the gunman's left hand dove for his gun, the six-shooter coming up in a blur, the deafening roar from his colt blending in with the booming sound from a rifle. Something punched into the lefty's chest, the breath going out of him. Pushed back, again something thumped his torso, followed by another booming shot, his body caving backward, his revolver spilling away from a limp hand without strength.

Buchanan felt his shoulder burn, his rifle thundering again, hearing shots coming from Seth and Adam.

Slammed backward to the ground, the mutton-chopped side-burns leader almost cleared leather when he died, his chest spurting bright red blood with each pump of his heart. Down, his blood no longer squirted.

Agile, the dark-bearded man almost made it behind the wagon. Hit by bullets, he spun around. Slumping, he sagged backward with a groan, his fingers leaving red claw-marks on the wagon's sideboard as he flopped against the wheel.

The potbellied man dropped to one knee, desperate, his shooting awry, hitting nothing. Torn by bullets, he crumbled into a heap, a gurgling sound coming from his throat.

Running, the lean man with the pockmarked face died from two slugs exiting his chest.

Spinning around, Scott saw the two men rummaging through the wagons dashing into the thicket. Pivoting, his rifle swinging at their running bodies, he sent a quick shot their way, their bobbing heads disappearing from sight.

Acrid smoke hung in the air, the stink from gunpowder assailing nostrils.

The potbellied man stirred, trying to lift his gun. Two guns barked, bullets tearing into the dying man.

Jacking open the action, Buchanan reloaded. Looking over at Seth and Adam, he gave a curt nod indicating a job well done.

Stokes felt his rope lashes coming off. For a second, he was at a loss for words. Wringing his hands to restore circulation, he stared at Buchanan, then at the dead bodies.

Buchanan moved away, working quickly. Keeping his eyes peeled in the direction of the departed looters just in case shooting erupted from the thicket, Wendell was freed next. Checking down the line, Scott saw Stuart's ropes were removed. Turning back, he approached Cliff, who was now barking out orders.

"Scott, you and Wes take Seth and Adam and go track them fugitives. Mitch, you and Santana unhook that dead ox killed by all that shooting and replace it with another. After you do, butcher up the dead one. We might as well have some fresh meat for the trail. Stuart, you and Wendell check out everyone and tend to anyone who's wounded. I'll get me some able-bodied men and drag them dead bodies where they can be buried."

Stephanie felt Tyler's arm around her shoulders, comforting her, his voice reassuring, "Relax, the shooting's over." He looked at her parents, concern in his voice. "You two okay, no one hurt?"

Both nodded, color not yet returning to her father's complexion.

Still shaken by the violence, Stephanie stared at the dead men, her voice agitated to a higher pitch, "How horrible, so savage!" She looked over at Mitch, eyes flashing, finally asking, "Why?"

A busy Mitch answered her, "Evil, is why."

Studying Mitch's grim face, Stephanie didn't ask again.

Still shocked by the unexpected violence, the wagon folks observed the men dragging dead bodies to be buried. Stephanie heard one of the men say it was a miracle none of them were wounded with so much shooting. How right he was, she thought, watching Stokes return.

"I want you folks to get back to what you were doing before this happened. I know it won't be easy, but staying busy helps. You can discuss everything while you work. My men are making sure none of them scoundrels will be doubling back. You folks got a lot to be thankful considering how none of us were hurt 'cept them bad guys. So let's get back to doing what we were before this ruckus happened." Taking a breath, Cliff squinted at the darkening sky, his voice urgent, "As for you ladies, let's plan on eating early. Those clouds are telling me we have some wet weather moving in." Seeing blood staining Scott's shoulder, Cliff asked, "You okay?"

"Nicked me is all."

"Wendell, bring the pot of water to a boil so we can bandage him up. I'm going over to try and get some identification before we bury them polecats." Suddenly pausing, he explained, "I knew you had to be close by. I was trying to think of something I could do, but they had me hogtied real tight. I felt pretty helpless. Thunder and tarnation, everything happened so fast!"

His eyes squinting, Scott's voice grim, "It had to happen that way. It was the left-handed gun who worried me most. I figured three against seven, along with the element of surprise evened the odds a bit. I thought about making my move after dark but couldn't afford to take chances with the womenfolk and all. If I waited, I worried they might use the women as hostages, or worse take liberties with them. I told Seth and Adam to kill everyone but us."

"Well, they sure enough did. How'd you know who to choose?"

Peeling his shirt off, Scott glanced at his shoulder while answering, "I remembered you telling me how those two volunteered before in case of Indian trouble. I also recalled you saying they were eager-beavers. Other than that, I didn't have much choice. I figured there was going to be a brief opportunity while those fellows were looting. If I didn't make my move before they finished, I didn't think the odds would improve. Like I said, I knew the left-handed shooter was bad news. The best way to get the edge on him was by surprise, same for their ramrod. Once he and the gunfighter cashed in, I was sure the rest would run for it."

Cliff nodded in agreement. "I'd say you figured it out pretty good. Glad you were right. I hate to admit this, but burying them no-accounts beats herding them on to the next settlement. I would have hated to keep an eye on those scoundrels while traveling."

Scott added, "Couldn't have said it better myself. They would have been scheming all the way. If they got free, there would have been hell to pay." He glanced back toward the rear wagons. "What about the three who got away?"

"Let them run for it. We have enough to do."

"You don't think they'll double back?"

"Not with their boss and top gunman dead, I don't."

Lightning split the sky, thunder rolled over the wagons, a breeze picking up, the dark cloudy storm not far away.

THE MORNING AFTER

The landscape still dripping from the heavy rains, Buchanan enjoyed the broken clouds whisking in a southeasterly direction across the sky. Occasional patches of blue sky peaked through the wind-driven front, the undersides of the clouds colored by an orange reflection, complements from the morning sun's filtered rays. Sheltered on the leeward side of the wagon out of the wind, Buchanan ran his hand through his hair, enjoying the smell and sound of percolating coffee. Reflecting on yesterday with all of its violence, Scott appreciated how Wendell's brewed coffee tasted special this morning. As he always did, he thanked the man. "Much obliged, Mr. Bartholomew."

Eyeing the distant river, the water dark and roily, Scott spoke to no one in particular. "Any riders trying to cross the river today better be ready to search both sides of the river for their possessions, that's if they don't drown first. Even from up here, the water appears to be raging pretty fierce. Trying to get across such a strong current would be suicide, water probably won't settle for several days."

Wendell stole a glance toward the distant river as he poured himself a cup of black coffee. As was his morning habit, he remained silent.

Approaching, Cliff waited until Wendell handed him a cup, repeating Buchanan's appreciation, "Much obliged, Mr. Bartholomew."

Staring at the rivulets of water cascading in the direction of the muddy trail below, Buchanan shifted his look to his boss, saying the obvious, "Based on what I'm seeing, I reckon we'll stay put until things dry up."

Cliff decided some fun was in order at his scout's expense. "We leave within the hour."

Scott's grunt was automatic.

Grinning, Cliff wryly confirmed what his scout already stated. "I'm glad you haven't lost your observation skills regarding trail conditions. How's your shoulder?"

"Stings a little is all. Truth is I'm feeling fortunate."

Watching Stuart's approach, Cliff asked his scout, "Because?"

"That lefty gunslinger's gun came up in a blur. If I didn't have the drop on him, Mitch would be saying last rites over me."

"You think so? I've seen you pull a gun. You're pretty fast."

"Not that fast."

Silence captured the moment; the only sounds came from dripping water coming off the wagon canvas.

Wes joining them, Cliff moved over to the fire. Pouring more coffee, he acknowledged Wes with a question. "What's the condition of the chuck wagon wheel? She all fixed up?"

"She'll roll fine. It was the rim on that wheel. Used what we saved from some old rims to fix her. The ones you insist on keeping."

"That's why I'm the wagon boss. You eat yet?"

"Matter of fact I did. Snuck over here early and Mr. Wendell took care of me."

"You're to be complemented. You've learned how to take advantage when you're assigned to scouting. Judging by your nose for food, my main scout said you have potential. I reckon he's right. I was just informed by Mr. Buchanan we won't be moving out until things dry up. In other words, he knows how to scheme like you. Have another cup of brew. According to him, we have lots of time."

"I'm not used to that luxury anymore. You two have me conditioned to be up at first light."

Cliff showed no mercy. "I hate to tell you this, but as of right now, I'm only going to use one scout."

"I was afraid of that."

Grinning, Buchanan teased him. "Now you can go back to eyeballing that blond gal for the rest of the trip."

All four laughed, Wes's laugh more subdued.

Buchanan's voice lost its merriment, "Will you look at what's coming."

Every head turned, following his stare. A line of horsemen riding single file were approaching. As they drew closer, badges glinted in the sun, the lead rider's deep voice bridged the distance, "Howdy gents, who's the wagon boss here?"

Cliff stepped forward. "I am, name's Clifford Stokes."

"Glad to meet you, Mr. Stokes. I'm Marshall Hatcher. Got a communication several days ago about some men with stolen money heading this way. We picked up their trail yesterday on the other side of the river. We crossed just before the heavy rains came, but lost their tracks after the storm washed everything out." Pushing his hat back, he scanned the wagons. "We did hear some shooting coming from this way yesterday. By any chance, you didn't happen to see who was doing all that shooting?"

Unable to contain himself, loud enough for everyone to hear, Wes blurted out, "So that's why those saddlebags were bulging!"

Hatcher's gaze narrowed, his attention drawn to Wes. "Say what, young fellow?"

Clifford answered for him. "Yes to both of your questions. Come with me." Turning, Cliff headed for the mounds of fresh dirt, pointing as he walked. "See those graves?"

"Now that you point them out, I see them."

"Some of the men you're looking for tried to help themselves to our supplies without our permission. As you can see, they ran into a lot more than they bargained for, some not making it. Their ringleader is under one of them mounds along with four others."

"We've been trailing eight men, I only see five graves."

"Three escaped," Clifford admitted.

Hatcher leaned forward in his saddle, wondering which ones were buried where. He asked, "Was one of those crooks a lefty?"

The wagon boss nodded. "He's under the second mound, the one closest to you."

Hatcher counted the mounds again. "And you say; three escaped?"

"That's right. Two ran away when the shooting erupted. One fellow escaped because he was guarding their horses out of sight. We never saw him. The two rummaging through the wagons didn't hang around to shoot it out when they saw their ramrod and the lefty gun-slinger go down. I'd say if you catch up with those three, you'll find the money they stole."

Hatcher straightened in the saddle. "You said they were after supplies. What type of supplies?"

"We don't know yet. Mostly they took food. I'm sure if they found any valuables they helped themselves. The wagon folks haven't finished taking an inventory yet. As for why they needed supplies, if I was to take an educated guess, and knowing what I know now, I'd say they were trying to meet their needs while avoiding the next settlement. Otherwise, they could have just gone on ahead without bothering us. Of course, it's possible they don't know where the next settlement is. Anyway, I reckon having stolen money is a good enough reason to stay out of sight."

Marshall Hatcher liked the wagon boss's conclusions. "Considering this was strange country to them, what you say makes horse sense. Before I can go after them, I think we should take a look at those faces under the dirt. I need to know whom I'm still chasing. By any chance was one of those men a tall fellow with overgrown sideburns?"

Clifford nodded. "Yep, and from what I heard and what my scout told me, he was the boss man. As for the digging, we only bury somebody once. Here's something that will make it easier for you. No need for you to dig up the whole body since all the heads are pointed uphill. The boss man with the mutton chopped sideburns is in the first grave, the lefty gunman next to him."

Liking the information, Hatcher cracked a smile, pleased he said, "Which means you've already eliminated two we don't have to uncover, leaving the other three. If you have shovels, I'd appreciate the use of them."

"We do. I'll have them fetched."

Clifford looked over at Mitch. "Mitch, if you'll fetch those shovels for the marshal, the sooner they uncover what they need to know the sooner they can pick up the tracks left by those robbers."

Buchanan followed Mitch. Staying busy was better than being idle.

Hatcher dismounted, asking, "How about their guns?"

Pointing toward a canvas bag, Clifford said, "Help yourselves."

The shovels fetched, they watched the marshal's men scrape aside the dirt away from the faces. Hatcher studied each, taking notes. Satisfied, he gestured for the men to cover the bodies. He turned, touching his hat brim. "Thanks for the use of the shovels. I'd be pleased if you'd start us off in the right direction."

Buchanan pointed in the direction his boss indicted, "They made their dash in the direction where the hill drops away to the north. We figured that's where they had their horses waiting. After the shooting, we made sure they didn't double back. Based on what you just told us Marshal Hatcher, I don't think they'll split up. Might, but I doubt it, especially since they have stolen money along with being in Indian country. After those heavy rains, your men should have no trouble picking up their trail. When you find a trail left by eight horses, three horse tracks heavier than the other five since they got no riders aboard, I'd say that's the trail them fugitives are leaving for you to follow. I'm also betting they stayed on this side of the river. Of course, they did flee before the deluge, which means they could have crossed right after they fled. I doubt it since the storm came shortly after they ran for it. I'm sure their primary concern was to get as much distance from us as possible before thinking to look for a river crossing. With the rain coming down in buckets, I'm thinking they didn't have enough time. Besides, from what I recollect, there's a few small border towns south of the river but none to the north, and they do need provisions. If I recollect correctly, there is a small settlement about a half day's ride from this very spot. Now don't hold me to what I remember from my last trip. Out here three years is a long time. A lot might have happened since I brought my last wagon train this way. For all I know the town might have been wiped out by Indians on the warpath. If it's still standing my guess is that town is a likely destination for them thieves. Regardless, you better hope they're on this side of the river. I imagine it'll likely take several days before the river quiets down for you to ford. Right now, I sure wouldn't advise anyone fording the river with it running so high and mean."

Hatcher tipped his hat, thanking the wagon master. "Much obliged, sounds like some more horse sense to me. Good luck to you folks."

"Same to you. Marshall Hatcher."

Carrying the shovels back to the work wagon with Mitch, Scott paused to watch the posse riding out, remembering the questions he planned to challenge this God-fearing man with. "Say, Mitch, I been meaning to ask you why your God allows for so much violence and killing. Why is that?"

Caught off guard, it took Mitch a moment to answer. "You said it right when you said—God allows."

"I'm not sure I follow you."

"It's not what God wants, but He does allow for choices between good and evil?"

"And why is that?"

Stacking the shovels neatly in the wagon, Mitch took his time, challenging Buchanan. "If you studied scripture like I do, you'd know why."

Scott was surprised by Mitch's tone. Usually he was very mild spoken. This time he sounded slightly agitated. Stubbornly, he asked again, "I still haven't heard an answer."

Mitch eyed Buchanan, not hesitating, "God gave man and woman choice from the very beginning and they chose future death. Why did God allow for such a bad decision? Because God wants humanity's obedience because of a proper attitude. In other words, man is more than an animal surviving on creature instincts."

"It still doesn't seem right to me. I can easily understand why animals act like they do, but not humans."

"Here's something for you to chew on. You admire Indian ways, right?"

"I admire how Indians are in tune with the land."

"And they can be crueler than the animal world. Isn't that so?"

"I suppose."

"I never heard you say anything negative about them, which makes you just as guilty."

"I guess you haven't. That is until now. I don't admire everything they do."

"Good, now we're making progress. No, it isn't right, and you're right about the animals. What's more, the Bible doesn't say violence is right, scripture says just the opposite. But here's something more for you to chew on. God's not doing the violence, man is, so stop blaming God. The Bible reveals we're in a constant battle over life and death because humanity chooses to be sinners. I guess you can say it is kind of a spiritual war in preparation for eternal life. I might add every person will end up in one of two places, either separated from God or in His presence. Most folks only think about temporal life. God offers us eternal life if man wants it. If you understood Bible truths, when bad things happen, it would make sense to you."

Brow wrinkling, Buchanan wasn't convinced. "Doesn't the Bible say God rained down fire and brimstone killing folks?"

"Yes, but always there was a warning first because of what they were doing. Bail worship was practiced back then which was sacrificing humans, so what they sowed happened to them. You need to study divine order."

"What's divine order?"

"A man reaps what he sows."

"So you say."

"I don't say that. It's what the scriptures say. Here's more food for thought. The Bible says that few people will choose to follow God, which is what you see, giving credibility to what the scriptures say. I know most people won't agree, but I have something else for you to digest."

"Stop, you're giving me a stomachache."

Undeterred, Mitch continued, "In the Bible, there is an answer for everything and I like that." Mitch's tone changed, suggesting, "Maybe someday you should read the Bible. If you did, then you wouldn't have to ask me so many questions."

Grimacing, Buchanan was aware he was being hammered pretty hard, glad to see Stephanie and her parents approaching. He glanced at Mitch, terminating the conversation. "Maybe someday I will."

Adam Clark acknowledged Mitch with a brief nod while talking to the wagon scout. "We want to thank you, Mr. Buchanan. You seem to have a way of arriving in the nick of time, all the time. We sure are grateful you possess such an admirable habit."

Norma added to her husband's appreciation. "I was very worried and fearful, especially the way one man looked at Stephanie with lust in his eyes. What he said horrified me."

Buchanan accepted their compliments humbly. "Thank you. The truth is, so was I. Thankfully things worked out okay. I reckon we all can be thankful. But please don't forget to thank those two men in the sixth wagon. They were also in harm's way, and without them, no telling how things might have worked out."

Adam was developing a growing respect for Buchanan. Apart from his obvious survival skills as a frontiersman, the man wasn't only thinking about himself.

Stephanie cast a glance at Scott, shifting her focus onto Mitch. "Tell me, Mitch, I saw the wagon scout listening to you. Did you have any words of wisdom for him?"

Mitch's face wrinkled into an ear-splitting grin. "I did make a suggestion or two, Miss Clark."

"And what were those suggestions?"

"I told him he should read the Bible."

"And what did he say?"

"He said that maybe someday he would."

Seeing they were having a little fun at his expense, Scott counterattacked, "Did you two plan this ahead of time?"

Both laughed, not answering.

Buchanan cast an eye toward Mr. Clark, adding, "Mitch did make such a suggestion. I said someday I might, but that's all I said."

Smiling, her eyes twinkling, Stephanie teased the wagon scout. "For a man half Apache and half Comanche, that's progress."

Having Stephanie's help, Mitch beamed. Not forgetting Buchanan's courage, he touched the scout's arm, sincerity dominating what he had to say. "Mr. Buchanan, I was sure glad it was you out there. I'm not one for violence, but you did what had to be done, I'm sure everyone is grateful including myself. Now, I have a few chores to do." Turning, he started to leave.

Buchanan's voice stopped him. "Mitch, I do have one request before you go."

"Gladly, what is it?"

"Please pay a visit to those two men in the sixth wagon and thank them. Without them helping me, things wouldn't have worked out like they did. Right now I'm getting all the thanks, but the fact is the whole wagon train owes Seth and Adam a debt of gratitude. I think they'd appreciate hearing it."

"Thanks for reminding me, I will do what you wish. And you're right, they showed great courage." Mitch saluted the Clarks. "If I can help in any way, please don't hesitate to ask." Turning, Mitch departed for the sixth wagon, pleased with his recent opportunity to witness for the Lord, humming the hymn "Amazing Grace" as he walked.

Listening to Mitch hum, Stephanie asked Buchanan, "I noticed you were wounded yesterday. Are you okay?"

"Nothing serious, a surface wound is all. I'm healing fine."

Stephanie's voice carried conviction, "We're glad you're okay. You're a fierce fighter, Scott Buchanan. I have to admit, just as Mitch said, we are all very thankful it was you out there."

Adam and Norma nodded in agreement.

Scott took a second to reflect on her statement before answering her. "Having fighting ability has kept me alive. You know, it's not my choice to fight, but I do like life."

"I guess," Stephanie, sighed, "often circumstances aren't what we choose, are they?"

"Well said. No, they're not. According to Mitch, there is too much evil out there. Seems like what he said is true."

Adam spoke up, "I guess Mitch's reasoning explains why towns and cities need law enforcement officers."

Buchanan added, "Unfortunately, until a posse shows up, people out here have to fend for themselves."

"Our recent experience is a good example," Adam agreed.

"Yes," Scott nodded, finishing with, "not forgetting we're dealing with people attitudes."

"I suppose," Adam wondered, "what you just said has something to do with dealing with wagon travelers."

"It does."

"I'd be interested in some examples."

Becoming philosophical, Scott did his best. "All too often I've observed how individuals become angry at someone because they were treated the same way they treat others. I call it a phenomenon." Seeing their confusion, he asked, "Am I making sense?"

Not sure what he meant, Stephanie questioned him. "I must confess I'm a little confused."

"Let me see if I can say it better. There have been times when I've purposely treated someone how they were treating others. When I did, they became upset, which suggests they should change their ways?"

How thought provoking, Stephanie thought. Her curiosity aroused, she persisted, "Tell me, Scott, did you have an ulterior motive why you treated them in such a way?"

"Not at first. I just figured that's the way they wanted it, so I respected their wishes. But when I observed how they didn't like it, I began using it to teach a lesson." Hoping he wasn't over his head in the literary sense, he added, "What's that old saying, poetic justice?"

More curious than ever, Stephanie pressed him, "Give us some examples."

"Mostly it's how rudely they talked to others and I would respond the same way. Another way was to ignore someone full of themselves. People who think they're important don't like to be ignored. Ignoring a person all swelled up in their own self-importance seems to be the most effective way to produce a change in attitude."

"When you talked to people like they talked to others, did they become aggravated? If they did, you ever tell them why?"

"Every once and a while, I'd explain if they didn't like to be treated in such a way, maybe they shouldn't treat others like they do."

"Did their attitudes change?"

"Rarely, though several improved slightly. I recall how one fellow kind of mellowed, not perfect, but better. A few acted like a side-winder rattlesnake feeling threatened. One thing though, I did notice how they treated me differently."

Fascinated how such a man of the wilds reasoned the way he did, Adam asked for an example, "In what way, Mr. Buchanan?"

"They left me alone."

Frowning, Stephanie realized Scott Buchanan was an observant man, a deep thinker, complimenting him, "Do you know you have a philosophical mind?"

"Someone once told me I should have been a philosopher. I don't know much about those types of folks. I guess being observant helps a man to understand more about others. Over the years, I've learned how little things can become important, very important. Out here, seeing what others miss keeps a man alive. As for me being a deep thinker, I guess having time alone allows for thinking and observing. Kind of becomes a habit. Seems like I'm always thinking about what I'm seeing, or what I should be seeing."

Stephanie smiled, realizing how much she enjoyed talking with Scott Buchanan, a man the wagon boss didn't think could adapt to civilization. She suspected he was wrong as she complimented him, "I would say being alone has its benefits if a person learns from it. And you seem to know how to use what you've learned, haven't you?"

"Most times, but not always, since a person can't get back time, might as well not waste it."

Fascinated by the scout, Norma Clark extended an invitation. "Mr. Buchanan, please have dinner with us tonight. You have such interesting insights. I would like to hear more."

"Thank you, Ma'am. I'm going to say yes, unless of course I find out the boss has other plans. If he does, I'll come by and inform you. Right now, I'm going to visit Seth and Adam. I haven't done what I've asked Mitch to do. Once I'm done there, I better check in and see what the boss wants. And again, thanks for all of your compliments."

Adam watched Buchanan go, speaking softly to his daughter, not wanting the scout to overhear him. "You like him, don't you?"

"Yes, I find him fascinating. There's something else about him."

"What's that, honey?"

"He's not such a wild man as people think. Yes, he knows how to live off the land, but I'm beginning to see he has more to his character than just being a frontiersman."

Adam looked at Norma, hoping for her support as he responded to his daughter. "You know honey, out here on the trail he's in his element, bigger than life. Tell me, how do you think he would adjust back in civilization?"

Stephanie looked into her father's eyes. "That's the real question, isn't it?"

"I'd say so."

"You know what I think Dad?"

Adam waited, Norma remaining neutral.

"I think he'd adapt fine. That's if he wants to."

"You mean, that's what you would like, don't you, Stephanie?"

She took a moment before answering, her voice wishful, "That too."

URSUS HORRIBILIS

The rank odor of large animals passing permeated the air. Buddy's nostrils flared, detecting another scent, a dangerous smell. Snorting, he blew the fear-causing scent out of his nose. Nervous and frightened, he fought the bit.

Pulling back on the reins, Buchanan settled his horse, also detecting a rank odor, one he was familiar with. Somewhere not far ahead, a buffalo herd had passed. Leaning over, he searched the ground, seeing nothing. Straightening, he checked the wind direction. Peering ahead, he urged Buddy into the wind. Standing in the stirrups, all Scott saw was empty prairie. Sure a herd wasn't far away, he cautioned himself to remain alert. It was always better to see before being seen, especially when pursuing hunted animals. Riding through the knee-high grass horse and rider climbed the highest point. No dark shapes appeared in the endless green. A stiff breeze bent the tall grass producing whisper-like sounds. The breeze subsided momentarily. Thanks to the sudden gust, the rank odor was stronger. Scott started his horse into the sea of green grass, fifty yards later he found a large swath of trampled prairie pointed southwest. From atop the saddle he saw the trail disappeared over a distant humpbacked hill.

Buchanan followed the crushed grass. Nearing the rise, he uncased his binoculars. He scanned west, then swung the lenses to the south, and finally north. Save for the breeze rustling the near bushes, the only signs of life came from a few startled birds flushing from out of the hip-high grass complaining as they flew away. The binoculars down, he studied the pale-green droppings in the crushed grass. The dung, a mixture of dark green and olive color, still moist in appearance, glistened in the sun. His right leg up and over the saddle, Scott settled to the ground. Kneeling, he lightly touched the dung. The hot sun having its way, the dung was drying around the edges. He estimated the herd had passed sometime during the midmorning hours. With a gentle touch, he stroked Buddy's neck to calm him. Buchanan kept his voice low as he talked to his horse. "The herd can't be too far away, old partner. Between my eyes and your stamina, shouldn't take us long to find them." Springing back into the saddle, he gently poked Buddy with his heels.

As he rode, he remembered Gray Coyote's invitation to hunt buffalo. Buchanan wondered if his new blood brothers had hunted this herd. Based on what he saw, he didn't think so. Buffalo can travel great distances when alarmed. From what he was seeing, every sign indicated a placid herd moseying along while grazing. Confident he'd see buffalo over the next hill, he unsheathed his rifle. Working the lever confirmed what he expected, a brass cartridge shined up at him. Closing the action, he placed the rifle in the crook of both arms. His excitement stirred, Buchanan reminded himself to savor the hunt. Life threatening experiences had a way of changing someone's attitude. His recent brush with death reminded him to appreciate the present. He always enjoyed hunting and now he savored the hunt more than ever. The rhythm of Buddy's steady walk relaxed him as they followed the trampled trail left by the herd.

Almost overhead now, the sun's heat triggered annoying deer flies encircling horse and rider. Buchanan turned Buddy as distant as possible away from the buffalo droppings. The farther they stayed away from the dung, the sooner they would escape the swarms of flies. Several minutes passed before the pests no longer buzzed overhead. Thankful, he and his horse were far enough away from the dung attracted flies; it was time to see what lay ahead. Buchanan swung Buddy for the nearest hilltop. As far he could see, all Scott saw was prairie. He marveled at the vast sea of grass which stretched out forever. The only way a man could judge distance in the big sky country was to judge one hill against another unless aided by occasional pockets of stunted growth providing points of reference. It wasn't easy to judge distance because of the numerous hidden swales. Pulling his eyes away from the green panorama, Scott looked for buffalo. He reminded himself how those swales created many hidden locations. Somewhere ahead, he suspected the herd was just out of sight in one of those unseen depressions.

The breeze ebbing, the sun hotter now, beads of sweat soaked Scott's brow. An occasional breath of air offered little relief. Reaching down, Buchanan lifted his canteen. Taking a gulp, the warm water made him grimace. Evaporation was a cooling process; he regretted not soaking the canteen's felt cover before he rode out. If they uncovered a spring, he'd dismount and soak the cover. In the meantime, warm water or not, his thirst was quenched. Finding some shade, he reined Buddy to a halt. He waited while Buddy extracted whatever moisture was in the grass. If the buffalo were near, he reckoned he wouldn't see them until he topped the next hill. Untying his bandana, Scott wiped the salty sweat running down his face. Several minutes passed before he lifted Buddy's head with a pull on the reins. It was time to see what was over the next hill, hopefully a herd of buffalo.

Buddy picked his way upward, Buchanan cautioning himself not to get careless. Hunted buffalo were spooky enough, no sense in giving them any advanced warning. If he spooked the herd, he would have to find them again. Alarmed buffalo meant miles of pursuit. Should he make such a mistake, the day would become a lot longer than he wanted. He remembered his early hunting days when his youthful impatience alarmed his quarry. Once alerted, the hunt was over. Nearing the highest point, he slipped from the saddle. A look at the grass told him the wind direction. Satisfied the breeze was favorable, he patted Buddy's shoulder. Rifle in hand, he started up.

Walking up the hill wasn't easy, the ground lumpy underfoot. Careful against twisting an ankle, Buchanan slowed his impatience down to a crawl. Finally at the top, he dragged down his hat brim. His eyes shaded, he drifted into view. Rifle dangling, he stared at the empty valley. For the longest time, he stayed still, silently protesting under his breath. Every sign indicated a contented herd, so where were the buffalo? Resigned, he swung back downhill.

Buddy eyeballed his stumbling master. Sensing his master's frustration, the big male muzzled Buchanan's arm. Slipping the rifle into the saddle scabbard, Buchanan led Buddy by the reins. He would stay on the ground to examine the trail left by the buffalo. Unless all his years of reading trail signs had forsaken him, the spoor wasn't old. Stopping, he studied the crushed grass. For some reason, the trail left by the herd no longer meandered. Strange, he thought. Despite the straight path left there were no signs of haste. Deliberately he walked in a wide arch as he looked for tracks left by calves. A hunter could often determine whether a herd was alarmed by studying the tracks left by youngsters. Usually the young frolicked as the herd grazed. Locating a small set of hoof prints, he saw the tracks indicated a calf keeping up with its mother. He followed them for a short stretch before he searched out another youngster's tracks. Finding several, he noted there was no frolicking. For whatever reason, the herd seemed intent on clearing the area despite ideal grazing grounds. One thing he was sure of, he wasn't going to catch them by following their tracks on foot. If he was going to provide fresh meat for the wagon folks, he'd better mount up and cover some ground. Bringing Buddy alongside, he lifted himself up into the saddle, their destination the next hilltop.

With a snort, Buddy suddenly side-stepped, neck arched, his eyes rolling up into his head. Muscles quivering, the gelding wanted to bolt. Buchanan stared down the hill, inhaling. A large humpbacked grizzly had his snout buried in the grass, the fur silver tipped, the bear's muscles shimmering in the sun. Now he understood why his horse had been skittish, and it hadn't been because of buffalo spoor, Buddy had smelled grizzly! The mystery was over why the herd had moved out. Stroking Buddy, he eyed the bear, the monster's head still buried in the grass. The huge bear's shoulders flexing, dirt and grass flew in every direction. Obviously, the monarch of the grasslands was intent on uncovering a meal burrowed beneath the soil. Preoccupied with his digging, the brute was unaware of their presence.

Buchanan brought his binoculars up as he judged the size of the humpbacked monster. From what he could tell, the grizzly was a huge male, undoubtedly the king of his surroundings. If the beast saw his horse, things could become dangerous very quickly. If the bear feared man, he would flee, if not, the grizzly would consider them a meal to be hunted. More than once, he'd watched grizzly raise havoc with a pack-train despite the presence of men with guns. He felt Buddy's muscles bunching, wanting to flee. It was time to put distance between themselves and the big bruin. Once they were out of sight, they'd swing wide and relocate the buffalo. Turning Buddy around, Scott urged a nervous horse away from the foraging bear. Scott kept his eyes on the bear as long as possible. Such a ferocious danger was nothing to lose sight of. Soon the hill began curving, the grizzly no longer visible. Keeping Buddy on the move until he settled down, they dropped off the hill, starting up the next incline. Hopefully, once they located the herd the brute of a bear would be long gone. Buchanan chided himself to forget the bear and stay focused on his intended quarry. If they spooked the buffalo, this hunt would end up miles from the wagon train. Any sudden exposure on the horizon would be a blunder.

Near the top, Buchanan reined Buddy in. Easing out from the saddle, he paused, mindful about the dangers in bear country. If there was one bear working the area, why not another, even worse, a mother with cubs. The last thing he wanted to stumble into was a mama bear bent on protecting her young. As for the big monster, he was doubtful the big bruin would change his line of travel. Despite his reasoning Buchanan cautioned, as long as he was in bear country, he'd better be armed with more than his pistol. Such a weapon wouldn't stop the fury from a mother bear or big male.

"Damn you, bear," Scott grumbled aloud to himself. Hadn't the brute complicated his hunt? In his next breath, he scolded himself to stop groveling, just keep a sharp eye out. He was sure the bear's presence made the herd more alert than normal. As long as a man wasn't aboard a horse, buffalo wouldn't be alarmed by a rider-less horse. The reins wrapped in hand, he led Buddy where he could see. Near the top, he dropped the reins, Buddy's signal to wait. Pulling his rifle, he started up the final twenty yards.

With each step, the hill steepened. Buchanan used his rifle butt to avoid falling. His brow sweat-soaked, he used his free hand to touch the ground for added balance. Ahead he could see lots of blue sky. The sudden appearance of a deer path offered an easier way to the top. Thankful, he followed it. The trick in not being noticed was to come into view gradually. He crouched at the crest, waiting for his breathing to catch up. Gradually, he rose.

Large brown bodies contrasted against the green hillside. Half the buffalo were grazing, the other half bedded down, a few calves frolicking amongst their mothers. Buchanan settled back into the grass. Out of sight, he scrambled back down the hill. Reaching Buddy, he attached the hobbles. Unlike the last time, Buddy sensed his master's excitement. Affectionately he rubbed the gelding's rump as he reached into his saddlebag pulling out a long leather strap looped at both ends. The one end would go through the ring on the forehand stock, the other around the butt stock. Rifle slung over his shoulder, he scrambled back up the hill. Like before, Scott rose gradually.

The herd was decent in size. From what he determined, a healthy herd, the right amount of bulls in relationship to cows, lots of calves too. Buchanan was thankful. Shooting four mature buffalo wasn't going to hurt their numbers. He smiled, thinking how Gray Coyote would approve since he only intended to harvest what was needed. If his shooting was accurate, he would ride back to the wagons for help. Unfortunately, from this distance, he would be forced to stand while aiming over the high grass. Yes, he was skilled, but not that skilled, especially from so far. Nor was he using a buffalo rifle which allowed one to shoot from long distance. Because of his nearness, once he started shooting, the herd would become alarmed and stampede. When that happened, no telling where his bullets would fly.

Buchanan studied the hillside. Halfway down, a finger of land jutted out. If he worked his way out to the end of the finger, the distance would be cut in half and shooting over the tall grass eliminated. Even better, from there, he could get comfortable and shoot from a prone position. Scott swung his gaze back to the herd. The animals seemed confident they had found a safe place to loll away the heat of the day. Sure there was no urgency causing him to rush, he rolled onto his side. He worked the rifle's makeshift sling over his neck and shoulders. The rifle comfortable across his back, Scott shifted onto his hands and knees. As he moved forward whirring wings exploded everywhere, all manner of insects fleeing before this strange intruder. Weaving his way through the miniature-like jungle with its inhabitants, he reached where the ground fell away. From here the buffalo were in full view.

Letting his breathing settle down, Buchanan wiped the sweat off his brow. It had been hot in the grass. A man had to admire how the animal world moved so easily compared to a stumbling man on hands and knees. His hand on the leather sling, Scott wiggled the rifle off his back. Stretching out prone, he picked out two standing buffalo.

Because the finger of land provided a natural funnel for any air movement, the steady breeze was now in his face. A gust of wind buffeted Buchanan, dying as quickly as it had come. The last thing he needed was a blast of air affecting his shooting.

Satisfied with his first two targets, Buchanan searched out two more buffalo, preferably ones bedded down. He eyed a large cow and bull bedded down shoulder to shoulder off to his left. Good, he thought, once the herd became alarmed his next two targets would be forced to stand before fleeing. Since Scott was a right handed shooter, the two lying down would allow him to swing his rifle naturally away from his first two targets. Squirming one elbow at a time into place, an annoying stone bothered his left elbow. Scott shifted away slightly, the annoyance gone. Shouldering the rifle, Scott took a deep breath, letting half out. Another gust of wind buffeted him, subsiding as quickly as it had come. He swung the iron sights just behind the near bull's front shoulder. The rifle blade steady, his trigger-finger tightened, the rifle slamming against his shoulder. The bull collapsed into a motionless heap where it stood. Buchanan swung the barrel onto the cow. At the boom of the shot, the cow's body slumped against the dead bull, the herd surging to their feet. Not in a rush, Scott swung the rifle in the direction of his next two targets.

The bedded cow and bull were now up, the bull's massive body partially obscured by the cow. Scott lined his sights on the cow. Slowly his finger tightened without knowing when, the lead messenger on its way. The cow's hide puffed, dust and blood spraying the bull. Alarmed, the big bull bellowed as he started to run. Tracking the quartering away bull with the front blade, the rifle bucked, the bull pitching headfirst down the slope. Rolling over onto his back, his four feet kicking feebly, the bull died. With the smell of blood, the herd stampeded, the ground trembling.

The ground tremors from the pounding hoofs reaching him, Ursus Horribilis rose full length onto his hind legs, his massive head turning in the direction from the distant shots. The bear's wet nose checked the breeze, his lips curling back, displaying his long yellow fangs. The monarch's age was old, his teeth blunt. A low rumbling growl escaped from deep within his chest. The bear's massive head swung back and forth, his dark snout sucking in air molecules as he sorted out the different smells arriving from a freshening breeze. A strong gust of wind brought the smell of buffalo to him. Forgetting the marmot still quivering within its burrow, he dropped onto all fours, his new destination the next hill where the enticing smells were coming from. The bear's muscles rippled across his entire body, his running strides creating a rolling movement, the tall grass offering no obstacle to his huge body. He covered the ground effortlessly, climbing the next hill. Again, he stood, sorting out the various scents carried by the air currents. Another low rumble came from within his chest, thick saliva drooling from his jowls. For the first time, he detected fresh blood, the smell intoxicating. Though his eyesight was poor, the bear's nose told him the exact location where the enticing smell was wafting from. Eager, he lumbered for the next hill, his weight crushing everything in his path. Near the top, a dangerous smell assailed his nostrils. Again, he towered onto his hind legs. The brute's front legs stretched out like he was reaching, his paws taunt, exposing long curved claws. Sucking air in deeply, the great bear hesitated, aware of the danger from the two-legged creature. Despite the presence of man, the king of his habitat decided he wasn't going to be denied fresh meat. Having lived long, the years had caught up with him, making it difficult for him to chase down larger game. The fresh smell of buffalo and blood was too enticing.

Walking up to the first buffalo, Buchanan poked the bull's eye with the rifle barrel. The eye didn't twitch. Satisfied, he headed for the second buffalo, flies already swirling around the cow's nostrils. Several shadows passed overhead. Eyeing the circling buzzards, Buchanan marveled how quickly death attracted scavengers seeking food to sustain life. Strange, he thought, how death benefitted the living, at least for those requiring death to sustain their existence. Scott moved around the dead cow, climbing up to the third buffalo. He pricked the cow's eye, seeing no signs of life. He started for the last buffalo, a heavily muscled bull. Satisfied, he turned for his horse. Reaching Buddy, Scott removed the sling, slipping the rifle into its scabbard. Settling down on one knee, the hobbles were removed. Anxious to check out the buffalo, Scott stuffed the hobbles into the nearest saddlebag. Mounting, he urged Buddy into a trot, going up and over. From the top of the hill he caught a glimpse of the rapidly disappearing herd, now just dark specks against the grassland. Descending, he rode up to the first carcass. Springing out of the saddle, Scott's hand settled around his Colt's handle. He hadn't taken more than two steps before stopping. He had better bring his rifle in case one of the buffalo still retained a flicker of life. On more than one occasion Scott watched a seemingly dead buffalo suddenly jump to life and gore a foolish hunter. He was sure all the buffalo were dead, but one never knew.

The grizzly stopped, his pig-like eyes focusing on the man below. The bear, unlike the other wild predators roaming the land was the most feared its strength second to none. Whenever the bear arrived at a kill, whether his or not, all other predators fled. The two-legged creature below was the exception. The huge bear understood the danger from the man. Long ago he had felt a hot fire in his side followed by a thunderous sound coming from the two-legged menace. He vividly remembered the searing pain, recalling how the puncture-like wound festered for months in his right side, the memory forever fresh in his small brain. The great bear decided he would not charge until he was close. There would be no warning growl when he rushed the strange creature. Settling onto all fours, he started down, quietly closing the distance; the only sound was the whisper-like noise from the blades of grass sliding across his fur. Despite his huge weight the bear treaded lightly. Feeling the smallest twig underfoot, his paws avoided any brittle stalks that might draw attention. Reaching where the land leveled off, the bear slowed. He eyed the man's horse. There was no danger from the horse, only the man. The great bear melted close to the ground, focusing intently on the man. For a moment, fear entered his cunning. Popping his jaws, he chased away the fear. There was no stopping now. Gathering himself, the grizzly worked his uncertainty into a rage, again popping his jaws, his bulging muscles coiled, then uncoiling, exploding into a blur of movement as he hurtled across the ground past the startled horse.

Buddy snorted, his eyes rolling up into the sockets. With a terrified whinny the gelding bolted, running for his life.

Hearing his horse, Buchanan wheeled around, his expression wide-eyed at the sight of the huge monster bearing down on him. There was no time to shoulder his rifle. He jerked the rifle around, the barrel pointing at the grizzly's chest, his rifle booming.

The bullet punched into the bear's mass of fat and muscle. A roar escaped the bear's gaping jaws.

Frantically working the lever, another bullet bolted into the chamber, Buchanan mashed the trigger rearward, unable to hear the faint splat as the bullet buried itself into the looming death. The grizzly didn't break stride, seemingly unaffected by the bullets. His head dropped low, his red pig-like eyes burning with hatred, his bear's huge body blocking the sun. Buchanan backed up, jacking one last bullet into the chamber.

The bear was on him, the huge paw clubbed him with a thump, claws raking across Buchanan's chest. Jolted backward, the rifle flew out of Scott's hands, everything a blur of brown and green with flashes of bright sunlight. Again, the bear clubbed him, Scott's feet leaving the ground. Skidding against the last buffalo, an eerie sound filled his ears. Stunned, Buchanan's hands instinctively found the ground, pushing him upward into a sitting position.

Momentarily the bear sagged. The first bullet, like the second, had found his heart. Drawing on his enormous reserve strength, jaws gnashing, he opened his carnivorous mouth, preparing to rip into the hated man's face.

Dazed, desperate to live, Buchanan saw the gaping canyon of teeth, a putrid odor washing over him. With jaws about to rip into his face, Buchanan's lips compressed into grim desperation. His hand finding his six-gun, he jammed the barrel against the roof of the bear's mouth, pulling the trigger again and again. The bullets wreaked havoc in the grizzly's brain. The jaws snapped shut, teeth grating against metal. The gun jerked from Buchanan's hand, his arm almost tore out of its socket, a searing pain shot up his shoulder. Slowly the huge head settled its great weight over Scott's chest, a shudder swept through the massive body

Buchanan's head sagging back, he felt numb, a warm wetness saturating his chest and armpits. His chin on his chest, Scott stared down. Blood was everywhere. Was it his or the bear's, he wondered. Dazed and numb from the bear's monstrous paw slamming into him, Scott raggedly sucked in gulps of air, his senses swimming back into focus. The numbness left, replaced with a throbbing pain. Damn, he thought, bring back the numbness. Not wanting to move, Scott did anyway. Bracing for more pain, he pushed out from under the huge head taking one last look at the brute. Blood still trickled from the bear's jaws and nose. Struggling onto one knee, he thought of Buddy, recalling his horse's shrill whinny of fear. Squinting downhill, Scott groaned. Buddy was nowhere to be seen. One thing was for sure, Buddy wouldn't be returning, not after escaping a rampaging grizzly, he wouldn't. There was one hope. If Buddy returned to the wagon train, Stokes would send out a search party. This was no time to feel sorry for himself, instead, a time to figure out a way to survive.

The blood from his shirt slowly pooling over the ground, Buchanan fought against dizziness.

With a sigh, he leaned against the buffalo's warm carcass. The soft body steadied him, at least for the moment. Closing his eyes,

Scott mulled over his plight, recalling a legendary mountain man who survived a grizzly mauling far worse than his own wounds. Buchanan scolded himself to toughen up and think clearly. The shock of his predicament and loss of blood overcame him. The blackness gaining dominance, Scott slumped out of consciousness.

Reins flying, Buddy raced across the hill. The grass offered no hindrance to his fearful escape. Thundering up the next hill, the gelding raced across the level ground heading for the next hill. Finally he slowed into a trot. Fright still upon him, saliva frothed from his mouth and nostrils. Sure the bear was no longer present, the big gelding gradually settled down from a gallop into a brisk trot followed by a hurried walk. His chest no longer heaving, Buddy topped the hill. Below the wagon trail beckoned, offering sanctuary through familiarity. He entered the trail, the scent left by horses and oxen his guide.

Gray Coyote and his companion reached the hill. Aware of the death scene below, he raised his hand. Two Bears rode up alongside, grunting, "Do you think the paleface lives?"

Starting his horse down the hill, Gray Coyote replied, "We will soon know."

Beyond the first two dead buffalo, Two Bears pointed. "The bear met the paleface here. See, over there lays his rifle."

Gray Coyote frowned as he stared at the rifle and two ejected cartridges. Observant, but remembering what he had heard, he gestured while speaking. "We heard more than two shots before he ended the devil spirit's life. The signs here tell us the battle was fierce." Despite his admiration for the man who had killed the great bear, he felt satisfaction, glad how this white intruder to their land had met his match because of the bear's devil spirit.

Near the stretched out man, Gray Coyote dismounted. For a moment, he admired the monster bear. Finally Gray Coyote moved past the huge grizzly. He settled onto one knee, suddenly aware who this paleface was—he was Eyes-That-See! Leaning over, he listened for sounds of life. He looked up at Two Bears, giving orders, "I can hear life. Go back and get the others. We have work to do. This paleface is our blood brother."

Wheeling his horse around, Two Bears raced away.

Mitch was the first to see Buddy. He turned his mount toward the rider-less horse, grabbing the loose reins. Turning, they trotted past the wagons. Halfway to the front, he saw Stokes racing toward him. Mitch came to a halt.

Stokes had a look of disbelief. "What the hell!" Gaining composure, he asked, "Where did you find Buchanan's horse?"

Mitch pointed toward the rear. "He came up the trail."

Stokes peered at the empty saddle, "Any signs of blood?"

"Nope, I didn't see any."

"I don't like it. Hell, his horse follows him around like a puppy dog. Stay here, I'll find Sammy. Hopefully we can backtrack and find out what happened."

Mitch watched his boss leave, aware of Stephanie Clark's approach. He could see the alarm in her face.

Stephanie stared at the empty saddle. "Mitch, where is Scott?"

"We don't know."

Hands pressing against her cheeks, Stephanie's voice barely audible, she whispered, "What are you going to do?"

"The boss went to get some help. We'll find his trail and backtrack. Hopefully, we should find him."

Both turned as the boss rode up with Sammy Tillman, Cliff ordering, "Mitch, you bring his horse, let's go."

As they trotted away, Stephanie turned at Tyler's arrival.

"Stephanie, what's all the commotion. Isn't that Buchanan's horse?"

"Something happened to Buchanan, his horse showed up without him."

Watching the departing riders, Harden shook his head.

One by one, the Kiowa braves astride their horses returned. Circling Gray Coyote, they waited for him to speak.

The wizened warrior looked into each face to make sure they understood his instructions. "Two Bears choose nine and go skin and quarter up the dead buffalo. Tall Oak, take four and dress out the bear. Do not forget its claws. Red Hawk, go retrieve his rifle and then come back, for you and I will save Eyes-That-See."

Buchanan's eyes opened, Gray Coyote's face swimming into focus. The old warrior congratulated him, "You have killed a great bear. The bear has the power of the devil spirit, a spirit that is without fear. Because of this, you have acquired his spirit and have grown stronger. Had the Great Spirit wanted the bear would be alive, not you. You have lost much blood but the spirit has spoken, you will live. There is one thing you must do to make sure you have the full power of the devil spirit's strength."

Red Hawk brought a cup up to his mouth. "Here, drink."

Scott drank, scowling. He had tasted blood before.

Red Hawk grinned. His eyes intent, he spoke with enthusiasm, "Good, you have the great bear's blood in your blood. Your spirit is far greater than before. I have also mixed in some herbs. Soon you will become drowsy."

Feeling the effects from whatever was mixed in the blood, Scott leaned forward as his shirt was removed. Firm hands applied something over his wounds with a cooling effect. He eyed the sun. The sun's position indicated it to be late afternoon. Mad at passing out earlier but not wanting to move, he stayed focused on Gray Coyote as his blood brother spoke.

"Your horse has fled. We will take you to a place to heal."

Nodding with acceptance, Scott's voice firm, "The wagon train needs to know what has taken place."

"If that is your wish, they will be told."

Glad he was back in control of his faculties, Scott asked, "What about the buffalo?"

"You killed four buffalo. Were they food for the wagon train?"

"Yes, they were meant to be food for the wagon train."

Gray Coyote took a moment before he decided. "The buffalo are being cut up as we speak. I and two others will go and tell your wagon chief. He shall know where the buffalo lay. What is the name of your wagon chief?"

"Clifford Stokes."

"What about the great bear? What do you want done with his hide?"

"Do as you wish."

"We will take the rest of the bear, but you shall have a claw necklace. What about the buffalo hides?"

"Do the same as with the bear." Buchanan looked into Gray Coyote's eyes. "It is good you found me, I'm glad to be a blood brother to the Kiowa."

Gray Coyote nodded with understanding.

"How long before I can return to the wagon train?"

"You ask what I do not know, perhaps in a few days. That is if you do as you're told. And now you must sit up so we can cover your upper body with a soft deerskin covering."

Straightening up, Scott suppressed any outward signs of pain.

Stuart watched his boss return with Mitch and Sammy, Buddy's saddle still empty.

Watching them dismount, Wendell strolled over. Hoping for the best, the cook chose his words carefully. "Anything I can do?" Worry crossed Wendell's brow as Cliff gave the bad news.

"We lost Buchanan's trail in a bunch of buffalo tracks. We tried to unravel Buddy's tracks from the road to the buffalo trail but failed. At daybreak, we'll pick up his horse's tracks until we find out what happened regardless if it takes all day. I would have liked to keep searching, but I didn't think there was enough daylight left, so we came back. No sense in following something you can't see. I have a hunch them buffalo will lead us to whatever occurred." Lifting his hat, Cliff rubbed his forehead, his voice adamant, "I'm sure Scott was after fresh meat for the wagons. Whatever happened, his rifle is still with him, a good sign."

His voice anxious, Tillman interrupted, "We got some Indians looking down on us, three to be exact."

All heads turned to see where Sam pointed. The Indians sat atop their horses observing the wagon folks upturned faces from the top of the hill. Aware they were seen, staying abreast, the three braves started down.

Looking for signs of hostility, not detecting any, Cliff instructed, "Easy, men, I think they're about to powwow. Keep your hands away from your guns. Let's see what they have to say."

Gray Coyote rode slightly to the front, the other two staying a horse length back. Nearing the wagon, he halted his horse, the other two alongside his flanks. Keeping his head high as a chief should, his look haughty, he spoke. "My name is Gray Coyote, blood brother to your wagon scout, Eyes-That-See."

Eyebrows arched, Cliff wondered what was next.

"Are you the wagon chief called Clifford Stokes?"

Cliff nodded.

"Eyes-That-See has sent me to find you. He fought a great bear. The bear is dead. We have taken Eyes-That-See to be healed. Your scout wanted you to know what happened. He also wants you to find the freshly killed buffalo. His shots were true. If you follow the buffalo trail over the third hill opposite where the sun rises, you will find four buffalo ready to be taken. You will need horses and men but not your knives. We have already cut up the meat."

Cliff just stared, astounded at what he was hearing. Mixed emotions flooding his brain, he questioned the old leader, "How bad are my scout's wounds?"

Gray Coyote answered quickly. "He suffers from the bear's claws on his left side. He will recover with our help."

Becoming tactful, Cliff revealed, "He has spoken very highly of you."

The old warrior chief nodded. "Yes, as you know, we are blood brothers. The great bear attacked while Eyes-That-See was checking his kills. The bear died after from your scout's bullets while attacking your scout. He needs the healing only my people can give. The devil spirit's claws went deep. I cannot tell you when he will return to you, so do not ask. We found him right after the attack. This was good. Because we did, he should heal quickly."

"I am pleased it was you who found him. We will go for the meat. You said over the third hill?"

A flicker of a smile played across the old warrior's lips. "Ah, your scout would find them easily, but his eyes are with us. We left small portions from the carcass out in the sun for the great birds to see, the rest we dragged under the nearest trees. If you have trouble, just follow the death in the sky, the great birds will show you the way.

This is all I have to say." Gray Coyote turned his horse, the other two following him.

Watching the three top the hill, Wendell's voice was the only spoken sound. "Well, I'll be! If Buchanan survives this he'll become a legend!"

Stunned and relieved, Stokes placed his hands on his hips, watching until Gray Coyote and his braves disappeared from sight. Wendell was right. Scott Buchanan was becoming a legend in his own time. Hearing the rustle of a skirt, Stokes turned, not surprised at seeing Miss Clark.

Stephanie wasted no time. "Mr. Stokes, I think you know why I'm here."

"Yes, I guess I do."

Crossing her arms in anticipation, she waited.

"Buchanan shot some buffalo for camp meat and got jumped by a grizzly."

Shocked, leaning forward, her voice alarmed, "Grizzly!"

Stokes nodded, offering no further explanation.

Stephanie's hands flew to her face, her voice strained. "Is he dead?"

Holding up his hand to calm her, Cliff added, "No, Miss Clark, he's not dead. His Kiowa blood brothers found him right after it happened. They've taken him to be healed."

"Shouldn't he be here with us?"

"No, ma'am, Indians have ways we don't understand. They know about herbs and such. You have to remember, they've been dealing with bears and the like long before us white folks came to this land. Fact is I'm thankful they found him."

Wendell supported his boss, "Miss Stephanie, the wagon boss is right. Buchanan was mighty fortunate to be found by them Indians, even better, by Gray Coyote's band. Bears have all sorts of rotten stuff between their teeth and claws, causing all sorts of infections. By them finding him right away he was as lucky as a man can be."

A little relieved, she sighed, her question directed at Mr. Stokes. "Will you go and see him?"

"Can't say I will since Gray Coyote didn't tell me where their village is. I suspect he doesn't want us to know."

"Why?"

"Indians don't want white folks meddling in Indian ways." Cliff hoped to calm her through reassurance. "You know, Miss Clark, we were just discussing how Scott Buchanan is becoming quite a legend."

"Oh… and why is that?"

"Because he survived a grizzly attack, is why."

Confused, Stephanie asked, "Being mauled by a grizzly makes a man a legend?"

"Yes, especially since he killed the bear while under attack. Indians admire such a feat. Killing such a creature means he will not only be talked about by the different tribes but also word will spread among the mountain men. I'd be surprised if he doesn't show up with a necklace full of bear claws. Such an ornament means his spirit is strong, a great honor, especially when it is the Indians who give the reward. Even more significant, when they give bear blood to a blood brother, the necklace wearer can enter into any council fire safely among different tribes by wearing such an honored adornment."

"Another spirit thing," Stephanie groaned.

Stuart chuckled as he added to the bear lure. "Yes, ma'am. Years ago there was this legendary mountain man working for a trapping outfit who got himself mauled by a grizzly so bad they left him for dead. The man's name was Hugh Glass. Seemed like every bone was broken in his body, plus half his scalp was eaten away. He came out of his coma, crawled hundreds of miles down the Missouri territory until he reached Fort Pierre, South Dakota. By the time he got to the fort, it was said he could run on all fours like a wolf. Anyway, he totally recovered, eventually going back to the mountains to hunt and trap."

Holding up her hand, shuddering, Stephanie concluded, "In other words, going back to his wild ways. Please, that's enough." Placing both hands on her hips, elbows pointed out, she leaned forward slightly as she questioned the wagon boss. "Mr. Stokes, exactly how bad are Scott's injuries?"

"Gray Coyote said he got clawed on his left side. That's all we know. The minute I find out more, I promise you'll be one of the first to hear."

Grimacing at the use of the word, clawed, Stephanie thanked him, "I would appreciate as soon as you know. If there is anything I can do, please ask me." Turning, she headed for her parents' wagon.

Stuart broke the momentary quiet. "Boss, it appears you need to do some more assigning. Who's going to scout out front when the wagons head up the trail?"

Mischief jumped into Cliff's thoughts. "Yeah, what else is new? You know what, whenever Buchanan gets back, I'm going to give him a cut in pay."

Wendell doubled over, his voice gushing out. "A cut in pay!"

A smile played over Cliff's lips, "Yeah, that's right, a cut in pay. The man's missed over half his responsibilities concerning scouting this month. And that's what I pay him for. Yep, I'm going to dock him, I surely will."

Stuart couldn't stop himself from laughing, followed by Wendell. Cliff looked over at both, joining in.

One thing they knew about the wagon boss, thanks to the countless hours on the trail, whenever it seemed like all hell was going into a hand basket, the man had a sense of humor. His attitude always seemed to help others during stressful periods.

The laughter subsiding, Stuart repeated his question. "So who is going to scout out front?"

"Who else but Santana? If we need a backup, Tillman will be next."

TWO MOONS

S upported by buffalo hides, Buchanan studied the tall warrior alongside Gray Coyote. The warrior's face had a stern look, his eyes dark and penetrating. The man's mouth was full lipped. Long black braids settled across his shoulders. A shiny medallion hung from his neck, bronze in appearance. The feathers and ornaments adorning his head and body indicated he was of the Cheyenne tribe. Scott guessed the man's regal presence indicated he was a man of importance. The warrior kept staring at the bear claw necklace around his neck, finally speaking, "Gray Coyote has told me you have killed a great bear. He also told me one of his warriors sought to take your spirit, but you now have his spirit." Pausing, the tall warrior let silence have its influence as he gestured toward Gray Coyote. "My warrior brother tells me you are now a blood brother to the Kiowa. He says you are a warrior without fear."

Buchanan knew he was about to be judged by this stern man. Knowing Indian ways often helped him as he sought to convey wisdom while appealing to warrior thinking. Hiding any nervousness, he waited a respectful time before responding, "A man without fear lacks wisdom. My fear departs when I fight. I am fearful before I fight out of respect for my adversary. I understand those who would harm me and why. When I kill, I grieve for the family of the one I killed. I took Lone Hawk's life because he hunted me. I killed the great bear because it too hunted me. That is honorable. Other than that, I only kill for food. When I shoot a creature for food, it is understandable. Tell me, what is your name so that I may know of whom I speak with?"

The Cheyenne warrior's eyes intensified. "My name is Two Moons."

For a second, Scott paused, aware he was in the presence of a legendary war chief. With a curt nod, he responded, "I have heard of you. You are the great warrior chief of the Cheyenne people. Isn't it true that you fight to protect your people and their way of life? Is it not so that you hunt the buffalo for food and garments, their hides providing shelter? After a successful hunt, you honor those creatures with dance. Tell me, Two Moons, have I not spoken with insight?"

Two Moon's eyes bore into Buchanan. "You have spoken wisely giving good answers. I fight because my people are threatened."

Pleased he had uncovered common ground for reasoning, this was the moment to see if he could establish a bond with such a great warrior leader. Taking advantage, Scott pressed on. "Then we are alike. Tell me, how far behind you are the army soldiers?"

The white-eye's knowledge caught Two Moons unexpectedly. He quickly masked his brief outward look of surprise, answering back with a question, "How do you know the long-knives follow us?"

"I am not sure. What I do know is when our wagons left the fort army patrols had been sent out. I also heard talk about a broken treaty. Your name was spoken."

Two Moons looked at Gray Coyote, his eyebrows arching ever so slightly. Crossing his arms, he spoke to Gray Coyote in his native tongue, their eyes only for each other. "He knows without knowing." He looked back down at the mauled wagon scout, shifting back into the white man's tongue with a question. "Why do you ask?"

"As a scout, I need to know these things. I would be foolish if I led the wagon train into a battleground where the army and the Cheyenne are preparing for a fight. Your warriors would not bring women and children into the area of battle, neither will I."

Two Moons appreciated the paleface's reasoning. "Tell me, Eyes-That-See, is that your only reason?"

The question was fraught with serious implications. Such questions almost always determine whether a man was friend or foe. However he answered, gaining Two Moon's trust was critical. Scott spaced out his words, appealing to the chief's mentality. "I would prefer not to know where you go. If I do not know, I cannot tell. I only want to know where you won't be."

Two Moons and Gray Coyote's eyes met, an unspoken meaning passing between them. Slowly both refocused on Buchanan. Two Moons questioned him about the grizzly, "Tell me how you killed the devil spirit?"

"My horse warned me. My rifle spoke twice before he was on me. My short gun finished him off as he was about to rip my head off. I was dazed and lost lots of blood. Gray Coyote came upon me and brought me here."

Satisfied, Two Moons nodded.

Gray Coyote broke the two way conversation, "Do you have a vision for Two Moons?"

Studying each face separately, Scott made an outward motion with his hand. "The white man's army can leave their women and children safely behind in the fort when they pursue battle, thus their families are protected. That is their advantage. But they must also return to the fort for more supplies, a disadvantage. The Cheyenne have only one disadvantage. Wherever you go, you must lead the enemy away from your village, this is not easy. Because you know the land, you are in your home. Like the deer being hunted, wherever the stag eats he is in his home. When the stag beds down, he is in his home. When he travels, he is in his pathway of life. The deer have a large home, stretching from hill to hill and beyond. Like the deer, you are always in your home. But unlike the deer, you have a warrior spirit like the great bear. That is your advantage."

Two Moons relaxed posture indicated acceptance of what was said.

Gray Coyote complimented his blood brother. "It is easy to see you were counseled by a wise chief as a young buck."

"I was also counseled by seeing things. The land and its inhabitants have taught me much."

Two Moons liked this white-eyes answers, asking him, "Killer of the great bear, have you considered what the Great Spirit has planned for you during your journey?"

Caught by surprise, Buchanan shrugged his shoulders as he talked. "I know little about such things. A man in my wagon train is a spiritual man. I spoke with him once, asking him questions about death."

Two Moons became eager, leaning forward. "What did this wise man say?"

"I asked him why would a great spirit, a God of all creation, which is what he believes, desire death, especially death of a warrior. Also, why does he approve of one warrior killing another?"

"What did this shaman say?"

"He said this was not God's desire. It was man's desire to become a god himself. The spiritual man told me that it was a man who first killed. He explained that this God of creation warned the man not to kill, but the man killed anyway. Even worse, he killed his blood brother. This God of creation did not like this."

"Why did this creator God allow the man to kill his brother?"

"The spiritual man told me it was because of choice. He said the creator God always gives men choice. He also explained a great mystery. He said this God of creation was a plural God."

"What type of Great Spirit is this plural God?"

"He said this God had a spirit, a father and son, three in one, all in one."

"I am confused. How can this be?"

"I also was confused. I asked him to explain. He told me this was because the creator God didn't need man, man needed him. He said that God had himself, a son, sending his Holy Spirit into those he wanted. He then told me how this God sent his people with their warriors into enemy lands to contend against evil. He explained there were twelve tribes, a different creature representing each tribe."

"What type of creatures?"

"I only remembered two. One was a wolf, the other a lion."

Two Moons crossed his arms, fascinated. "Those tribes must have had great victories."

"He said as long as those tribes depended on this God of three, they were victorious. The spiritual man told me it didn't matter the number of their enemies, as long as they depended on their God. If they were obedient, they would never lose a battle."

"So then, they were always victorious."

"No, they became scattered, driven from the land."

A frown creased Two Moon's brow, the story reminding him what was happening to his own people. "How did they become scattered?"

"They became stiff-necked, prideful about themselves, so God let their great village fall and their enemies enslave them. They were led far away as captive slaves."

"Tell me, bear slayer, will they forever remain slaves?"

"This spiritual man said no. He said these people will one day return to their great village. After they have returned, all killing will stop. This will happen when this creator God swoops down on a white horse destroying all evil. That is what the man told me."

Suddenly, Two Moons kneeled, peering deep into Buchanan's eyes. "Tell me, Eyes-That-See, is this creator God angry at my tribe?"

Looking into the warrior chief's face, Buchanan hoped his answer would satisfy the chief. "You ask what I do not know. Perhaps someday the three of us will visit with this Christian man. When we do, we shall all ask him questions. Such a council meeting may answer questions we do not know."

Rising to his full height, Two Moons was pleased with this pale-face. "I would like that. For now I must leave. One day Gray Coyote and I will seek you out. Together we will listen to this spiritual man. Concerning my people, you are right. Wherever the Cheyenne ride, we are in our home. That is our advantage." Turning, Two Moons left, Gray Coyote following.

Massaging his right shoulder, Buchanan struggled to his feet. Each day the pain lessened, the stiffness in his shoulder almost gone. Underneath his arm and along his ribcage, he experienced itchiness, an indication healing was progressing. Every morning and evening one of Gray Coyote's wives entered, replacing his dressings. Every time she did, the itching stopped. Twice a day, she gave him a bitter broth, full of herbs. Whatever was in the broth and in the dressing was working. He recognized the one substance covering his wounds was a green type of moss. Before dark, she would return and use thick bear grease while massaging the muscles along his upper back, being gentle when working the upper part of his wounded arm. During her last visit, she informed him tomorrow he would be allowed to walk around the village for the first time. Originally having protested his confinement, she scolded him by explaining if he was up and about his wounds might tear.

Outside Buchanan heard the voices cease. Sure Gray Coyote would return any minute, he settled back against the hides.

The flap rustled, Gray Coyote squatting in front of Buchanan. "Two Moons has departed with his warriors. Tomorrow morning our village will move closer to the white man's town. In this way, the army will not bother us. Also, this white man's village is where your wagon train is heading. If when the sun comes up you walk well and ride without great pain, before the sun descends on the new day we will return you to your chief, unless of course, you choose to stay. If that is your wish, you may choose a wife from among our village."

Pleased with Gray Coyote's offer, Buchanan smiled. For a moment, he thought about Stephanie. He nodded at Gray Coyote, careful to be respectful. "Such an offer is a great gift, but I must return. I have given my word to my chief. A man is only as good as his words have meaning."

Gray Coyote understood.

"I am eager to walk and ride again. A man laying down all the time feels like he has no purpose."

Understanding and sympathetic, Gray Coyote stared at the open flap, the sun's rays flooding in. "My squaw tells me your wounds have no fever. You would be wise to do as she tells you, for she is a great healer. Soon you will prowl the land as you did before. When you do, you will once again have purpose." Rising, he left.

Watching the flap close, Buchanan studied the tepee's structure. What a marvelous, mobile home, he thought. The tent was made out of many buffalo hides, the leather both soft and stiff enough to ward off weather. During the night everyone gathered near a small fire, the warmth captured while the smoke drafted out the small opening at the top. Since the fire was always small, maximum fuel efficiency was achieved. During the heat of the day, the oppressive heat dissipated through the top. Because the structure drafted so well, when the rains came, the water shed outwardly. Leaning back, he closed his eyes, falling into a deep sleep.

Awakening, Buchanan watched Gray Coyote's squaw enter. Sitting up, he accepted the lukewarm cup of broth. Scott tilted the cup, grimacing. The squaw's face was without expression. She watched him sternly, never smiling. If she spoke at all, it was an order. During her healing visits she remained unfriendly. Today, Buchanan decided to see if he could change her attitude. Able to speak the Kiowa language, he asked her, "Tell me your name?"

Gray Coyote's squaw didn't look at him when she answered. "My name is Healing Spirit."

"Your name tells me a lot about you."

"We are given names by our talents."

"Tell me, Healing Spirit, why isn't the broth hot?"

A flicker of a smile played on the corners of her mouth, quickly it ended as it had appeared. Her look again stern, she scolded him, "Why do you want healing water to be hot—to burn your lips?"

Buchanan made a face. "So it doesn't taste so bitter."

"We prepare it warm so the body absorbs it easily. If it is hot, the body must cool it before receiving it."

"Oh."

Healing Spirit rose. Going behind him, she lifted up his newly made buffalo-skin shirt. Working on his muscles, she complimented the wagon scout, "My husband has told me you have defied death many times. He is honored to have you as a blood brother."

"I too am honored. Gray Coyote has lived long in this land. Such a long life tells me he has a strong spirit."

Gray Coyote's wife became quiet.

"Tell me, how many wives does Gray Coyote have?"

"Once he had many, now just a few."

Aware she hadn't answered his question, he asked again, "Why so few?"

"That is all he needs."

"In our way of life, we only have one."

"Our way is better. More minds, more wisdom."

"So Gray Coyote has become wiser because of his wives?"

"Yes, and because of those he has chosen. He wants women who strengthen his wisdom. He speaks often with us, not afraid to ask questions. At his age he no longer needs children."

Buchanan felt his shirt being pulled back down. She had massaged his back and shoulder for a long time. He thanked her. "Your hands truly have a healing touch. For the many days I have been on my back, yet I feel little soreness. Thank you, Healing Spirit."

Healing Spirit slipped through the flap, pulling it closed, her voice drifting back, "Your body needs rest before the sun rises."

Sure the broth had something in it besides healing herbs making him feel drowsy, Scott's chin settled on his chest, minutes later he slept.

The barking dog awoke him. Healing Spirit was back, starting a fire. Buchanan looked past her. The outside light was gray. He had slept long. For the first time ever, she smiled at him, but only for a second, handing him a clay pot. The clay was warm to the touch. The bear meat smelled good. Using his fingers, he ate. The flap opened, Gray Coyote the sudden arrival. He spoke to Healing Spirit. "Is he ready for the morning?"

"We will know in the morning," She replied.

Stuart and Stokes watched the wagons circling up, the boss's facial expression reflective; his thoughts lingering on Buchanan's return. As if reading his mind, Stuart expressed what was on his boss's mind. "I'm anticipating we should be seeing our chief scout soon. According to my memory, it's near going past the third week since we saw him last."

Cliff lifted his hat, running his hand through his hair. He had no answers. "I've given the same thought. The truth is we got no control over where or when he shows up." Looking toward the plains, he sprinkled in a little humor. "Since we have no control over his dereliction of duty, at the very least we can do something we have control over, which is to help Wendell get a fire started. Once he gets to cooking, the faster our hunger departs."

Stuart smiled. "I got no argument with good old common sense." Dismounting, they tethered their horses. Cliff was looking forward to a change in menu, careful to keep those thoughts private. It is not good to stir up Wendell's ornery personality. For over two weeks, they had been dining on salted-down buffalo steaks. Good food to be sure, a lot better than the normal trail provisions, but even fresh meat became boring unless prepared another way. What the heck, Cliff reasoned, didn't Wendell eat the same chow they did? Sooner or later he would become tired of the same old fixings, his fixings. The cook had said he was going to change the way he cooked the meal tonight, it would be smart to restrain his mouth.

As Wendell made the dumplings, Cliff congratulated himself for managing a tight rein on his frustration. The sight of fresh dumplings fueled his digestive juices. He could almost taste the savory meat blended into the newly made dumplings. Turning his attention back to the business at hand, he gave an order, "Come on, wagon foreman, let's go fetch some firewood for Mr. Bartholomew. Wood smells a lot better than buffalo chips, cooks faster too."

Lately wood was getting scarcer and scarcer because of the number of people heading west. The constant scavenging along the trail by settlers and prospectors was depleting the land. Thankfully, the recent supply of dried buffalo chips had made the difference. Still, wood added a special ambience around the evening fire.

Having no idea where to find wood, Stuart deferred to his boss, "What makes you think we'll find any?"

"When we rode in, I spied a grove of trees off to the south. Let's wander over and have us a look see. Bring the horses 'cause I sure ain't planning on lugging an armful of wood from such a distance."

Aware Tyler Harden was on his way for a visit; Stephanie smiled in his direction, his approach not stopping her from talking with her mother. "You know, Mom, every time I eat this buffalo meat I can't help but think about the wagon scout. I keep wondering if the

Kiowa will keep their promise." She smiled, greeting Tyler, "Hi, are you hungry?"

"No, I've got my partner cooking up dinner, thank you anyway. I wondered if you heard anything about Buchanan?"

With a negative shake of her head, Stephanie turned back to her mother. "Mom, what do you think about my question?"

Norma sighed, "Honey, I have no idea. Indian ways are so different from ours. I do believe he has earned their respect. If I were you, I'd go and ask Mitch Robinson to pray for his safe return."

Liking her mother's answer, Stephanie was glad she asked. "That's exactly what I'm going to do."

Tyler listened quietly before stating, "I asked Mr. Stokes if he'd take me to see the dead bear."

Wondering why he hadn't asked sooner, Norma questioned him, "Why so late?"

"I did ask a while back. He told me the Kiowa had only left a few skeleton parts. I guess there isn't much to see."

Glad to see Tyler, Adam Clark walked out from behind the wagon, his greeting a question, "Did Stokes explain how big the bear was?"

"He said the bear was huge. He estimated the grizzly to be past his prime."

"Did he describe anything else?"

"Based on the shell casings at the scene, he thought Buchanan shot at least twice with his rifle. He also thinks he may have emptied his six-shooter. The chief leading the Kiowa told Mr. Stokes the bear died at Buchanan's feet."

Stephanie interrupted. "If the bear died at his feet, then how did Scott get hurt?"

"Stokes doesn't know. He came to his own conclusions by reading the signs at the site. Of course we won't know until Buchanan shows up. The wagon boss thinks Buchanan's initial shots were lethal before the bear plowed into him."

Cringing, Stephanie asked, "How could he tell all that?"

"Like I said, he saw rifle casings in one place and the dead bear carcass about twenty feet beyond, not forgetting what the Kiowa chief said."

"Oh."

Picturing him in such a situation, Tyler's face became grim. Feeling sympathy for the wagon scout, he expressed as much, "This has been one hell of a trip for Buchanan. After this, he may want to try another profession."

Adam almost agreed but changed his mind, his thoughts becoming a statement, "I doubt it. I haven't forgotten what his boss said about him. Do you remember what he said?"

Stephanie answered her father. "Yes, I remember. Mr. Stokes said Buchanan is half Apache and half Cheyenne."

Nodding in agreement, Adam concluded, "He ought to know, he's been with him for a long time. Out in this wild land, the man's in his element. Considering Buchanan's skills, where else would he be as comfortable making a living? I think Mr. Stokes is right."

Thinking about what Tyler and her father were saying, Stephanie considered their reasoning was valid. If Scott Buchanan wasn't scouting for a wagon train, how else would he earn a living?

Norma's voice stopped the speculation. "The food's ready. Please join us, Mr. Harden, I cooked more than enough."

Refusing, Harden thanked her, "Perhaps another time, Mrs. Clark. Per my instructions, my partner's whipping up enough chow for two. If I show up not hungry, I'm going to need an awfully good excuse, so I better return hungry."

Watching Tyler leave, Adam shifted his stare away from the simmering meat in the pot to his daughter. "You're right, Stephanie. Every time I smell buffalo meat cooking, I think about Scott Buchanan. I hope he's recovering okay."

Stephanie was thoughtful before responding, "You know, Dad, Scott Buchanan has taught all of us something about life, hasn't he?"

"What do you mean honey?"

"He's taught us how important it is to make friends through courage."

Interesting evaluation, Adam reflected. Curious, he asked his daughter, "What brought such a conclusion to your thinking?"

Stephanie looked at her father. "It just came to me. He fought the Kiowa who stalked him, then took the Indian's body and delivered it to their chief for a proper burial. That act was a very courageous thing to do. He then bargains with his life against the chief's life, also threatening to kill a younger brave. By doing such a brave act he gained their respect."

Adam was fascinated. "Go on, honey."

"Because he gained their respect, the Kiowa considered him worthy, making him one of their own. When they found him after the bear attack, because he's a blood brother they took him to be healed." Stephanie finished with a smile, "He turned his enemies into his friends. Now do you understand why?"

"You're right, honey, he taught all of us a valuable lesson. Courage can make friends even from a man's enemies."

Gray Coyote, Two Bears, and Buchanan sat atop their horses watching the village depart, Three Feathers in the lead, finally the last group passed. Soon they were gone from view. The only signs of Kiowa's passing came from dust kicked up by the travois being dragged across the ground.

Gray Coyote turned his horse. "Come, the day is early. We will find the wagon train."

Two Bears moved to the front. They traveled quietly; bird songs filled the morning air, an occasional snort from one of the horses interrupting the serenade. Apart from the birds, the only other sounds came from the muffled hooves dislodging an occasional rock.

As the sun climbed higher, the bird singing subsided. High overhead, the shrill piercing scream from a solitary red-tailed hawk broke the silence. Moving along the crest of the hill, Two Bears turned his horse, flanking the canyon wall before swinging north.

At every change, Buchanan checked each new direction, including the sun's position. Again, Two Bears changed the line of travel, entering a series of draws before swinging upward. Single file they took their time.

The sun was now almost directly overhead. Buchanan noticed how quiet the horses had become, as if they understood the need for silence. Not even an occasional snort disturbed the stillness. Smiling inwardly, Buchanan couldn't help but think he must have some Indian blood in him. He traveled as they liked to travel, without sound, attuned to the natural. Up ahead, Two Bears reined in his horse, Gray Coyote moving alongside. Below, the river sparkled in the noon sun.

Pleased with his opportunity to show Gray Coyote his ability to lead, Two Bears pointed toward a point of land sloping toward the river. Now it was time to show proper respect. From here on, he would follow the wise old leader. Waiting until Gray Coyote's attention shifted on him, Two Bears gestured with a head motion toward the river. "The wagon train lies just beyond the high ground where the mighty water bends."

Grunting, Gray Coyote complimented Two Bears scouting. "You have done well. It is time to join our blood brother to his wagon chief, Clifford Stokes."

Gray Coyote taking the lead, Two Bears and Buchanan followed. Keeping the slope between themselves and the river, they remained out of sight. Nearing where the land dropped abruptly, Gray Coyote's horse surged to the highest vantage point. For the first time, Buchanan moved to the front, staring at the wagons below. He waited for Gray Coyote to speak.

High above the red-tailed hawks piercing scream came again, as if his escort was necessary to announce their presence. Not sure what words he would say, hearing the hawk's scream gave Buchanan an idea. He would use the hawk's cry as a good omen, one he would take advantage of as he said his goodbyes.

Gray Coyote broke the silence. "It is good we part here. Take your rifle, for I must return the horse to its owner. After you reach the wagons, we will depart. Go in peace. When you return, seek us out and we will celebrate."

Sliding from the horse, Buchanan took his rifle. Again, the hawk's shrill call drifted down. Briefly admiring the circling bird before speaking, he studied Gray Coyote's face as he had his say. "Fate has crossed our paths. Because of this fate, I'm a better man than before. During our ride, the hawk has screamed three times. Perhaps the three-gods-in-one is in harmony with the Great Spirit of your people. I think the hawk is announcing we will meet again. When this happens, we will have much to say to each other. Tell Healing Spirit I am grateful for her healing touch. After I am gone, tell your braves I go with Kiowa blood in my veins. This blood will take me far. I ask one last thing. Wait until I reach the bottom so that I can raise my rifle to salute your journey."

"This we will do, go in peace."

Without further talk, Scott wheeled around. Aware the people below were watching him, he picked a narrow path down the hill.

Stokes greeted him with wry humor. "It's about time, Mr. Buchanan. I told Stuart I was docking your pay for not being on the job."

Casting a bland look, Buchanan faced the hilltop, raising his rifle.

Gray Coyote and Two Bears held lances aloft. Moments later they were gone.

Facing around, Buchanan threw in a retort. "Who said I wasn't on the job? Fact is, according to my job performance, you owe me."

"Is that so?" Cliff challenged. "And why is that?"

"While I was healing, I negotiated for a safe passage with Two Moons." Winking over at Stuart and Wendell, he finished off his boss with, "And you know who Two Moons is! I'm thinking I'm due a raise... a substantial one. How's that for an answer?"

Stokes laughed. "I hope you are fully recovered, 'cause we got no doctors here, especially cranial surgeons. I'd say your mind seems a mite muddled, what with stories about Two Moons and all!"

Enjoying himself, Buchanan fought back. "I not only met the Great War Chief, I and the preacher man are going to confer with him."

Cliff wasn't stumped. "Save it for when we get some food in you 'cause I'm thinking you're hallucinating from a lack of nourishment."

A grin splitting his face, Buchanan loved the point he was about to make. "Speaking about nourishment, have all of you been enjoying

those buffalo steaks you've been eating? I even had it cut up for you."
Spreading his hands, he polished off his boss, saying, "More evidence
showing me doing my job. Yep, I guess a pay raise is proper. Since I've
been dining on bear meat for some days, what's on tonight's menu?
Hopefully, not beans and hash."

"Why don't you ask, Wendell?" Cliff suggested.

"Wendell?"

Wendell didn't hesitate. "Bear stew."

Doubling over, Buchanan laughed softly. Straightening, he
prodded him with a suggestion, "How about some ox meat. It is the
closest in taste to beef. Before I left I recall one being cut up."

Enjoying himself, Wendell added to his fun. "While you was
resting after your latest escapades, not forgetting being waited on
hand and foot with no responsibilities by some Indian squaw, we
already ate the one killed in the shootout. If you'd been around, you'd
have eaten your fill. Of course, had you been around, most likely
you'd be complaining about eating ox meat every day."

Chuckling, Scott fought back. "So you think."

"Nope," Wendell grinned, "based on experience."

Curious to know details, Stuart broke up the verbal contest.
"How about giving us some lowdown about the bear encounter and
meeting up with Two Moons? You might even explain about the bear
necklace draped around your neck."

Stokes checked the sun, aware it was past time to get going. He
decided to put the story on hold until the night, his voice interrupting the banter, "Scott, hold on to that story. Tonight you can enter-
tain us around the campfire. Whatever you have to say should be
mighty interesting. Besides, I want someone else to listen in besides
me and the crew. If it's okay with you, I'm going to ask the Clark
family over to hear what you have to say. Stephanie has been over
here more than once since you met up with that grizzly. I'm kind of
getting the impression you have a secret admirer."

Pleased about Stephanie more than he should be, Scott agreed,
"Sure, why not. She's more than earned an invitation, especially after
keeping a watch fire going for me. You go ahead and do all the inviting you want. Right now I'm going to saddle up my horse before we

move out. Today was my second day in the saddle and it felt darned good to ride again, gives a man a feeling of being back in control."

High overhead, the red-tailed hawks piercing whistle drifted down.

Stokes followed Scott's gaze, watching the bird of prey hovering in lazy circles above them. Finally he asked, "A friend of yours?"

Scott was slow in answering, "I think we kind of bonded."

Cliff looked at his foreman. "Stuart, go tell the Clarks about tonight. After that, send Mitch over. Soon as that's done, we move out. Wendell, give our delinquent scout some leftovers before we head up the trail."

"Want me out on the point?" Scott asked.

Cliff grunted. "That's what I pay you for. You'll find Santana out there. He'll be busting at the seams to hear your story. The rest of us will just have to wait."

Striding over to Wendell, Scott waved off a plate. "Just give me something to chew on till the evening campfire. Once I settle in, then I'll eat."

The evening came soon enough.

The fire dying into hot coals, everyone leaned back, the Clarks attention on the wagon boss as he introduced the subject. "Our wagon scout is going to tell us about his latest adventure. I expect you folks have a right to be curious. I know I sure am. After our curiosity is satisfied, I'm asking everyone to pass along what you learned to the rest of the travelers. In other words, you're going to save me the trouble." Stokes shifted his attention to Buchanan. "Okay, Scott, if you would, let's hear about it."

Buchanan cleared his throat. "Found buffalo tracks about a quarter mile south of the trail. I estimated the herd passed sometime during midmorning. I was sure they were just over the hill. No such luck. Neither were they over the next hill, or the next one. The sign was red-hot, but no buffalo. I couldn't figure it out until I came upon a big grizzly. It was then that I realized the buffalo must have gotten a whiff of bear odor, motivating the herd to clear out. The bruin was feeding between two grassy slopes. I was glad Buddy alerted me before he saw us. The big fellow kept moving away, feeding as he went. Considering how he was going in the opposite direction, I stopped worrying about him. I finally caught up with the herd and shot four buffalo. By now, the bear was the furthest thing from my mind. Turned out I shouldn't have forgotten about his nose."

Looking around, Buchanan let silence capture the listeners as he relived the moment in his mind. "After I shot the last buffalo, I rode down to make sure they were dead. What saved me was I grabbed my rifle just in case one of them buffalo came to life and tries to gore me. As I was heading to check the last buffalo, Buddy gave out a terrified whinny. I spun around seeing the bear almost on me. I managed two rifle shots from the hip before he whacked me with that big paw of his. Clubbed me twice, sent me spinning through the air. The only thing that saved me was how I landed. Ended up on my back, slightly dazed, but not out. Fortunately for me it was a soft landing because I landed on the last buffalo. I still faced the bear. Had I landed any other way, I'd have been a goner. When the monster opened his mouth, I shoved my pistol barrel against the roof of his mouth, emptying my six-shooter. After I crawled out from under, I became woozy, everything spinning around and around. The next thing I know, Gray Coyote was hovering over me. I reckoned they must have heard the shooting. If he and his Kiowa braves hadn't found me, what with my horse being gone and all, I doubt I would have made it. One thing I was sure of, after such a scare, I knew Buddy wasn't returning."

Stuart protested, "Now hang on, we'd have found you."

"I considered the possibility. I reckoned my best hope was Buddy finding his way back to the wagons, but I couldn't be sure." Pausing, Buchanan rubbed where the bear's claws had raked across his chest, his voice reflective, "Indians sure know how to heal up a man with herbs and such. Once they got me back to their village, one of Gray Coyote's squaws fixed up my wounds while giving me a bitter broth to drink. While I was on the mend, Gray Coyote introduced me to the great Cheyenne war chief, Two Moons."

Looking around, Buchanan's eyes settled on Mitch. "Mitch, I told Two Moons about this God you believe in. He wanted me to ask you if your God was mad at his tribe. I told him that one day the two of us might go visit for a powwow. He and I have questions for you." Rocking forward slightly, a twinkle captured Buchanan's expression. "Mitch, you got time, because right now the army's chasing him. So you can rest easy for the moment while you try to think up some answers for what's on our minds. You might even want to get prayed up so as you can be prepared, 'cause they got their own beliefs and I got my doubts, anyway, that about sums up what we talked about."

Stuart wanted to know more about the grizzly. "What was going through your mind when you saw the bear bearing down on you?"

"Not much, everything happened so fast. One thing I remember was the foul odor coming out of his mouth. Man, he stunk. I can still see his jaws opened wide and them big yellow fangs."

Reaching down, Scott lifted the bear necklace. "As you can see, he was an old-timer. I'd say he was somewhere near eight hundred pounds, give or take a little. It was his length that was unbelievable. He measured out a tad more than nine feet long, bigger than most grizzly bears."

"You mentioned you never heard him until your horse warned you? Seems with him being so big and all you'd have heard him coming."

"When a big bruin wants they can be like most wildlife, real quiet and stealthy. Their paws can feel everything underfoot. Remember, I was checking on those buffalo and not aware of what was behind me. All I can say is, thank the good Lord that grizzly ran past Buddy before he reached me."

Stuart marveled for a minute, before asking, "When he walloped you, it hurt much?"

"Just two big thumps, then I was airborne, the pain coming later."

"Where'd your bullets end up?"

"According to Gray Coyote, both ended up in his heart. The grizzly would have died later but not before he tore my face off. Emptying my pistol into his mouth is what saved me from a worse mauling."

For a moment, the only sounds came from the fire's popping coals.

Stephanie spoke softly. "Scott, what did the Indian woman use to heal your wounds?"

"I'm not sure. Her name was Healing Spirit. She used a green type of moss, along with some broad-leafed plants and something wet and gooey, very thick. She changed my dressings three times a day. Whenever she changed the dressing, it always came off easy. Also, the stuff went on cool. I was amazed."

"You didn't ask her?"

"Oh, I asked her. She would never tell me."

"What about the broth?"

Buchanan laughed, "She scolded me when I complained it wasn't hot enough. I told her it tasted bitter and suggested it should be hot."

"What did she say?"

"Informed me it was the right temperature for my body to absorb. She asked me if I wanted to burn my lips."

Smiling, Stephanie wished she could meet this woman.

Clearing his throat, Mitch asked, "Tell me, what prompted your conversation with Two Moons about the Lord?"

"He asked me if I ever considered the Great Spirit in my journey. Gray Coyote was present when we talked. I told him about you, explaining how you are a spiritual man, said I didn't have answers to such questions. I suggested how one day all three of us should sit down for a visit with you and ask those questions. Another thing I mentioned was how you believe in a three-gods-in-one. It was then Two Moons became real keen. Like most Indian chiefs, he's spiritually minded. He asked me if your God was mad at his tribe. Does that answer your curiosity?"

Thoughtful, an idea jumped to the fore in Mitch's mind. "You want to ride over now?"

Buchanan chuckled, not surprised. "No, they're gone. We might see Gray Coyote and his band in the next town, but not Two Moons. The Kiowa village is moving toward the next settlement to avoid being near any fight between the army and Cheyenne. As of right now, Two Moons is on the run."

Silence settling over the group, a curious Tillman asked a question. "Tell us about that bear necklace you're wearing?"

"Glad too. Many tribes consider the bear to be an Indian warrior reincarnated. Such a necklace shows a man's courage having conquered a great creature while at the same time gaining a departed warrior's spirit. From what I understand, Indians avoid tangling with grizzlies unless attacked. After my experience, I can see why." Pausing, Buchanan grimaced, recalling, "After I was sufficiently revived, Red Hawk had me drink the bear's blood."

The women gasped, Norma squeezing her daughter's hand.

Tillman was more fascinated than ever. "When you first saw the bear, what did you think?"

"When I saw the grizzly digging in the soil, I figured him to be a big male. Buddy got real skittish, so we moved away. I kept my eyes on him until we were out of sight. I can assure you, when I first saw the bear I wasn't a happy camper. Since the brute was going in the opposite direction, I was sure he'd be long gone by the time I located the herd. I actually became more worried about accidentally bumping into a female with cubs."

"Until you saw him bearing down on you?"

Correct, until I saw him bearing down on me. Right then I got busy shooting from the hip. There was no time to shoulder my rifle, just pivot, pull the trigger, work the action, pull the trigger."

"Pretty good shooting, I'd say."

"So do I. Hell, I never practice shooting that way. I guess the brutes closeness helped, tough to miss such a big target. After I was healing, I reflected about how he got the jump on me. I'm flat out convinced the big fellow stalked me."

"What brought you to that conclusion?"

"The brute never made a sound until I put a bullet into him. He sure enough roared then."

Norma shuddered as Stephanie asked, "How are your wounds?"

"Pretty much healed. Even better, I don't have much in the way of scars, something to do with the herbal potion. I still feel some soreness in my shoulder and back muscles first thing in the morning.

Once I loosen up, I have full range of motion. Considering what happened, I can't complain. That pretty much sums up what happened."

No more questions coming, Cliff dismissed the gathering. "Now all of you know as much as me. Save me a lot of time if you'd pass the story around."

As the Adams family left, Stephanie slid past Buchanan, whispering, "I expect a visit."

Scott nodded yes.

Parting Ways

The following week the rains came continuously, fierce thunderstorms drenching the land. The grassy plains turned into a rich tapestry of various shades of green with wildflowers springing up everywhere. As far as the eyes could see, the hillsides were dotted with gold and purple-colored asters, surrounded by pockets of prairie coneflowers with their pale pink petals. As the rains reinvigorated the parched earth, the birds seemed the happiest, their songs constantly serenading the landscape. Wildlife dotted the plains, especially deer and antelope, giving Buchanan opportunity to provide fresh table fare daily.

Because of the soaked earth, the wagon train's progress slowed. Often the wheels became mired in mud, the oxen straining, all progress becoming slow and tedious. Searching ahead, Buchanan directed his boss around the numerous quagmires. Despite adding to the distance by detouring, as long as the wagons kept moving the morale remained high. Adding a variety of fresh meat to the diet was a major consolation. Finally the rains ceased, the soil hardening, the wagon trail once again the shortest way to cover distance.

Passing through miles of rolling prairie, the wagons arrived at a bustling settlement in northern Colorado territory. Here was a place where the trail forked, allowing merchants to profit by supplying travelers with necessary provisions as they proceeded north or west. It was at this juncture that Cliff's wagons would begin a wide swing north before retracing their route east. Having kept schedule, Cliff secured arrangements for those settlers connecting with other wagon masters whose experience he trusted. For those continuing on to California, they would experience a lengthy trip crossing two mountain ranges before traversing desert country. For Cliff, it was time to restock food supplies while picking up folks heading for Wyoming territory, including a few bound for Oregon.

A hint of mischief in his eyes, Cliff handed Scott his supply list. Expecting a protest, he gave his orders, "Make sure we have these supplies ready for pickup by this afternoon."

Scott didn't reach for the list. Knowing the wagon boss never gave him such a responsibility, he waited for some sort of an explanation.

Cliff didn't miss the look. "After you place the order, I'll send Stuart and Mitch to pick the supplies up." He added, "There's a good reason I'm sending you."

Scott questioned his boss. "The reason is?"

"There's somebody waiting to see you at the supply house."

"And who might that be?"

"Why don't you venture a guess?"

There was devilishness in his boss's words and expression, Scott coming up with a name. "Would it be Stephanie Clark?"

"Yes, it would be Miss Clark. She told me that she and her folks are heading out within the hour and she wants to see you. And since I don't want you wandering around without a purpose, I came up with something that needs doing, making you the lucky person. I told her you'd be at the Jackson Supply House within the hour, so you better get going."

Scott studied the list, Cliff's voice stopping the scout's curiosity. "I said you better get going. The list isn't going to change, just the clock's ticking. I suggest you don't keep the lady waiting."

Working his way through the crowd, Buchanan saw Stephanie seated on a bench outside the large double doors. Nearing the entrance, he enjoyed the smell of cured hay and livestock feed permeating all the way out onto the boardwalk. As for the human noise, that was another thing. Listening to the dull roar from so many voices, he didn't question why he enjoyed being out on the trail by himself. Smiling, he caught her attention, raising his voice louder than the noise from within. "How about we cross the street, that way we can hear each other."

Jumping up, she slipped her arm through his, her voice enthusiastic. "I'd like that."

Dodging the busy human and horse traffic, Scott pointed to a broken down wagon providing a place to sit. The human voices fading, he dusted off a spot with his hat. Hoisting Stephanie up, he questioned her, "Cliff told me you're about to move out. Isn't it kind of late in the day?"

Laughing, Stephanie confessed, "I lied. We're not leaving until the morning, but I wanted to make sure you'd come." Taking a deep breath, she scolded him. "Weren't you going to come and see me before I leave?"

Scott liked her question. "And what brought you to that conclusion? Matter of fact, I checked with your wagon master. He told me the wagons aren't leaving until tomorrow morning, which means I intended on visiting this evening. Therefore, your stretching out the truth was unnecessary."

"So you say."

"You don't believe me?"

"I'm not sure. Tell me, Scott Buchanan, why is it men always wait until we approach them first?"

Shrugging, Scott looked into Stephanie's face. "I can't speak for every man, just myself. I guess if a woman shows interest, it gives a man a measure of courage." Laughing, he admitted, "We hate to be told no—it's tough on the ego."

Stephanie's laugh was soft. "So when it comes to us, you men are cowards?"

"Something like that."

"Well, since you're such a coward, I'm looking for a promise. I'm extending an invitation to you. I want you to come visit me when my family is settled in San Francisco."

Scott answered back with a question. "Does that mean you're going to wait and not go off and get hitched?"

"If you promise me you'll come, I'll wait."

"Even if Tyler Harden proposes?"

"Scott, didn't I promise to keep a watch fire going until you returned?"

"Yes, you did keep your promise."

"So tell me, are you going to come and see me?"

"You know, Stephanie, it won't be until early summer the following year before I could visit. I've made a commitment to return with Stokes and I keep my word." Shifting his eyes away, he stared at the distant horizon, wondering what her reaction would be concerning what he was about to say, managing to get it out. "That's a long time for someone to wait."

Stephanie glanced toward the same horizon. Knowing she'd already considered such a possibility, she answered him back, "You taught me patience by requesting I keep a watch fire going until you returned. I guess I can say you trained and prepared me for such a wait." Returning her eyes to his face, she insisted, "Please say yes."

Moved by impulse, Scott reached up turning her chin. "Since you insist, I'll come." Leaning forward, he kissed her cheek lightly.

Surprised, Stephanie leaned into the kiss, her voice tinged with enthusiasm. "Good, now that you promised, I can be excited about next year." Now it was her turn to hope what she said next came out right. Unsure, she said it anyway. "Scott, I'm a confused person. Do you know why?"

"Tell me."

"The reason I'm confused is because I constantly find myself thinking about you."

"Just me?"

Stephanie answered truthfully. "No."

Scott laughed. "Is this a test?"

"To be fair to you, yes."

"So there is no guarantee."

Stephanie had an unexpected answer for him. "If you asked me out there on the trail, I would have said yes."

Caught by surprise, he collected his wits. "But back in civilization, in high society, you're not sure?"

Wrapping her hand around his, Stephanie's voice was affectionate. "Yes, I'm not sure. But not because of what you're thinking. There's another reason why. Would you be interested in knowing why?"

"Sure, go ahead."

"I'm not sure you want to give up certain things. Tell me, would you be willing to give up life on the trail for a woman who wants a home in a village with lots of children?"

Scott teased her. "Gray Coyote promised me a wife if I stayed with his tribe. Now, if I accepted his invitation, I could remain a wild man while avoiding becoming civilized. What do you think about that?"

Stephanie squeezed his arm, scolding him. "But you didn't stay, did you, Scott Buchanan? You're dodging my question?"

Not sure himself, he took a moment before answering her. "Sometimes a person can't have everything despite wanting it all. And you're right, you've asked a fair question." Pondering a way of life he thrived on, he studied the distant haze settling over the hills, choosing his words carefully. "What with me liking the open trail so much and not forgetting my type of personality, that's reason for concern from any woman." Studying her face for a reaction, he confessed, "Right now I'm going to muddy up the water a little bit. Thinking about you lately has got me to thinking about settling down. The truth is, Stephanie, I haven't made up my mind yet. Sorry for my answer."

Snuggling close, Stephanie's wistful response gave him encouragement. "That's what I admire about you. You're truthful. My father is convinced you can never give up the wagon train way of life. He's positive you'll never adapt away from so much adventure."

The man was astute, Buchanan conceded. He thought about his golden rule, the one he wasn't obeying at the moment. Her father was right, that was the test—the real test.

Staring at the cloudless sky, Stephanie's voice broke the momentary silence. "You know, during the gunfight with those robbers, you were so intense. At first I was frightened, almost falling to the ground to avoid the bullets. But I didn't. It was so strange because all of a sudden, I saw something very amazing. During the violence, I observed how every person reacted. It was as if I saw everything in slow motion."

Interesting, Scott thought. "Tell me, what did you see?"

"Well, I saw you and the other two men shooting. Mr. Stokes was desperately attempting to get into the fight by freeing himself. Wendell and Stuart showed no signs of fear, watching everything. Mitch was standing, his lips moving, I could see he was praying. Everyone else was trying to get behind some type of shelter."

How fascinating, Scott thought, asking her, "How about Tyler? What was he doing?"

Laughing, she pressed against him. "He was looking at me while crouching behind a wagon wheel. I could see he was concerned for my safety."

"You must have liked his concern."

"At first I did."

"That's an interesting contradiction."

"Perhaps it is, but I would have been more impressed if he was like Stuart or Mr. Stokes, even Wendell. You know, still standing while showing his concern."

Eyebrows arched, Scott pursued his curiosity. "I'm thinking you're leaving something out."

Stephanie shrugged. "I just thought how he took care of himself first before showing concern for me. What he did wasn't terribly wrong, but compared to you and the others, I wasn't as impressed with his actions."

"Talk about understanding body language and what it means, you sure are observant." Teasing, he added, "If you were a man, I would have advised Cliff to use you out on the point instead of Wes Santana."

Letting out an audible breath, Stephanie remained serious. "Thanks, but, no, thanks. I don't like all the danger along with so much killing. Tell me, Scott, doesn't killing bother you?"

"It does, I don't go looking for a fight desiring to kill someone. For me this has been the worst trip dealing with danger and killing. As for me killing, when it's forced on me, I defend myself because I like to remain among the living. Kind of reminds me of my army days during the war."

"What made you want to join?"

"Maybe I was young and foolish. I saw it as a very brave thing to do. It didn't take me long to have a belly-full against killing."

Almost not wanting to ask what was on her mind, she asked anyway. "Were you good at it?"

"Better than most."

"You feel the same way about hunting?"

"During my youth, I was always fascinated by hunting and trapping as a way of life. Such a skill makes one part of the land. As time went on, I patterned my love for hunting after the Indians. They use everything they kill. I mean, they don't waste anything." Buchanan's voice became reflective. "I had a conversation with Mitch Robinson about human's killing others and animal hunting."

"What was his response?"

"He told me, with God, attitude is everything."

"By saying such a thing, he meant?"

"He gave me an example in the Bible."

Stephanie waited.

"Mentioned a passage in the Bible where God says a diligent man shall roast his game."

"I'm confused. What does the passage mean?"

"In other words, a man is not to be wasteful."

"Like the Indians."

"Yes, like the Indians. As for some folks who object to such a way of life, they live in a make-believe world."

"Why?"

"Most of nature is about killing. Insects kill insects while eating plants. Animals eat plants, while meat-eating animals hunt plant-eating animals. Everything is survival of the fittest, including people eating animals. That's just the way it is."

Stephanie liked the Bible's reference about not being wasteful. "Mitch does seem to have answers, doesn't he? What did he say about men killing men?"

"He told me everything has an origin and so does evil. Said I shouldn't feel guilty before the Almighty about killing those thieving men because they were evil. Same for the Kiowa brave. Mitch said he left me with no choice."

"Did you like his explanations?"

"Seemed like reasonable answers."

Absorbed in Mitch's reasoning, Stephanie asked, "Do you think Mitch is right?"

"I don't know. What I do know is what I see, and I like being among the living. Other than that, you'll have to ask Mitch. Maybe we should call him the answer man."

"He does seem to have profound answers, doesn't he?"

"I'd say so." Scott squinted, his eyes looking into hers. "Tell me, Stephanie, what else did you observe?"

Wondering how he'd respond, she said what was on her mind. "I saw who I want to be with."

Not wanting to ask, he did anyway. "And who is that?"

"You."

Buchanan's emotions surged, afraid to continue their conversation, he placed both hands around Stephanie's waist, helping her to the ground. "Come on, I have to go place that order or the boss man will skin me alive. After I'm done, we can talk some more."

"You're such a coward." She laughed.

Afraid his emotions would spill over, Buchanan avoided responding.

Most of the afternoon was a busy time, the wagons being inspected, small repairs completed, provisions loaded. Both Cliff and Buchanan were pleased how many folks came by to thank them before departing to their new wagon trains.

Finished tying a knot, Buchanan observed Tyler Harden's approach. Surprised, he wondered what was on the man's mind. Moments later, he was even more surprised when Harden expressed his gratitude, the newspaper man extending his hand, his voice sincere, "I want to thank you. You're the best man I've ever traveled with."

Grasping the hand, Scott smiled. "I figure you should be in San Francisco within a couple of months. I reckon when I visit your town, I'll buy a newspaper and read what you have to say."

Smiling broadly, Tyler encouraged, "If you do visit, I expect you to drop by for dinner."

"I just might take you up on such an offer."

"You do that. I have to admit something to you, Mr. Buchanan. I'm attracted to Stephanie and so are you. I respect you as an honorable competitor." Harden's eyes twinkled as he added, "Maybe I'll be more fortunate with you gone."

Was Harden fishing for information, Buchanan wondered. He kept Stephanie's recent invitation to himself. After all, it was her responsibility to tell Harden, not his. A smile highlighting his face, he found common ground. "Can't say I blame you, Mr. Harden. She is worth the competitions."

Not satisfied with such a benign response, Harden probed, "Are you planning on visiting San Francisco?"

"When I do, I'll visit and see how things worked out for the Clarks and yourself."

Tyler's face took on a confident look. "I'll look forward to your visit. My wife and I will insist you come for dinner." A sly look drifted across his face. "I mean, Stephanie, of course."

Scott's head rocked back, his laugh explosive. Eyeing Harden, a chuckle continued as he spoke. "The advantage is all yours, at least for the time being." Becoming serious, he complimented the man. "Not very many folks volunteered like you did while on the trail. Such an attitude says something about a man's character. As for Stephanie, you're a forthright man. I can't say I blame you."

"Coming from you, that's quite a compliment."

Scott decided it was time to close this conversation with a request, a request he was sure Harden was planning on doing anyway. "If you don't mind, I have one request."

"I'd consider your request an honor. What can I do?"

"I'd be obliged if you would keep an eye on Stephanie and her folks while crossing into California. Once you pass over the last mountain range, the trail will become fairly short and easy, but those mountains can be a test of endurance. While you're keeping an eye on the Clarks—I'm also wishing you good luck."

"Tough to refuse such a request, you can count on it and good luck to you."

Watching the man leave, Buchanan couldn't help but think how the man had done him no wrong. Reflecting on Tyler Harden, he had to admit the man had a way of endearing people to him, in many ways, a very likable person. Not exactly his type, still, one had to admire such a personality. By Harden going out of his way to visit before departing was a perfect example. He hoped everything went well for Tyler—almost everything. Aware how time was getting away from him, it was time to check in with his boss. Tonight he would visit with Stephanie and her folks. Tomorrow, he'd see her off and then catch up with the wagons.

Knowing his boss, Scott had no doubt the wagons would be on the trail right after the morning meal. Clifford Stokes was a man who liked to establish a routine, a disciplined way of making it known who the boss man was and what was to be expected. Shifting his thoughts, an anxious feeling seeped into his heart. Was he being stupid concerning Stephanie and Tyler by encouraging the fox to guard the henhouse? Shrugging, he discarded such thoughts. Harden would do it anyway. Besides, it was the Clark family safety which mattered most.

Up early, Buchanan completed his chores. All that he needed now was to fill his stomach before seeing Stephanie off. He stared at the loosely scattered wagons, thinking how this was the first time he wouldn't be introduced to the new travelers while listening to Stokes give his traditional opening speech. The wagon boss always laid down rules for the good of safe travel. After his speech ended, he introduced his foreman and chief scout, allowing them a brief opportunity to say a few words. Buchanan always enjoyed the moment, but this time he wouldn't be there. Shaking off this missed opportunity wasn't difficult considering what really bothered him. Not seeing

Stephanie anymore was causing him more concern than he'd anticipated. He had to admit, he'd found her presence more than just stimulating. Now she would be gone, a void in its place.

Picking up his bedroll, Scott walked over to Buddy, talking to his constant trail companion. "You think I'm in trouble, old buddy. Seems like I've forgotten my golden rule, don't you think?" All he got was a blank look. No sympathy there, Scott grimaced. The gelding always sensed his moods, followed by a comforting nuzzle. Not this time. Apparently Buddy wasn't sympathetic concerning his master's strange new emotion. Pausing, he stroked his horse as his mind wandered. Reaching for the bit, he became aware Buddy was giving him his what-are-you-doing look. Scott caught himself. Didn't he always secure the blanket and saddle first before securing the bridle? Tossing aside the reins, he smoothed the blanket over Buddy's back, followed by the saddle. Buckling the cinch, he waited for Buddy to relax, giving the cinch one more pull. Satisfied, he attached his bedroll. Bringing the bridle up, he worked the bit between the gelding's teeth. Grabbing the reins, he led Buddy to the back of the chuck wagon. Wrapping the reins, Buchanan's thoughts returned to the competition between himself and Harden over Stephanie's affections. Hell, he thought, the man was a viable attraction. Harden offered far more advantages to a woman than he did. Such a successful man was a great catch. As for him, out here on the trail, the advantage was his. Unfortunately, his tactical opportunity was about to end. A voice broke his concentration.

"Morning, chief scout, when are you planning on riding over to see Stephanie off?"

Erasing his startled expression, Scott answered Cliff, "After the morning chow if you have anything needing doing, now's the time, 'cause you won't be seeing me until I catch up with you somewhere along the trail."

"You're not staying for my sage but necessary introductions?"

"Nope, not this time."

Cliff nodded with a smile. "I thought as much. As for any last-minute chores, we'll get by. One thing though, just make sure you say goodbye for me." Gesturing, he started toward the chuck wagon. "Come on, let's help Wendell. I don't want you blaming me for missing the Clark wagon."

Already Wendell had the fire down to hot cooking coals, including having piled up another armload of firewood nearby. A large iron skillet sat atop a cast iron grill over the coals, a wrought-iron pot suspended by a tepee tripod at the other end. Both were large and heavy, many a meal having come from those monsters. It took two hands to lift either, their mass ensuring even cooking temperatures. Even better, the years over countless cooking fires assured all sorts of flavors were stored within those iron molecules.

"What needs doing, Mr. Bartholomew?" Cliff asked.

Straightening, Wendell eyed his boss. "Fetch me some washing-up water so I can heat up enough for the cleanup. That's about it. As for breakfast, in a moment, I'm going to throw on some antelope steaks... for which we can thank Mr. Scott Buchanan. Along with them steaks will be fresh eggs along with spuds and bacon, compliments from the town store. Other than that, the coffee is brewed, every man for himself."

"Whew," Cliff gushed, "a meal fit for a king."

Picking up a full plate, Buchanan became hypnotized by the sun breaking over the hills. The sun's rays were bathing the wagons in a golden hue, each man's breath captured by the slanting rays.

All talking ceased, everyone becoming spellbound by the unfolding beauty. Steaming vapors rose from every coffee cup, the vapors turning into shimmering gold-like crystals drifting toward the ground. Everywhere horses and oxen stood, their breathing showered golden vapors over the dew-covered grass, every blade like a sparkling icicle.

Sipping his coffee, Scott imagined hearing the sound of tinkling ice as the vapors settled over the ground. During such a scene, he wished he was a skilled artist. How nice it would be to capture such a moment on canvas. The sun's strengthening rays spreading their warmth, the golden vapors disappeared as if never there. The sunrise no longer casting its spell, an ox bawled, several more on the other side of town.

Stuart advanced his cup as Cliff lifted the coffeepot, the gurgling sounds of coffee a pleasant sound to his ears. Buchanan was next. Studying the golden brown liquid, he was mindful how the color almost recaptured the brief beauty of the early morning. He gave the boss his usual thank you. "Much obliged."

Wendell appreciated the heat. His old bones worked better as the day warmed. Guarding against burning his lips, he sipped his coffee, mischief in his mind. He eyed Buchanan. Perhaps he might have some fun at the wagon scout's expense relating to Stephanie. Instead, he decided against it. Sometimes it paid to keep a man's mouth shut. Wendell kept his thoughts to himself. He took another sip of coffee. Turning back to the business at hand, the skillet hissed to life, antelope steaks placed on its surface. For Wendell, cooking time was critical. A cook worth his keep shouldn't let himself become distracted. Once the men were fed, as was his habit, he'd be the last to satisfy his hunger

No one spoke as they fed their faces, the only sounds coming from knives and forks clinking against plates. Wendell knew silence meant the food was good. Hell, he contemplated; breakfast was time when men chewed their food while thinking about what was to come, a time to keep one's thoughts private. Night time chow was different. When the day was done, that's when stories needed to be told. It was his turn to eat. He lifted the last steak from the skillet. Next on went the potatoes with bacon and eggs, no one disturbing him.

Buchanan stole a look toward the town street. People were scurrying around as they prepared for a day of business.

Wendell's voice broke Scott's concentration away from the street. "Mr. Buchanan, you be sure to say goodbye to that Stephanie gal for me. And while I'm at it, let me remind you how important it is to finish your obligation to this wagon train." Wendell paused to wink at him. "We fully expect to see you back here mucho-pronto despite your attraction to such a pretty filly."

Buchanan winked back. "Thanks for reminding me of my obligation."

Stuart and Cliff chuckled in the background.

"You're welcome."

Stuart had the next say. "The same goes for me."

"Which part, the Clarks, or getting back here?"

"Both."

Draining his cup, Cliff became serious. "You tell Mr. and Mrs. Clark I'm planning on visiting San Francisco, and when I do, I'd appreciate a tour."

Buchanan looked at his boss. "Consider it done." Rinsing his plate, he asked, "When are you heading up the trail?"

"If I have my way, within the hour."

"You usually do have your way. Like I already said, I'll catch up with you on the trail."

"I do recall you saying as much. Another thing, it would please me if you say goodbye to the Geming family for me. They sure are decent folks. I wanted to walk over for one last visit. I became overly busy and forgot to wish them good luck during the rest of their journey. Also, tell them I apologize for the scare caused by those thieves."

"They'll like that, anything else?"

"Like Wendell said, make sure my goodbyes include the Clarks, especially Stephanie."

Walking away, Buchanan lifted himself into the saddle. Entering the main street, Buddy picked his way around the hurrying people. Livestock clogged the street everywhere. Amused, Scott watched a frustrated man pursuing a plump, leghorn chicken, the clucking bird artfully dodging the man's best efforts. Near the town's outer edge, he saw small groups of Indians. Curious, he scanned each group, hoping to see Gray Coyote and his braves. No such luck. Before he caught up with the wagons, he would swing wide and see if his Kiowa brothers were camped outside the town. Up ahead, he saw oxen being hitched to wagons, a waving hat catching his attention. Turning Buddy, he headed for the hat.

Greeting him, Stephanie admonished him with a cheery voice, "It's about time."

Buchanan teased her, "Glad you're still so eager considering my visit last night. First, I've been instructed by my boss to say goodbye to the Geming family. As soon as I do, I'll be right back. You happen to know where they are?"

"They've been placed at the back of the wagon train. I don't think I like that."

Reining Buddy around, he said, "Like it or not, some things only change with time. Once they get to San Francisco, they'll be among their own kind."

"I don't like that either."

"Well," Scott began; his face wry in appearance. "Look at it this way, folks in high society feels the same way about me, which suggests, it's smart to be around your own kind. You know, Stephanie, there are lots of different types of prejudice. Be back in a minute."

Stephanie made a face as he left.

As expected, despite the size of the Geming family, they were the lone family waiting for the word to move out. Scott had no doubt such readiness had to do with their culture. As he neared, the patriarchal leader stepped away from the group. He greeted Scott's arrival with his customary bow.

Taking his hat off, semi-bowing from the saddle, Scott spoke respectfully, "My boss has instructed me to wish you and your family good fortune on your journey. Being so busy he forgot to say goodbye. He wishes to convey his apologies and asks for your forgiveness."

Pleased, Geming bowed lower. "Tell Mr. Stokes we understand and are honored. Inform him we also wish all of you much good fortune." He smiled as he straightened.

Scott nodded in appreciation. Wheeling the dun around, he saw Stephanie with her father and mother by her side. Booting Buddy forward, he approached at a trot. Sliding from the saddle, he greeted both, "Good morning, Ma'am, Mr. Clark."

His hand outstretched, Adam stepped forward. "Have you eaten yet, Mr. Buchanan? Norma hasn't put the bread away yet."

Grasping the hand, Scott politely refused. "Thank you, but Wendell stuffed us pretty good, almost like royalty. Seems like the sky is indicating good travel weather ahead for you folks. I was told to say goodbye to you and your family. Everyone wishes for your family to have a safe journey for the rest of the way. Those wishes include all the hired workers from the wagon train. However, my wagon boss has a special request."

"A special request, you say?"

"Yes, but before I forget, my boss hopes you forgive him for such a stressful journey."

Husband and wife looking at each other, Adam shrugged as he spoke. "Please tell your boss and his men how fortunate we were to have selected his wagon train to get us this far. It is unfortunate we will be unable to continue on to California under his leadership and your scouting."

"Thank you, sir. I will express your gratitude."

"And now, what is Mr. Stokes's special request?"

"When he visits your town, he'd like a tour."

Adam laughed. "Not only will he get a tour, tell him we will be honored to have him as our houseguest." Pausing, Adam's expression became serious. "My family also wants to thank you, Mr. Buchanan. We all agree you are a man of great courage. After your visit last night you became the subject of our conversation." Hesitating, he looked for Buchanan's reaction, seeing none.

Knowing a compliment was coming his way, Buchanan stayed quiet. Long ago he'd learned to accept compliments humbly.

Sounding almost philosophically, Adam explained, "My daughter expressed something I've never considered before. She brought it to my attention how courage brings respect, and how such a quality can establish unexpected friendships. After she spoke, I realized it was not by accident why a roving band of Indians, who might have intended us harm, made you a blood brother. Because of your actions, we were guaranteed a safe passage. Such a thing would never have happened except for your exceptional courage. We are all very grateful and I'm extending the same invitation to you as I have to your boss. Please come and visit with us. When you do, it will be our privilege to provide lodging. If you do visit, like your boss, you shall have a tour."

Hat in both hands, Buchanan expressed appreciation. "Thank you for the invitation."

"No, thank you. You have taught all of us a life lesson. The truth is, Mr. Buchanan, Norma and I have always been choosy who we think is socially acceptable. Your recent evaluation regarding character values was very profound." Adam smiled, continuing on, "It took a trip out here in the wilds to teach us how life can be very shallow and superficial. We've learned to depend on different types of people during this trip. More important, they are every bit our equal. Please tell your boss that our family is forever grateful."

Surprised and impressed with Clark's sincerity, Buchanan glanced toward Stephanie as he spoke, "He'll like that and so will the men."

"Good, you do that."

"I think there is someone else we're overlooking."

"Who might that be?"

"I'm sure you've heard the saying, not far from the tree the leaf falls."

"Yes, I'm familiar with the saying."

"May I submit the name Stephanie Clark."

All three stared keenly into the wagon scout's face. Adam and Norma waited for his explanation.

"You know," Scott began, "I've been part of a wagon train long enough to know when someone's been raised right. Most women as beautiful as your daughter have a way of getting stuck on themselves while becoming social butterflies that look down on others. If I've seen that once, I've seen it a hundred times. You just admitted as much. But I'm thinking you taught Stephanie something else, that something else being a person who respects others despite who they are. And I might add, I make a living observing people. I know good character when I see it. Now, when you mix beauty and good character together, that's real beauty."

Norma Clark's face beamed. Unable to contain herself, her words gushed out, "How nice of you, Mr. Buchanan."

"You're welcome, Mrs. Clark." A twinkle in his eyes, Scott added, "As they say, the proof is in the pudding." Becoming serious again, he had more to say. "Some of the most beautiful folks I've had the privilege to know were those who helped others without ulterior motives. I think you know what I mean. Most folks only help others if there's something in return for them. That's superficial and selfish. But the people I'm talking about are people who help others in need without expecting something in return. I've always admired such a quality as special."

Feeling slightly guilty, Adam agreed, "You're right Mr. Buchanan, a very humbling statement."

Having heard enough, Stephanie grabbed Buchanan's hand. "If everyone will now excuse us, we've only a few minutes before the wagons move out. Besides, all this talk about me is embarrassing. I can become very selfish, like right now." Pulling Scott's hand, she headed for a lone tree absent from any human activity.

Trailing half a step behind, Scott teased her. "What's the matter, don't you like compliments?"

"Only after I hear about them, not when I'm present."

"I'd say you're making my point, aren't you?"

Shaking her finger in his face, Stephanie scolded him. "No more talk about my character." Satisfied they weren't visible to everyone, she spun around, stepping forward. "Now, I expect a real kiss. Not like the one in town."

Their lips met, the kiss long, Buchanan finally stepping back. His hands around her waist, he asked, "How was that?"

Snuggling, Stephanie sighed. "Better." Staring into his eyes, she inquired, "You said you'll come. Promise me you'll keep your word because I will wait for you."

"Just like you promised to keep the watch fire going, I keep my promises."

"Good. I've got to go now. Please escort me to my horse." Holding his hand, Stephanie started for the wagon.

Aware her folks were watching, Buchanan whispered, "Tell me, do you think your folks will approve of me as a family member?"

Not hesitating, Stephanie's answer was quick. "You taught them one lesson, why not another? I doubt they've changed what they want for me. The family part you'll have to earn. Does that answer your question?"

Grinning, Buchanan said, "Pretty much."

"Mom and Dad think once we get to San Francisco, I'll settle into town life and find the right man."

"Like Harden?"

"He qualifies."

Reaching Stephanie's horse, Scott held the reins as she mounted. Handing up the reins, he gestured at a distant curve in the wagon trail. "You see where the road bends?"

"Yes."

"I'll wave to you from there." Smiling, he reminded her of her promise. "You said you'd wait and since we're holding ourselves accountable, I'm holding you to your promise."

"If you want, you can come with me now."

"Can't do that, I have to keep my obligations." Giving her hand a squeeze, he walked to his horse. Mounting Buddy, he swung the gelding into a trot. Reaching the bend, he hauled back on the reins.

On the other side of town, he heard a familiar shout announcing Cliff's wagon train was already on the move. Yep, as usual, boss Stokes had made schedule. Shifting his attention to the near wagons, Scott watched the lead team enter the trail. Gradually the wagons were strung out in a single line. Tyler Harden's wagon was fourth in line. Tipping his hat, Scott acknowledged both Harden and Cooper's wave. The Clark wagon was next, Stephanie riding alongside, her face turned his way.

Scott raised his hand, their eyes locked onto each other for as long as possible. Finally obscured by the rising dust from turning wheels, he dropped his hand. As individual wagons rolled past, occasionally a hand was raised in his direction. He acknowledged each with a wave. Finally the last two wagons neared, the Geming family rumbling into sight. Buchanan lifted his hat high.

Slowly the wagons shrunk into the distance, becoming smaller and smaller. Scott briefly avoided thinking. The feeling didn't last long. The Clarks still faced miles of difficult terrain before reaching their final destination, including going over two mountain ranges. There was one thing he'd heard which offered promise. Recent reports out of St. Louis mentioned train service about to connect Carson City to the coast. If that was true, Stephanie's travel might become a lot safer and quicker. Funny, he thought, despite disliking the coming invasion from advancing civilization bringing all of its noise and smoke, concerning the Clarks, he hoped it was so. Weather and ambushing Indians wouldn't pose much of a problem for railroad travel. One thing he was sure of, there was no way in hell he'd ever depend on such a noisy contraption over a good horse.

Trains have to follow tracks, but a man's horse followed any trail. Another thing, a man can't talk to metal. What's more, no hunk of metal ever warned anyone concerning danger. Nope, it was tough to beat a good horse. Knee pressure turning Buddy, he started him forward with his boot heels.

Hopefully, he'd find Gray Coyote's band before hooking up with Stokes. His mind still somewhat in turmoil, he urged the gelding into a trot. Adjusting to his horse's rhythm, they swung south. If he was lucky, finding Gray Coyote's band would offer some distraction for what was bothering him.

THE LOSS OF A FRIEND

Leaving Fort Laramie without Scott Buchanan's presence, the wagon train made good time as it came upon a long line of workers. Curious, Cliff ordered an early stop for a midday meal. Slouched in their saddles with their horses side by side, the wagon boss and his foreman listened to the sound of sledgehammers and grunting workers laying railroad tracks.

Shifting in the saddle with a grunt, Stuart crossed one leg over the other. Sitting sidesaddle despite his horse fidgeting, he rolled a smoke. Dragging his thumbnail over a match, he puffed the cigarette to life, the tip glowing red. Watching the industrious workers, Stuart suggested, "Are you thinking what I'm thinking?"

Cliff knew exactly what was on Stuart's mind. "You're thinking the end of an era."

Stuart nodded as he took a long drag on his smoke before he complained. "Won't be much need for taking travelers up and down the trail with wagons once all those rails are in place."

Cliff didn't doubt he was right. He was not quite agreeing but almost. He found some common ground as he reasoned, "I reckon we got us some time if we want. Folks with money will still need to travel while wanting their possessions with them, but you're right.

When the train companies connect the east to the west, goodbye to this way of life. Once those huffing and puffing monsters start belching across the land, travel will be a lot faster, most likely three times as fast, not forgetting a lot more comfortable."

Stuart sighed in agreement. "A lot safer too. Like you said, common folk will still need a cheaper way of travel. From what we've observed, we passed single wagons with folks walking alongside as well as larger groups of wagons moving homesteaders all the time. Intelligent reasoning tells me train travel will take care of the money people."

"Stuart, like I've often said, it doesn't pay to argue against good old common sense."

"I guess we might have some time before trains become a cheaper way of travel, but the writing's on the wall for the future. How about your freight business?"

"Someone's got to haul freight to the trains, so it might as well be me, at least for the time being."

"So you aren't worried?"

"I've made my money."

"How about Buchanan?"

Cliff grinned. "The man's a miser for sure. You can bet he's stashed every penny. Nope, money won't be his problem. His problem will be dealing with a new lifestyle."

Stuart gave Buchanan credit. "At least he saved his money."

"Yep, he saw into the future. Like I said, money's not his primary concern."

"You're saying that concern will be in Frisco?"

"It is. He's smitten for sure."

"You think Stephanie will wait especially with that Harden fellow living in the same city?"

"I'm inclined to think so. She did say she'd wait for him to show up, and from what we've observed, I became convinced watching how she kept that watch fire going. Yep, she impressed me for sure."

"But," Stuart suggested, "it'll be tough if Buchanan rides all those miles only to find she's up and got married. He's got to cross two mountain ranges to reach San Francisco. Depending on the time of year, and from what I've been told, crossing those mountain ranges can be tricky. Imagine riding all that distance only to find she went and got herself hitched."

His eyebrows arched, Cliff hated to think of such a thing. "You're right, Stuart. If Stephanie isn't waiting, it'll be a long ride for naught. Knowing the man like I do, he would recover from such a disappointment. Like I've said on many occasions, his trouble will be adjusting to a cluttered way of life while being surrounded by civilization. The man has catamount blood in his veins. Every time he sees new sodbusters, he has something negative to say. Complains about the noise people make, doesn't like to be crowded. Whew, there are some big adjustments coming Buchanan's way."

Stuart chuckled, giving some thought to what Cliff said and acknowledging the boss's points. "He'd have been better off if he'd taken up on Gray Coyote's offer and taken himself a squaw. That way, he would remain free while satisfying his personal needs."

"Can't tell a smitten man what's best for him," Cliff responded.

"I guess not. One thing though, it's been said how a long spell of time's been known to help reduce the heart's desires."

"Yeah, but every man's got his memories. It's tough when a man falls head over heels in love and then expect him to ride off and forget the woman he's been smitten by. A better solution is to find some gal whose parents live in a place where a man likes, 'cause a daughter always wants to be near her mother. If I were to offer a young fellow some wise advice, I'd suggest he find a territory he likes, or some town, and then run into a gal who lives there. That way, he'd avoid any tug-of-war and be able to settle down along with his bride being satisfied where she's at. As for Buchanan not being sure where to settle down, more than once I've told him there will always be a job for him in my freight business. I even mentioned how he could be my foreman."

"What did he say?"

"Thanked me, told me he'd let me know. He talked about scouting for the army, maybe guiding hunting parties and such."

"Apparently he's given his dilemma some thought."

Cliff nodded. "My proposition was serious, I already knew his answer would be no when I asked. Now Stuart, don't take it personal, but you are next on the list for foreman in my freight business. I'm sure you understand how Buchanan and I go way back, kind of like a father and son relationship. Not forgetting all the danger we faced while serving together during the war. Stuart, you're just as capable, but my first deceased wife, as well as my second bride, adopted Scott Buchanan, moving you into third place."

"Considering all you've said, no offense taken. Fact is, I'm flattered."

"Well, you earned it."

"Speaking about Buchanan, where is he?"

Turning around in his saddle, Cliff faced south as he spoke. "Buchanan heard there's a bunch of Kiowa over that far hill. He rode out early hoping it was Gray Coyote's band."

"Ah, that would be pleasing to him."

"What's more, when he gets back, I've got a surprise for him. I'm telling him ahead of time so he can get his mind ready for a change. I'm going to release him from his scouting after we return from the upper Snake River at this very juncture."

Stuart rocked in his saddle, a touch of shock in his voice, "Releasing him!"

"That's my intention, and now you're wondering why?"

"God Almighty, yes I am!"

"Here's your answer. Why would I make him travel all the way back from where we started at Independence Missouri only for him to have to turn around and ride all these extra miles back here before heading to San Francisco?"

"You have a point there, one I hadn't thought of."

"Rest assured I've given it plenty of thought. Right now we're at a juncture that would cut his riding distance in half, so I'm releasing him after we return from the upper Oregon Trail."

Stuart looked at his boss. "You know how Scott always fulfills his obligations."

"I expect he'll protest, but only mildly."

"Because he's smitten."

"Something like that."

Intrigued, Stuart admitted, "That's one conversation I'd love to be present when you inform him, 'cause he'll be knocked out of his saddle when he hears your decision."

"Then stick around 'cause as soon as he gets back I'm telling him, and I'm doing it this-a-way so his thoughts can adjust."

"Suppose he insists on finishing the whole trip?"

A twinkle appeared in Cliff's eyes. "He'll agree with me once I inform him he's not going to get paid anymore. Besides, I still need him for the upper trail. Knowing such, Scott will understand he's fulfilled his obligations."

"You wouldn't dare."

"Watch me. I know how to motivate him especially since he's such a miser."

Scratching his chin, Stuart chuckled. "Knowing you, I take it back. Seems like you've thought it out."

Cliff took his time as he spoke, "To tell you the truth, when Buchanan goes, I'm going to miss him. Like I said, we go way back." Hat in hand, Cliff dusted off the brim, concluding, "Sooner or later, a stallion takes on his own herd. You know, it is part of being a male, and a male needs a mare. Well, we will know soon enough how things went during his visit before I explain his new plans to him. Be very interesting to see how he reacts. Come on, my new freight foreman, that's if you want it. Let's ride back to the wagons and finish our responsibilities."

Buchanan hauled out his binoculars. Focusing, he scanned the Kiowa village for trouble. From what he could see below, all appeared calm. Considering how the Kiowa were so close to town, those braves had to be of a peaceful mindset. Still, caution never hurt. If the village included Gray Coyote's band, he could relax. If not, he'd best stay alert. One of the braves was looking up at him. Scott searched for a known face but saw none. Friendly or not, it was time to ride on down and find out. He started the gelding down the gradual slope. Several mangy dogs began barking, the fiercest leader of the pack moving his way.

A crowd slowly gathered awaiting Buchanan's arrival.

Knowing a mongrel packs' primary purpose was to sound an alert, ready to flee if threatened, Scott ignored them. Reaching the village's outskirts, he searched several of the nearest faces, unable to identify a friend. Keeping Buddy heading forward, he suddenly recognized Spotted Pony. Glad he had located Gray Coyote's band, he greeted the tall warrior. "I am pleased to see my blood brother."

Spotted Pony welcomed Buchanan. "Eyes-That-See, it has been a long time. Come down and join me."

Easing out from the saddle, Scott noticed a lone squaw watching him. The squaw was Healing Spirit. He waved, suddenly feeling at home, grateful to recognize those who were special to him. Eager to see Gray Coyote, he asked for him. "I have a lot to say to Gray Coyote. Where is he?"

Sadness reflected in Spotted Pony's face, his words deliberate. "He has departed into the presence of the Great Spirit."

With his face tightening, Buchanan blurted out, "What happened?"

"A sickness came upon his body, his age unable to fight off such an attack. He lingered bravely before departing. Come, you must walk with me as we speak. Have you eaten?"

"I have forgotten about food in my eagerness to find my blood brothers."

"Good, as our special guest and blood brother, we will feast. But first you must meet our chief, Thunder Cloud. Before you speak with him, I must warn you."

"I'm listening."

"The brave you killed, Lone Hawk, was one of Thunder Cloud's many sons."

"I'll be," Buchanan frowned, "what will be his response?"

"He does not hold this against you, but you should be wise in how you answer him. You must win him over. When this is done, I have something else to tell you about Gray Coyote. He left you a message to be told through me."

Somewhat relieved that Thunder Cloud would not seek revenge, Scott considered possible responses. It would be smart to think before he spoke. He questioned Spotted Pony, "You're sure he harbors no vengeance?"

Spotted Pony answered the question indirectly. "You have been around our people long enough to know how to answer."

Shifting his mind away from what he would say, Scott's thoughts returned to Gray Coyote. "You said Gray Coyote left a message for me?"

Walking toward the center of the village, Spotted Pony answered Buchanan. "Yes, he entrusted it to me. Also, Healing Spirit has something to tell you."

"I am eager to hear the both of you."

Dropping his voice, Spotted Pony whispered, "We are at the chief's lodge."

A lone man stood in the shadow cast from the tepee, his face lined with wrinkles indicating his years.

Spotted Pony introduced Buchanan. "This is our warrior blood brother adopted by Gray Coyote. His Kiowa name was given to him by your son, Lone Hawk. He is Eyes-That-See."

Intensity flickered in the man's alert eyes. "I am Thunder Cloud, chief of this village. I have acquired my title because I have always struck in battle as do the storm clouds that suddenly appear in the sky with bolts of lightning. I have lived long. Are you not the one who killed my son Lone Hawk?"

Buchanan kept his face passive as Spotted Pony spoke for him.

"He knows you are Lone Hawk's father. A man always grieves when he outlives one his sons, as you do now. He comes without fear looking forward to this meeting. Gray Coyote chose to make him a blood brother because of his courage. I will let him speak for himself."

The chief's eyes bore into Scott. Buchanan had his cue. "Although your son was brave and without fear, it was his desire to do battle, not mine. He left me no choice."

Studying Buchanan's face, Thunder Cloud's response was slow. "By giving you the name Eyes-That-See, this showed he respected you. He would not have given you such a name if he thought little of you."

"I honored your son's bravery by asking Gray Coyote if I might keep the name given to me by your son. He granted my wish. I returned your son for a proper burial, a warrior deserves as much."

Thunder Cloud's intensity relaxed, indicating he held no grudge, his voice firm, "I know this is true because I have heard it from others. I do not hold his death against you. My son died as he wished, such is the life of a warrior. It was brought to my attention you are a slayer of a great bear. Had my son known you would kill the devil-spirit bear, perhaps you and he would have ridden together?"

"I would have liked riding alongside him."

His right arm pointing toward the entrance, Thunder Cloud extended an invitation. "You are welcomed into my dwelling as a blood brother because of your courage." He paused, adding, "I understood my son was headstrong and overly eager for battle. I had hoped Gray Coyote could temper his aggression, but it was not to be. Come and sit as we wait for others to join us. We will smoke the pipe and talk." Pointing over his shoulder, he gave orders to Spotted Pony. "Go bring the others."

Soon, the circle within the tent was full of sitting braves.

Finished packing the pipe, Thunder Cloud lit the bowl. Facing left, he blew a puff of smoke out. Turning right, another puff went out. Swinging around, again he sent out more smoke. Turning back to the inner circle, he blew smoke to the center, offering the pipe to his guest.

Seeing the curiosity on Buchanan's face, Spotted Pony explained, "Thunder Cloud has honored the many warriors from the past who have gone to the four corners of the earth. This custom is not necessary for you."

The group waited until Buchanan exhaled a puff, passing the pipe to the brave next to him. Soon the pipe returned to Thunder Cloud, who took one last puff. Finished, he asked, "What has Eyes-That-See noticed on his journey?"

"I have seen what your people call the 'iron horse.' As I rode here, I saw workers laying a path made from hard metal."

Thunder Cloud frowned. "This is not good."

His voice sympathetic, Scott nodded in agreement. "I'm afraid this way of crossing the land is here to stay. Bad or not, the men are at work day and night."

Glancing beyond the flaps at the distant hills, Thunder Cloud's voice became very subdued. "Our way of life is threatened in many ways, first by slow-moving wagons and now by an iron horse." He faced Buchanan. "You are fortunate because you are one of them."

Giving thought to what the chief said, Buchanan answered honestly. "I am not as fortunate because I'm more like my red brothers. I like to roam and listen to what is around me."

The chief's eyes expressed appreciation, followed by a nod of agreement.

Looking at the circle of braves, with each word, Scott included every man. "Like your people, I'm skilled at hunting. The white man's villages roar with noise. When one walks down the street, you can be run over. In a Kiowa village, one can hear the singing of the birds despite men and women moving about. Occasionally, there are sounds from horses and barking dogs, even so, one can still hear the peaceful sounds from the wind brushing the tall grass outside the village."

Thunder Cloud's eyes twinkled at Buchanan's description of the white settlers' villages. Seconds later, the twinkle disappeared as he challenged the wagon scout. "Then why do you help bring these people to spread their noise?"

Buchanan took a second to answer. "You have asked a fair question. I came for the same reason they come. And like you, who were here first, I now resent their intrusion."

Passing over the pipe, Thunder Cloud allowed for the wagon scout to collect his thoughts.

Thankful, Buchanan puffed twice before passing it on. Aware of the scrutiny from the others, he completed his response. "But not at first. In the beginning, I was no better than many of the new people arriving. There is one thing that makes me different from the settlers."

"What is different?" Thunder Cloud asked.

"I love being free to roam where I want, and when I want."

The tension broken, the chief rocked ever so slightly. Focusing on Spotted Pony, he started the humor in motion. "Even we have never had such freedom. I wonder if there is such a tribe."

The circle of braves laughed, one brave nudging the man next to him.

Joining in their soft laughter, Scott waited until the humor passed, changing the conversation. "I am saddened to know about Gray Coyote's passing. I have been told he left a message for me."

Thunder Cloud looked toward Spotted Pony.

Spotted Pony saw the look. "The message he left is this: he wanted you to know he died with all his body parts. Therefore, he would not be wandering around looking for a hand, a leg, or an arm where he has gone. Because of this, he will meet you when you arrive. He said it was good the mighty bear left you whole. In that way, you are like him, not having to wander about putting yourself back together again. He also left instructions for you."

"What were those instructions?"

"When you meet with Two Moons, do not forget to bring the spiritual man from your wagon train. As for Gray Coyote, he will not need to listen to such a man, for now he is in the spirit world."

His eyes sweeping the circle of faces, Scott asked, "Tell me, where is Two Moons?"

Spotted Pony answered him. "He was forced to surrender to the army for the good of his people. They have been sent to an agency."

More bad news, Buchanan sighed. His voice firm, he declared, "I will find Two Moons and honor Gray Coyote's wishes." Thoughtful, his finger making an aimless circle in the dirt floor, he asked, "I would like to visit with Healing Spirit. I was told she also has a message for me. Is it proper for me to pay her a visit?"

"Of course," Spotted Pony suggested. "She is widowed and available."

The circle of faces laughed.

Buchanan added to the laughter.

Thunder Cloud continued on with the merriment. "I will instruct our people to make the arrangements."

The laughter became louder. Not at a loss for words, Buchanan conceded, "It is good to hear laughter even if it's at my expense. I think Gray Coyote's spirit lives on in this house of buffalo skins. I think one visit will be more than enough. As you know, I like to roam."

Spotted Pony kept it going. "You mean you like to flee." Several minutes passed before the laughter subsided.

One brave named Big Horse encouraged, "Come back after your visit and we will eat." Unable to resist one last touch of humor, he added, "If you do not return, we will understand."

Buchanan rose to his feet. It was good the men enjoyed laughter at his expense. Because they did, he had been accepted. With a smile, he excused himself. Nearing where he'd last seen Healing Spirit, he saw her. Buchanan quickly closed the distance.

"It is good to see Eyes-That-See. You have kept your promise."

"I too am pleased to visit with Healing Spirit again."

"How are your wounds from the devil spirit?"

"Thanks to your touch, I'm whole and without pain. I'm saddened because I looked forward to listening to Gray Coyote's wisdom."

Healing Spirit's response was a statement. "He will be remembered around the many council fires."

"Yes," Buchanan agreed.

"Already, Gray Coyote's name is burned into our peoples' scroll of history," she finished.

Buchanan thought about what she said. "Good, he has earned such an honor. I'm unhappy regarding Two Moons's surrender. Hopefully, I'll see him again."

"He would like that."

"I'm glad you're well. I have been welcomed by Spotted Pony and Thunder Cloud. I remembered you telling me how Gray Coyote accepted your counsel. I'm sure you made him comfortable in his last days."

"He had a warrior's spirit. The most I could do was sooth his sickness while listening to his death chant. He died as a warrior without fear. More than once he thanked the Great Spirit for you as a blood brother."

Feeling a rush of emotion, Scott steadied himself, his words thankful. "I'm a better man having known the both of you."

She nodded. Moisture briefly filled her eyes. Suddenly it was gone, replaced with her ever stoic look. Buchanan saw it and it pleased him. He reached out with a gentle touch. "No man can journey without the right people around him. Gray Coyote chose wisely, you being one of his choices."

Healing Spirit changed the conversation. "Have you come to stay?"

"I'm bound from where I came. After, I will return and cross over the mountains."

"Why are you returning to cross the mountains?"

"Because of a woman."

Interest kindled in Healing Spirit's eyes. "Tell me about her."

"She is a lot like you. Not in healing gifts, but in wisdom."

"You have chosen a long journey to see this woman, a very dangerous journey."

Buchanan shrugged. "She said she'd wait for me."

"Because your journey will take much time, this is a good way to test her."

Buchanan changed the subject. "What about you?"

"My gifts are always needed."

How profound, Scott thought, mentioning a difference, "In our way of life, a man has only one wife. I think the one who waits for me will be a woman who understands purpose."

Healing Spirit's face was expressionless. She asked, "You are not sure of her words?"

"I will know better when I find her. As for purpose, only time will tell. I was told by Spotted Pony that you have a message for me from Gray Coyote."

"Yes, a message and a gift."

"You say a gift."

"Come, follow me." Turning, she stooped as she entered her shelter with Scott following. "Sit," she gestured.

Sitting cross-legged, he observed a leather bundle in Healing Spirit's hands. She settled across from him, extending the bundle with both hands. "This is his gift."

Unwinding the leather thongs, Scott peeled back the layers. The knife's blade had a dull sheen in the subdued light. He lifted his stare, his eyebrows arched.

"He wanted you to carry this knife wherever you travel. In this way, his spirit will always ride with you. The knife has seen many battles. Its spirit is strong."

"I'm honored."

"Gray Coyote respected you as a blood brother. Many who rode with him have asked for his knife."

"What did you say to them?"

"I told them the knife has been spoken for."

Scott nodded.

"Gray Coyote had another reason he wanted you to have his knife."

"What was his reason?"

"We often sat here while talking about what the future is for our people. We both agreed that before long, we will be herded into reservations—our freedoms a thing of the past. This will not happen to you because of the color of your skin. You will remain free, and as you travel, so too will Gray Coyote's spirit be at your side while remaining free. He wanted his knife and its spirit to ride in freedom through you aboard your pony. Besides, there is another advantage."

"Tell me about this advantage."

"Gray Coyote's name is known by many warrior brothers from other tribes. As you journey, whenever you ride into another's camp, show them the knife and you will be honored as a friend."

Staring back down at the knife, Scott's voice became hushed. "This is a great gift."

Healing Spirit smiled. "A man earns his gifts from others because his heart is right. Gray Coyote's other message was for me to tell you he saw your heart was good. Like Gray Coyote, you do not kill solely for pleasure."

His head nodding yes, Buchanan appreciated her insight. "It would seem that the Great Spirit brings together those who share a common bond."

Healing Spirit was pleased. Rising, she concluded their conversation. "I have nothing else to tell you."

Standing, Scott expressed his gratitude. "It was good I found your village. You have lightened my heart despite the passing of Gray Coyote. When I return to cross the mountains, I will seek you out one more time." Turning, he stepped into the late afternoon sun. Several yards beyond hearing, Spotted Pony waited.

It was obvious the sinewy brave had made sure Buchanan and Healing Spirit had a private conversation. Following the brave's lithe movements toward the center of the village, Scott asked, "Why do they call you Spotted Pony?"

"Why do you think I have such a name?"

"Because every horse you ride has different colors."

"You have seen the types of ponies I ride, but I was not given my name for such a reason. I am called Spotted Pony because I always spot pony tracks by another tribe that would attack our village. My advanced warnings are why I was given such an earned name."

Ahead loomed the chief's tent. Outside, the food was being prepared. Scott was sure he was about to experience more fun at his expense. The fun at his expense was brief. Mostly he was quizzed about his past. The meal completed, he assured Thunder Cloud and the rest he would return in the near future. Escorted by Spotted Pony, Buchanan voiced, "My visit, though brief, has strengthened our friendship. When we meet again, I will be anxious to listen to what you have to say."

Spotted Pony gripped both of Buchanan's shoulders as he faced him. "Go ride with the Great Spirit. Carry Gray Coyote's knife at your side, for the old warrior's spirit was strong and so shall it be for you."

Up in the saddle, Buchanan left the village with Gray Coyote's knife belted to his side. The subtle pressure from the knife made him feel as if the wise old leader's spirit rode with him.

Spotted Pony and Healing Spirit drifted together as they watched Buchanan's shoulders, then his head disappear into the haze.

Healing Spirit was the first to speak. "Like other warriors from our tribe, one like them departs."

Arms folded, Spotted Pony grunted. "Eyes-That-See's warrior spirit is strong. We shall see him again."

Topping the hill before slowly descending, the village now obscured, Buchanan's thoughts reflected back on his journey in life. During a man's ride into maturity, there are special people who come into one's presence, men and women one never forgets. Gray Coyote was such a man. Who would have thought that a fight to the death would allow him the privilege of becoming a blood brother to a type of people he always admired? His hand reached down to touch the knife's handle.

Scott gave thought to the old Chippewa man who had taught him the art of observation, a lesson he never forgot. There was an older boy who rooted for him when he fought a bigger lad during a noon break in the school yard, a boy who was popular with the other classmates. The older boy didn't interfere. Instead, he yelled encouragement. Such support was something Scott never forgot. Despite never seeing him again, to this day he still recalled the boy's first name.

Scott recalled a neighbor who had taught him to trap and hunt before he'd headed west. Age being a factor, Scott wondered if he was still alive. No matter, the man, like a few others, had been a positive influence in his life. Such people weren't many, but just enough to be remembered as special.

So too there were a few men during his army days, men he fought side by side with. It was during this period of his life that he'd forged a relationship with his army superior, a captain by the name of Clifford Stokes. Later, the captain's wife embraced him as a son. Nope, he reckoned, a man didn't need a lot of hangers-on, just a few people with sand in their craw, the type of people you could count on.

A glance at the sun told him it was well past noon. Another hour passed when Scott caught up with the wagon train. He rode

Buddy alongside Cliff's tethered horse. With lithe quickness, he was out of the saddle. Glad for company, the mare whinnied in appreciation as he tied Buddy next to her. The reins wrapped, Buchanan noted every eye turned in his direction. He studied the welcoming committee, seeing curiosity in each face, several already aware of the new knife tucked along his belt.

"Once again," Cliff chided, "our scout arrives just in time for a late noon meal after cleanup."

Wendell chimed in, "Yes sir, the man's consistent, that's fer sure."

Always observant, Cliff said, "I see you have an extra weapon stuck in your waist. Want to tell us about it?"

"I have to admit, you fellows don't miss much. Unfortunately, I had a sad visit."

"How so?" Cliff asked.

"I was looking forward to my reunion with Gray Coyote, but sickness got hold of him and he passed away."

Feeling for him, Cliff offered his condolences. "I'm sorry to hear of his passing. How about the rest of the village?"

"Just a few of the elderly died. Gray Coyote left a couple of messages for me along with his knife."

Obviously, for Buchanan to be given the knife was a great honor, Cliff thought.

Seeing Mitch walking across the semicircled wagons, Scott yelled, "Mitch, come over here. I have something to tell you." Waiting until Mitch stood before them, he explained, "I understand Two Moons has been sent to an agency. I believe it's up near Fort Kearney in Wyoming territory. Gray Coyote's gone to the happy hunting ground because of a sickness, but I'm to convey a message to you."

"I'm sorry about Gray Coyote. What is the message?"

"Spotted Pony told me that Gray Coyote wants us to keep our promise to visit Two Moons."

Frowning, Mitch asked, "How are we going to do that? We will have left Wyoming territory far behind."

"Darned if I know. You're in the miracle business, not me."

Cliff felt this was the time he wanted, interrupting both, "That's not all. Here's something else for our chief scout to consider."

Scott eyed his boss. "What exactly does that mean?"

"I'm going to tell you something ahead of time. When we arrive back here at this very junction, whenever that is, you will no be longer scouting for me. In other words, I'll be releasing you."

The sudden silence was almost eerie. Scott wondered if his boss was joking. Seeing no humor in Cliff's face, he questioned him, "Releasing me when we return here before swinging east? Is this a joke?"

"Nope, so as you can head for San Francisco. I'd release you now, but I need your scouting considering what lies ahead up along the Snake River. We have a few remaining folks bound for the Willamette Valley Settlement. They have made arrangements to be picked up halfway along the trail. When we return to Fort Hall, I'll give you a cash advance and send the rest when you want it. Right now, you would save a heap of miles by turning west at this very juncture. There is no sense in you having to backtrack to see that Stephanie gal. As I just said, if I didn't need you farther along the Oregon Trail, I'd release you pronto."

Momentarily unable to concentrate, Buchanan collected his thoughts, making a mild argument. "You know I always finish my obligations."

"You will have finished your obligations when we return here. My mind's made up. Just slightly northwest of where we're camped lies Fort Hall and slightly beyond is where the Oregon Trail can connect you to the California Trail. Once there, you'll actually be in the southern pass. Your other option is to stay with us farther on our return where you could pick up the Santa Fe Trail, but you'll have to traverse some difficult terrain. You may avoid some weather but add miles of travel. If you listen to me, you'll shorten the miles using the South Pass when riding through the mountains. The way Stuart and I figured it out, you might run into an early snowstorm this side of the Sierras. Should that happen, Fort Churchill provides a proper place to wait it out."

Pushing aside any potential objections, Scott thought intently before accusing his boss and foreman. "It seems like you two have been in cahoots!"

"Nope," Cliff defended. "Just me. Most likely you'll reach the coast by late winter or early spring. From what Stuart and I saw, there is a good chance the Clark family might have shipped the rest of their belongings and bought passage on the railroad by then. Anyway, no sense you traveling all those extra miles. I'm telling you now so you can get it settled in your brain. In the meantime, why don't you finish telling us about your visit, not forgetting to tell us more about the knife?"

Seconds passed before Buchanan attempted to focus on what happened by answering, "Healing Spirit gave me the knife with a special message from Gray Coyote. She told me his warrior spirit would always ride with me on life's journey. He said because I was white, I wouldn't be forced into a reservation like his tribe will be one day. She also informed me how Gray Coyote was well-known by other tribes. If I show them the knife, I'd be welcomed amongst them. Also, Spotted Pony told me Gray Coyote would meet me on the other side as long as I kept my body parts." Pausing, Scott checked each face, admitting, "What made me feel so special was how he didn't forget me during his last days."

"Body parts!" Mitch exclaimed.

"Certain tribes mutilate their dead adversaries as a way of hindering those warriors whom they killed, so when they enter the spirit world themselves, those adversaries are still collecting their own body parts before seeking revenge."

Shaking his head in disgust, Mitch declared, "So it never ends."

Scott took the plate Wendell handed him. Looking around for a convenient place to sit, asking, "Mind if I get off my feet and eat while I talk?" He found a seat next to Stuart. Comfortable, he eyed his boss. "I suppose you've already figured out how I and the preacher will meet up with Two Moons, haven't you?"

"That's why I'm the wagon boss."

"Did you hear that, Mitch? The boss has the miracle part figured out for you. This should be good."

Shifting his stare away from Buchanan, Mitch prompted, "Do tell us, Mr. Stokes."

Wondering what the miracle was, all eyes focused on the wagon boss.

"The railroad is how. By the time both of you get married, the Central and Union Pacific will be connected. All the two of you have to do is ride the rails and visit Two Moons. Simple as can be, mission accomplished."

"I'll be," Stuart chuckled.

SOUTHERN PASSAGE

S cott constantly battled with his mind concerning change as the wagons moved northwest. Thankfully, his years of scouting were instinctive. Despite mulling over his coming change of life, his sixth sense still prevailed concerning his surroundings.

As they moved northwest, a series of severe thunderstorms produced rivulets of mud cascading across the trail. Mud was everywhere. Leaving the violent storms behind offered no respite. Continuing up the Oregon Trail, the wagons ran into mist-like dark clouds scudding across the lower atmosphere producing raw wet weather without relief. Rain slickers were the order of the day. Finally, their halfway destination reached, a small town offered hot food along with a measure of civilized comfort. The few remaining passengers destined to continue on came by to express their gratitude wishing both Clifford and Buchanan well.

Finally alone, eyeing his boss, Scott prodded despite already knowing the answer. "When do we head back?"

"First thing in the morning," Cliff laughed. "What did you expect me to say?"

"If you said anything else, I'd consider you picked up some fever along the trail." Changing the subject, Scott mentioned their surroundings. "It sure has plenty of distant grandeur up this way, lots of shades of green contrasting against the slate gray. So much lush foliage must be because of the rain, don't you think?"

Cliff allowed for some thought before responding. "Truth is, I've never been this far up the trail. From what others have told me, most of the wet conditions slide along the coast the far side of the mountain range, so I guess our luck ran out concerning weather. Of course, as a scouting man, would you rather deal with bears, Indians, or weather?"

"How about none of the above!"

"Yeah, I should have known better to ask. Well, let me mosey over to the men explaining how I'm allowing them to have dry lodging along with hot grub on me before we head back down the trail come morning."

"Me included?"

"You sure earned it this trip, that's for sure."

"Man, a hot bath would be like heaven sent down from above."

"Don't tell Mitch," Cliff laughed.

The following morning broke with a welcome sunrise. Leaning against the door of the eatery, Scott felt a rush of concern for what lay ahead considering how his scouting days were nearing the end. For a brief second, he felt a nervous twitch in his stomach. Minutes later, he shrugged it off. After all, he still had a few scouting miles left before they reached Fort Hall. Most of all, he hoped Stephanie and her parents were doing well. Being of a nature of not wanting to wait things out, the sooner he started into his next journey with all its uncertainty, the more he would be himself.

Stepping away from the door, he pushed his hat on before starting for the wagons at the far end of town. From this distance, he could see Cliff already gathering the new travelers bound for Fort Laramie and beyond. Unlike their beginning departure out of Trumansburg when he was absent uncovering concerns, Scott reckoned he'd be introduced as the chief scout.

Waiting for Buchanan's approach, Cliff turned addressing the assembled men and women. "Folks, I'm a stickler for leaving on time.

If the wagons don't start out timely, it's difficult to make up lost time. I can't say it simpler than I just did. Squander time, and she'll repay you likewise. Same is true when and if we stop to eat. Notice I said if. Should we be fortunate covering some miles, then stopping for a nice lunch is a certainty. If not, my advice is to either wolf down your food come morning or cook something you can eat as you travel. The reason I plan on departing first thing without wasting time is because the payoff is arriving before the sky darkens allowing enough daylight for evening meals together with some socializing."

Pausing, Cliff motioned in the direction of his grouped together men. "Let me introduce my crew. All these men are seasoned travelers with work to do so don't hesitate to get acquainted with them after working hours. Notice I said after working hours." Touching Stuart, who stood nearest, Cliff introduced him. "My foreman here is Stuart Whitman. Seeing as how you folks now know Stuart's my foreman, if you have questions and can't find me, go see Stuart. Stuart, take a step to the fore and say hello."

Removing his hat with a flourish, Stuart's drawl captivated all.

"Next is Mr. Bartholomew, who is my trail cook. If anyone has questions regarding provisions and such, don't ask me, see Wendell. Wendell, make yourself known."

Doing as he was told, Wendell made a statement. "I won't cook for you, but I do know provisioning tricks for the trail. I'd be glad to share them."

Cliff enjoyed his next introduction. "We even provide spiritual guidance if needed. Let me introduce Mitch Robinson. During trying situations along the trail, he offers spiritual encouragement. Fact is, Mr. Robinson is preparing to enter the ministry. Mitch, step forward and take a bow."

Pleasing looks appeared on numerous faces, especially the ladies.

Cliff gestured with his thumb over his shoulder. "The man leaning on the wagon wheel behind me is Scott Buchanan who happens to be the best scout who ever led the way. Unfortunately, he'll be leaving us bound for San Francisco via the Southern Pass when we stop to replenish any needed provisions at Fort Hall. Before he speaks, I'd like to introduce you to Wes Santana. Wes will be taking over the scouting after we continue down the trail. Guess who trained Wes? If you thought it was Buchanan, you'd be right. Wes, take a step forward so the good people will know whom I'm talking about."

Wes smiled as he stepped forward.

Half turning, Cliff addressed Buchanan. "Scott Buchanan, you have something encouraging for the folks?"

Easing away from the wheel, Scott intended to savor the moment. Most likely, this would be his last opportunity to address folks as a wagon scout. Taking his time, he eyed each person before he began. "It's been my pleasure to work for the best trail master the good Lord ever produced, and that's a fact. If you want info on the trail, the chain of command is Clifford Stokes. If you can't find Mr. Stokes, wait until you do because it is still Mr. Stokes. As a last resort, locate Stuart whom you just met." With a smile Buchanan admitted, "Once you do, most likely he'll wait to see Mr. Stokes before he answers whatever's on your mind. If you considered that it's still Mr. Stokes, you'd be right. So there you have it."

Laughter broke out.

"Why am I telling you this? Because Mr. Stokes knows everyone and everything happening at the same time. Since we all report to him, he's your best source. I'll close by repeating myself. You are fortunate to be traveling with the best wagon master the Lord ever produced, and that's a fact. To be quite honest, Mr. Stokes and this wagon train have been family to me and after you get dropped off at your final destinations you will also feel like you've been part of family. I'm talked out. It is a pleasure to meet all you folks."

With a nod, Cliff turned around, asking, "You folks have any questions before we head out?"

One fellow at the far end held up his hand.

"Go ahead, I'm listening."

"You always travel with scouts?"

"I have ever since my army days. Tell me, did you get here on your own?"

"Not exactly, but not with any scouts."

"Well then," Cliff smiled, "I reckon having some scouts should make you feel more secure."

Once again, pleasing looks appeared on the ladies' faces followed by several amens coming forth.

"Are there any other questions or concerns?"

The faces were silent.

With no new question coming forth, Cliff continued, "During our travels, should any concerns come up, save whatever's on your mind for the night camp where I'm always available. If an emergency occurs, that's different. Now, I want all you travelers to listen very carefully. At this precise moment we are about to start our practiced habit of leaving on time. I kid you not when I say any stragglers will have to catch up because we are leaving within seconds." Pausing for emphasis, Cliff ordered, "Go to your wagons right now!"

Approaching Scott, Cliff suggested, "Well, chief scout, you know the drill."

"Boss, I was wondering if you were going to allow me the opportunity for my final trail talk."

"Well, you missed the last opportunity, so I figured you're entitled. I'm glad I made sure you had your say seeing as how you added some compliments regarding family. That family part was special, and we all feel the same way regarding you. Scott, when I get back home to my wife and business, I've a big change waiting for me also."

"At least you'll still have your freight company."

Cliff half grimaced, pointing out, "Maybe so, but age is at my doorstep and the adventure part of life for me is about to be a thing of the past."

Understanding only too well, Scott grunted. "I'm kind of wondering if I'm about to experience likewise. Anyway, I'm already saddled and ready, so I'll see you out front after I send out your soon-to-be head scout."

Watching Buchanan walk away, Cliff headed for his horse. Mounting, he nudged the mare toward the rear wagon at a slow walk before starting up the line. Pleased that all the travelers' eyes were on him appearing ready, he reached Stuart, his voice soft, "Move them out, foreman."

Stuart's voice echoed down the line.

Scott rode up to a waiting Wes. Pulling back gently on the reins, he spoke with authority, "Go ahead, the wagon boss's next chief scout, do your job."

Dumbstruck, Wes spoke after a second. "From where I sit, you're still chief scout"

"Maybe so, but only until we reach Fort Hall. So move that pony of yours down the trail. I'll catch up with you later in the day. Besides, it's time you realize soon there will be no one but you. Don't stare at me, chief scout, start scouting."

With a half smile, Wes wheeled his horse around. Booting the grey into a gallop past Stuart and Cliff, hat held aloft, Wes whooped.

Stuart eyed Cliff, speaking with a chuckle. "It does appear it will soon be official."

"Seems so," Cliff agreed. Aware Buchanan was approaching, Cliff swung the mare around. Moments later, they rode side by side, Stokes mentioning, "I noticed you've shifted some responsibilities."

"Yep, something I learned from you."

"Right now, how is your mind-set?"

"Best way I can describe the feeling is twitchy. How many years have we ridden together?"

"My bride keeps track of such information. I'll ask her when I return home."

"Including running your freight business when you're away?"

"She is meticulous with the bookkeeping and staying on top of costs and profits. I couldn't do this without her."

"Real special lady she is. Attractive too," Scott added.

"I'll be sure to convey your compliment. You and Stephanie will stand out pretty handsome likewise."

Buchanan took his time before answering. "You sound pretty sure she'll be waiting for me."

"Knowing her, I'm as sure as sure can be."

Changing the subject, Scott injected, "Riding for you has allowed me plenty of freedom along with independence."

Cliff took his time before responding. "Life eventually brings changes to everyone. You are plenty young enough to adapt while making another mark besides scouting. Just as I'd bet on Stephanie, I'd gamble my freight business on you. How'd you like that statement?"

"I suspect you are right. The problem for me will be my ability, or lack of such, to propose. Tell me, how in God's good name am I going to do such a thing?"

With a chuckle, Cliff said, "I heard you were Prince Charming during the dance back on the trail. I'd bet my monetary stash against yours she'll lead you right where you want to go anyway. The ladies have a way of doing such a thing. Care to make a wager?"

"Nope, considering how Stephanie persuaded me to visit her so far away."

"I wonder if you're telling me everything."

"I've already told you enough."

Cliff grinned, confessing, "Since life is a teacher, being led into the corral happened to me. Love is a strong emotion which tends to take over, and no one is immune. The only question being, are you two right for each other? I'll tell you this. I doubt you'll find a better mate than Stephanie. The same goes for her regarding my soon-to-be former scout."

"You make a convincing argument, that's for sure."

For a stretch, both rode in silence, the only sounds from swishing tails chasing annoying deer flies. Cliff's curiosity finally got the best of him, asking, "Tell me, wagon scout, what are you going to miss the most?"

Seconds passed before Scott said, "All of it."

"Do you know what you just revealed?"

"I'm sure you're about to explain."

"Just this, all these years were worthwhile. Do the same with what lies ahead and you'll have no regrets."

More silence followed before Buchanan added, "Lots of horse sense in such thinking. I think I'll mosey ahead and find what high ground Wes chose to scout from. Once I know, I'll cover the opposite terrain. See you later at the campfire."

Despite the improving weather, the progress down the trail slowed into numerous stops because of repairs. It seemed the latest travelers hadn't chosen the more expensive and durable Canastota Wagons. Cliff fumed inwardly because of his fanaticism regarding schedule. Finally, Fort Hall appeared in the distance.

Sitting atop his horse, Wes eyed Scott, a question in his expression.

Staring in the direction of Fort Hall, Buchanan rubbed Buddy's neck, acknowledging the look. "Yeah, the job's all yours now, Wes. Let's help the boss settle the wagons and then we can satisfy our curiosities. Maybe I'll shop around and find something Stephanie will like."

Alone, the afternoon wearing on, Buchanan wandered amongst all the hustle and bustle. As he neared the general store, a voice hailed him.

"Say, mister, aren't you Scott Buchanan?"

Turning, Scott faced a stout-looking fellow wearing buckskin tops and bottoms. With a nod, he questioned, "Whom do I have the pleasure of conversing with?"

"Name's Harold Collingsworth. We met some time ago along the Platt River. We kind of enjoyed each other's wagon trains for a spell."

Stepping closer, Scott recognized the face. "You have more whiskers than before."

"That I do, that I do," Harold laughed.

"Where are you bound?"

"Where there are wide open spaces. City life wasn't for me."

"What city?"

"I got me some relatives in Frisco. I was glad to vamoose."

All sounds suddenly seemed distant. Scott asked what he didn't want to know. "Why?"

"I felt trapped with city folks crowding all around me. Now, don't get me wrong, 'cause it is an interesting place. But a man has to want to be surrounded with wall to wall folks bumping into one another while their breathing produces suffocating perfumes. I declare, it takes a good week in the wilds before one can smell the good earth again. Say, where are you bound for, Scott Buchanan?"

Digesting those words, Scott answered with, "I'm heading where you just came from."

Studying Buchanan's face, Harold couldn't help saying what came to mind. "I can't see a scout like you heading for such a place. Is it temporary?"

"Maybe, maybe not."

"Sounds to me like there's still hope, you have relatives there?"

"Truth is, I met a lady heading there and got smitten."

Nodding in sympathy, Harold stated, "I declare such a thing can happen to a man. If you kind of feel claustrophobic like what happened to me, you can always mount up on your horse and cover some miles getting away from all the noise. If'en you desire to shoot some large game where a man can breath, bring your long gun considering how the hills are pretty treeless. Well, I'm guiding some hunters north, so I'd best get going. I'm wishing the best to you, Scott Buchanan."

Watching a fellow man who loves the trail hurrying away, Scott mumbled, "Geez, lots of noise, suffocating perfumes, people bumping into one another, claustrophobia, and no trees."

With a shrug, Buchanan started for the familiar supply house where he and Stephanie had made promises. Nearing the hustle and bustle, he enjoyed the healthy aroma from livestock feed wafting out into the still air. Across from the store remained the very wagon where he and Stephanie discussed commitments. If nothing else, recalling the moment lifted his spirits. Besides, if he couldn't adjust, there was no law requiring him to stay. Tonight he'd discuss his plans with Cliff in preparation for the morning. For a brief moment, he thought about boss Stokes, a man who inspired one's respect. Such a lifetime relationship was irreplaceable. Yes, he would miss the camaraderie.

The day slid by too soon. As the numerous camp fires burned down, Scott took his plate over to Wendell with a compliment. "I'd be more than willing to help in the cleanup seeing as how you always gave me priority."

"Nope," Wendell explained. "I just used you against the trail boss is all."

"So I was of use?"

"Somewhat," Wendell needled.

Shifting his stare at Cliff, Scott started a conversation he had been avoiding. "So tell me, boss, when have you figured I'm supposed to ride out?"

Cliff was ready. "First thing in the morning. Wendell will fill you up with bacon and eggs. After you're stuffed, we'll make sure you have adequate provisions for the trail."

Nodding, Scott explained, "I know you allowed me plenty of time to adjust my thoughts and it's much appreciated. Nonetheless, I'm still wrestling with this change."

"For a man like yourself, you've had more than enough opportunity to realize such a change is right for you. We've already drawn up a map. Besides, we stopped early so you could relax including spending the evening amongst the best trail friends a man could ever want."

The faces around the fire nodded in unison.

Scott eyed the diminishing rays of light. Other than what he'd just confessed, if someone asked him what his thoughts were at this very moment, his answer would be that he was rattled. He'd always had a place to spend the night, people he knew, food never being an issue. There was one other time of uncertainty. He still remembered it well. It was the day he had left home during his youth.

Wendell broke Scott's concentration. "Here, have more coffee."

Thanking Wendell, Scott's mind returned to his past, recalling how he'd survived when he left home. For a second, he felt another one of those twinges deep inside. The moment passed, replaced with anticipation. This time, he had someone waiting for him, and if Stephanie wasn't waiting, he had a place to come back too. Looking over at his boss, he questioned Cliff with, "Tell me again how long it took you to come up with your decision for me."

"Kept nagging at me, so it all made sense."

Scott conceded, agreeing, "I reckon it does at that."

Stuart prodded Scott, "Just think, no more morning assignments as chief scout."

Scott would be glad when the dawn came. For the first time in over a month he felt useless, recalling that same feeling prior to

Stephanie's departure. Come morning, he and his horse would start out for one last visit with his Kiowa brothers and then on to a bustling city. He grimaced. Stephanie had better be waiting or else!

Despite a restless night, the morning came soon enough, the sun bursting over the hilltops. Up and about, Scott handed his empty plate to Wendell. His stomach full, he looked into the old man's eyes, kidding him, "Wendell, you sure enough have spoiled me. I hate to admit it, but I'm going to miss your lousy cooking."

Wendell chided back. "I did it on purpose for a moment like now. It seems like a man's never appreciated unless he's being spoiled by someone, thus causing the spoiler to be appreciated."

With an emphatic shake of his head, Buchanan agreed, "I'm flat-out admitting it. You have been like an old mother hen to me. And yes, I'm spoiled."

A touch of affection in the cook's voice, he gave an order. "After you get settled, you come back for a visit, you hear?"

"I will, Mr. Bartholomew, I will." Turning, Scott approached Buddy, finding room in his saddlebags for his personal wash-up gear amongst the already loaded provisions for the trail.

His head canted sideways, Buddy sensed a different morning was about to happen. Stepping back, Scott was satisfied nothing was forgotten. He watched Cliff and Stuart approaching.

Cliff started the conversation. "Stuart and I got to prod the folks into action, so we'll say our goodbyes now. Like Wendell said, we expect a visit. I reckon in life timing is everything and with the railroad a fact, visiting in the future will be a lot faster and convenient. Since you can't scout for me anymore, it makes sense for you to see how things will work out for you and Stephanie."

Scott laughed, "You been making decisions for me as far back as our army days. What's more, I always appreciated your motives."

Cliff laughed back, admitting as much. "I owed you as much. Also, seeing the railroad did that. Stuart's going to run my freight business unless you want it. I've got no illusions about you wanting to work for me because of that Stephanie gal." Grinning, Cliff finished with, "I'm betting you two are going to tie the knot, which means the only way I see you again is for a social visit. However, before you come for a visit, I do expect a letter."

"I guess I can manage to scratch out one."

Cliff stuck out his hand. "You just received my last orders, my old army scout."

Stuart's voice interrupted, "If we don't hear from you, we will come-a-looken, all three of us."

Addressing the foreman, Scott's expression was meaningful. "Stuart, I'm leaving family, you being part of it. Family deserves consideration and you can bet you'll hear from me."

Touched, Stuart thanked him, "Glad I contributed."

Almost forgetting Cliff's wife, Buchanan apologized with, "I almost forgot to ask you to say goodbye to the misses for me."

"I'll remember to convey your goodbye."

Buchanan kept his stare back on his ex-boss. "You been like a father to me. Can't say anything better than that. I'm a lucky man and I know it. Good or bad, you'll hear from me as soon as possible." Watching the rest of the men approach, he greeted Wes, "How's it feel to be the new chief wagon scout?"

"I had a good trainer. I hope I learn to read trail sign as well as you."

"You'll do. Like I said before, a man gets better at anything when he depends on himself." Shifting his stare to Mitch, he said, "Since it requires a preacher man to be wed, when Stephanie and I tie the knot, you'd better be ordained so you can officiate. What's more, I do expect to be invited when you get hitched to that schoolteacher whose picture you carry around in your breast pocket."

Mitch grinned, countering, "After I do, I'll have a story to tell my congregation. I'll explain how I married an untamable frontiersman to a sophisticated lady."

A soft laugh swept through the men.

"You do that. I also suggest you find a place somewhere between my ex-boss and me to start up your ministry. By you choosing such a location, it will make traveling much easier, especially when we go visit Two Moons."

"So I'm back in the miracle business, am I?"

"If you want to be a preacher, you'd better be."

"If it's in the Lord's will, it will happen. There is a saying how God listens to our plans and then laughs."

"Well then, you go and have a serious talk with him."

The surrounding men burst into laughter, even a near horse snorting, producing more laughter.

Serious, Mitch's voice assumed authority, "Scott Buchanan."

Sensing the change, Scott encouraged, "Go on."

"You've had several close brushes with life over death. You might want to consider salvation for your soul."

Respecting Mitch, Scott answered thoughtfully, "Okay, and of course, I can find out about this salvation for my soul in what you call the Holy Scriptures."

"Yes, it's in the book of John, chapter three, beginning in verse three to be precise."

"Does this John fellow have a last name?"

"His official handle is the Apostle John."

"I see. Well, right now I have a lot on my plate. Hopefully, this will satisfy you. When we hook up to see Two Moons, you'll have your opportunity."

"I'll look forward to it."

Adjusting his focus away from Mitch to the rest of the gathered men, Scott had his final say. "I've been blessed to ride the trail with a special group of men. Every one of you in some way or another taught me something. Much obliged."

The nodding heads showed appreciation.

Slipping his foot into the stirrup, Scott rose into the saddle. Swinging Buddy around, he looked down with a nod. "I can't think of anything more worthwhile to say, so adios until we meet again."

Nudging the gelding gently around, Buchanan and Buddy headed in the direction where he hoped the Kiowa village still remained. He had told Healing Spirit and Spotted Pony there would be one last visit before heading west, and since Scott was known to keep his word, it had better happen. Yes, some time would be lost, but promises were meant to be kept. After he visited the village, there was only one commitment left which was located in California.

Casting a backward glance, Scott held his hat high with a wave, urging Buddy into a trot.

Part of his life leaving, Cliff frowned. Good for Buchanan, he thought. The man-stallion was heading for his mare, and a stallion needed a mare to build his own herd. He was of the opinion his scout had some good bloodlines to pass along.

For a brief moment, Scott looked back at the men, the rising sun reflecting on their faces as they observed his departure. Turning in the saddle, he let the rhythm from Buddy's mile eating trot relax him.

Keeping his eyes on Buchanan's departure, Cliff instructed Mitch, "I want you to pray for the best scout and trail partner a man ever had."

"Every day?" Mitch asked.

"Yep, every day."

Deciding to push his boss, Mitch suggested, "I didn't know you believe in prayer."

"I've asked you to say last rites, haven't I?"

"Yes, you have, but I was thinking that's because of traditional reasons."

Considering Mitch's point, Cliff confessed, "No dispute there, but what matters is how you believe in prayers. More than once you've expressed as much, so that's your assignment. Besides, praying does seem to give a measure of peace."

"It does do that," Mitch agreed.

Taking a last look, Buchanan becoming smaller in the distance, Cliff knew the next toughest moment would come when he informed his wife they would no longer be setting an extra plate at the Sunday dinner table. Eyeing Stuart, Cliff asked, "What did that fellow say awhile back on the trail?"

Stuart's frown accented his concern. "Seems like all this wet weather has had an effect on the South Pass, appears to be lots of rock slides, plus some snow piling up at the higher elevations."

Not good, Cliff thought, following with another question. "Did the man happen to reveal anything regarding the Sierras?"

"He kind of hinted there was unusual weather happening all over." Thinking about the weather, Stuart continued, "What's more to worry about concerning Buchanan, the weather or running into some shady characters along the trail?"

Taking one last look in the direction his scout had departed, Cliff shrugged his shoulders as he spoke, "Scott's a master at finding trouble before it becomes a problem. Trust me, he can locate trouble like no other man and then avoid it. Another thing, you ever notice his stare when he gets irritated at someone? Such a look can freeze a man's mobility. Besides, most traveling folks are of a mind to be helpful. Yep, the weather will be the key, and of course, if Stephanie's waiting."

Stuart considered he couldn't have said it better himself.

Striding back toward the chuck wagon, Cliff became his old self, barking out orders.

LATE SPRING

The gentle breeze greeting her, Stephanie moved out onto the porch, the balmy morning temperatures providing a reason to be outside. Settling into the long wooden rocker, her gaze wandered over the grassy hills, the land stretching out in a panoramic view. Split-rail fences surrounded the ranch house. A few horses, thoroughbred horses, grazed on the green grass. They too were surrounded by split-rail fences. Beyond the horses, a small herd of beef cattle drifted across the landscape. Stephanie rocked slowly, the sofa creaking. Reflecting on the previous year, she studied the tops of the hills. Would she ever see Scott Buchanan again, she wondered. She had told him she would wait, and she was waiting. Three times Tyler Harden had asked for her hand in marriage, each time she flirted with saying yes. Unable to keep Buchanan out of her thoughts, she found a way to stall. Recalling the scout's teasing, she remembered him saying how love and proximity go hand and hand. She also remembered another of his statements. He had said that absence makes the heart grow fonder. Right now she was experiencing the latter. The question was, how much longer would she feel that way?

A lone bawl from a distant steer drifted her way, the creaking sound from the rocker finally replacing the dying bellow. Her father wanted her to marry Tyler Harden. Dad's reasoning was simple. The man was highly successful. Stephanie's mother agreed with her father. Both believed such a marriage would introduce their daughter into the world of high society, a very proper life for her. She knew she couldn't wait forever. Even worse, she was attracted to Harden, often questioning her hesitation. More recently there had been other suitors, most quite handsome and charming. All were accomplished men of importance. Was she being foolish, she wondered. No, she scolded herself. She had made a promise, therefore she would wait, at least until Buchanan came or didn't come. He had said he would come and she believed him. The trip across the frontier had been one of her greatest experiences. She recalled how she kept her watch fire promise and how Buchanan complimented the spirit within her for keeping her commitment. Stephanie remembered something else the wagon scout had said. He explained how time exposes little things, rewarding those who were willing to wait. She had kept her promise back then and wait she would. Patience was a virtue testing one's character. There was something about Buchanan that fascinated her. The man was exciting, seeing everything, always ready to act on what he saw.

Absorbed in past thoughts, she recalled the wagon boss saying how Scott Buchanan was half Cheyenne and half Apache, indicating a man harboring an untamable nature. Suddenly worry crossed her mind. Despite Buchanan's considerable skills and instincts, something might happen to him? If her experience on the trail was any example, he could be dead. No, she reminded herself, he was too good at what he did. The real question was, if he came, would he be willing to settle down and raise a family?

Her gaze shifting, Stephanie focused on her favorite horse. The chestnut-colored mare was staring her way with ears perked forward. The sun shining on her burnished coat, the mare snorted in her direction. What a beautiful horse, she admired. Smiling, Stephanie knew the mare wanted her attention. Tempted to go for a ride, she decided against it. There were ranch chores needing to be completed before heading for town. Having promised to meet with her parents for lunch, she scolded herself for daydreaming the morning away.

Stealing one last look at the horizon, Stephanie froze, the wooden sofa coming to a halt. A lone rider sat atop the distant hill. Even from this distance, she could see the horse's light brown, dun color. Stephanie's heart begins to pound as the rider began dropping down, slowly closing the distance. Standing, her heart still hammering, she descended the steps.

It seemed like an eternity since Buchanan had seen Stephanie Clark. The minute he saw the distant figure on the porch he had no doubt who the woman was. Had she become impatient, he worried. Had she married despite saying she would wait? His other concern being, was he about to make a fool of himself? Well, he thought, there was only one way to find out. Gently, he nudged Buddy with his boot heels.

Holding the bottom rail, Stephanie waited.

As he neared, Scott stole a glance at Stephanie's fingers. Looking for a ring, he didn't see one. Reining Buddy in, he slipped from the saddle. Leading his horse, he was relieved seeing her face break into a radiant smile. He recalled the first dance with her, remembering that very smile as he approached her and her escort, Tyler Harden. He remembered how her smile had relaxed him, and seeing the same radiant smile again, he experienced that same identical feeling of relief. Smiling, his voice breached the distance, "Stephanie, I'm seeing that belle-of-the-ball smile again."

Starting forward, flirtation in her voice, she asked him, "What took you so long, Scott Buchanan?"

He laughed. "Your trail led into town, not here."

"Are you still following two sets of tracks?"

Again, he eyed her ring finger before stealing a look into her eyes. "Tell me about this ranch. I didn't know you liked wide open spaces."

"Scott, may I ask you why you keep looking at my fingers?"

Pausing, he answered her, "I was looking for a ring. I guess I'm wondering if Tyler Harden's still around."

Stephanie took a step closer. "I see him. He keeps asking me to marry him."

"And?"

"I keep stalling him. Do you want to know why?"

"I'm hoping it's because of me."

Loving his answer, Stephanie half turned gesturing at the land. "Scott, my Father bought me this ranch from a man in debt because of excessive gambling. Dad wasn't interested in owning a horse ranch despite knowing I wanted to raise horses. He told me yes if the primary reason for a ranch was to raise beef." For a second she stared at her mare before continuing on. "Although Dad's business in town is doing well, whatever he finances has to make money. He doesn't think there is much money in horses. However, he is pretty certain there are serious profits in beef." She turned back, her voice throaty, "Scott, do you know the other reason why I wanted a ranch?"

"No, tell me why."

"I couldn't expect a man who is half Apache and half Cheyenne to live in town. I know that type of man needs wide open spaces. So tell me, Scott Buchanan, why are you here?"

Emotions soaring, Scott moved forward. Reaching out he drew her in. "Why do you think I'm here?"

"Was it because you promised to come?"

"I did do that, but that's not the real reason."

"Then ask me, because I'm waiting to say yes."

"Marry me."

Their bodies melted together, lips brushing; Stephanie's voice whispering, "Yes."

Buddy whinnied, heading for the mare.

Stepping back, he held her shoulders. "I saw your parents briefly in town. They were very cordial."

"Did they ask you to stay?"

"They did."

Stephanie snuggled her head against his shoulder, warning him, "It's a good thing you have their respect considering you're about to change their plans for me."

"Is our getting married going to be a major problem?"

"I think they already know. Since they're expecting me for lunch, you can ask for their blessing when we dine."

"Dine, is it? Are you beginning to educate me socially?"

"Didn't you once tell me life is a constant learning process?"

"Seems like I did."

"I think over time you'll surprise yourself."

"So you are trying to change me, aren't you?"

"If I am, don't let me. I like you the way you are."

"Any instructions how I should ask for your folk's permission?"

"Just be yourself."

Grasping her hand they started for the barn, Scott kept humor in the conversation, "Let me help you get saddled up. Then we can go... dine... with your folks and receive their blessing."

Her heart soaring, she snuggled as they walked. For a moment, Stephanie felt concern. When her parents introduced Scott Buchanan as her life-long partner to his socially correct business associates, it was going to be difficult for her dad. The adjustment that was about to happen would affect everyone, Scott and herself included. For a brief second, she hoped love would conquer all. Pushing aside all negative thinking, she squeezed Buchanan's hand.

ACKNOWLEDGMENTS

Special thanks to Dave Henderson for his fellowship along with proof reading help. A writer always needs another set of eyes and Dave not only was a major help, but his enthusiasm concerning the novel was a constant motivation for me. Especially when Dave expressed I'd wrote another winner!

Much thanks to Pat Reap for his invaluable computer knowledge, and yes, proof reading. So thank you Pat for being such a persistent 'pest' regarding details which improved the novel. Stay healthy because I'll need you in the future.

Meredith Arnold. After reading my first novel she never stopped asking me when my next book would be published. I mean, she never let up even over long periods of time including up to the present! It seemed like every time I turned around there was Meredith asking me to please hurry up. What encouragement, thank you so much Meredith!

I better not forget Bill and Jane Massey. Talk about neighbors who kept badgering me for my next novel every time I see them, or talked with them down in Florida. I'm beginning to wonder if they met Meredith, or maybe Meredith met Bill and Jane. Regardless, I'm finally complying. Thanks to both of you for being such encouragers.

Sharon Dorn's words regarding my first novel were, "I couldn't but the book down." During our recent Christmas conversation, when she found out my next novel was about to be published, she insisted she be amongst the first to purchase, "Life over Death." Such enthusiasm is encouraging. Thank you Sharon

Neighbors like Steve and Diane Wakefield, along with Peter and Sue Jordan, including the newest neighbor, Jim and Katie Kelly. After reading my first work, they too are insisting on reading my soon to be published novel, "Life over Death." More encouragement!

Thanks to Pastor Hal Jensen and his wife Nancy. Both promoted my first fiction novel, "Last Assignment." Nancy expressed my story read like real life with Christianity appearing during critical moments. Like the above mentioned, they too want my second work.

I asked my wife, Sharon, to proof read a chapter. When she gave the paper back to me, I noticed an obvious error. I asked if she had proof read the chapter. Sharon admitted she became so caught up in the story, she forgot my request. I'll take such encouragement anytime.

When Yvonne Bailey told me she read my book to a shut-in, my day shined brightly into the following week. Using my novel for such an instrument for a person in need exceeded my expectations!

Jay Carbonaro expressed there was one thing he didn't like about, "Last Assignment." When I inquired what it was, he said he didn't want the story to end. Obviously, such a response is very encouraging for my future writing!

I know there are others and I'll catch up the next time, and there will be another time.

ABOUT THE AUTHOR

After Bruce's honorable discharge from the Marine Corp, he enrolled in the Famous Writers School located in Westport, Connecticut, later attending the Central Business School in Syracuse, New York. In April of 1991, Bruce had a feature article published in a national outdoor magazine. The following year, he had a second published. After retiring from American Airlines, Bruce wrote his Western fiction novel titled *Last Assignment*, which received local success with constant request for his next work. His latest novel titled *Life over Death* answers those requests. Bruce and his wife, Sharon, reside on the beautiful shores of Otisco Lake, located in upstate New York.

CPSIA information can be obtained
at www.ICGtesting.com
Printed in the USA
FFHW020822230719
53814743-59506FF